THE SILVANA CHRONICLES

THE

SILVANA

CHRONICLES

The Turning

Belinda Mellor

CP
BOOKS

Map by Karen Nolan mizzwinkens.com
Cover and interior illustrations by Holly Dunn hollydunndesign.com

Revised Edition published November 2025
First published June 2015
by Copy Press Books, Nelson, New Zealand
Copy Press Books, 141 Pascoe St, Annesbrook, Nelson, New Zealand

ISBN 978-1-0671129-2-9 (International Edition)

COPYPRESS

Designed and distributed in New Zealand by CopyPress, Nelson, New Zealand.

www.copypress.co.nz

For Iona

Dreaming

(For Belinda, after reading *Silvana: The Greening*)

Some anthem
deep within the mystic groves of sleep,
echoes through the slumbering wildwood
and trembling among the fallen leaves,
ceases.

Some song,
risen from the valleys of the heart,
soothes itself against a memory,
then plucking at the chords of thought,
quietens.

Some music,
carried on the sleeping wings of night,
deep inside the silence of the soul,
lingers until morning, then
vanishes.

Then dreams,
tuned from the broken lyre of hope,
creep through the being, clutching at the mind,
and toll the ancient silver bell of love,
till all the sleepers wake,
and find their peace.

J. S. Johnson

Fabiom toyed with the amber paperweight on Ravik's desk then replaced it carefully, holding out his hands palms upwards as he turned to face the prince.

"The historian Jerynn was right, Silvanan blood he called it. Poetry is all very well but tears that are spilled can be dried. Blood is another matter. And my hands are dripping with it. It will not wash away."

Part

I

Chapter One

PALE SHAFTS OF light illuminated the ash grove. Casandrina could feel each leaf respond to the sun's dew-drying rays and her great tree's almost imperceivable growth. Roots delved deeper, sapwood expanded, bark stretched, branches reached out, seeds formed.

"If your father's hold-house was not virtually *in* our woods, you would see him less often, and your brother would not spend all his time here. If that were so, I doubt you would be considering taking a husband for many seasons, if ever. You have had too much contact with humans." The words were directed at her daughter, who chose not to come out of her tree into the grove. Casandrina paid that detail no heed; she knew Elzandria could hear her. "Your father is worried you would choose unwisely. I have warned him that, with your lack of seniority, should a young man come who would be worthy of you he would likely be desired also by another Silvana – and the other would take him."

With that, Elzandria came to stand near her.

"What should I do?"

"Wait," Casandrina suggested. She was being unfair, she knew. It was not her place to interfere in Elzandria's decisions, and playing on the young Silvana's affection for her father was really interference, nevertheless –

"I thought he would want me to be able to live with you," Elzandria said, moving away from Casandrina, in and out of the trees, touching each with her hand as she went.

Casandrina sighed. "He does."

"He has said so?"

"Yes, more than once," Casandrina admitted, compelled to tell

Elzandria the truth. "Yet he fears for your safety should you be challenged, as do I. And he cannot bear to think of you being less than completely happy should you succeed – less happy than I am." She had to smile as she said the words and Elzandria bowed her head.

"I know. I want that happiness for myself too."

"And so you should," Casandrina told her. "Wait. You know there is a cost for taking this path. Ask Narilina, or any other who has taken a husband, who has become substantial for a human lifetime. At least if you do take it, make it worthwhile – so that at the end you have no regrets. That is what Narilina told me."

"Did someone call me? I heard my name."

Casandrina inclined her head towards her own mother's tree as Narilina stepped into the grove. Like her daughter and granddaughter, she appeared as a young girl, but her huge tree was deeply ridged, and Narilina spent much of her time resting.

"No. Talking about you, not to you," Casandrina confessed.

Elzandria hesitated, then said. *"Knowing you will not regenerate, that you will end with your tree, that choosing to be a wife, a mother, you also chose to die. Is it hard? It feels easy to me – now – when my tree is so young."*

Narilina laughed – a melodic sound that caused several songbirds to trill and warble in response – before lifting her face skywards, to gaze up at the topmost branches of her tree. Unlike in past years, few seedpods formed amid the bright leaves. *"I have no regrets, little one. But you need not rush into anything. Be patient. Grow. That is what we Silvanii do best."*

⊰⊱

Sorting out service quotas was among Fabiom of Deepvale's least favourite tasks, however, it was one he insisted on doing himself; although this year he did have his son's help.

"Three thousand, is that right?" Lesandor asked.

Fabiom glanced up from the ledgers. "Um, about that number, yes."

"And Prince Ravik gets ten percent: three hundred."

"Uh huh," Fabiom agreed absently.

"And you have to choose each one of those individually?"

Fabiom gave his son his full attention. "It's about balance. Our needs, weighed against the Prince's needs; plus his opinion of us. That he thinks well of us is, in a way, part of our need. So we send him three hundred or so good, keen, trustworthy men, adept in a variety of skills. On the other hand, we have our own holding to run; we can't afford to send him all our brightest and best."

"You have Plino the carpenter and Rubus the weaver down to go to Fairwater, and I know you think very highly of both. Surely their service should be here."

"They both requested to go. As far as I can, I let those who want to travel to the capital do so. Most of them bring their skills and experience back home eventually. I certainly wouldn't deny anyone that opportunity without good reason."

Lesandor twisted a stylus between his fingers. "But I do not get a choice, do I?"

"No, you don't. As a son of a high house you are automatically the Prince's to command for two years. And it's just as well; you can't spend all your life in the woods of Deepvale."

"I don't see why not – did you know some badgers have moved into the copse where the big oak fell last winter? They have three cubs." He played with a ball of scraped wax as he gazed out of the window. "I cannot imagine spending even a month in a city."

Fabiom chuckled. "There are beautiful beech forests around Fairwater, as you well know if you've done any studying at all. After all…."

"Prince Lincius met and married Sulmarita there. I know." Lesandor chewed the end of the stylus. "Your friend Gwillon – his mother is a beech Silvana, is she not?"

"No. She is of a birch. Do you not recall her hair – a mix of dark grey and silver white, like the bark of her tree? You were fascinated by it when you met her at Gwillon's wedding."

"I was five," Lesandor reminded his father. "I barely remember." He paused, stylus poised above his wax tablet. "Why do you think Gwillon did not wed a Silvana himself? You do not think…. I always get the feeling they like me. But, what if…."

"Stop! I'm not having this conversation with you for at least another year. You've enough to think about now without that."

"I wish I knew why Gwillon had not tried."

"Maybe he did," Fabiom said, then, as Lesandor drew a sharp breath, immediately regretted the words. "Though I doubt it. I can't imagine he wouldn't have succeeded, had he tried."

"Yet maybe he did and his mother protected him. She would, wouldn't she? And his sister?"

"I would imagine so. I cannot imagine *your* mother or sister, or your grandmother, letting any harm come to *you*. But, we're not talking about this."

"So, maybe he did try, and was not chosen. Maybe they only like men who are human-born. What would I do?"

"Lesandor!"

"But what would I do?"

Fabiom put aside his work. "Your mother's woodmaids adore you, if that's anything to go by. I can't imagine for one moment that the Silvanii don't already feel the same. Come on, concentrate. Service quotas. It's important you learn all of this."

"Why? I will not need to know it for years."

Fabiom looked away, but not before Lesandor saw the creased brow and set jaw: the tell-tale signs of his father's displeasure.

"Why are you angry with me?"

"I'm not angry with *you*." Fabiom sighed. "It's just…. When I was your age I thought exactly the same thing. A year and a half later, your grandfather was gone and I was responsible for – everything. You need to be prepared."

"Don't say that! I do not want to think about you not being here. Look at Masgor. He must be at least a hundred and he is still waving that willow stick of his around and insisting I recite the names of every ruler of Morene since the days of Starven, and the finer details of the Treaty with Gerik. He will go on for years yet. You will live just as long."

"He's only eighty-five," Fabiom said, his mind still on his own father. "And you get off very lightly where that stick of his is concerned. He has a soft spot for you, or he's mellowed with the years, I'm not sure which. He was less gentle when I was a student."

"That is because you were such a daydreamer – he has told me."

Fabiom snorted. "And you're not?"

"Apparently not, at least by comparison."

"His memory is playing tricks on him," Fabiom asserted, opening the second ledger. "Now these are all manual workers, builders and the like. We need to send a slightly higher percentage to the capital than normal: there is a major refit of the port in Fairwater and Ravik has specifically asked for workers for that project."

Lesandor finally took the hint and started inscribing names.

❋

Later that afternoon, leaving Lesandor to go off with three of Casandrina's woodmaids to check on the badger family, Fabiom joined his wife and daughter in their grove. Sitting in the shade of the ash trees, Fabiom unfolded a parchment.

"What is that?" Casandrina inquired.

"It's a missive from the chief magistrate in Windwood: they are adamant that Lesandor must go to the holding for two years. My latest offer to redeem him was turned down. I'm out of options."

Casandrina touched the paper, her fingers tracing letters she could not read. "Have you told him?"

"Not yet. He's having enough trouble coming to terms with the idea of spending two years in Fairwater on his official service."

"*If only I had succeeded in saving that foolish nephew of Marid and Tarison's,*" Narilina murmured, startling Fabiom, who had not noticed the ancient Silvana approach.

In a flurry of pale hair, gold limbs and mauve silk, Elzandria danced around her parents and grandmother. "*It is a nonsensical demand. You did nothing wrong, Father, and Lesandor certainly did not. Can you not make them change their demands? Prince Ravik is your friend; ask for his aid.*" She stopped mid-twirl and looked at Fabiom imploringly.

He shook his head in pretend despair – he was at a distinct disadvantage, he felt, when both his wife and daughter could persuade him to do almost anything with so little effort.

Casandrina saved him on this occasion. "Perhaps it is for the best," she said. "The seasons turn; Turning and Greening and one more Turning

7

and he will reach manhood. Though I would keep him at home forever, I must not. We have done enough damage already – he has hardly any friends his own age, he is forever in the woods – I have been remiss."

"You have been an exceptional mother," Fabiom told her. "However, you are right about one thing: he ought to go away for a while, but not bounden to Windwood – not his very first time away from home."

There was one possibility, not that they could put off the inevitable. In reparation for the loss of Windwood's heir, Lesandor was bound to go to the western holding for two full years, yet it need not be his first extended leave from Deepvale.

"I *shall* speak to Ravik," Fabiom decided. "Lesandor may not be old enough for his official service yet, but the prince may take him to Fairwater nevertheless. Even a half-year in the capital should widen his perspective of the world. And with Yan there to watch out for him, and take over his education, we would need have no worries. If he meets new people, forms new attachments, he will be more prepared for the new lord holder of Windwood at least."

"*I do not want him to go anywhere. And, if there is a new holder, surely the old one's edicts do not stand?*" Elzandria pouted.

Fabiom laughed shortly. "If only! It's one of Herbis's nephews who inherited the holding, and the outstanding services owed. His name's Yasdon. I've never met him, but Tarison has and he seems to think he's a decent enough man, if a bit soft."

Not soft enough to concede to Fabiom's plea that Lesandor be spared in return for an extremely generous payment of amber and produce, however. It puzzled Fabiom that a holding never known to be wealthy would so quickly turn down such an offer.

Chapter Two

LESANDOR WAS NOT overly enthusiastic when his father put the idea of going to Fairwater to him; less enthusiastic still about going to Windwood for two years. He tried not to think about leaving home, and found it surprisingly easy as he had never been anywhere save occasional visits to the holdings that bordered their own and once, aged five, to Riverplain. For fifteen and a half years his world had been a carefree one of adventures in the wildwood, indulgent parents and woodmaids, two doting grandmothers – one human and one Silvanan – and a sister who adored him. Even his studies were pleasant enough, despite an unpromising beginning with an inexperienced tutor who had failed to understand that neither reading nor writing came easily to him. For the past four years Fabiom's old tutor, Masgor, had lived with them and had taken over his education; the old man cheerfully put up with his erratic spelling.

Resolutely, Lesandor pushed thoughts of Fairwater – and Windwood – to the back of his mind. He had other things with which to occupy himself, such as helping his mother in the mulberry coppices, and Darseus – their farm manager since his father Kilm retired – in the vineyards, picking over and tying up the plants in preparation for the ripening fruit; or Nissus – cousin Kita's husband – in the medicinal herb garden his grandfather had struggled to establish, his father had developed, and which now flourished with a multitude of beneficial herbs from many lands.

Nissus, however, was quite enthusiastic about Lesandor going to the capital.

"You'll enjoy it, once you're there," the young physician assured him.

"I certainly did. Naturally, I missed my family and friends, and Deepvale too, but there are plenty of compensations. It's a marvellous place – and the woods are beautiful."

"And…." Lesandor prompted, as he carefully repotted a tray of blue-flowering starwort.

Nissus grinned. "And you can be of help to me. Your cousin Yan has been more than kind: he has brought my herbal treatise to the attention of all sorts of influential people and it is now widely published. But, you know Yan. It's all books with him these days. I'd be grateful for another pair of eyes and ears, looking for plants, listening to stories of how they are used in this place or that – for good and ill. Who better than you? You are a natural herbalist."

"Do you think you would have room to grow anything else here?" Lesandor asked dubiously, looking at the crammed potting shelves all around them.

Nissus chuckled. "Seeing how my interest in plants…."

"Obsession," corrected Kita, who was showing her five-year-old daughter, Keran, which herbs would make a tonic for her younger brothers, for the twins had nasty coughs.

Nissus ignored her. "My *interest*, is almost entirely due to my wife's influence, I am sure I'll be able to talk her round. If I'm nice to her she'll let me build another glass room." Grinning, he glanced over his shoulder at Kita.

"I might," Kita replied. "If you are *exceptionally* nice. And if I am satisfied by your explanation as to what these 'compensations' were that Fairwater had to offer while you were supposed to be studying at the school of apothecary there."

Nissus winked at Lesandor. "I was thinking of the culture and the architecture and the wonderful entertainment, my love. What else?"

It was not at all coincidental that, just twenty days later, Prince Ravik and Princess Maedrim came to visit. With them was Raidan, recently turned sixteen years, the youngest of their five sons. Raidan, who took after his Varlassian mother far more than his father, was a slight, hazel-eyed boy with startling red hair, a sprinkling of freckles and a wide grin.

Lesandor was glad to see him. They had met on several occasions before and had always got on well. He was glad, too, of company his own age; most of their visitors were much older than he.

With both being easy-going and cheerful, Raidan and Lesandor's friendship was immediately renewed, as if they had seen each other only days before, not well over a year.

As the day wore on, the two boys tired of the conversation of their elders and Lesandor suggested they go to the woods. It was a glorious summer's day and Raidan readily agreed, especially when Lesandor mentioned the river.

Laughing, and mock-fighting, they chased across the garden, barely hesitating to strip off before plunging into the River Swan to cross under, rather than over, the stone bridge, bundled clothing held high above their heads.

"Ugh! It's cold!" Raidan gasped. He threw his clothing on the far bank and lunged at Lesandor, pushing him under.

As Lesandor surfaced, spluttering, he caught sight of his sister, watching from among nearby trees.

"The current is strong," Raidan said, deftly avoiding Lesandor's attempts to retaliate. "Is it safe?"

Elzandria smiled.

"Yes, we're very safe," Lesandor promised, pushing water from his hair with both hands.

"The woods here feel different, somehow," Raidan observed once they were dressed again and some way from the river. "The ground's rougher, more up and down, and the trees feel closer together. But it's friendly, isn't it? You'd like Fairwater's woods. Since Pharrell married Luthrina, I've got to know our beech woods well. They're different, as I say, but just as beautiful."

"Might you follow his example?" Lesandor asked. He knew Ravik and Maedrim had consulted his mother when their middle son had expressed his desire to seek a Silvanan bride. While she had been unable to guarantee his safety, Casandrina had shared her belief that, of all their boys, Pharrell was the most likely to succeed. Lesandor also knew she believed Raidan would have a very good chance, should he so choose.

"That boy could do anything he wanted," she had told Raidan's mother the last time the royal family had visited Deepvale. Unlike Lesandor, Raidan had not overheard the conversation.

Raidan pulled a yes-no expression. "I'm tempted, I guess. I mean – the Silvanii are lovely. But no, probably not. I think I'd rather wait – a long while. After all, Father has all the heirs any prince could want. I can see myself getting married at, maybe, thirty. That would be a good age."

"That is one of the best things about marrying a Silvana," Lesandor pointed out. "You get a beautiful bride at seventeen, and the responsibilities of fatherhood in your mid-thirties. That would suit me!"

"That's true. But I want to travel. I want to explore all of Morene, and then further afield. I might spend a year in Varlass, with Grandfather. And Father has a good relationship with King Feeard of Malandel so perhaps I'll visit the Sunlands. Who knows where I'll go?"

"Even Gerik?" Lesandor asked with a grimace.

"Even Gerik!" Raidan replied laughing. "You can come with me."

Lesandor stripped a chunk of creamy-coloured fungus from a nearby oak and threw it at him. "Thanks. But no thanks."

"Not to Gerik, idiot! To Malandel. Is this edible?"

Lesandor snatched the fungus from Raidan's hands. "No." He looked around. "But this one is."

With that, they realised they were getting hungry and began foraging. In time they located some tiny strawberries, a dozen stalks of asparagus, some watercress and more edible fungi; not enough to satisfy them, but more enjoyable for being found.

It was late by the time they returned to the hold-house, laughing together at some joke. Only hunger had brought them back, and they were pleased to be greeted by the news that supper was about to be served. Over the meal, Prince Ravik suggested to Lesandor that he might return to Fairwater with them and stay in the capital awhile, as companion to Raidan.

"I'd be glad to, my lord, thank you," Lesandor replied, discovering his resistance to the notion had vanished completely.

"We will take good care of him," Ravik promised Casandrina and Fabiom four days later as he, Maedrim and the two boys made ready to leave. "He'll enjoy Fairwater. And, as none of our three youngest have seen their grandfather for two years, I thought we might take a trip to Varlass for a brief visit. A voyage would be just the thing to widen Lesandor's horizons. And it would be good for Raidan to have the company of someone his own age."

"Do you plan to visit Gerik also?" Casandrina inquired.

"Ah, my lady," Ravik rebuked mildly, "if I should, I shall send your son back to you first; I would never ask that of Lesandor."

Chapter Three

THEY ARRIVED AT Fairwater Port on a balmy afternoon, after a leisurely four-day voyage on board Ravik's ship, *Galingale*. During the voyage the Ruling Prince had taken the opportunity to visit several of his favoured projects along the coastline.

Lesandor was already awed. In Silverbeach, where the fine white sands furnished not just the local glassworks but pane makers and glassblowers all over Morene, he had had his first glimpse of glass plate manufacturing. Further along the coast he had seen the vast salt flats and evaporation pans at Brinespring. Despite those wonders, as *Galingale* rounded the coastline, its blue sails catching the warm breeze, the vista that opened up before him made Lesandor catch his breath. The sheer number of ships and smaller vessels, and the multitude of dock workers and builders was almost overwhelming. He found himself looking out for the men from their own holding, sent away on service, but it was impossible to see any one person among the throng. Beyond the port was the city, bigger even than he had imagined, and above both was the gleaming white palace.

With care, Lesandor washed his hands in the red marble basin in the palace heart room and, with a slight bow, acknowledged the four doors, one facing each of the winds. That done, he touched the sturdy beech stand that supported the basin: a bough of Sulmarita's tree. She had been wife to Prince Lincius, the first man in Morene to wed a Silvana. His action was partly in homage to her memory, but equally in the hope of gaining courage to face the very different life that lay on the far side of whichever of the heart room's four doors he would be led through.

With a smile, Princess Maedrim indicated the east door. "Welcome to our home."

They had barely gone through to the family's private quarters when Dilon, the youngest of Raidan's brothers, burst in with a delighted cry of "Visitor!"

The three older brothers followed close behind. Two looked at Lesandor uncertainly but the third broke into a broad grin of recognition and grasped Lesandor's right upper arm in the customary salutation of adult men.

"Lesandor! Welcome."

Lesandor returned Pharrell's grip, delighted he should be thus greeted.

It was two years since Pharrell and Dilon had been to Deepvale, longer still since Lesandor had seen Romarus or Laurens.

He had feared he would be unable to tell the two oldest apart, but their bearing marked them easily and he greeted them by name, earning a surprised eyebrow lift from Romarus and a thoughtful half-bow from Laurens. Though none was particularly tall, all four were taller than Raidan, and all were darker-skinned than their youngest brother, in both factors taking after their father.

Face-to-face with the brothers, Lesandor quickly reviewed what he knew of each: Raidan had given him information about the four on board *Galingale*.

"Romarus takes being the first-born far too seriously," Raidan had warned him. "He takes everything far too seriously, to be honest – himself most of all."

Lesandor was not surprised to hear that, he was aware that Fabiom did not think Romarus was the best of Ravik's sons to inherit his father's title.

With reference to his second brother, Raidan had said: "Laurens takes *life* far too seriously – which is not the same thing."

Lesandor already knew that Laurens, whom Casandrina described as 'a gentle soul', had been a pupil of Yan's until very recently, and the two were close friends.

Lesandor had needed no reminder of the middle son. Two years earlier Pharrell had become the first prince for nearly a hundred years to win the hand of a Silvana, and Lesandor was delighted at the prospect of meeting his bride, Luthrina.

The fourth brother was Dilon. Barely two years Raidan's senior, Dilon was Ravik and Maedrim's wild child, and Raidan's chief tormentor and closest ally both.

That night they feasted in a magnificent hall where twenty-seven life-size images of Silvanii and woodmaids adorned the walls. The room was not normally used for informal dining and Lesandor knew it had been opened up for his benefit.

More welcome even than the Silvanan frescoes was the company of Pharrell's wife. Lesandor had never before seen a Silvana shorter than himself. Of a height with her husband, Luthrina was otherwise almost exactly as Lesandor had imagined: her eyes the soft green of a beech tree and her hair, darker than his mother's, shot through with copper tones that reflected the hues of her tree's closed buds. Her presence comforted him. As night fell, she sang a gentle song that lulled all present into a state of postprandial relaxation and his last feelings of unease evaporated.

It did not take Lesandor long to discover there was much to do and see in the capital. Having cousin Yan as his tutor, whilst strange in a way, helped ease the feelings of homesickness that occasionally crept up on him; besides which, Princess Maedrim happily looked after him.

"One more makes no difference," she told him once, when he thanked her for her care. "I lost count years ago," she added. "When *your* time comes to marry, Lesandor, be kind to your wife. If she gives you two or three strapping sons, be grateful. Don't insist a little girl is needed to finish the family off nicely. There are no guarantees in this life."

Raidan heard her and snorted indignantly. "Thank you, Mother."

She tousled his hair and Lesandor laughed, but did not reply. If his plans went aright, and he won his Silvanan bride, one son and one daughter were to be his future. If he failed, he would have no future to worry about.

Despite Lesandor having his heart set on seeking a Silvanan wife, and Raidan's avowed aversion to early marriage, the two attractive, well-bred young men on the verge of adulthood attracted a lot of female attention, as much from mothers of eligible daughters as from the daughters themselves.

Having endured one awkward gathering, the next time the two observed a group of ladies arriving at the palace they fled to the stable block, up against the outer wall of the garden, before Raidan's mother could suggest they meet any of her guests.

At what they hoped was a safe distance from the palace, laughing breathlessly at their close escape, Lesandor admitted he knew nothing about talking to girls, though his father's hold-house was full of them.

Raidan guffawed. "I noticed, and very pretty ones."

Before he could respond to that comment, something caught Lesandor's eye. "What in the world is that?" He peered into the nearest stall where a large black shape loomed out of the shadows. What looked like a huge, long-maned donkey put its head over the door. Lesandor stepped back.

"It's a horse," Raidan said, patting the animal's nose.

"Where is it from?" Cautiously, Lesandor held his hand out and the horse nuzzled his fingers. Its ears were smaller and hair much shorter and stiffer than a donkey's but, like the smaller animals with which he was familiar, it enjoyed having its jowl scratched and soon had its neck stretched upwards, its eyes closed, enjoying the attention.

"When Feeard of Malandel visited us some years ago, Father told him he had never seen a horse. The king sent this as a gift. They say he is a small one, but I can't imagine anything bigger, can you?"

The horse was fat and friendly and, when it was inside, shared its stall with an equally fat donkey, who – seeing the two boys – came over to get a share of the attention.

"He's called Tali. It's a Malandelian word. It means gold."

"Which is a stupid name for a black horse, is it not?" Dilon remarked from the doorway. "I thought I'd seen you two come in here. I presume, like me, you are hiding from Mother's friends and their terrifying daughters. She really should give us more notice when she is planning a soiree. I was nearly spotted this time!" He offered the horse a wisp of hay. "You can ride him, if you want," he said casually, but Lesandor heard the challenge in his voice.

"Have you?"

"We all have," Raidan admitted. "Even Laurens, would you believe? Father doesn't know. Tali had only been here a week when Romarus got on him in the paddock, tried to make him gallop, fell off and broke his ankle. Since then, we're forbidden to sit on him, even in the stable yard."

"I presume Romarus has not got back on since."

Raidan and Dilon exchanged glances.

"Don't you believe it," Dilon said, with a laugh. "Our eldest brother is quite smitten with the idea of being a horseman. He thinks he would look *majestic*. He's fallen off since, as well."

"He looked less than majestic then," Raidan pointed out. "Though he didn't break anything those other times –"

"More's the pity," Dilon muttered.

"So Father doesn't know," Raidan continued, as if his brother had not interrupted him.

"Well?" Dilon opened the door of the stall and gestured for Lesandor to enter.

"You don't have to," Raidan said.

Lesandor hesitated, but Dilon's expression told him the older boy did not believe he would dare – so how could he refuse?

Afterwards, they all admitted he had fallen off very gracefully, which Dilon attributed to his being the son of a Silvana.

They returned to the palace, laughing, shoving and joking, merrier still when Maedrim upbraided them for their absence, as some of her friends had asked that they might be entertained by her youngest sons' musical talents, and they were nowhere to be found.

Of Princess Maedrim's five sons, Raidan alone had inherited her star-reading gift. That skill fascinated Lesandor and the two spent many nights lying out on the grassy hill of the palace gazing up at the spangled heavens, with Raidan pointing out all the stars in their groups and telling his companion the Varlassian names for the constellations, and from time to time reading signs and portents in the night sky. Happily engaged in that pursuit, Lesandor did not notice his friend's occasional reluctance to speak of what he saw, or the worried look that sometimes shadowed Raidan's normally cheerful visage.

Lesandor had been in Fairwater some two months when Raidan came to his room in the early hours one morning and woke him. The light of countless stars shimmered through the open shutter of the small window.

"Something bad is coming, I've seen it in the skies. Mother saw it too. I woke her, for I thought – I hoped – I must be mistaken. Something that bodes ill for you; or someone who wishes you ill."

"Whom have I upset? Who would wish me ill? I can think of no one," Lesandor protested sleepily, pushing himself up onto one elbow against the softness of the wool-and-hyssop-stuffed mattress.

Raidan regarded him for a long moment. "I am worried for you," he said, around a mighty yawn. "There have been other things...."

"Have you not been to bed yet?" Lesandor asked. "Can we worry about this in the morning – the proper morning?"

"I suppose so," Raidan agreed reluctantly. "I just thought you should know. Move over, then." With that, he climbed onto the bed, curled up on his side and immediately fell asleep.

Lesandor found it impossible to go back to sleep himself after that and, having thrown a blanket over his friend, spent the cold predawn hours wondering what or who could be the cause of Raidan's disquiet.

The answer came before noon the next day, with the arrival of Raidan's aunt, the Princess Jaymna, come with her ten-year-old grandson to celebrate the forthcoming birth anniversary of Prince Romarus's first-born son, heir to the principality.

Raidan hurried to tell Lesandor the news. "Just keep out of her way. Father thinks you should stay with Yan while she is here."

"I have never even met her!" Lesandor pointed out. "She has no reason to hate me."

"Maybe – but you do know what your mother did to her garden, don't you? It's never been the same since. Most of the fruit is inedible: looks gorgeous, tastes disgusting. And most of the grounds of her house are just run wild. Whenever she speaks of your family – which she manages to do every time we see her – it is not in pleasant tones, believe me;

though I never did learn what was behind their falling-out." He looked at Lesandor expectantly, but Lesandor shook his head.

Actually, Lesandor knew very well; it was just that he could think of no way to tell Raidan without sounding offensive.

"I do know Mother gets a very funny look in her eyes if ever your aunt's name is mentioned, and Father quickly changes the subject," he allowed, which was certainly the truth.

Whilst Jaymna was staying in Fairwater, the two boys could only meet during the day, and in secret. Within the palace, the Silvana-fresco hall was their favoured haunt; outside the palace, Yan's lodgings offered the best refuge. On one of these days – halfway between the palace and the street where Yan lived – they chanced upon the arrival of an elaborately draped litter, borne by four pied donkeys and accompanied by a sizable entourage of servants and guards. They watched the procession with interest.

Later, mentioning what they had seen to Dilon, they discovered Lord Yasdon of Windwood had arrived in the city to ask for the aid of Prince Ravik in settling a land dispute in his holding.

"It's an odd thing," Dilon said. "According to Father, Lord Yasdon has managed to avoid coming here whenever he was supposed to, for his testing by the Assembly before his appointment as holder, for instance. And yet he turns up now."

"Didn't he try to offer his daughter in marriage to cousin Larse?" Raidan remembered. "But Larse was already betrothed."

"Perhaps he's come looking for another royally-connected husband for her," Dilon suggested.

Raidan elbowed his brother. "You and Laurens are the only ones of us old enough and neither married nor betrothed, Dilon. It's unlikely to be Laurens, so must be you."

Having learnt who it was that came to the capital in such style, Lesandor determined to get a closer look at the holder of Windwood, regardless of Jaymna's presence in the palace. He had long-since told Raidan of the service he was bound to do and the young prince suggested they secrete themselves on the balcony above the fresco hall where Yasdon was going to be entertained by one of the members of the Assembly that very evening. All went according to plan, and when they did get the opportunity to spy on Yasdon, Lesandor was pleasantly surprised at the smallish, jolly man the Lord Holder turned out to be.

Raidan put his mouth close to Lesandor's ear. "Well, I suppose if the situation was reversed, Yasdon's son might have more cause to be nervous meeting *your* father for the first time than it seems you need be of meeting Yasdon," he suggested, watching the holder of Windwood tuck into a sweet rice dish with great enthusiasm, sharing jokes with his fellow diners and the serving-men alike.

"Really?" Lesandor asked.

"Lord Fabiom is an imposing man, is he not? I don't think anyone would describe Lord Yasdon thus."

Lesandor smiled wistfully; Fabiom was a gentle father, yet perhaps that was not how someone unfamiliar would view him. It was an odd thought.

"Does Lord Yasdon have a son?" Lesandor asked, equally quietly, really thinking for the first time what it would be like to go to a strange holding for two years.

"Yes," Raidan whispered back. "A bit younger than us, thirteen or so." He pulled a face. "Petron's his name. I met him about two years ago – horrible boy!"

The afternoon following Lord Yasdon's arrival, Yan – having just finished some lengthy research at the academy – invited Lesandor and Raidan to go with him to the theatre and then back to his lodgings for supper. Raidan had to decline supper for he was expected at the family celebration to mark the first birth anniversary of Romarus and Tanalia's infant son, Davin. Nevertheless, he gladly joined the outing to the theatre and the three of them enjoyed themselves enormously.

Afterwards, when Raidan had gone, Yan's mood changed.

"I think we should drink to the health of Prince Ravik's grandson," he suggested. But he scowled as he spoke. "A lot is expected of heirs," he muttered as he poured them both a cup of wine from his own father's cellars.

"You got out of it," Lesandor reminded him.

Yan tasted the wine appreciatively.

"Yes. Thankfully my sister turned out to be more than capable; but if she hadn't been, or if she had married away from the holding...."

"Something is troubling you," Lesandor guessed.

Yan sighed. "Yes, it is." He twisted the cup round and around in his hands. "You and Lord Yasdon of Windwood. *That* is something that can't be got out of. Have you met him?"

Lesandor shook his head. "No, but I saw him. He looked pleasant enough, and quite friendly, though not very fit. Windwood must be a very prosperous holding if Yasdon's arrival is anything to go by."

"It never was prosperous in the past. Yasdon may have wealth of his own, that I don't know. If he has, it's from his mother's side. His father, Nimo, was a wastrel by all accounts." Yan pursed his lips. Ever since he was old enough to be aware, Yan had known his father was concerned at the demand made on Deepvale by Windwood: that Fabiom's first-born son should be bound to the western holding for two years. Since he had joined the academy in Fairwater, eight years previously, he had made a point of finding out all he could about the new lord holder of Windwood.

"Rumours suggest Yasdon is devious. I'm not even sure the holding should have passed to him. There were a number of relatives with equal claims. And Mother always maintained there had been something odd about the death of my cousin Dala, though no one seems quite sure what." He passed Lesandor a bowl of olives. "There are no real facts to be had. Aunt Riann went off to a small house, away from Windwood's municipal centre, when the last really bad fever hit there. It killed her husband, as well as Dala, and Dala's husband, Lambrose. That must be oh, fifteen years ago. Since then, Riann has taken no further part in the holding's affairs. She was some ten years older than Mother, which would make her about seventy now. As far as I know she is still caring for Giar. Apparently he's been her only interest since Herbis' and Dala's deaths, though he never made any recovery."

Lesandor swirled the blood-red wine around in the cup and stared at it intently.

"When you say 'odd', with regards to the death of Lord Herbis's daughter, you don't mean Lord Yasdon had some part in it, do you?"

"No, no! Well, that's never been suggested," Yan hastily assured him. "Even a hint of something like that and Ravik would have had to intervene. No, just timing, or inheritance. Remember her mother and brother are still alive. Nothing of hers should have passed to Yasdon – whether goods, land or title. All I'm saying is – when the time comes and you must go there – be careful."

"Was there something about Dala and my father?" Lesandor asked.

Yan frowned, remembering. "Something," he muttered. "I think the meal is ready."

"Yan! Tell me."

"I was very young, nine, ten at most."

"Yan!"

Yan threw up his arms. "They were betrothed; according to Lord Herbis anyway. Fabiom had different ideas, that's all."

Lesandor's plans to keep well out of Princess Jaymna's way were proceeding perfectly, until the second day of Lord Yasdon's visit.

Windwood's holder was exploring the palace, commenting loudly and enthusiastically on everything he saw, and Lesandor and Raidan were following him – at a safe distance, or so they believed.

They came around a corner and found themselves face-to-face, not with the holder of Windwood but with Princess Jaymna.

"Raidan, I was looking for you. I want you to have supper with me tonight, on my boat. Oh," she paused and scrutinised Lesandor, "and who is your friend?"

Before Raidan could think of some way of *not* introducing Lesandor to his aunt, her expression became incredulous.

"I know you," she said. "Lesandor of Deepvale. I am right, am I not?"

Lesandor made a polite bow, berating himself for being stupid enough to get caught like this. "I do not believe we have met, your Highness," he managed.

"Perhaps not," she allowed. "Nevertheless, I do know you. I remember I sent you a gift when you were born."

His mind raced – he had no recollection of any gift ever being mentioned. "I am sorry, my lady. I was not aware of that." He wondered what it could have been: a peace offering? Pacifying a Silvana was not easily achieved – he could well recall the fire in his mother's eyes last time Jaymna's name was mentioned – yet maybe the princess had tried to make amends.

"Thank you," he said, rather belatedly, hoping that was the right response.

She smiled. "You are welcome, Lesandor."

Much to his surprise, Jaymna invited him to join Raidan and Dilon for supper on board her river boat that very night. Raidan looked worried, and Lesandor knew his friend's premonition was preying on his mind. He trusted Raidan's instincts and was loath to accept the invitation, yet what could he do? Had Prince Ravik been there, he might have intervened, however there was only Raidan, and he could offer no assistance.

"From bad to worse," Lesandor groaned as he stepped onto the brightly lit boat and noticed Windwood's portly holder already ensconced on board.

"Told you: husband hunting!" Dilon poked him in the side. "You, me and Raidan – all gathered together for inspection; all fair game."

"I am fifteen," Lesandor reminded the young prince. "You, on the other hand, at eighteen, are now quite eligible."

"But you'll be sixteen in what, five days?"

"Yes, and still a year before my coming to manhood." He accepted a wooden skewer of baked grapes and shrimps from a servant. "Are you eager to marry, so young?"

"Probably not. Though they say Yasdon's daughter is very pretty. So I could be tempted – if I wasn't having so much fun *not* being married. Speaking of which, I see Aunt Jaymna has brought some quite attractive handmaidens with her, so, if you will excuse me..."

Lesandor would rather Dilon had stayed close by, for he had been deprived of Raidan's company as soon as they boarded. Urged by his aunt to entertain her guests, Raidan had sent for his favourite instrument, a shell and ox-horn lyre inlaid with mother-of-pearl, and then been obliged to spend the remainder of the evening sitting at his aunt's feet, playing. Fortunately there were just enough people for Lesandor to be able to avoid both Jaymna and Yasdon for most of the evening, though Yasdon kept smiling at him in a rather alarming way every time they set eyes on each other.

Happily, Yasdon's attention was mostly taken up elsewhere – he was enthralled by Jaymna, talking away to her animatedly whenever he got the chance. During one such occasion, Lesandor felt the princess's eyes boring into him as, at her side, Yasdon reclined, his hands articulating his tale as much as his words. Though Lesandor could not hear what they were saying, he could read Yasdon's gestures well enough – he was telling the story of his cousin Giar's descent into madness, and Jaymna was taking in every word.

When, eventually, Yasdon stopped talking, Jaymna turned her full attention back to him. She patted his arm as she made some reply; immediately Yasdon was beaming and nodding with delight at whatever she had suggested.

With Raidan occupied and Dilon nowhere to be seen, Lesandor cut himself a piece of cheese and wished the night was over.

"Her Highness would have a word, sir," a serving-man informed him.

Lesandor glanced across. Yasdon beckoned him urgently, while the princess raised a languid hand.

Lesandor took a deep breath and made his way to them.

Jaymna patted the cushion beside her seat and, having little choice, Lesandor sat.

"Lord Yasdon thinks you should visit his house very soon. He'll take you back there with him immediately. Isn't that a splendid idea, Lesandor? That way there won't be any nasty surprises – when you go later."

Raidan glanced up from his lyre and frowned.

Lesandor looked from the princess to Lord Yasdon. What could he say? Where he went, what he did, was up to Prince Ravik. For the moment he had nothing to worry about. Nevertheless, he had a rather uncomfortable feeling.

Chapter Four

THOUGH HE HAD firmly rejected the suggestion that Lesandor should return to Windwood with Yasdon, Prince Ravik made the decision to accept Yasdon's invitation to go to Windwood himself, to help resolve a land dispute that had arisen in the holding. He agreed that, when he went, Raidan and Lesandor might accompany him. Both boys were destined to be statesmen and it was about time they learnt the ways of such matters. His wife was not so enthusiastic about the idea. However, for once, Ravik agreed with his sister, and felt that a gentle and relatively brief introduction to the holding of Windwood would do Lesandor no harm.

"This is an excellent idea," Yasdon enthused as he made ready to depart. "You can get to know us, and we you," he added, in case Lesandor had missed the point.

"And I shall know exactly where you are," Jaymna said quietly, as she stepped away. She too was leaving.

Ten days after Yasdon and Jaymna's departure from the capital, Ravik joined his five sons and Lesandor for a noon-time meal. They were in a private dining alcove adjoining the city's great bath house, where the younger men had spent a good part of the morning.

"I shall see you at the palace. Don't be long," Ravik told Raidan as soon as they had eaten. "We leave in two hours and you need to say goodbye to your mother. You, too, Lesandor. Maedrim would take it amiss if she didn't see you before we depart."

As his father left, Pharrell sat up and poured more well-watered wine into their cups. "Rather you than me," he said. "I can't imagine either of you are overjoyed at the prospect of sitting, possibly for days, listening to interminable and tedious arguments over borders and rights of way."

After the freedom the two had enjoyed for the past months, they had to agree. Though, as neither of them had been to that part of Morene before, they were quietly excited, too.

"Be wary of Lord Yasdon. He seems meek, but he is ambitious," Romarus said. He emptied his cup in one gulp, put down the empty vessel, wiped his mouth and stood. "Travel safe," he added as he left the room.

"One ambitious man recognises another." Laurens, twenty-three and by far the most serious and studious of Ravik and Maedrim's sons quoted the philosopher Merites – just quietly enough for his older brother not to overhear as he shut the door.

Raidan chuckled.

Lesandor frowned. "How can a man destined to be ruling prince be ambitious? What could he want that he does not have?"

"Gerik," Dilon replied without hesitation.

"He wants to gallop about on horseback, like the Malandelian king is said to do," Raidan added.

Dilon slapped him on the shoulder, hard enough to knock Raidan sideways. "Ah, you said it – 'king' – that's it. He wants to be more than a prince. He wants to be a king."

"That hurt!" Raidan complained. "And no, he doesn't. Not even our big brother is *that* ambitious – or stupid." He picked up one of the cushions he had been reclining on and threw it at Dilon.

"He can call himself what he will. The Silvanii won't bow to him," Pharrell pointed out, deftly saving the earthenware wine jug from a poorly-aimed cushion. "And speaking of Silvanii, I too must wish you a safe journey and take my leave. I promised my wife I would return by midday, and I fear I am already forsworn."

"If she is anything like my mother, she has little notion of time," Lesandor said with a laugh as Pharrell drained his cup.

"True enough. Be safe."

Laurens glanced up from the small book he was reading even as he finished his meal. "Names matter. What a man calls himself affects how he behaves, how he sees himself." He stared at the closed door, as if seeing his brother beyond it. "You might be right, Dilon."

"Which would be a small miracle of itself," Raidan said with a laugh, rubbing his shoulder theatrically and then ducking to avoid a further slap.

⬦

Ravik's party arrived in Windwood shortly before noon on the fifth day after setting out. Lord Yasdon made them most welcome and, despite the fact that he had had so little time to prepare, presented all sorts of diversions: fire jugglers, musicians playing lutes and pipes, even a poet who, to Lesandor's delight and Prince Ravik's amusement, recited several of Fabiom's poems, describing them as 'odes of the wildwood, collected in the eastern holdings'.

Yasdon was a jovial man who laughed readily and provided lavish meals for his guests, starting with a great feast to which he had invited the holding's most notable citizens.

The meal and the entertainment went on throughout the remainder of the day. Having already eaten well of fish and poultry, Lesandor was amazed when great bronze platters of roast meats were carried in to the dining room. His amazement turned to concern when their host came over to where he reclined on one of several blue velvet-draped settles and confided, "This must seem a poor show to you, Lesandor, compared with what Deepvale is able to provide. Alas, Windwood is nowhere near as wealthy as your father's holding."

"No, not at all. You have been most generous to us, my lord. This is splendid."

"Excellent." Yasdon patted his arm and beamed at him.

When the lord holder moved on to speak to other guests, Lesandor leant over to Raidan. "My father has never gone to such trouble to entertain yours," he whispered anxiously. "Should he have done so?"

Raidan speared a piece of tender goat meat with his knife. "My father visits Deepvale often, he hardly ever comes to Windwood – what does that tell you?" He regarded the diners lounging around the room, some on settles, others on sumptuous cushions. "I'd say this is all for show." His voice, already low, dropped further. "I recall my brother Laurens saying something about this holding being less than prosperous. Perhaps this is Yasdon's way of making a lie of such rumours, or at least trying to."

Throughout the meal, Yasdon watched Lesandor carefully. He had realised the young man was on extremely good terms with the ruling prince and his son but could not decide if that was a good or bad thing. His interest grew the next morning when Lesandor trounced the holding's best young archers in a contest held as part of the festivities. Yasdon took such skills very seriously, even though he preferred not to take part in much physical activity himself. The fact that the boy was just turned sixteen years impressed him immensely and when, that afternoon, Lesandor proved that he was not only capable against a set target but expert at the chase as well, Yasdon knew he had made the right decision when he turned down Fabiom's attempts to buy Lesandor's service back.

That night they feasted well on wild boar. As the meal drew to an end, the visitors were invited to entertain the gathering. Lesandor's mellow voice – hinting of his maternal inheritance – and the song of the woods he chose to sing, which he had learnt from Elzandria, sealed his reputation, and his fate.

The next morning all pleasures were put aside and business resumed as Ravik listened to the facts of the land dispute that had arisen and in which Yasdon had requested his intervention. The matter took five days to hear and decide. Lesandor attended all the sessions and comported himself admirably. His father had trained him well and he was more interested than he had expected to be, for the case concerned the possible eviction of six households and the destruction of a wide tract of woodland.

On the final day, Yasdon sent for him. He was smiling broadly when Lesandor entered his private room.

"A satisfactory conclusion, don't you think?" Yasdon inquired, referring to the proposed compromise reached in the case, which had resulted in the relocation of four of the families onto better land and the cessation of the felling. Ravik's graphic description of the poor, thin soil on the treeless plains of Gerik had seen to that. The prince had not mentioned that Lesandor had taken him into the woods and shown him how close some of the felling was to Silvanan haunts, or that the boy had pointed out nearby woodmaids' trees to himself and Raidan, much to their delight.

"Most satisfactory," Lesandor agreed. "I thank you for allowing me to see and hear the wisdom shown these last few days. I hope that in my life I may make good use of this experience."

"I hope so too," Yasdon agreed.

It should have been a casual remark but Lesandor heard great intensity in the words and he frowned slightly.

"I have a – how shall we say – yes: a *proposal* to put to you, Lesandor. Sit, sit. Now, from my late uncle's papers, I understand you are to spend two years with us here in Windwood. An unfortunate business, most unfortunate. Yet there we are and, if we wait, as you probably expected, well, I don't quite know what we shall do with you to make your time here both worthwhile for us and not too unpleasant for you. However, even the worst situations can be turned to the good, eh? You see, there's Petron. You have yet to meet Petron. He's fourteen and he is, what shall I say, for it pains me – *difficult*, I suppose – if I am honest. A situation for which I hold myself to blame entirely. His mother died when he was born and I have over-indulged him. Now it is time to change that. He needs both guidance, which I trust I and his tutors may give him, and example – which he could gain from you. So, my suggestion is simply this: that your service begin right away. All I would be asking of you is to demonstrate how the heir of a high house should conduct himself, the value of learning, the arts and skills a young man of breeding should display." He paused and tapped his fingers against his lower lip. "I also have a daughter, my dear Mysha. A lovely girl. She is soon sixteen – you would like her, I think."

"Absolutely not!" Ravik said, that evening, when Lesandor went to his chamber and told him what Yasdon had suggested. "Yet, by your expression, I think you are not averse to the suggestion."

Lesandor shrugged. "I do not really know how I feel," he admitted. "But it seems to me that, rather than two years of punishing labour or demeaning tedium – as I had feared – Lord Yasdon is offering me two years of comfort and relative freedom, doing what I do best. And I could cope with that."

Raidan, who was sitting strumming his lyre on the balcony beyond the open window, chuckled, as his father smiled broadly and said, "Punishing labour or demeaning tedium? I would not permit either of those eventualities to befall you, Lesandor."

"Nevertheless, he is right, Father," Raidan pointed out. "And Yasdon's knowledge of treelaw seems woefully inadequate, Lesandor could help rectify that."

"I would certainly try, my lord," Lesandor promised.

Ravik nodded hesitantly. "I admit these points are valid, but your parents may not be happy to learn I brought you here for a brief visit, and left you for two years."

"They might not mind too much," Lesandor reasoned. "I am sure Father will be glad if I can discharge my service in Windwood early, and then life can go on, with this behind us. I will be of more use to Father in two years' time, as well – for surely I must learn something useful if I remain here."

"Very astute," Ravik agreed. "Very well, I shall let this decision be yours. And I must confess there is a potential benefit for me in this: when his time comes, Morene will need Petron to be a better holder than Yasdon currently is. If you can help accomplish that, I shall indeed be grateful."

As they broke their fast the next morning, Lesandor gave Windwood's holder his decision.

Yasdon beamed in delight and leant forward to clasp Lesandor's hands. "Excellent! Excellent!" Then, noticing the ruling prince looked less than pleased, asked anxiously, "My lord, you do not approve?"

"I am undecided whether I approve or not. Nevertheless, I give my consent – on the understanding that the boy is treated with the respect due to his birth, and not in accordance with him being in bounden service."

"Of course! Of course!" Yasdon agreed. "I had intended nothing less, my lord, I assure you. While he is here, Lesandor will be like a son to me."

That afternoon, as his party made ready to leave, the prince composed a letter to Fabiom and Casandrina. He reasoned that Windwood was no more than six days journey from Deepvale and there was nothing in the agreement which would preclude Lesandor from returning home if occasion demanded. Indeed, Lesandor had had only one request, which was that his next birth anniversary should be spent at home. Although Yasdon had tried to object, Ravik had made it a condition of Lesandor staying – insisting a young man should be with his own family when he celebrated his coming to manhood. The irony hit him even as he said so: had that been the case with Giar, had he not been left in Fabiom's care, Lesandor would not now be in this position. Thirty years ago, Ravik had not approved of Herbis's demand of 'a son for a son', though he had little choice but to sanction it in order to avoid more serious conflict, for rarely did antagonism between two holdings not spill over to others. Time had passed, and Yasdon was not Herbis; he had no personal vendetta against Deepvale. Indeed, Giar's loss of sensibility had resulted in Yasdon's ascendance. Ravik sealed the letter, praying that his belief expressed within – that Yasdon would treat the boy fairly – was correct.

For Lesandor, the hardest thing was to say goodbye to Raidan. It had been good to have the company of someone his own age, someone to share things with, to joke with.

In token of their friendship Raidan suggested they exchange cloak pins until they should meet again. He offered Lesandor his finely-wrought gold clasp set with a black Varlassian opal, but Lesandor shook his head. He only had the clasp of silver-mounted amber that his father had loaned him on the day of his departure from Deepvale. It was not his to give away.

"Is the amber from your mother's tree?" Raidan asked, when Lesandor explained.

Lesandor nodded and swallowed hard as a sudden pang of homesickness knotted his insides.

"A loan then," Raidan suggested, putting an awkward hand on his arm.

"Yes, I would like that," Lesandor agreed.

"It won't be for long," Raidan said, trying to sound reassuring. Then he grinned. "Don't let Yasdon overfeed you, or your mother won't recognise you when you *do* get a chance to go home."

Lesandor unfastened the silver pin. "You will come back here, won't you?"

"Yes, I promise! And I will take the greatest care of this until I do. But – are you sure?"

"I am. I have another piece of amber from her tree – I always carry it with me – and my bow is one Father and I made together. I would like something of yours too." He smiled wistfully. "Everything is so different here. And we were having fun, weren't we? Yasdon laughs a lot but that is not the same thing."

"No, it's not, but you'll find things to enjoy," Raidan insisted. "I wish I could offer to stay awhile but we're off to Varlass almost immediately. I wish you were coming too." His grip on Lesandor's arm tightened. "I know what we'll do – when the time for your official service comes about I'll persuade Father that we should serve together."

Lesandor was pleased with that suggestion, especially given Prince Ravik's promise that, unlike Fabiom, he would not end up in Gerik.

He pinned Raidan's gold and opal clasp onto his shoulder. "That, I shall look forward to. Meanwhile, wish me luck with Petron."

Raidan's grin widened and his eyes sparkled wickedly. "Oh, I do, for you'll surely need it," he said.

Chapter Five

AN OPAL-SET CLOAK clasp was not the only piece of jewellery Lesandor received that day.

The royal party had not long departed when Yasdon sent for him. With some trepidation, Lesandor made his way to the office that Yasdon maintained in his hold-house. Without any allies there, it had occurred to him that he had no idea what the future held in store.

"Come in, boy, come in." Yasdon was smiling broadly. "It's just you and me for now. We can get to know each other properly, can't we?"

For a moment, Lesandor froze as thoughts came to him of his father's first encounter with Princess Jaymna – which, though he had suggested otherwise to Raidan, he had in fact heard about in explicit detail from Fabiom's old friend Philon on more than one occasion. Lesandor could see no way of escaping Yasdon's clutches if the lord holder had amorous intentions.

"I have something for you," Yasdon continued. "Come closer, come closer. Don't look so alarmed."

Trying to appear more confident than he felt, Lesandor made his way to where Yasdon was unwrapping something shiny from a piece of yellow silk.

"Isn't this a fine piece?" the holder asked. He held up a bronze armband with two tightly wound spirals, one above, one below, each with a small sapphire at the centre.

"Indeed it is, my lord," Lesandor agreed, relieved.

"Try it. Try it," Yasdon urged, regardless of the fact that Lesandor already wore a leaf motif band around his right upper-arm and a plain band around his left.

Lesandor reached for his left arm, but Yasdon stopped him. "The other one."

The entwined oak and ivy band had been a gift from his grandmother Vida on his fourteenth birth anniversary. Reluctantly, Lesandor removed it and laid it on Yasdon's desk, then replaced it with the spirals and their bright, eye-like centres.

"While you are here, you will keep that on."

It was not a suggestion.

While Lesandor was in Yasdon's study, his belongings were moved to the guest suite Prince Ravik had vacated only that morning. Dismissed by the holder, Lesandor stood and looked at his reflection in the polished metal mirror. His right arm, the most visible. Even with a cloak on it would be seen. Yasdon had claimed him. The band was part gift, part symbol of servitude. For two years his will was to be subject to Yasdon's. This was the sign. A constant reminder.

Lesandor fingered the spirals, tracing one inwards to its centre. Then he swapped his plain armband for the leaf one he had removed earlier. He had said nothing of his Silvanan heritage to Windwood's holder, nor had Yasdon made mention of it. Being the sort of man he was, Lesandor could only surmise that Yasdon did not know. In that secret lay a sort of freedom and Lesandor resolved to say nothing of the matter.

For the next nine days, Yasdon took Lesandor with him wherever he went – to the offices in the municipal centre, to the courtroom, to his business interests. Together they visited craftsmen, merchants, the holding's elders and Yasdon's farm manager. That still left a good amount of time, for Yasdon was happy to leave as much work as possible to others.

Lesandor divided his spare time between exploring the wildwood and trying to see what could be done with the remnants of Lord Herbis's foray into sericulture. The stands of thirty-year-old mulberry trees – a gift to Windwood from Deepvale on Fabiom's return from service – were overgrown and neglected, while the silk mill – built at great expense – was producing little of real value or quality, and that mostly from cocoons reared on farms elsewhere in the holding. Yet the basis was there, and he had two years. If Yasdon was keen, and Lesandor guessed he would be, building up a small yet viable silk business was something that could easily be accomplished. It was even something he and Petron could, perhaps, do together – which would satisfy the holder's demands, surely?

Yasdon's children had been staying with an elderly aunt of their late mother's, and were put out when they returned to learn that they had missed the royal visitors. Petron was also disturbed to find Lesandor had taken over the silk mill and had, in the brief time he had been there, seemingly won the hearts of the entire household. He went to say as much to his sister.

"I know. I've heard all about him. Have you seen him, Petron? I did – just briefly – from the window. He has the blackest hair, and he's much taller than Father, and very handsome." Mysha glanced at her brother, short and skinny, with bad skin. "My maids were telling me he sings beautifully and, despite his deep complexion, his eyes are the brightest shade of blue."

Mysha gazed at her dimpled reflection in the mirror and began to brush her soft brown hair.

"You've already done that."

"I want to look my best. After all, I might just bump into him in the corridor. He's been given the lavender rooms...."

"He's what? He's here on service!"

"Oh, Petron! Don't be silly. He's the son of a holder. Where do you expect him to sleep – with the donkeys?"

"Right. Where's Father? Why wasn't he home when we returned? This is ridiculous."

"I'm home now," Yasdon answered, sweeping into Mysha's room and her embrace. "What's ridiculous, Petron?"

"This person – Lesandor. You've given him the best rooms, the servants are running around after him. He's supposed to be here on service – working!"

"He *is* working," Yasdon replied mildly, smoothing Mysha's hair as

36

he spoke. "He has already reorganised the rearing rooms in the silk mill and has started pruning the trees in the orchard."

"Well, isn't he wonderful? And that's another thing. What's this about me working with him? The silk mills! Do you honestly think I'm going to start picking mulberry leaves or boiling cocoons?"

"Well, yes, Petron. As a matter of fact, I do."

Up until then, Petron had been looking forward to a holder's son being around for two years' service; the thought had amused him greatly. He had not envisioned that would entail the takeover of one of the best suites in the house and every privilege being bestowed on the visitor, let alone that he himself would be required to work on the silk farm.

"No. Let him do it. Let him sleep out there too. He's the one who is paying us back for what happened to Giar."

"Come now, Petron. You are quite aware this matter of service is a formality. Lesandor was in no way involved in my cousin's demise. He was not even born at the time! Just this once, take my advice – make a friend of Lesandor. And learn about silk production as well. It could turn into a profitable business. Goodness knows, we could do with *something* being profitable around here."

Petron had no such intention and instead went off with his friends to a tavern in the municipal centre from which he did not return for two days.

In contrast, Mysha did not share such misgivings and quite agreed with her father that their visitor should be looked after as well as possible. Once she had met Lesandor, as she did that evening at supper, she was even more certain.

From the moment they were introduced, Lesandor discovered that Mysha would be his constant companion had she not had other duties to attend to. Yasdon did nothing to discourage his daughter's obvious attraction to their guest, and Lesandor sensed impending disaster.

It was not that Mysha was at all disagreeable; indeed she was very comely, neat and courteous. It was just that she could never be accused of being clever, or witty, or inquisitive, nor did she share any of his interests, except for a small fondness for poetry. Furthermore, her curvaceous prettiness was not particularly attractive to Lesandor, who was more enamoured of the lithe beauty of his mother's woodmaids; for Mysha took after her father, caring nothing for the outdoors, and she was rather delicate. And then there was Petron. Even without other plans for his future, the prospect of having Petron as brother would not have appealed to Lesandor. His initial hope that they might be friends had been short-lived and the younger boy was one person he did not encourage to keep him company. Not that Petron needed much discouraging – he soon learnt to admire Lesandor but, unlike Prince Raidan, he was quite capable of resenting him at the same time. As his resentment took no practical form, Lesandor paid it no heed; he even hoped Petron's antipathy might serve him as a means to escape any closer involvement with Lord Yasdon's family.

Unfortunately, Yasdon was not easily put off. Within half a year, when Lesandor had proved himself the ablest bowman and among the best orators in the holding, Yasdon began to speak openly about long-term plans and ideas – together with vague comments about two years being little compensation for the loss of a holding's heir.

Close to his seventeenth birth anniversary, Lesandor had quite a task to persuade Yasdon to let him return to his parents' holding; Yasdon was all for inviting them to celebrate Lesandor's coming to manhood in Windwood.

"Ask them here. We'll throw a great party. Ask them to come."

Lesandor explained, without explaining, that his sister was unable to travel and he would not wish to spend such a momentous day apart from her. Reluctantly Yasdon let him go, but not without a full escort.

"Come back to us soon." Yasdon's hand gripped the bronze and sapphire band he had bestowed upon Lesandor. Despite the smiles and the convivial arm-clasps that followed, it seemed more like a command than a parting pleasantry.

Chapter Six

FABIOM WAS WAITING at the hostelry at Watersmeet, near the shared border with Fairwater and Alderbridge, for he had been warned of Lesandor's impending arrival by Casandrina's woodmaids. What he was not expecting was that his son would be accompanied by six fully-armed men.

"Is there trouble?" Fabiom asked, returning Lesandor's enthusiastic embrace. It had been years since travellers had been harassed on the roads and no word had come to him that there had been any recent occurrences.

"No. Lord Yasdon is just very cautious," Lesandor assured him.

Greetings over, Fabiom had some trouble persuading the mistress of the place that she could accommodate and feed so many, for the hostelry was already full. But, on the promise of an amphora of the season's best wine, he finally got his way.

While the woman prepared a hasty meal, her two children served watered-wine, bread and spiced almonds.

Fabiom addressed the escort captain: "Tonight you will stay here. Tomorrow I will make arrangements for you and your men to be accommodated in the municipal centre. Present yourself to the clerk there at noon and he will show you to your lodgings."

Clearly uncomfortable with the arrangements, the captain was, nevertheless, well-trained enough to realise he could not argue with the local holder about where he and his men might go, or when.

"Why are we staying here? There is time to get home before dark," Lesandor said, taking a mouthful of the hurriedly-prepared meal. The mistress of the hostelry had solved the problem of how to cater for her unexpected guests by cutting up the little meat she had left and mixing it with a mess of cooked lentils, chopped olives and fresh herbs.

Fabiom moved some food around on his plate, but did not eat. "We're not. They are. Eat. We should be going. As you say, we can get home before dark, but to do that we need to leave soon."

Across the room, the men – seated on large cushions – ate with gusto.

Fabiom stood and drained his cup. "Is there anything in your belongings you need before the morrow?"

Lesandor shook his head.

"Good. Bring my son's things," Fabiom told the captain, then threw down a handful of coins on the table. "Are you ready?"

Lesandor looked at his own meal, mostly eaten, and his father's, barely touched.

"I'm not hungry. Let's go," Fabiom insisted.

The confluence of the rivers was at the very edge of the wildwood. Within forty paces the shortcut path to Deepvale's hold-house disappeared between the trees.

They had not been travelling long when Lesandor stopped and glanced about. "I can sense Silvanii, I have done since we entered the woods, but I have seen none. How strange."

"We can't tarry," Fabiom warned. "Come, we need to keep moving."

"Is everything all right, Father? You seem distracted."

Fabiom tried to relax, failed. "Let's get you home. Your mother is anxious to see you."

Half-roused by quiet voices, Fabiom was fully awakened by Casandrina slipping from his embrace, and their bed. The dim light that filtered through the slats of the shutters suggested dawn had not yet broken.

"I am sorry." She leant to kiss him. "I did not mean to disturb you. Kir'h saw Lesandor go out of the house, so I am going to...."

"Make sure he does not cross the bridge," he finished for her. "I'll go. I should be with him."

Casandrina considered. "Yes. Perhaps that would be for the best," she agreed.

A mist hung over the garden and the grass was sodden with dew. Everything was silent. Fabiom shivered, pulling his cloak closer. As he had expected, Lesandor was standing by the stone bridge that led from the gardens, across the Swan river, into the wildwood.

"Mother says I must not ... must not...."

Hinting at dangers she refused to elaborate upon, Casandrina had insisted he must not present himself in the woods on his birth eve, saying only that he had to trust her. He had argued with her, though he knew she cared only for his wellbeing, but she was adamant and, finally, he had given his word.

"I know," Fabiom said, putting an arm around Lesandor's shoulders. "It's hard."

It was hard too, to know what words to use to comfort his son. Fabiom remembered that when he set his own heart on winning a Silvanan bride he was not prepared to listen to any objection. If someone had come up with a genuine reason why he should not pursue that course, he had no idea what he would have done.

"Did you know she would forbid me? You did, didn't you?" Lesandor pulled away from Fabiom's embrace. "That's why you were distracted yesterday."

"I – Yes, I did. But only very recently. We had never discussed it. I always thought you would; she always knew you couldn't. Neither of us guessed the other thought differently. And I am so sorry."

Fabiom turned his gaze to the mist-shrouded forest beyond the bridge. Since earliest memory he had thought of the wildwood as benign, the place where he went to feel safe. He could not reconcile that feeling with his wife's dire warnings to keep their son from venturing there.

Earlier, as he dressed, he had asked her, "Would it really be so dreadful if he presented himself on his birth anniversary?"

She answered without hesitation. "Yes."

"Just 'yes'?"

The bronze pin he was trying to fasten snagged on the fabric of his tunic. She took it from him and secured the shoulder.

"Would you see the line of Laurrus broken? Even if Lesandor succeeded, how could his son live in the world of men, be a lord to men – such as you are? Such a child would care nothing for commerce or politics. Reading, writing – Lesandor has trouble enough with such things."

"But that is not your main objection, is it?"

She traced his jawline with her fingertips, a reminder of the very first time she touched him. "Darling man. I still bear the scars from not being alone in wanting you. Every Silvana in Deepvale would lay claim to Lesandor. *Every* one. It would not be a rational decision – they would be drawn to him, even those who would claim no desire to leave the wildwood. The damage would be devastating."

Not knowing how to explain any of that to Lesandor, Fabiom said simply, "That's why I came to meet you yesterday. Your mother did not want you coming through the woods unaccompanied, nor did she want you lingering there."

"So – I have lost the wildwood, too, is that it?"

Fabiom gripped Lesandor's shoulder. "No, of course not. Just for this time. I do not fully understand it either, but I trust your mother – as you must."

"I do," Lesandor said quietly. He picked up the bow and quiver he had brought out of the house with him and shot three arrows into the nearest target, letting them fly with such force that they ended buried up to their fletching in the tightly-woven reeds the target was made of.

"If I return to Windwood, unmarried, I am afraid Yasdon will expect me to wed his daughter – he has hinted at it more than once. If I do not return he will take it as a gross insult, and we will be guilty of dereliction."

"Let him be insulted then," Fabiom insisted, shaking his head as his son offered him the bow. Lesandor's shots had been erratic and off-centre, and Fabiom was not inclined to outshoot him on this occasion. "You have been there, what, fifteen months? As far as I'm concerned the debt is as good as paid in full."

Even as he spoke, he was conscious of the soldiers who were now put up in the most comfortable of the municipal centre hostelries. He had a distinct feeling their purpose had been less to see Lesandor safely to Deepvale than to make sure of his return to Windwood.

Fabiom did not voice his thought, saying only, "We would not save you from one ill-starred fate simply to cast you into another. If you do not care for this girl it would be unfair to her, as much as to yourself, to take her as wife."

Lesandor said nothing as he made an unsuccessful attempt to pull his arrows out of the target. Finally he resorted to pushing them through, ruining the fletching.

"Anyway," Fabiom continued, "you are far too young. If you are not to wed a Silvana there is no need to think of marriage for years yet. But, tell me, does Yasdon keep a full military force?" As the sun rose and the mist lifted, revealing dew-spangled gossamer webs bedecking every tree and bush, he began to calculate the number of men-at-arms he could muster.

Lesandor managed a brief smile. "Yes, he does. I understand he maintained the level of soldiery Lord Herbis had. I will not ask why you ask – I can guess what you are thinking, Father."

Fabiom's humourless laugh confirmed that guess. "It would not be my first choice, nevertheless, should it come to it, I am certain we could match him strength for strength. And Ravik would not argue with me for that: he wrote to me of his concerns about Yasdon's suitability to be a holder when he first left you there."

Lesandor shook his head. "There is no need. I shall go back to Windwood long enough to discharge our debt, but make it clear to Yasdon I have no intention of settling down for several years. Though as soon as my time is done, I would be grateful if you could find some urgent reason for me to return home."

Fabiom looked at his son with respect, and promised he would do as Lesandor requested. Yasdon could hardly gainsay him – once the two years were over.

Given his mother's prohibition, Lesandor presumed he would have to spend his birth anniversary confined to the hold-house. Instead, on his birth eve, they set out for Valehead, to pass the occasion with family there.

Autumn had come late that year and the leaves were only just turning, soft golds and reds among the green. The day was warm and the breezes wafted delicate scents towards them.

"I used to take all this for granted," Lesandor sighed.

"I too, when I was your age," Fabiom agreed. "There's nothing like a year away from home to make you appreciate what has been around you all the time." He plucked a sprig of honeysuckle laden with purple berries and studied it closely. "Every single blade of grass, every flower, is unique and yet the *whole* never seems to change."

Lesandor smiled, remembering Masgor complaining only that morning – "Your father still thinks like a poet rather than a politician" – while his old eyes shone with delight.

In Valehead, Kita and Nissus's children were in high spirits and that, besides the generous gifts he received from his grandmother, great uncle and cousins, and the lavish meals Marid prepared, were balm to Lesandor's aching heart, at least for the time he was there.

They returned to the hold-house the following evening and, at last, Lesandor ventured into the woods. He went with his mother, to take his leave of his sister and grandmother. The wind blew in fitful gusts, sending leaves showering to the ground.

Barely had he laid a woven fern wreath about the branches of his grandmother's tree when Casandrina said, "We will not stay long."

Instead of arguing, as Lesandor had expected, Elzandria agreed, *"No. And I shall accompany you a way back towards the house."*

"I, too," Narilina said.

Lesandor was taken aback. The ancient Silvana rarely left her tree, let alone the grove. "Something is wrong," he whispered, suddenly afraid.

Casandrina turned her head one way, then another, listening.

"Come," Elzandria said, leaving the grove. *"They were expecting you – last night."*

"What do you mean? Who were?"

"Gracillia, especially," his mother murmured. "She is strong enough now. She wanted your father but I had two advantages over her – seniority and the fact that he had already formed an attachment to my tree. Even then, it was not enough to prevent her challenging me."

"You said 'they'," Lesandor reminded Elzandria, trying to take in what his mother was saying as they hurried through the wind-pummelled tracts between the trees.

Elzandria said nothing but, as the bridge came into view, Casandrina stopped and faced him.

"Silvana son," she whispered, taking his face gently between her two hands. "Do you not understand? They would destroy each other, for you."

Wind-whipped branches cracked over their heads and Casandrina turned to Elzandria.

"And now do *you* understand the dangers?"

Elzandria bowed her head as a sheet of lightning rent the sky.

"Be strong," Narilina told Lesandor in parting. *"You have been my joy."*

He imagined he felt the soft brush of her lips on his forehead, then she and Elzandria were gone.

❦

"I would say you left us a boy and returned a man, except there are few men in this holding I would have accounted your equal anyway."

Yasdon was glad to see him back, and pleased to hear all in Lesandor's family were well, his sister especially. He had assumed she was rather frail, hence her inability to travel. Lesandor did not dissuade him from that belief.

"We missed you," Mysha announced as her greeting. It was clear she meant *she* had missed him. Lesandor doubted that Petron had missed him at all.

Denied the chance to throw a party for Lesandor's birth anniversary, Yasdon decided to give him a 'welcome back' celebration instead, two days hence. Mercifully, from Lesandor's point of view, it was not to be a large affair, for at year's end Mysha would be celebrating her seventeenth birth anniversary and a particularly grand party would mark that occasion.

Lesandor felt Yasdon was trying to claim him, but he could not prevent them honouring him, however uncomfortable it might make him feel.

The afternoon before the party, Lesandor was at the silk mill – where a small extension was being built to accommodate extra rearing trays. Having sorted broken cocoons and left-over fibres to be sent back to the hold-house for spinning, he was passing time with the holding's chief carpenter. Well-versed in treelaw, the genial craftsman had recognised Lesandor's Silvanan heritage the moment they met, and, since then, made a point of overseeing any project Lesandor was involved in.

A figure appeared in the distance, coming from the direction of the hold-house.

"The little lady is looking for you," the carpenter said, with an ill-concealed chuckle.

Mysha waved. As she got nearer, Lesandor saw she carried a sealed scroll.

"This arrived for you," she told him breathlessly. "Master carpenter," she acknowledged.

The man made a polite bow.

"I told Father I would deliver it, as I needed to come here and check on those new girls who are learning to reel."

Out of her line of vision, the carpenter grinned.

Lesandor had encountered the new girls. It was the results of their initial efforts that made up the bulk of the silk he had collected for spinning. "Two of the girls seem to be learning quickly, the third might need more tuition. Thank you for this." He broke his father's seal and scanned the letter. "My…." He drew a short breath. "My mother's mother has – died."

The carpenter bowed his head as he touched his hand to his heart.

"Had she been ill?" Mysha asked, solicitously touching Lesandor's arm.

"No, but she was very old." He pictured the fern wreath he had woven for Narilina the day he left Deepvale. The next wreath he made for her would be for her fallen tree. It was impossible to imagine her not being there.

Mysha interrupted his thoughts. "Old people are funny, aren't they? The seamstress has no teeth at all, I can't understand a word she says. So I nod a lot. Did your grandmother have all her teeth?"

Despite the solemnity of the moment, Lesandor could not help but smile at the image Mysha's words evoked.

The carpenter coughed and turned away, as Lesandor – who was trying hard not to look at the older man – replied, "Well, in truth, I could not always understand everything she said, but I suspect that was because she was very wise and some things she said were too profound, not because of her teeth."

With the party looming, Yasdon kept him busy for most of the day, but Lesandor finally managed to escape through a small wooden door that led from the garden to the wildwood.

He dared not be away from the hold-house too long so he did not go as deep into the woods as he would have liked. Nevertheless, it was not long before he found a particularly pretty dell where an ash tree grew beside a whitethorn and a holly, and a small spring bubbled between moss-covered rocks. There he made a shrine of flat stones on which he placed a crimson sprig of feathery, late-flowering beebalm. As he said a blessing, he sensed the comforting presence of woodmaids nearby.

Despite the drizzle and the growing chill, Lesandor would have liked to have stayed the night, but guessed that already his absence would have been noticed. He had no wish to explain where he had been or what he had been doing.

As it was, the only comment his late arrival to supper earned was, "Ah, there you are!" from Yasdon. For that, at least, he was grateful.

The party commenced shortly after dawn with the arrival of the first guests. They drank hot wine and laughed and talked loudly, ignoring the fine drizzle and the grey sky. They were excited by the prospect of the entertainment ahead, for Yasdon had arranged that they should begin the day with a hunt before returning to the hold-house for a lavish feast. Lesandor guessed Yasdon was hoping he would display his skills for the guests to admire. He did not relish the proposal, but neither could he bring himself to miss in the chase, or fail purposely. He was what he was and he would live with that – whatever the consequences.

Petron, too, was becoming quite skilled in the hunt. He had allowed himself to learn from Lesandor and so, rather than refusing to go out for fear of being shown up, he went willingly, keen to demonstrate his prowess. Lesandor noted the improvement with a mixture of satisfaction and dismay, presuming it would only endear him to Yasdon more. For some time the suspicion had been growing in his mind that Lord Yasdon did not really like Petron very much, though the holder indulged his son shamelessly.

The morning was drawing to a close and the chase had thus far been enjoyable but unsuccessful, when Petron's servant, Trisran, came running towards the main body of the hunting party to report that his master had fallen into a narrow ravine. Petron had seen a crown stag across the valley and had tried to track the animal alone, save for Trisran, only to slip and fall into a steep-sided hollow from which he had no means of escape.

"Is he hurt?" Lesandor asked, as he ran with some of the others back to where Trisran indicated.

"He thinks he may have broken his leg," Trisran gasped, struggling to keep up. "He says he can't move."

It was not the state of his leg that was causing Petron the most anxiety. By the time Lesandor and the others reached him, his precarious ledge was crumbling away. Below him was another, far deeper, far less accessible drop.

"Petron! We are here. Try not to move," Lesandor called, looking for any means to help the boy.

"If you hold my arm I might be able to climb down to him," Trisran offered.

"That is both a brave and noble suggestion," Lesandor said. He did not need to add that Petron had never done anything for Trisran that would warrant such loyalty on his servant's part. "Yet there may be an easier way." He lifted a hanging ivy vine growing from a nearby tree and tugged on it.

"It will not support you," one of his companions objected.

He was right, too, yet there was a way of changing that. With one quick glance down to Petron, Lesandor stepped away from the edge and towards the trees.

"I need a rope to take my weight," he said softly. He knew there were woodmaids here and, as he spoke to them, he could sense their amusement. He was not sure he could trust them, they were well known for their capriciousness and these did not know him personally, yet he had no choice but to seek their aid. "Please, ladies," he whispered.

They must have sensed his breeding for their laughter subsided and when they came towards him they seemed almost respectful. They did not speak to him but they held out a length of rope made from woven ivy, one end of which they kept hold of and wrapped round the trunk of a large elm tree. The tree was not Silvanan, there were no Silvanii around. He could only hope his own presence was enough to keep the woodmaids in order.

"Is he all right?" he asked Trisran as he returned to the ravine edge with his end of the vine rope. Trisran nodded. "This is strong and well secured to a tree close by." Lesandor looked around. He appeared to be the lightest in weight. Even Trisran, who he guessed to be some years younger than himself, looked heavier-built than he was. "I shall go. Help me down."

The earth crumbled beneath his feet as Lesandor inched his way towards where Petron lay, fingers buried in the loose earth as he clung on as hard as he could. Petron's left leg was twisted unnaturally beneath his body and there was blood on his cheek. As Lesandor came closer, some small stones fell onto Petron's face and the boy whimpered with terror. Lesandor did not fault him for that, he could feel his own heart pounding in his chest and his palms were wet with perspiration as he lowered himself onto the ledge. Roots protruded from the side of the ravine and Lesandor gratefully took hold of some that looked strong and firm.

"I am down," he called to the others waiting above. "All right, Petron, give me your hand." Somehow he managed to pull the boy to an upright position and, very carefully, he manoeuvred the rope under Petron's arms and tied it. "Hold on," he instructed, calling, "Pull!" before Petron could reply; then grasped the roots once again as more of the ledge crumbled.

Below them, a tributary of the River Grebe flowed swift and treacherous. Lesandor tried not to look down. He could sense it was a long way to the bottom, though he had no desire to know exactly how far.

It took some time and much effort to pull Petron free, for he was afraid and his leg was painful. The vine rope held. Lesandor had never been more relieved than he was at the moment the rope was lowered once more and he could clamber to the top, onto safe ground. Petron lay nearby, groaning.

"It's not broken," one of Petron's companions told him, as two of them helped him to his feet. "Just badly sprained and bruised, still, we'd better get you back to the hold-house."

Across the valley a huge stag regarded them disdainfully before turning and disappearing into the dappled woods.

"Thank you," Lesandor breathed as they left the area. Girlish laughter greeted his softly-voiced gratitude. He saw Trisran's head turn quickly and a puzzled look come into the lad's eyes.

"Be careful!" Petron scolded. Trisran was supporting him and, as his attention wandered, his hold on his master had loosened.

Lesandor gave him a comradely grin.

They questioned Lesandor about the speed with which he had fashioned the rope and he said, truthfully enough, that he had learnt the way to acquire such a rope long ago. He did not elucidate further and was saved from having to answer more questions by Petron complaining about his plight.

Celebration for Lesandor's return turned into a rejoicing for Petron's rescue. Yasdon poured Lesandor's drink and selected the finest morsels of food for him, allowing no one else to wait upon him.

"You, whom I treasure as if you were my own son, have saved the beloved son of this house. What father could be happier?"

Lesandor had no answer to that, though he guessed his own father might not appreciate Yasdon claiming him so utterly.

"Honoured guests!" Yasdon called. Silence fell. Yasdon stood over Lesandor, hands firmly grasping the yound man's shoulders. "Dear friends, I am glad you are with us on this occasion. You came to welcome Lesandor back to this house and instead you can join me in my heartfelt thanks for his courage and quick thinking. I am going to do something now that I had thought to do in a short while anyway. I cannot wait, and why should I? Lesandor, I must reward you with the highest honour, the greatest gift at my disposal. You have already brought much happiness to my house, now I ask you to make that happiness complete."

Lesandor realised he had been holding his breath and that he needed to breathe. For one horrible moment he thought he had forgotten how.

"I...." he gasped.

Yasdon took no notice. He had already taken one hand from Lesandor's shoulder and was holding it out to Mysha.

"Mysha, my daughter."

She stood and came towards him. She did not look at Lesandor but kept her eyes demurely downcast, nevertheless Lesandor was in no doubt she knew exactly what was happening. This might be unexpected to him but she seemed not at all surprised.

"What greater honour can a father bestow?" Yasdon asked the assembled guests. They were smiling, delighted. "For all that you have come to mean to us, Lesandor, I give you the hand of my daughter, Mysha."

Yasdon's hand slipped from Lesandor's shoulder to the ornate arm band that circled his right bicep, his action clearly reminding Lesandor that he was owned and Yasdon could ask anything of him.

Lesandor scanned the assembly. Only Petron seemed less than happy. Some of the guests were cheering already. If he refused, he might not leave there alive and, if he did, could even Prince Ravik prevent Yasdon turning Windwood against Deepvale? Wars in Morene had been caused by far lesser insults. He looked at Mysha, who was still studying her feet. He rose to stand before her.

"If the lady is willing," he said stiffly. The sliver of hope, that she would not be, was vanquished by her smile as she raised her eyes to gaze adoringly into his.

"The lady is more than willing," she declared.

Chapter Seven

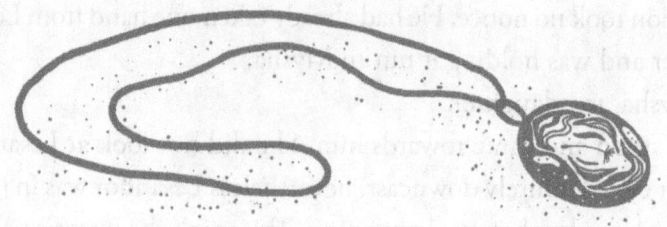

LESANDOR'S ONLY REMAINING hope – that Prince Ravik would not sanction his marriage – was quenched four days later when Yasdon received a scroll, delivered in the hands of a chilled and exhausted courier who hunkered down before the blazing fire in the main room of the hold-house.

As the courier wrapped his hands around a beaker of steaming, spiced wine, Yasdon broke the seal and scanned the document, nodding vigorously. "Good, good. All is in order." Carelessly, he cast the scroll onto the fire where it crackled and burnt.

"My lord!" The courier sprang to his feet.

"What was I thinking!" Yasdon took two steps towards the blaze, then two back. "Get it out! Get it out!"

Before anyone could find something that could safely retrieve the document, the reed parchment crackled and turned to ash.

"Ah. How foolish of me." Yasdon tapped his forehead. "Too many thoughts, too many plans. Never mind, never mind, it's done now. It is of little consequence. The scroll is read and you are all witnesses." He indicated the courier and the two servants standing by, as well as Lesandor.

At that moment, Mysha came in. Unusually, her hair was piled on top of her head, bound there with wide ribbons of yellow and blue, leaving her neck bare. "Did I hear right, Father, that word has come from the prince?"

"You did, my sweet. Have you the silk?"

Lesandor looked at the skein of scarlet silk she held out. Now that the prince had given his consent, he must weave a betrothal band for her. With shaking fingers he wrapped six strings around her neck, then knotted and threaded the intricate pattern that claimed her as his. So close, she smelt sweet and her skin was softer than the silk. He let his fingers linger on her neck and throat, and she reached up and touched his hand. Warring feelings strove for precedence within him. Yet when he was done and she stood on tiptoes and kissed him, it was a far from unpleasant sensation. At that moment, he was perfectly content that their marriage night was not far off. It was what came after which concerned him.

Later, while Lesandor read and Petron reluctantly completed a set of geometry problems his tutor had set him, Mysha reclined on a settle in the library, gazing into a hand-mirror as she brushed her hair. She was not looking at her reflection but at the two young men behind her.

"You will try to get along with each other, won't you? For my sake."

Lesandor was taken aback by her question. By the look on Petron's face, he was not the only one.

"It would mean a lot to me," Mysha continued, giving neither her husband-to-be nor her brother a chance to reply. Then she dropped both brush and mirror and clapped her hands in delight. "It could be your wedding present to me!"

"Right," Petron muttered. "I had thought to give you a white donkey – but if you'd rather…."

"A white donkey? Truly? Oh – I'm almost tempted. Can't I have both?"

"No. It's one or the other."

Mysha pursed her lips. "I would have liked a white donkey. You know I've always wanted one. But it seems I shall have to do without."

Petron nodded. "If you are sure."

"Yes, I'm sure."

Petron rose from his desk, went over to Lesandor and stuck out his hand. "Looks like your bride has spoken."

Mysha's face was lit by a beatific smile as Lesandor rose to his feet and the two clasped each other's right arm.

Petron broke contact first. "Well, the easiest way to ensure you get your wish is for me not to be here. I shall see you both at supper."

"Your study?" Mysha's reminder was answered with a noncommittal grunt.

As Petron sauntered off, she turned to Lesandor. "Thank you."

"What are you thanking me for?"

"Making friends with Petron, of course."

He sighed. "Mysha, we're not friends. No, wait –" he went on hurriedly as her lip began to quiver. "Hopefully, by making an effort for the duration of the wedding festivities, we will learn to at least tolerate each other. But beyond making an effort, I can promise you nothing more. I will do my best – if it means so much to you."

"It really does," she whispered, her eyes filling with tears. "And I don't understand why you don't get along."

He dropped a quick kiss on her forehead. "Some people just do not like each other. It is no one's fault."

❦

Lesandor and Mysha were wed on the day she reached seventeen years.

Yasdon had invited the holding's elders, along with influential landholders and many of the senior trades and craftspeople. He had also invited his late uncle's wife, but Riann had sent her apologies, along with a small but exquisite statue of a young man and woman holding hands around a mulberry tree – symbol of love and prosperity.

Once the guests had presented their gifts, they were ushered out into the central courtyard where four large braziers were aflame and a dais had been set up. Accompanied by five unmarried men, Lesandor was led out of the hold-house and up the right hand steps of the dais, while five young women led Mysha up the steps from the left.

Not at his best after a sleepless night, when he had seriously contemplated trying to escape and make his way home over the snow-clogged passes, Lesandor nevertheless had to admit his bride looked beautiful. Her light brown hair and honey-gold skin were set off by the deep amber hue of her heavy velvet wedding robes. Having resigned himself to the inevitable, Lesandor had stumbled out of bed that morning determined to focus on the positive aspects of his situation: Mysha was easy on the eye and she liked him. His situation would be far worse if Yasdon's daughter was more like Yasdon's son.

To the delight and approval of all those assembled, Lesandor presented his bride with a pendant: a piece of pale amber within which a dandelion seed had been captured for eternity.

The silver-haired magistrate chosen to perform the ceremony took a step forward and put his hand over the couple's hands and the bridal token. "So appropriate – the delicate and the resilient, the temporal and the permanent, the seed of a new life and the residue of one finished – everything in balance." His voice carried around the courtyard.

Puzzled by the last pair the magistrate had pronounced, Lesandor hardly registered that the man had taken his right hand and was speaking about duty and fidelity. He had just realised the magistrate must have presumed the amber had come from a fallen Silvanan tree, as most amber did, when he found Mysha's hand in his and their marriage being pronounced as lawful and binding.

"I will be true to you, in thought and deed, until my dying day." Mysha's voice was barely a whisper. Lesandor's, when he repeated the vow, was hoarse. The deed was done.

From the moment the musicians began playing and the newly married couple stepped off the dais, and back into the relative warmth of the hold-house, everyone wanted to engage them in conversation – although in Lesandor's case those conversations consisted largely of less than subtle comments about the upcoming wedding night. Mysha was swept away by giggling female relatives and friends who persuaded her to dance with them. Lesandor tried to be polite, laugh at appropriate times, and agree when that was what seemed to be expected.

As Mysha danced past, her amber pendant catching the bright winter sunlight, her father waylaid Lesandor. "Such a generous gift," Yasdon enthused. "Wherever did you get it?"

"I –" Lesandor had no intention of telling his father-by-marriage that the piece was from Elzandria's tree: a tear shed the day he left home to go to Fairwater. "I brought it with me. It was a present from my sister. I had nothing else worthy of a bride-gift."

"It was well done. Very well done. Generous." Yasdon beamed. He turned to the table beside them, piled with sweets and honeyed delicacies.

"Yes – very generous," Petron agreed. He picked up a date stuffed with honeyed curd, put it back and contemplated the array.

"Speaking of generous. Were you really intending to give your sister a white donkey?" Lesandor inquired, as Yasdon moved out of hearing.

Around them, the wedding guests chatted and mingled, drinking morat and picking at candied fruits and other sweet morsels.

Petron nearly choked on the handful of raisins he had just thrown into his mouth.

"Don't be an idiot! Oh, don't look so disapproving. I was teasing her. Even if I had the coin – which I don't – I wouldn't waste it on something so useless. You could have sold that necklace you gave her and bought one with the proceeds, I shouldn't wonder."

"Perhaps," Lesandor agreed. "But that amber is not for sale."

Petron raised his brows, then grinned. "You don't have a license for it, you mean."

Lesandor hesitated. "You are right, as it happens. I do not."

A servant passed with a laden tray. Lesandor took a glass beaker, surprised to discover it contained morat and not wine. The fermented mulberry and honey drink was his father's favourite and reminded him too much of home. He could see Petron working up to say something and wondered how he could prevent him from pursuing the issue of the amber, but that was not the thought concerning Mysha's brother.

"You won't hurt her – tonight – will you? I know you don't like her. You don't like any of us. You think you're better than everyone here. But, she's –"

Lesandor cut him off. "What are you talking about? Hurt her! Why would I...? Why would you even think that?"

Petron shrugged and looked away. "I'm asking. That's all. It's not easy for me."

"No, I can imagine."

Petron opened his mouth and closed it again before walking away. Across the room, Mysha scowled. Lesandor schooled his expression into a smile and took a deep breath. She did look lovely. And while Petron was not entirely wrong – about anything he had said – the last thing on Lesandor's mind at that moment was hurting her.

Winter held the country in its thrall. Snow on the mountain passes isolated each holding from the rest so that no communication was possible.

In their marriage bed it was warm enough to distract him, but when he was elsewhere, Lesandor longed for his family.

It was almost a month before a letter arrived from Fabiom. It came on a crisp blue day that had started with a heavy frost and had turned bright and almost warm by mid-morning, as many such days did, before evening descended with a cold hand and the fires were relit once again. On this day, Yasdon's household was enjoying a noon-time meal, gathered in the dining area. The doors were wide open, revealing a vista of distant mountains, their tops white against the brilliant sky. The courier arrived through the open doors, accompanied by the house-steward.

To Lesandor's surprise, the scroll he was handed was not a reply to the letter he had sent home as soon as the mountain passes had thawed sufficiently, but word that the ruling prince required his service immediately and that his first duty would be aboard a ship of Ravik's fleet.

"Two years!" Yasdon exclaimed, half-choking on a mouthful of roast venison. "So soon?" He picked up a cloth and wiped his mouth.

"It is his due," Lesandor pointed out, wondering if Raidan had managed to secure a place for himself on the vessel, as he had promised. "And if I give the prince my time now, I will be free." He did not add that his own father had never quite been free of the prince's demands.

"When?" Mysha asked, her eyes filling with tears.

"His vessel will be by these shores in" – he consulted the letter – "seventeen, no, sixteen days."

"Is that all it says?" Yasdon asked. "Not where, or why?"

"The letter is from my father, not from the prince. Father had not received *my* letter, I think; he makes no reference to our marriage."

Yasdon picked up his beaker with a shaking hand, "I had hoped we would meet your parents soon – and now this!" He took a deep draught.

Mysha regarded Lesandor uncertainly. "Will you go?"

He poured some wine into his own cup and handed it to her. "What I would choose to do, what I would not choose, what I might want – none of those things are of any consequence. In this matter I must do as others would have me do."

Fabiom received Lesandor's missive the very day he sent his own. He arrived in Windwood just one day after his letter. Cold, tired and hungry.

"Your mother is very angry," were his first words to his son.

Lesandor blanched. "She did not come, did she? No, it is too far. But she might, if she really wanted to. She would hate to be so far from her tree – but she could."

Fabiom shook his head. "You are right: she could. But, no, somehow, and to be honest I am not sure how I did it, I persuaded her to stay at home." He glanced around. They were by the gate lodge, but out of hearing of the elderly gatekeep. "I do not believe Yasdon sought, let alone obtained, Ravik's permission. If you have not consummated the marriage … but you are seventeen and I hear she is a pretty lass. I would find it hard to believe."

Lesandor briefly met his father's eyes and half-laughed.

"Even so – I could petition Prince Ravik for you to set her aside. Under the circumstances he might agree. You were coerced, after all."

Lesandor kicked a stone, then grimaced. "What would be the point? It's not as if I have any other plans."

Fabiom raised his brows. "That is your only reason?"

"It would shame her, would it not? And cause great trouble for you. I would not wish either."

"Good. That is a man's answer. So now you will have to find your own contentment."

Lesandor sighed. "I shall, I suppose. I have no choice."

At that moment, Mysha saw them and came over to greet Fabiom. She blushed when he spoke to her, and giggled; Lesandor felt his jaw tighten. Fabiom touched his arm. "Is it too much to hope that one of you will offer me food and a hot drink – indoors? It's cold walking these paths."

Later, when they were alone, and he was bathed, changed and well-fed, Fabiom told his son, "She is just a girl. She will have grown up in the time you are away. Be kind to her, be patient."

"Woodmaids have more sense," Lesandor replied sullenly.

"Woodmaids are wiser than we tend to allow, and have the advantage of age – despite their appearance. Do not expect the cossetted daughter of a clinging man such as Yasdon to exhibit the wisdom or sense of such as they – less still of a Silvana."

Lesandor smiled wryly. That was the point: he had wanted something he could not have and felt dissatisfied, which was hardly Mysha's fault.

Furious with Yasdon, and aware that it would do his son no good to let his antagonism show, Fabiom remained in Windwood a mere three days. Yasdon seemed oblivious to his visitor's feelings, which did nothing to improve Fabiom's mood. At least he would be able to return to Casandrina and say that Mysha seemed pleasant enough. For certain, she adored Lesandor and Fabiom saw some sign of hope in that. He was more concerned by her brother's attitude, fearing it did not bode well for the couple, and also by the fact that Yasdon seemed to think Lesandor should stay in Windwood indefinitely. Now was not the time to dispute the issue, but Fabiom was determined that once Lesandor's service with Prince Ravik was concluded he, and his wife, would come to Deepvale, whether Yasdon liked it or not. With so little time to spend together he chose not to share his anxiety over that matter with Lesandor, though he doubted his son was unaware of the problem.

They made their own pathways through the edge of the great woods that gave the holding its name, both of them at ease among the trees and the woodland life.

Fabiom paused to admire some dusty-gold hazel catkins that were braving the early spring frosts.

"Yasdon showed me your coppiced mulberries – they wintered well. He seemed delighted at the prospect of a decent harvest this year. Despite how I feel about him, when things are running smoothly I thought I might send him some additional eggs for rearing, even lend him someone with experience for a season."

Lesandor grinned. "Someone other than me?"

"Definitely someone other than you! That's the point, it will ease your leaving. Anyway, you've little more interest in sericulture than I had at your age. Be honest."

"It is Silvanan...."

"Yes, exactly. So it's fascinating, and the product is wonderful. But the work is somewhat tedious and thus it is preferable to read about it in a book, or watch others do it, than get too involved yourself."

"Father!" Then Lesandor laughed. "Now I know why Grandmother says how surprised she is we have a business at all, let alone a prosperous one."

"All credit to your mother, and to Kilm and his sons. It's a question of finding what you're good at," Fabiom muttered, turning over a rotten log with his foot. "You'll do well with Prince Ravik. He knows you, knows your strengths and will use them. You might get to travel farther than Varlass, even to Malandel. Wherever you go, just make the most of the time ahead – and enjoy yourself!"

The following day, Fabiom took his leave of Lesandor with a heavy heart. It was almost a year and a half since his son had set out for what was supposed to be a short sojourn with Ravik. They could not have believed then that he would be leaving them for four years. Yet Fabiom was not sorry that Ravik should call on Lesandor's services. It was not so much that Mysha would have matured in the interim that mattered, more that two years' distance from his frustration and disappointment should make Lesandor more tolerant of his new wife, less likely to compare her unfavourably with his mother.

⁂

Despite his father's words, and his own best efforts over the next five days, Lesandor was relieved, as well as surprised, to see the blue sails of Prince Ravik's ship on the horizon. He had gone down to the port, to the merchants who traded there, to select some last few items he deemed necessary for his forthcoming time away. The *Galingale* was a day early. Only fifteen days had passed since the letter had arrived from Fabiom, Lesandor had been counting. If he was honest with himself he was not so unhappy with Mysha that he should count their days together so assiduously, it was just that he wanted to get away from Windwood. He needed time to try to come to terms with events that had overtaken him, and he feared the prince might excuse him when he heard about his marriage, especially if Yasdon had any influence.

Before the ship was secured in its moorings, Yasdon had arrived. He had arranged that word be sent to him as soon as the royal pennant was spotted.

"Good, good, you're here." He put his arm about Lesandor's shoulders. "We'll persuade him to wait, just a while. I know you said about getting it over with, but not yet. Not yet."

A young lad with copper-brown hair ran down the ramp and began to make fast one of the ropes. Lesandor thought he recognised him from somewhere, though he could not say where.

"Boy! We must see Prince Ravik at once," Yasdon shouted.

"He's not here," the lad replied.

"He must be. You are mistaken. His pennant is flying from the masthead."

The boy glanced upwards and shrugged. "Wrong pennant." Then he grinned. "Prince Ravik is my great-uncle. I'd know if he was on board."

Yasdon went visibly pale when he heard the news. "Who's in charge?" he demanded.

"Lesandor? Lesandor!" Raidan called out in surprised delight. "What are you doing here? I heard you'd gone home, else I would have brought your amber clasp back for you. I didn't want to risk it on a sea voyage. It's good to see you've survived so far!"

Lesandor flashed a grin and a warning gesture towards the young prince but Yasdon had taken no heed, busy as he was questioning those disembarking.

Raidan, among the first onto the quay, grabbed Lesandor's arm.

"It's good to see you." Raidan grimaced towards the ship. "I could do with some amiable company on board, I wish you were coming."

"But I am."

"No, you can't!"

Lesandor laughed. "You just said you wished I was."

"No. I didn't mean it. I meant I would enjoy your company. You can't come on this trip."

Lesandor scowled. "I had a letter of notification delivered to me: I am required to join your father's service, immediately."

"There must be some mistake," Raidan muttered absently and seemingly to himself.

"Sorry to disappoint you."

"I.... What? No! I didn't mean that the way it sounded. But Father always said he would never ask this of you under any circumstances. And this trip isn't even particularly important – it's just a glorified trading run. Lesandor – we're bound for Gerik!"

Gerik. The very name made Lesandor's blood run cold. "So, there has been a mistake." Relief mingled with disappointment. "Well, I am glad you are here, though sorry we won't be sharing service time yet." He grinned and looked around; the lord holder was out of hearing. "Yasdon was planning a big feast for tomorrow, but he is an expert at such things, I'm sure he will manage to put together something decadent even a day early. Though he shall be fretting about not having huge pieces of meat roasted for you all... Raidan, what's wrong?"

"My cousin, Larse. He's in charge. He has obedience down to an absolute art. If he believes my father intended you to go, then nothing but my father's word will prevent his insisting that you should."

Lesandor looked across to where he could see Yasdon talking earnestly with a handsomely-dressed man in his mid-thirties who seemed to be making conciliatory but nevertheless negative gestures.

"Lord Yasdon appears to be arguing with Larse," Raidan observed.

"Yes," Lesandor sighed. "And it looks like he has lost." Everything within him told him he could not go to Gerik.

Yasdon turned to look at him and shook his head.

"Is he trying to prevent your going?" Raidan asked curiously. "Very commendable, but why does he look so very unhappy about it?"

"That is a long story," Lesandor replied. "But he wants me to stay here. I thought I wanted to leave – and yet suddenly I agree with him."

Raidan rubbed his jaw. "The best we can do is send letters – though my father is away from the capital for several days. To Lord Fabiom, then. Yes, write to your father – he will know what to do. He has influence; he'll get you home." He looked at his cousin and the holder who were still talking, though less animatedly. "Larse will not be swayed, no matter what Yasdon says about your blood."

"Yasdon does not know – about my mother, I mean. I do not know why I didn't tell him. No, I do know. That, too, is a long story." He considered Yasdon's defeated stance. "I suspect I shall have time to tell you any number of long stories though."

Larse strolled over to the two young men, leaving Yasdon standing, forlorn.

"Lesandor of Deepvale?" He grasped Lesandor's upper arm. "You have your service missive?"

"I do –" Lesandor returned the greeting gesture. "I just wondered if there could be a mistake."

Larse shrugged. "Everything seems to be in order. We sail in the morning. I'm sorry it's so soon after your marriage. You two know each other?"

He glanced at Raidan who answered, "We do. Lesandor was at the palace as my companion last year."

"Then perhaps you'd like to travel together," Larse suggested.

"Yes," Lesandor and Raidan replied as one.

"Thank you." Lesandor added. He took a deep breath. "Lord Yasdon is waiting for me, I expect we shall see you up at the hold-house shortly. I had better go there now, excuse me."

As he turned and walked away he heard Raidan say to Larse, "Did you say 'marriage'?"

"Please do not cry, Mysha." Lesandor climbed into the bed beside her and held her awkwardly.

He had put aside his intention to spend his last night in Morene in the woods; her misery was genuine and he would never have wished to make her unhappy. Until that moment he had not thought how she really felt about his leaving. "I do not want to go. I have to." He was glad to be able to say so, even if his reasons were not the same as hers. She did not have to know that. "I am sorry."

She moved just far enough away from him to be able to wipe her eyes. "I'll try to be brave," she promised. "You won't want to see me crying in front of everybody at the port tomorrow, will you? Did you see, I didn't weep at all at the feast? I knew your ship's officers and the lords and princes were all looking at me. I wanted to, all the way through the meal, but I didn't. I'm sorry I could not dance for them though, I would have wept if I had. Did I disappoint you?"

"Oh, Mysha!" he sighed, stroking her hair, almost in tears himself, glad he was able to hide in the darkness of the night. "You did not disappoint me. Of course not! I do not want you to be so sad. It does not matter what anybody else thinks."

"Thank you," she whispered indistinctly, and he held her closer still, letting himself take comfort in one last night of intimacy, wishing he could feel the same way about her as he knew she felt about him. It all seemed so unfair.

Mysha did weep at the port, but only a little. Lesandor wanted to console her, yet he wanted to leave Windwood – though not to go to Gerik. While he was trying to untangle that bundle of knotted emotions, her father almost pushed between them. Yasdon held him tightly. Lesandor longed for Fabiom's embrace.

Part II

Chapter One

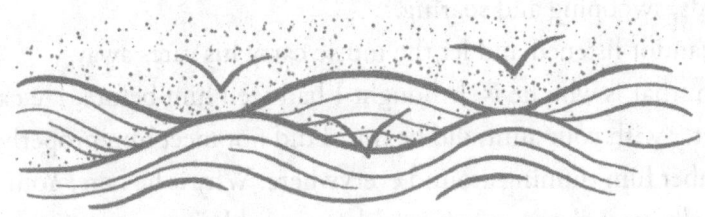

ALINGALE SAILED AWAY from Morene, heading south-west into uncertain waters. Standing near the prow, Lesandor looked over the wide ocean towards their destination while his heart already yearned for the shores receding into the hazy morning light behind them. He raked his hands through his wind-swept hair and listened to the lonely cries of the gulls following hopefully in their wake. Raidan came to join him.

"Which story do you intend to begin with?" Raidan inquired. "You've certainly been busy since we last met."

Lesandor groaned. "Nothing has gone right since then. I was so certain of my future. And now – look at me now!"

"You don't love her, do you?"

Lesandor started. "How...? It's not so obvious, is it?"

"No. Not when we left. But I think you would have told me yesterday, if you'd been really happy; it seemed as if you wanted to leave – until you learnt where we were headed."

Lesandor stared at the water-stained deck. "I did not know how to refuse." He looked up to meet Raidan's eyes. "Like being here, headed for Gerik. Marrying Mysha was exactly the same – feels much the same, too. Yet I need not feel guilty about not wanting to go to Gerik – *it* could not care less whether I want to be there or not. Still, we are on our way now, I cannot change that." He forced a wan smile. "I promise, I shall not be a total misery." He spoke without much conviction, but Raidan was satisfied.

Sweet music drifted along the deck and Raidan grinned.

"That's Tegun, Larse's nephew – he's twelve. He doesn't want to let

Larse catch him playing his pipes." His smile faded. "Larse is so hard on him, it's not fair. The boy hardly asked to come on this trip."

The music of the waves played in the boy's piping, the flight of the sea birds, swooping and soaring.

Lesandor listened and let the music carry his cares away.

"Ah, that is who he is. I thought I had seen him before. He came to Fairwater with your aunt, did he not? I did not meet him properly, but I remember him running around everywhere. Why is he here? Your father has hardly started conscripting twelve-year-olds."

Raidan glanced over his shoulder; no one was near enough to overhear them. "For the most part he lives with his grandmother, my Aunt Jaymna. As she's away at the moment, Tegun should be at his own home. However, his mother – Larse's sister – asked Larse to bring him. She was widowed last year and I think Tegun's presence was cramping her new social life. Larse was none too pleased, and he's taking it out on the boy."

As the day drew to a close and the grey shapes that were the bow-riding dolphins merged with the grey of the sea and of the sky, Lesandor and Raidan went below decks.

"We can share this cabin; it's a bit cramped but it's only for one night. Here, you have that berth." Raidan pointed to the port side of the cabin and the lower berth there. Something in his expression made Lesandor curious.

"Do you not want it, there is more light on this side?" He sat on the edge and realised that it was not terribly comfortable.

"No, you have it."

Later, when darkness had swallowed up the ocean completely and they had turned in for the night, Raidan asked, "Why did you not tell Yasdon about Casandrina? Why so secretive? You should be proud of being a Silvana's son."

"I am!" Lesandor protested. "Oh, I do not know. There were all sorts of reasons. As you know, there was – trouble – in the past, between our two families, to do with the Silvanii. That is how I came to be in Windwood. Apart from that, Yasdon is so *proud* of me, shows me off like a prized hunting trophy. I could not give him anything else to boast of, and I needed to have something of my own, something he had no part in. He thinks he knows me so well but he does not know that one very important thing, so he does not know me at all." He laughed lightly at that, his mother's laugh, and Raidan grinned. "Anyway, enough of me. You must have some stories too, it has been over a year, after all."

Raidan sat up and swung his legs back to the ground. "I'll let you in on a secret of my own. But it really is. Promise to say nothing."

Intrigued, Lesandor promised.

"Last summer I was in Rushford – Father wanted someone to go and see the marble quarries – and I met this girl. I'm not sure Father will approve. No, actually I'm certain he won't. Her family history is less than ideal. But – well – he doesn't know and it's too late now. You're not the only one who's married."

"You too! What do you mean Prince Ravik doesn't know? You are high born – you cannot marry without his permission."

"Well, that's true. But there was a magistrate, a retired one granted...."

"And you did not tell him who you were? Who your father is? That you need permission to wed. Does your *bride* know?"

"No, I…. Don't say it like that. She is my true wife."

"Perhaps," Lesandor said, unconvinced. "So, what happened to waiting until you were near thirty?"

"Cuivah happened."

"That is her name – Cuivah?" Lesandor wanted to believe he had misheard, but knew he had not. His tone betrayed his emotions.

"Ah – you know."

Lesandor laughed bitterly. "Well, let me see. It is not a common name, and you said her family history is less than ideal. So I might make a wild conjecture; perhaps her" – he did a quick calculation – "grandmother, I am guessing, betrayed our land – your father's land – by selling the secrets of silk-making abroad, and in doing so jeopardised the relationship between mankind and Silvanii? Oh, yes, then there was that part about the family being banished for all generations, without any possibility of mercy if they returned, because, you know, the whole relationship between mankind and Silvanii thing...."

"At least I didn't let myself be married off to some simpering, preening, barely literate girl – against my will."

"She –" Lesandor thought of his father's words when he had expressed much the same opinion himself. "Yasdon has cosseted her. She will grow into a different woman. We shall go home and my mother will see to that. You do not know her."

There was a pause before Raidan said, "You're right. I don't know her. I'm sorry. That was petty."

"Forget it."

Another long moment of silence passed.

Raidan sighed. "Will you let me at least explain what happened; how it happened?"

When Lesandor did not say otherwise, Raidan chose to take his silence as agreement.

"We met at a stone carver's studio. The quarry master had taken me to several such places, to see the holding's stone being worked. A young woman was there on her own – a ward of the carver's she said. She showed us around. She was funny and clever and beautiful. We met several times after that. It wasn't easy, she was living with the craftsman and his family. He is a relative – one not implicated in the scandal, before you ask. The quarry master hadn't told her who I was, so I didn't either. It would have complicated things, and our relationship wasn't supposed to be serious. I went home, but I couldn't stop thinking about her. Then, a few months ago, Father needed someone to go back to Rushford – so I volunteered. We met again and we couldn't deny how we felt about each other, so we married. I promised her I'd be back before summer's end. It's a promise I mean to keep, for our child is due then."

Lesandor sat up and hit his head on the unused bunk above him.

"Your father is the Ruling Prince of Morene and you haven't told him even that you are married. What are you planning to do – present him with a grandchild and hope that will mollify him?"

"Actually, yes," Raidan admitted. "And don't sound so indignant, Lesandor. You know I've four brothers older than me and two of those are married, Romarus already has two sons of his own and Pharrell is guaranteed one." He chuckled. "Ideally, Cuivah will bear a girl-child

70

so I can present Father with his longed-for granddaughter; that would smooth things considerably."

"That is true," Lesandor agreed, lying down again. "And – despite everything – I am happy for you – if you really care for her."

"I do, more than I can say. She's very special." There was a moment's silence. "I'm sorry you don't feel the same way about your Mysha. I hope you will, in time. I'm sure you're right about your mother's influence."

I wish I was sure, Lesandor thought. "What are you doing?" he asked aloud, hearing a scraping sound coming from the other side of the narrow cabin.

"It's common practice for men on these ships to carve out the names of loved-ones left behind. Feel under the ridge of your bunk."

Lesandor groped around the wood until he felt the unmistakable shapes of lettering.

"I gave you that side for a reason," Raidan explained. "I think it was once your father's."

It took him some time to find his mother's name but it was there, quite distinctly shaped.

Lying in the dark, Lesandor admitted to Raidan that he was right about Mysha. After a moment's hesitation, he told him about his seventeenth birth anniversary, his dreams being dashed, his mother's prohibition and, finally, his return to Windwood and Yasdon's insistence on his betrothal to Mysha.

"And so I said yes."

"There was probably little else you could do, without risking your life or starting a war," Raidan agreed.

"But to fall in love – I hate to admit it, but I am jealous of you, Raidan."

"You won't be so jealous when I have to face my father."

"I could be with you when you do."

"Ha! You only want to see what he'll do to me."

"Absolutely."

"Tell you what – you can do the talking. In fact, how about you tell him and I'll – I don't know – go and visit my grandfather in Varlass maybe...."

"Raidan, I love you dearly, but there is no way in the world I could face your father and tell him you have fathered a child on a girl from that family. I am not sure I shall be able to tell *my* father, for that matter."

Raidan chuckled as he settled down. "Well, that's all in the future. For now we've got to get through this trip. And I'm sorry for what I said, especially with what's ahead of us. But it will be all right. Larse is tolerable, not much fun – no sense of humour for one thing, though that's hardly surprising given his background – but not a bad officer. We'll be home soon – back to the wildwood – and our wives."

"Yes." Lesandor sighed as he traced his mother's name again with his fingers, and wondered if she knew where he would be this time tomorrow.

❧

"Gerik!"

"So his letter says." Fabiom flung the paper onto the table and folded his arms across his chest, shaking his head as he did so. "I don't understand. Ravik wouldn't…. Even if I had offended him, and I am not aware of doing so, he wouldn't do that to Lesandor."

"No," Casandrina agreed. "Ravik would not."

Fabiom had been staring out of the window, biting his lip in consternation. It took a moment for her words to register.

"I think I must go to Fairwater, see him in person."

"We should never have believed Jaymna would forget. She has been waiting all this while," Casandrina whispered as she came to stand beside him.

Her head rested on his shoulder and they looked out at the rain falling, soft as tears, on the garden. Fabiom never had believed the princess would forget or forgive, yet they did not know for certain that she was behind Lesandor's commission. Only Ravik would be able to tell him that, and bring Lesandor home.

❧

"We've landed in the middle of a war!" Larse informed them. "Oh, they're not calling it that, of course; it's business as usual according to the local officials, but there are people getting killed and it's getting worse." He leant his elbow on the table and rubbed his chin. "The question is: what do we do?"

"Go home," Lesandor muttered under his breath. Even as he had stepped onto the jetty a wave of nausea had hit him, worsening when the wooden planking over the water gave way to the packed earth of the blighted island. Since being ashore, the nausea had not dissipated, nor had the headache that had come on within the first hour of disembarking. Even if his father could get him home, he knew it would not be for several days. Somehow, he had to push past the sickness in the land that seemed to be manifesting in his body.

The inn was like almost any similar establishment in Morene: worn leather couches set around low tables, piles of stained, oversized cushions piled in the corners for customers not quick enough to get a couch, narrow shelves set around the walls for those who would rather stand to lean against, and for bowls of dried fish slivers, olives and salted almonds. Lesandor tried to make himself believe he was at home. It was not easy.

"We could go home," Larse was saying. "But no. Trade links are trade links, whoever's in power. We'll stay."

"If the rebel faction succeed in their power bid, the treaty could be void. We might have to start negotiations over again," Raidan pointed out. "Better to go back now, and return when we know more."

Lesandor thought of his father, camped on the plains to the east of where they now were. Twenty-two years old. Half a year watching and waiting. Half a year of bad dreams until the treaty was sorted out. It had stood since then, unviolated. But now....

"We could try to gather information about the rebels and how the war is going," suggested Ellish, *Galingale's* captain.

"Don't forget why we're here." Larse picked at the olives and almonds, offered to provoke customers' thirsts. "They can grow nothing like this any more. Gerik imports a lot of food, not enough of it from Morene and we've got to change that."

"How can we, if we don't know who'll be in power here in the future? Unless we take sides, and hope we made the right choice," Raidan protested. "Let's just go back, tonight."

"The only side – the only people we can trust – are those who signed the treaty, which is the current authority, don't ever forget that," Larse countered. He looked at Raidan for a long moment. "I'm staying here for a day, then going south to Fallowridge. You can take nine or ten men and go elsewhere. Choose somewhere safe; ask where that might be. There are good trading points inland and history suggests that hostilities in one area are not even heard of half-way across this country. You said you wanted some responsibility on this trip. You have it."

Defeated, Raidan glanced at Lesandor then back to Larse. "Lesandor comes with me." He was ready to argue the point but Larse merely shrugged.

"As you wish."

Larse began to drum his fingers on the table. "Now, what about you?" he muttered, glaring at his young nephew. "I told your mother that you'd only be a nuisance; she wouldn't have it. Still, I can hardly blame her for wanting rid of you for a while."

"I can help," Tegun said. "There are lots of things I can do."

"Don't be stupid! What can you do, except get in the way? I don't want to hear a word from you. Just keep quiet and do as you're told."

Tegun cowered.

"He can come with me," Raidan said quietly.

The relief on the lad's face spoke volumes.

Like Tegun, Lesandor was glad to be going with Raidan, as glad as he could be about anything, given the circumstances. He watched a group of men across the room, earnestly engrossed in some activity. At first he thought it was a type of game, with stones, such as he had played as a boy. However, before any game could have been concluded the various coloured stones were packed away carefully and Lesandor realised that it was a sale he was watching and the men were not all together. Their clothes confirmed that fact, now that he came to study them more carefully. Two of them were quite obviously not local at all, dressed as they were in robes adorned with intricate stitching of a type he had never seen before.

The rustle of paper beside him disturbed his appraisal of the traders as Raidan spread a large map out on the table and pointed to a black mark on the west coast.

"This looks like a sizable town, Stonehaven they call it." He indicated over his shoulder with his head, towards the group Lesandor had been watching, "There are some traders in port from there, like those in the far corner. According to the barkeep here they'd be happy to take us – for a small fee." He shook his head. "Apparently, everything they say about Gerik is true: there's nothing that can't be bought or sold. Anyway, Stonehaven is far enough from Fallowridge, the capital. We shan't be in Larse's way and we'll be more likely to gain different intelligence. I tried to talk him into letting us stay here for a few days, despite the unrest, but he won't have it. We start out in the morning."

Tegun was dozing off and Raidan's nine other chosen companions nodded in agreement then started talking among themselves. Raidan regarded Lesandor sympathetically.

"I am all right," Lesandor muttered. "At least we have something to do."

The traders' initial reluctance to be their guides was overcome at the cost of four good elm bows, but they warned the Morenians it would take three days to reach Stonehaven, for they had stops to make and would be staying overnight in towns along the way. Should they choose to go alone they might make it in two or, then again, not at all. Raidan had no intention of taking his men through Gerik unaccompanied; he hardly needed the traders' barely concealed warning to convince him of that, and small towns were exactly the sort of place where they could discover something to their advantage. Larse might still have his mind on forging new trade links, as he had been commissioned to do, but Raidan was sure his father would be far more interested in the power-play being staged in Gerik, and that was what he intended to find out about.

The leader of the four traders, a stout, unshaven fellow called Troi, asked them their business, but with little real interest. A trade mission, Raidan explained, truthfully enough, going into a few succinct details about Morenian crops and produce. That seemed satisfactory. Indeed, by the time they went to their beds, another of the traders, Brune, was already making plans for a new venture involving the importation of Morenian wine.

That night, the wind moaned under the slates of the roof and hissed through the cracks in the shutters. Lesandor tossed in his bed, pulled the covers up around his ears to shut out the noise and failed to sleep.

The next morning they rose early. They were to make the journey to Stonehaven on foot, walking beside the traders' pack donkeys.

"Plainest clothes, no ornaments," Raidan instructed.

The day was dreary, with a heavy sea mist hanging over the land, cold and cloying.

"At least you can't see the scenery," Raidan whispered to Lesandor as they set off, wrapped against the weather. The bell on the lead donkey clattered hollowly from some way ahead.

"I wouldn't want to get lost in it though," Lesandor muttered in reply, increasing his speed unconsciously.

Raidan lengthened his stride to keep up.

As far as it was possible to tell in the mist, the morning passed. Still they went on walking.

"My stomach says it's lunch time," Tegun complained.

"Mine too," Raidan agreed. "I suppose these fellows know where we're going. For all we know, we've passed through half-a-dozen towns and settlements without realising."

Lesandor did not feel hungry. He had not felt hungry enough to eat breakfast either, nor supper the night before. Nevertheless he agreed that a stop was due, if only to warm up and try to dry out a bit. A fire would be a pleasant comfort, a log fire, blazing wood, the scent of resin....

"... well, it's true, isn't it?"

Lesandor realised that the question, whatever it was, had been aimed at him. The speaker, Syjan, was awaiting a reply.

"I'm sorry," he apologised, embarrassed. "I was thinking."

The man grunted noncommittally. They walked on.

Eventually, buildings materialised through the mist and Troi called a halt. "Right. This is it for the day."

"For the day?" Raidan said, surprised, though the colour of the day gave no indication as to what the time might be.

Troi misundersood his tone. "Business. We warned you – business comes first. This is Crossford, our first stop. By the time we're done here it'll be too late to go farther."

The fire was made from dried goat dung, and the meal might well have been, too, for all the appetite Lesandor displayed. Raidan watched with concern as Lesandor pushed his food around on the plate and pretended an interest in the bargaining going on between their escort and the local traders nearby. The prince leant across the table to help himself to another piece of flat bread and the movement caught Lesandor's attention. He grinned halfheartedly at his companion, then pushed his plate away.

"Take my mind off of all this," he suggested quietly. "Tell me more about your lady. I was thinking you could start with how you first enticed her away from her guardian's house."

Raidan glanced about, no one was paying them any heed. So he nodded and pulled his stool closer to Lesandor's and told his story in more detail. After that, the evening passed pleasantly enough and, by the time they thought about turning in for the night, Lesandor was sufficiently relaxed to take a bowl of gruel and tired enough to sleep properly after it.

Fabiom travelled on foot, for he could make better speed than with the donkey cart, yet Fairwater had never seemed so far away. It rained incessantly. The two nights it took to make the journey he passed in roadside taverns, pausing only long enough to get some sleep and dry his clothes. He ate on the move; walked, ran, walked, ran. Eventually the river widened into the estuary that led into the sea.

Set atop the highest hill, built all in white marble, the royal palace overlooked the shining city, though Fabiom had neither time nor inclination to be awed by the splendour. He stripped off his travel-soiled clothes, washed as well as he was able with the last of his water, fastened on a clean tunic and finished his journey. As he rinsed his hands in the ornate basin of the palace heart room he requested an immediate audience with Prince Ravik.

Ravik was entertaining a diplomatic delegation from Malandel, who had arrived only that day, but he left them and came to meet Fabiom.

"This is a pleasant surprise. More pleasant than the other surprises I've had sprung on me today, for certain! There's new trouble brewing in Gerik, I fear, or so my sources tell me. But – something is wrong. What is it, my friend?"

"What sort of trouble?" Fabiom demanded. "I'm sorry, my lord, I forget myself. It's just.... No, I must know. What trouble?"

"Not here. Come." Ravik opened the door to a comfortable ante-chamber, where his wife sat at a small loom threaded with a pale ochre warp, their youngest grandson asleep in a cradle beside her. Maedrim looked tired, though she smiled warmly when she saw her husband.

The prince hesitated, then ushered Fabiom inside.

Maedrim rose from her weaving stool and embraced Fabiom, kissing him on both cheeks.

"How is it with you, my lady?" Fabiom asked quietly, glancing at the cradle.

The princess shook her head. "Do not be anxious on his account – he is not for settling. We came in here for some peace for my sake, not his. He is my excuse."

"You seem weary, my lady. I trust you are well."

"*I* seem weary! I take it you have not seen your reflection," she retorted. "For myself, recently I have not been sleeping. That is all that ails me."

"You do look dreadful, Fabiom," Ravik agreed.

"And unshaven, too, which is not like you," Maedrim added.

Fabiom ran his hand over a jaw covered with three days' stubble. "I travelled fast. I wanted to get here as quickly as possible. My prince, please tell me – what have you heard from Gerik?"

Ravik handed Fabiom a cup of well-watered wine. "Rebel forces are massing, even in the towns. Robstrom's name is being spoken openly once more. There is talk of a new order, even if it must be achieved by civil war. That is what I have heard."

Maedrim let out a shuddering breath. "I have seen troubling things in the stars – terrible forebodings of destruction – so that I cannot sleep. And you, Fabiom, you do not look like a man who brings good news."

Ravik had sat down and he watched Fabiom pace towards the window, to stare down onto the city and out to the ocean beyond.

"Lesandor is in Gerik. I can't believe, no, I *don't* believe you sent him there, my lord. Yet he was given no option. He sailed from Windwood, with your youngest son."

Maedrim gave an inarticulate cry and the colour drained from her face.

Fabiom turned to look at his prince. "His mother fears for his safety. Gerik – Gerik could destroy him."

Ravik briefly covered his eyes. "I know that!" he hissed. "It isn't even my venture. Norgest organised it. Larse his son, step-son, is in command. It's a trading voyage. Believe me, Fabiom, there is no way I would have sent Lesandor to Gerik. He should have been on board the *Spikenard*, which sailed for Varlass six days ago. Raidan *should* be with him, I had intended them both to go to Varlass. Raidan was away in Rushford, on my behalf. I sent a message to him there, to go to Southernport and take ship, I told him they should go together. But why – why would he think that meant to Gerik?" He muttered the last, almost to himself.

Fabiom slumped down on a settle. "You may not have sent them, but please – bring Lesandor home. My lord, I will do anything...."

"No." Ravik held up his hand. "You need offer me nothing, Fabiom. You are my friend. Even if you were not, I do know enough about the people of this land not to send such a one as Lesandor to Gerik." He paused and shook his head. "Just as Jaymna knows it. I'm sorry; this is unforgivable and there will be restitution. Meanwhile, of course I will bring him home. I'll send a ship with the next tide. Unless, that is, you would go to him yourself?"

Fabiom considered that option, remembering how he had hated Gerik, the nightmares he had endured; only able to guess what effect the place was having on his son, Casandrina's son.

"If you give me leave then, yes, I will go. They have an eight-day head start but with luck they will still be near the port if it is trade links they are seeking to establish. And, if the trouble you have been hearing about is anything like as bad as the rumours would have it, I will bring Raidan home too. A royal hostage would be too strong a temptation for any Gerik dynasty striving for recognition or power."

"Come and eat." Maedrim stood and lifted the babe from his cradle. "You have some time before the tide turns."

Ravik opened the door for his wife, and indicated Fabiom to follow her. "Those Malandelians who arrived earlier, they came via Gerik. They have information, some of it may aid you. As for supplies and men, I will give you whatever and whomever you need."

Fabiom needed the repast. The food was certainly an improvement on what he had eaten on his journey, besides which, he had been so anxious for the past two days. To sit and relax, knowing something practical was actually going to be done, was relief indeed. The visiting Malandelians provided good company. Their leader, a young, neatly-bearded nobleman by the name of Jowan, listened with sympathy and concern to Fabiom's tale and spoke animatedly about his own voyage thus far, including the brief stop they had made in Gerik where they gathered a good deal of intelligence on the situation there, before sailing on to Morene.

"There seems no question that opposing factions are heading for a serious confrontation," he told Fabiom, filling him in on what they had already been discussing with Prince Ravik. "Some say Robstrom has gathered a huge rebel force to his banner, that things will be finally settled this time, but it will be bloody. Like you, we have people there we want to get out. I was planing to set sail for Gerik tomorrow, one day sooner will make little odds. My ship, *Sunbow*, will make good speed – she is at your service."

It was a generous offer and Fabiom accepted it gratefully. Ravik was relieved too, for he knew Jowan to be a good man and one with contacts in Gerik that could help them. The more he heard, the more anxious he was that all their people, but Raidan and Lesandor especially, should be safely home on Morenien soil.

The meal was concluded somewhat hurriedly, and while Jowan was making last minute preparations and sending word to the rest of his men and crew, who had not been expecting to sail until the morrow, Fabiom organised what supplies he needed and wrote a letter for his house-steward to read to Casandrina.

Sunbow sailed before dusk.

Chapter Two

THEY STEPPED OUT into a white world of swirling fog that made grotesque shapes out of nothing, and obscured everything that was really there. Lesandor stood for a long moment, trying to get his bearings, but he had taken little notice of the layout of Crossford town when they arrived last night, so that he could not say where he now was in relation to anything. Cutting through the shrouding silence came the clear tinkling of the pack donkeys' bells. Beside Lesandor, Raidan let out his breath. He too was uncomfortable in this sightless, formless void.

"Keep close by the beasts. Let's go," Troi's voice urged.

Lesandor took hold of the strap of a donkey's pack as the animal passed close to him. "Raidan?"

"I'm here. Everyone together?"

Voices of affirmation greeted the prince's question as they set off through the gloom.

"Good. Tegun, stay close to me."

The morning passed with only muted sounds for distraction: the monotonous beat of hard hooves broken occasionally as the donkeys stepped onto loose stones or negotiated rough banks, low voices that kept the group in touch but never in conversation, and footsteps – the sound of thirty-two leather-clad feet.

Lesandor walked as if in a dream, staring ahead but seeing nothing, stepping out, left foot, right foot, on and on, listening to the sound of his own tread and the hollow clop of the little donkey beside him. The sounds lulled him, numbing his senses, and he retreated into the rhythms.

Hunger roused him from his trance-like state. His left hand was warm from resting against the donkey's soft coat, his right hand chilled to the bone. It took a moment to realise something was different and, even when that fact registered, he could not immediately say what it was. He stopped walking. One pace on, the donkey halted. Silence.

"Raidan? Troi? Where the.... Raidan!"

No voice answered his call. The donkey tore at some thistles it had discovered, otherwise there was no sound at all. Lesandor took a deep breath, to call again. Instead he let it out, slowly, and strained to hear any sound that would give him a clue as to his companions' whereabouts. Nothing. The donkey seemed unconcerned at having deserted its fellows, obviously satisfied with Lesandor's company.

"I don't suppose there would be anything to eat in that pack?" Lesandor wondered aloud.

The two heavy panniers were seemingly crammed with nothing but bronze oil jars. Just to make certain, he took a few of them out and slipped his hand inside to feel around. His fingers closed about something familiar, warm and smooth.

Beneath the top layer of jars, the basket was filled with amber — pieces too big to be formed except by the felling of a Silvanan tree. Tears sprung to Lesandor's eyes and for a moment he thought he was going to be physically sick. Mercifully, the moment passed. He unstrapped the panniers and lowered them to the ground.

He would wait for the fog to clear, there was no point in going on blindly. Troi had assured them such weather always blew over within a couple of days. This was the second day.

Refusing to think about what they contained, Lesandor propped himself on top of the two baskets and waited. Relieved of its burden, the donkey rolled in the damp grass, then went back to eating.

As the fog darkened with evening, Lesandor shivered, cold and hungry. By now the others would know he was missing. Had he gone so far astray that they could not find him? He pulled his cloak tighter still and felt the fabric damp and clammy. Morning seemed a long way off.

"Maybe Stonehaven will live up to its name," Raidan suggested. "You might feel better in a place not built out of the destruction of the forests. I know I will and it must be far worse for you. Lesandor?" There was no reply. "Lesandor, are you all right?"

Troi called a halt, his annoyance evident. "Call him. He can't be far."

"One of the beasts is missing," Troi's brother, Syjan, said, after repeated shouts of Lesandor's name had elicited no response. "The one with the – the valuables."

"The little thief! Are you in on this?" Troi rounded furiously on Raidan. Nearby there sounded a whisper of metal against leather.

In the fog, Raidan could not be sure whether one of his own men had drawn or one of Troi's. It made little difference, in the opaque world they traversed, an attack by either side would be suicidal. His father had taught him to be a diplomat first, a warrior only in necessity.

"Lesandor has not stolen your *valuables*, whatever they are, or your donkey. Believe me, he would be the last person to intentionally wander off in Gerik. He must have trusted the beast would stay with the others. They're lost. Rather than argue, should we not retrace our path and, if not 'look' for them, at least call?"

Troi snorted contemptuously at Raidan's assurance that Lesandor had not deliberately purloined the donkey and its cargo. "We haven't time; we've already lost half a day in the fog." He scratched his neck, thinking. "We'll split up. I'll not lose more of you and have to look for you. If you want to search, you do so on your own account, otherwise come on with me and Gart. Syjan and Brune can go back. We'll meet up in Bridgetown tomorrow evening. Hopefully we can then all get on to Stonehaven, as planned." His voice was heavy with sarcasm.

Raidan was indecisive. The thought of leaving Lesandor appalled him, yet, until the fog lifted, there was nothing that men unfamiliar with this land could do. It would be of little help to Lesandor if they, too, went missing.

"Very well," he agreed reluctantly. "We'll go on to, where was it? Bridgetown? If I have your word that your men will look until they find him."

"For a price," Troi retorted with a covetous glance at Raidan's yew-wood bow.

"Naturally," Raidan agreed, with no surprise.

Lesandor dozed, woke, dozed again. The fog seemed to have thinned and the darkness of the night was a more natural hue. Each time he woke he listened, but no sounds carried on the night air other than the stirrings of the donkey and the occasional rustle of some small nocturnal creature. When morning came at last, it did so with a featureless grey sky but at least the fog was lifted and it was possible to see.

What he saw did little to ease his discomfort. Away to the north-east were the low outlines of rounded hills, otherwise nothing, except flat land of small shrubs and tough grass. Within the circle of his vision not a single building was visible. The path he had travelled wound away towards the hills and he knew he had walked too far north, that the others would have gone westwards. He stood, uncertain whether he should try to find his own way to Stonehaven, which he knew – from the maps he had seen – lay to the south-west of his present position, at the mouth of the River Prosperous. He could try to find the river and work his way along that. If there were any settlements in this part of Gerik they would most likely be found alongside the river. Yet he knew Raidan would not just abandon him. If anyone was out searching for him they might go back to where he turned off the main highway. But the fog had covered the land all day yesterday, they could hardly have looked for him in that, and he seemed to have walked well away from where he judged the river to be, where the road should be. Finally he decided there was no point in waiting and took hold of the donkey's halter.

"Come on, then. This way." He did not reload the little animal but left the panniers where he had dropped them, hoping they might alert whoever came searching for him. Then he set off south-west, as best as he could judge. The grassland was not hard to traverse. All the while he walked he was looking out for anything he might drink or eat, whilst at the same time trying not to notice the dead landscape. It was a hard task.

At home, there would be curled fern fronds in the shady nooks beneath trees, tender shoots of asparagus hidden in the undergrowth of the riverbank. Instead, he had to compete with the donkey and make do with a few burdock and dandelion leaves, and the smallest, least prickly thistle-heads.

By midday his tread had become leaden. His feet were sore, his body and mind equally weary and still the view remained unchanged, unbroken by buildings, hills or trees. "It would be useful if your legs were longer, or mine less so," he told the donkey.

He had finished the diluted wine in the flask at his hip and, apart from the few bitter greens, he had eaten nothing since early the previous day. He stopped more and more frequently, doubting his decision to go on, knowing he could not find his way back.

The stream flowed silently beneath an overhanging bank and he might have stepped into it had not the donkey put its head down to drink almost before it had stopped walking.

Relieved, Lesandor knelt and drank, then washed his face in an attempt to clear his mind. It was not the River Prosperous but it surely had to be a tributary. Reason said that if he followed it he would come eventually to the parent river, the river that led to his destination and, hopefully, a speedy reunion with his companions.

A darting movement caught his attention: silver-bright fish hiding beneath the bank, food if he could catch them. Raw fish, for he would find nothing with which to build a fire. The thought was not appealing, yet his empty stomach persuaded him to try.

The water was bitterly cold and the fish darted through his benumbed fingers. He was wasting both time and energy and achieving nothing. Giving up on that, he pulled a dozen threads from his travel cloak, knotted the ends together and tied one end to the lower nock of his bow, the other about the shaft of an arrow. In no time at all he managed to land two fish. Out of the water he could see they were not silver at all, but iridescent blue and gold. They had large eyes and turned down mouths and as he ate them he knew he had never tasted anything so unpleasant in his life. He also knew he had to eat if he was to go on, and he had to go on. Though he was far from satisfied with his meal, he could not bring himself to catch any more fish but only filled his flask with stream water and started on his way again.

As the sun began its descent he was violently sick.

He drank nearly all of the water in his flask in an effort to cleanse his mouth, though it did little good. His head throbbed and lights danced behind his eyes while his stomach was gripped with shooting pains that seemed to reach down even through his thighs and up into his chest. The stream lay some way to his left, for the stiff grass grew thickest there and it had been impossible to walk close by it. He needed more water; it was the only thing he could think of to try to ease the agony. And if, as he suspected, the fish was to blame for his discomfort, he needed to make himself sick again. Pushing his way through the tangled clumps of grass he reached the water and drank deeply. Before he could decide what to do next, he passed out.

The wooden walls of Bridgetown loomed before them, stark in the gloom of the evening. Impatiently, Raidan watched the gates open. They were late, the town was closed up for the night, but Troi was well known and had assured them they would be admitted. Raidan wondered why this town should be walled at all; it appeared to be in the middle of nowhere.

"Are they here? Did you ask?" he demanded. Troi had returned from speaking briefly with the gateman.

"Be patient!" Troi told him. "I'll have to inquire in the Townmaster's offices. The rest of you go on to the inn." He grinned at the expression on Raidan's face. "The Townmaster's not partial to strangers, as you may have deduced from the fortifications. He's particularly wary of Morenians, high-born ones especially."

Raidan nodded wearily, ignoring Troi's last remark. "Very well, I'll wait." He had little choice.

Troi seemed to be gone a long time. The Bridge, as the inn was unimaginatively named, was crowded and noisy, and among those present there was no one Raidan recognised; certainly neither of the two who had been sent to look for Lesandor were there. His heart sank. Troi returned eventually.

"Some good news, some bad." He took the mug Gart handed him and drank half of the contents before continuing. "They found your friend – that's the good news."

"And the bad?" Raidan asked, annoyed to have to play games but relieved beyond measure.

"He was unwell, I have no details. Possibly no more than a soaking out near the marshes. That's why we had to head south for a way, to avoid them. I was worried he might have gone north, we'd never have found him then. Anyway, facilities here are basic, as you can see. Syjan thought it best to go on to Stonehaven. We'll all meet up there. Your friend should be recovered by then, I'd say."

❦

"Lesandor?" The voice was cajoling, insistent almost. Lesandor did not want to be disturbed. He muttered in his sleep and turned onto his side.

"Lesandor, come on!" Other voices joined in and he reluctantly opened his eyes and got to his feet.

"Where are we going?"

"To the woods, come on. The Dancing Glade."

His drowsiness left him at that, and he followed the voices, now raised in song. In and out of tall trees, down twisting paths, under hanging boughs, until he came at last to the Dancing Glade. The woodmaids who had led him there drifted away, laughing to themselves. He watched them go, then sat down on the soft grass and waited. And the Silvanii came and danced.

They were not substantial, as his mother was, but he could see them all clearly, as he had never seen any save his sister or grandmother before. That puzzled him but he spared the matter little thought, caught up as he was in the hypnotic steps and movement of the swaying bodies. One of the Silvanii danced close by him, smiling at him so that his heart ached. Another beckoned him forward, holding out a slender hand. Before he could respond, her expression changed, eyes widening in horror as she fell with a soul-piercing cry and faded from his sight.

The others danced on, oblivious. He scrambled to his feet, backing away from the dancers. Behind him was a solid wall of briars, through which he could not pass. The Silvanii moved towards him, surrounding him and, though he was not aware of having moved, he found himself in the centre of the glade and the undulating figures. Another screamed and fell, so close that he reached out to catch her, but his arms closed on empty air. Again her sisters took no notice, though their pace quickened and their steps became more complex still. The third to fall did not fade away but lay moaning piteously. He could not touch her, for it was as if an invisible barrier stood between them, through which he could not reach. Every cry, every strained movement found an echo in his own body and he wept for her and for himself.

As he looked up, trying to find help from those still dancing, he saw, across the glade, a gap in the briar hedge. He could do nothing for the fallen Silvana; perhaps he could do something for the others. The briars gripped and tore at his face and arms and legs, bringing up angry welts on his skin, whilst white petals fell about him mockingly. He pushed through, regardless of the thorns, coming out upon a scene of carnage, of broken, fallen trees, and amber pouring from gaping wounds, hardening in the air even as it ran. One young elm had been uprooted by the fall of a larger tree, and he realised that had to be the tree of the Silvana he had left in the Dancing Glade, dying. He stood, appalled, as he heard the unmistakable sound of an axe biting into living wood. Behind him, beyond the briars, another scream rent the night. The sound of the tree's fall came to him from across the river and he pushed his way forward, clambering over the corpse of a felled ash, down to the river bank and into the icy flow.

Rushing and roaring, the water swept him off his feet. He caught at a branch and tried to force his way across but he was pushed beneath the water and hurtled downstream, and the cries and the axe blows were left behind.

"Silvanii do not dance in the dark. They do not dance in the dark."

"Hush, young fellow. You're near drowned. Stop fretting yourself. It's been many a year since Silvanii danced here, day or night."

"What? Where am I?" Lesandor tried to sit up but his head spun and his stomach threatened to rebel again. He rested his head back on the pillow with a groan, only then becoming aware of the fact that it was a pillow he was lying on and that a heavy pile of warm blankets covered his body. His clothes had been taken from him. From the way the lamplight reflected off the walls, he appeared to be in some sort of stone hut.

"No questions now. You're lucky to be alive. If I hadn't found your beast, I'd not have come looking for you, and if I hadn't, likely as not, no one would. Not until it was too late. The Prosperous is a dangerous river to go swimming in, especially in the dark."

A hefty, middle-aged man, with a mop of unruly chestnut-brown hair, a scarred cheek and a cheerful grin, was bending over him.

"I thought I was somewhere else," Lesandor murmured as his dream came back to him all too vividly. "I had a terrible dream. I think I was sick earlier, unless that, too, was a dream. I ate some fish, it tasted horrible … I do not know."

"Blue and yellow fish?"

Lesandor nodded, then regretted moving his head so suddenly.

"You're even luckier than I thought. Rest now, anyway. I'm Pob by the way, well, that's what everyone calls me."

Lesandor did not reply but fell asleep again, without dreams.

Late the next morning he awoke to the smell of cooking, and felt his stomach turn ominously. When Pob came over to his bedside with a bowl of something steaming, he tried to push it away, but the older man was insistent. To his surprise, Lesandor did manage to swallow a few mouthfuls of what turned out to be a mild broth, without any adverse reaction.

"Do you good, if you can keep it down," Pob told him casually. "You'll have no objections I trust, but I borrowed your bow to get us that meal – easiest duck I've taken in months. What sort of wood is that then?"

"Ash." Lesandor had brought his plainest bow on the trip, in preference to any better one he possessed, choosing it simply for its wood the moment he discovered where they were headed.

"A rare thing in this land. Only the wealthy have bows here, and only the really wealthy have wooden ones. Marks a man out indeed. It'll be worth a bit if you're ever stuck."

Lesandor smiled wistfully. "I hope it does not come to that, but who knows – given my present circumstances. I suppose it was foolish of me to leave the saddlebags."

Pob looked at him quizzically. "What was in these saddlebags?"

"Amber," Lesandor replied without hesitation.

"That you left out there, somewhere?" Pob asked, just to be sure he understood correctly. "Of course, being Morenian, it offended your sensibilities."

For an instant, Lesandor felt his anger flare until he realised Pob was not mocking him, he just did not understand. "I left them as a marker. You saved my life, you find the amber, you keep it. You explain to Troi...." he muttered.

"It can wait." Pob replied with a short laugh. "But I'll not risk that much hard currency falling into the wrong hands. I'll find someone to go and look for it. As for this Troi, well we can worry about him later, whoever he is. By the way, I've sorted out some fresh clothing for you. Utility stuff but warm and clean."

Pob was quite content to travel with Lesandor to Stonehaven. He had been going that way anyway, he said. To Lesandor's surprise, when they left the hut – which turned out to be one of about a dozen clustered together – they headed off north again, as far as he could tell retracing the way he had come yesterday.

"Marshes," Pob explained. "No way through down there." He laughed. "You probably hadn't gone too far adrift when you lost your friends. Of course your swim took you a bit nearer Stonehaven. If we had a boat we could continue that way, otherwise this is best." He chuckled again. "It's a good thing the river bends as much as it does, most people get washed ashore the way you did."

"Most people?"

"Oh, you weren't the first. Won't be the last. You were certainly one of the luckier ones though, as I say."

"You saw no sight of anyone who might have been looking for me?" Lesandor asked, after a while.

Pob shook his head. "I live out here, know all about it. No one's been off the road in days, apart from you. No signs anyway."

The journey from Bridgetown to Stonehaven was made by boat and seemed interminably slow. According to Troi it would only have taken two days, had a chance to do some business not come up on a settlement near the marsh edge. Raidan tried to argue but Troi would not listen. He claimed that, while Lesandor had been found, the donkey and its load had not, and – unless it was returned within four days – compensation would have to be paid in full for that. He was not losing business too.

Raidan said nothing. He knew by then what the 'load' was. Late the previous evening, two of the traders had been discussing the amber and the trouble there would be if it was not recovered. They had taken no notice of young Tegun, curled up beneath a rug in a corner of the room, whom they wrongly assumed to be sound asleep.

Tegun's revelation had set the Morenians debating among themselves whether the amber might be old, from the trees that had once graced Gerik, or newer, somehow taken from Morene. The possibility that it might be the latter set off calls for action, and Raidan had difficulty keeping his men from doing anything rash. But he prevailed, arguing that, for Lesandor's sake, they could not risk antagonising Troi and the other traders.

That night was spent in a stilted marsh hut where it was impossible to stand upright. Grimy cobwebs festooned the roof beams, lowering the ceiling further still. They ate a bland supper around a cheerless fire while the wind blew at them from all sides, lifting the rush matting as it came through cracks in the floorboards. The building was old, the wood rotting. There was nothing to repair it with. Every year the stilts had to be shortened, the decaying wood at the base cut away. It was a contest as to whether the hut would reach the surface of the water still intact, or collapse above it.

The inhabitants were seemingly as miserable as their home, though that hardly surprised the Morenians. Raidan fervently hoped Lesandor had not come this way; he did not wish to contemplate the effect the place might have had upon his friend's sensibilities.

"Is there another way from Bridgetown to Stonehaven?" Raidan asked one of their hosts – a bald, wizened man, named Hettor – glad to have thought of something to say, for the conversation had become strained and awkward soon after the introductions had been made.

"No, not unless you go way round, and it's a long ways. Marsh to the north, marsh to the south. The river is the only road." Hettor laughed mirthlessly.

"Then you'll have seen Troi's brother, and two companions. One of them perhaps not too well. When did they come through here?"

"No one's been since three days ago. Quiet this time of year, better later. No, I've not seen Syjan since he passed this way going to Westmouth with Troi and all."

There was a river toll. If Lesandor and his rescuers had passed through, Hettor would have known. Troi had lied. It did not take too much imagination to work out why. What had he to gain from finding Lesandor, apart from retrieving his amber? And he was going to make Raidan pay for that anyway. Troi, who had not overheard the conversation, soon became aware of Raidan's eyes boring into his back and he turned his head to nod amiably in the direction of the young prince. They were outmatched as well as outnumbered, yet Raidan could not just leave Lesandor to his fate. Stooping to avoid the filthy roof beams, he worked his way across to Troi's side.

"You lied to me."

The trader did not even blink. "Perhaps I did."

"Why? I would have gone back. I would have found him!"

All around, heads turned to stare, Raidan's companions open-mouthed as the implication of his words sank in.

Troi was no longer smiling. "I have things to do. Time is my master. You say you have come to trade. That's your story, maybe it's true, I don't know. I don't much care either. But some people do, and they wouldn't want you and these roaming loose through Gerik. Would you have a dozen of us in Morene, going wherever, doing whatever? I don't think so. So, I lied." He shrugged. "He'll make his own way to Stonehaven if he has any sense. It's not hard to find. And if he cares about his health, and yours, he'll bring our merchandise with him."

In case Raidan had any ideas about arguing, Gart took his short knife from his belt and used the tip to clean his fingernails.

Chapter Three

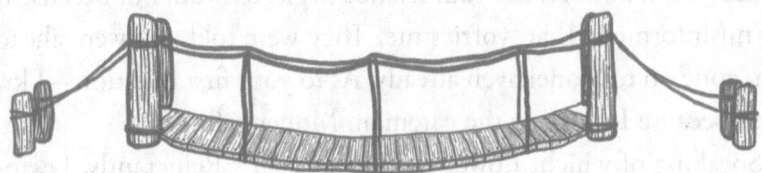

A S SOON AS Lesandor and Pob reached Bridgetown, Lesandor inquired after Troi and his party. His questions were politely but unhelpfully answered: many people passed through Bridgetown, going and coming from Stonehaven. Eventually, he was directed to the Townmaster's offices. When, some considerable time later, he returned to the small room Pob had rented for them, he was thoroughly disheartened.

"I don't believe this place!" Lesandor exclaimed. "They kept me waiting for ages, then I had to fill out a form. A form! I only wanted to know if the others had been through already, and if Raidan had left me a message. I thought he would have done." He said the last quietly, disappointed there had been nothing of the sort, either in the Townmaster's offices or at the inn.

Pob regarded him mildly. "And did you learn anything?"

"Nothing. They said they didn't know. I do not believe that. Eleven strangers came through this town, one of them...." he paused, but Pob finished his sentence for him.

"A prince of Morene."

"Yes. How did you...? Never mind." What had he said while he was delirious, he wondered? Yet for some reason he trusted Pob.

He was too wound up with frustration at the machinations of the bureaucracy he was having to endure, to care much about anything else at that moment anyway. "*They* would know that, wouldn't they? This country is on the verge of a civil war, they would know *everyone* who came and went." He threw himself down onto a sagging couch, blue eyes bright with indignation.

"They did come through, and left again, two days ago," Pob said casually.

"How do you know? Was there a message?'

"No – in reply to your second question." Pob rubbed his jowl and frowned. "And not because your friends neglected you, but because they were misinformed. That worries me. They were told you were ahead of them, gone on to Stonehaven already. As to your first question – I know all this because I spoke to the gateman. Money talks."

"Speaking of which, I owe you a great debt." Reluctantly, Lesandor indicated his ash bow beside his pack. "You said such things were of value. It is yours. The donkey and the amber were not mine, so they hardly count."

Pob laughed. "Forget it! And I'll not take your bow, beauty though it is. You may have need of it yet. Now you're recovered, more or less, I'll have some stories from you. I move about, remember, I'm often looking for a meal or a bed. No better currency for a man on the road than a store of good tales. Buy almost anything they will. Deal?"

"Deal," Lesandor agreed, relieved at not having to part with the bow. "What sort of stories had you in mind?"

"Well, let me see. What was the first thing you said to me as you woke up after your dip? 'Silvanii don't dance in the dark'. That sounds like a good place to start. As we can't go by river, it'll take us at least three days to get to Stonehaven. That should give you plenty of time to explain. We'll set out first thing tomorrow."

So Lesandor traded his stories of the Silvanii for a safe passage through Gerik. To begin, he recited the tale, known to every child in Morene, of Prince Essher. A tale already half-forgotten in Gerik.

"Essher, the youngest son of a foreign nobleman had, by chance, travelled to Morene and Gerik when he was very young and had realised there was something extraordinary about these lands. His travelling companions, even his father, had been afraid, but Essher kept returning. And so it was that he was here, in Gerik, on his seventeenth birth eve, at which time he met and won Jarisella, an elm Silvana, as his wife...."

Pob listened, fascinated, every now and again asking a question or commenting on the tale he was hearing.

"Yes, Essher, I've heard the name. His great-grandson was Cylanus who became the first Ruling Prince of Gerik. Go on, go on."

Lesandor went on. "Over the years, as Jarisella taught her husband about forestry and the secrets of silk, he became very wealthy. Others came and stayed and thus the colonisation of our lands began. The Silvanii were content, for they were respected – indeed they were glad of the protection the colonists afforded them. Up until that time, timber had been regularly cut by visiting ships. Even in Morene today there are few Silvanan trees near the coasts."

Pob nodded slowly, enthralled. "All I knew of that time was Essher's name, and that Cylanus, Essher's great-grandson, died childless, and his twin younger brothers each had one son – the princes Lensen and Starven."

"Quite so, and Starven was the first Ruling Prince of Morene and his son, Lincius, was the next of that line to marry a Silvana. And none of them styled himself 'King' because they understood that they ruled neither land nor Silvanii but men only."

"What sort of tree was Prince Lincius's wife from?"

"A beech. Her name was Sulmarita."

"What is a beech tree like?"

As they traversed the barren plains, Lesandor told Pob about the different trees that grew in Morene, that had once flourished in Gerik, and about their Silvanii and the woodmaids. From then on the history of Prince Lincius mingled with incidents from his own family history. Episodes from the upbringing of Prince Lincius's son, Tibbeau, and from Lesandor's own childhood ran side by side. Other stories, from other sources, passed the time until Stonehaven loomed large on the horizon.

"I thought...." Lesandor took a deep breath through clenched teeth. "*Stonehaven*, the name. But there is not a single stone in the place, is there?"

"It takes its name from the cliffs on which it stands. I'm afraid this town, like most others in Gerik, was carved out of the forests, literally."

A wooden swing bridge spanned the Prosperous. The town of Stonehaven lay on both sides. It was vast and sprawling and in the light of the setting sun the wood with which it was built glowed gold as if it dripped with amber. How many trees had fallen to build such a place, Lesandor could only guess. How many of those had belonged to the Silvanii, he did not wish to know.

Pob touched his arm. He had never seen a forest, let alone known the Silvanii, but Lesandor's tales of the past two days had touched his heart and he could see in the young man's face the horror that lay behind something he had always taken for granted.

"I am all right," Lesandor said automatically and steeled himself to go on functioning. He would meet up with the others here, they would get the information and secure the deals they had come for and then – then they would head back. He did not dwell on the prospect of the long trek across Gerik, just on the notion of reaching Westmouth and boarding ship once more for Morene. He would go to Deepvale, he decided. Before he returned to Windwood or reported to Fairwater for his next assignment he would go home, and in the great woods of Deepvale he would restore his sense of being. Maybe Pob would like to go with him.

"Too much military activity here for my tastes," Pob muttered as he observed a group of soldiers crossing the bridge. "We need to get to the other side; I have friends there, but I think we'll wait awhile. Come on, we'll get something to eat on this side."

"Is there something you have not told me?" Lesandor asked.

"A lot," Pob replied. "But now's not the time, and anyway, it's stories for services rendered, isn't it? Mind you, you might well get the chance to save *my* life before we're through here, in which case I'll owe you a few tales."

He led the way down a narrow street and out into an open square, bordered on all sides by two-storey buildings with balconies all around. Three other lanes led out of the square and Lesandor had the feeling it was a good place to exit in a hurry.

"Why did you tell me you wanted to come to Stonehaven when it is obvious this is not the safest place for you to be?" Lesandor asked as they came to a halt outside an open-fronted carvery where diners sat on benches set around low tables. Though he was not particularly hungry, and was still only able to eat the lightest dishes, he knew he must have something, so he followed Pob inside to take a place at a half-filled table.

"Needed, rather than wanted," Pob explained succinctly, then turned to the woman who was serving and ordered two dinners. "There are people here I have to see."

"And people you have to avoid, by the looks of things," Lesandor added quietly.

"Exactly. Ah, that looks good. There's not much choice here, but at least they don't serve fish."

Before they had finished their meal, which consisted of some sort of game bird – Pob said it was snipe – in a bilberry and herb sauce, they were joined by three men and a woman, who all greeted Pob cheerfully. They seemed pleased to see him, the woman especially so. She was young, perhaps a year or so older than Lesandor, tall, slender and quite beautiful. Her hair was chestnut brown, caught back in a thick plait that hung over her shoulder almost to her waist, and her eyes were the colour of dark honey. Lesandor found himself staring and made himself take notice of her male companions instead. Two of them were a similar age, the other a few years older, all three of them were quite deferential towards Pob. Lesandor could not help but notice the woman was less so.

"I fished him out of the river," Pob said by way of introducing Lesandor. "It was worth the effort: he's told me some good yarns." With that he turned to Lesandor, "These reprobates I wouldn't get my feet wet for, but they might be good for a drink later on. I suppose they're hungry, as usual."

They'd already eaten, the youngest of the men claimed, and were just on their way home. The woman told Pob they expected to see him later and extended the same invitation to Lesandor, who, reluctantly, declined. As soon as he was finished with his meal he intended to find Raidan and the others.

"Before you leave then," the woman suggested – she glanced at Pob, who gave a minute nod – "go to the baker's shop on Half Hill; say you're looking for Sirsha and someone there will direct you."

Pob directed Lesandor to a tavern called the Gull, which was situated on one of the main wharves and was known to be a frequent haunt of Troi and his associates. He promised to join Lesandor there later, to see he was indeed safely reunited with his friends and to take his leave. He had his own business to attend to meanwhile and so they parted company with a warm arm-clasp and each went his own way.

The Gull was a large, square building, quite noticeable by virtue of its being limed to a brilliant white. Having found it easily, Lesandor pushed open the heavy doors and went inside. As he did so, he realised this was the first time he had gone into any place in Gerik unaccompanied and, as dozens of heads turned to look in his direction, he could not help but wonder if he had done the wrong thing. It took barely an instant to perceive that he was not the only foreigner and, judging by the costumes and accents he could detect, many had travelled far greater distances to get there than he. Curiosity, not hostility, motivated most of the customers to look towards the opening door and soon their attention returned to their food, drink and interrupted conversations. Lesandor looked around. He could see no sign of anyone he recognised.

A young lad came over and offered him refreshments. When Lesandor inquired after the traders, the lad said he knew Troi but had seen neither him nor any of those who worked for him for many days. At Lesandor's insistence, and the procuration of a handful of small coins, he promised to ask around. The look on his face said Lesandor was wasting both his time and his money.

"Oh, I know Troi, all right. He was here briefly, but then he set out again," the keeper of the Gull said; uncle to the lad Lesandor had sent off to make inquiries. "He did visit the tavern – with his brother – but it was just the two of them; no foreigners. You'd be best to ask at the Townmaster's offices."

Lesandor's heart sank. Stonehaven was three times the size of Bridgetown, and something told him finding any help in the administrative centre would be at least that many times harder. Still, he thanked the innkeeper, threw a few more coins onto the damp countertop and set out for the bridge and the Townmaster's offices, which lay on the far side.

The soldiers stationed on the bridge regarded Lesandor coldly. Though his borrowed clothes were inconspicuous, he knew his ash bow marked him out. With so much unrest in the country, he was not surprised they were wary of strangers.

There were more soldiers in the toll booth on the far side, still more on the streets. He asked the way to the Townmaster's offices and was answered civilly enough. Straight on through three crossroads, into an open square, he would not miss it. He did not ask but wondered if, like the Gull, the municipal centre was painted white, that it was so obvious.

The building was not limed, yet in its own way it was more noticeable still. Even from the outside, Lesandor could see that Stonehaven's municipal offices were quite different from those of Bridgetown. There was an air of authority rather than bureaucracy about the place which set warning bells resounding in his mind. Then he went through the open doors into the vestibule and all such thoughts went from his head. Wood of every colour, from every tree he had ever seen, and some he could not even name, covered the walls, floors and ceilings and, over the wall panelling, veneer designs of fruits, flowers, wildlife and landscapes vied with each other for sheer magnificence. Each piece of furniture that stood upon the patterned wooden floor-tiles was of a different grain and, as in the rest of the decor, the colours ranged from softest creams and greys to deepest red and midnight black. Lesandor stared, aghast, yet he could not deny that it was beautiful.

As he had feared, there were forms to fill in saying who he was, what his business was in Stonehaven and the nature of his enquiry. He was told the forms would be passed to the appropriate person and the matter dealt with as speedily as possible. It sounded as if that could be several days.

"I just want to know if a message was left for me. Please, check. There has to be something. There were ten men and a boy, their leader is young: a shortish man with bright red hair. Someone must have seen them!"

He had raised his voice and a couple of well-coiffured heads turned in his direction, eyebrows raised. He returned the looks unwaveringly, at the same time noticing the insignia of rank, the purple-edged robes. Perhaps he could speed matters along.

He turned back to the clerk. "A trade delegation, consisting of eleven Morenians, has gone missing in Gerik whilst in the company of men of this town. Men who, according to good authority, have returned to Stonehaven recently and departed again. I became unintentionally separated from this party some days ago."

"Unintentionally separated, you say?"

Lesandor ignored the snide tone. "I intended to meet with them again, here, but now I am concerned for their wellbeing, as I am sure his Highness, Prince Ravik, would be if he were aware of the situation."

His tirade, and the import of his words, caught the attention of the two dignitaries who had been passing. One came towards him and, with a nod, dismissed the clerk.

"I am Townmaster Florim. I could not help but overhear that you had become separated from your group and are desirous to rejoin them. You are...?"

"Lesandor, of the Morenian holding of Deepvale. Thank you, Townmaster, for your interest. You will appreciate my concern. I expected to find my companions waiting here for me."

"A delegation from Morene, from the Ruling Prince you say. Missing? That is unfortunate indeed. I am sure it is a temporary situation, a misunderstanding. Yet we cannot be too careful in these troubled times. There are those in Gerik who would be glad to cause dissension between ourselves and his Highness. I have an important meeting now, I will raise the matter with my colleagues. Tomorrow I will have word for you. Will you return then?"

Lesandor had no choice but to comply.

The afternoon passed slowly though Lesandor made numerous inquiries after both the Morenians and Troi's associates. He learnt nothing, other than that the keeper of the Gull had been correct: Troi and his brother had been seen around Stonehaven for just one day and had headed off upriver again. Thinking about the Gull reminded Lesandor that Pob had promised to call in there that evening. He made his way back across the bridge and down to the southside wharves and had only just arrived when Pob walked in.

"Alone?" Pob inquired, and Lesandor told his tale.

Pob scratched his jaw thoughtfully. "Very strange. Well, we won't stay here. You're welcome to bed down with the friends who are looking after me, one more or less will make no difference. They might know something. I know people who keep their ears and eyes open."

Lesandor was not at all surprised to hear that.

Early the next morning, Lesandor left Pob's lodgings, though he had gone to bed late enough. There had been much coming and going and everyone who came was questioned but no one knew anything about the missing Morenians. The Townmaster was Lesandor's only remaining hope. With mounting anxiety, he retraced his way to the spectacularly-decorated building to wait in the vestibule.

A door opened, unexpectedly, in what had appeared to be an unbroken wall of greens and greys, and the Townmaster, in a full-length, purple-edged robe, approached.

"Thank you for coming back. Please, this way." He indicated the door through which he had just entered. "Sit, please. I am sorry you have been so inconvenienced. As I promised, I inquired about your friends and nowhere are they to be found; no one has heard mention of them." He rubbed his lips with his fingertips and looked searchingly at Lesandor. "Tell me again why they, why you, came to Stonehaven."

"Townmaster, I explained all that yesterday. We seek to expand our trade links with your country. We have a surplus of many crops which no longer survive in Gerik." Lesandor looked meaningfully at the walls of the audience room they were in, a room no less resplendent than the vestibule and one that spoke of the mass destruction of almost as many trees. "I became parted from my companions in the heavy fog, but I know they came on this way. I expected to meet them here as soon as I arrived."

"And your father is a lord holder and a member of the Morenian Assembly and is friend and confidant to the Ruling Prince, whose youngest son also happens to be along on this simple trading mission. Come now, Lesandor, this won't do. You can hardly expect me to believe that is the truth, can you? I'd rather not draw Morene into our affairs, but your very presence here suggests that your masters have already become involved." He leant back, lowered his hands and smiled, almost amiably. "An idea has just occurred to me. If you lead me to Robstrom, I'll find your friends and you can all go quickly and safely back to Morene. Otherwise, I'm afraid things might get unpleasant. I haven't time for you to make up your mind to be cooperative. You'll tell me what I want to know today, or tomorrow, no later. And, if you'll heed some very sound advice, you'll tell me today."

Bewildered, Lesandor stared at the man. "Townmaster, I have no desire to find out what methods of persuasion you employ here in Stonehaven, but I have never heard of 'Robstrom'. I do not even know what Robstrom is."

"*Who* Robstrom is, Lesandor. Who. And I want him, today. I'll not argue with you; we both know you have met him, dealt with him. I'll warrant he is behind this entire venture of your Ruling Prince into Gerik. He is the enemy of Gerik. A traitor. If you protect him, you too are an enemy and will be treated as such. Do as I say and I will know you are a friend. It is simple. I will send someone to meet you at the Gull at sundown. Be there."

Pob would know, if anyone did. They had met so many people, quite a few of whom had not been introduced by name. Lesandor walked slowly along the road leading from the Townmaster's offices. The threats had not overly frightened him; it had seemed too bizarre to be taken seriously. Yet, should this Robstrom turn out to be a friend of Pob's, Lesandor was not about to betray him. He wondered if maybe he ought to be afraid.

Pob listened to Lesandor's account of the morning's events with a grim expression, shaking his head as the narrative ended.

"He's lying about Prince Raidan and the others. He must be, if, as you say, you told him nothing yesterday about there being a Morenian prince among your party. So, he must know where they are. It's them for Robstrom. And, as he knows *he's* lying, I doubt if he'll give you credit for telling the truth."

"But I *do not* know who this Robstrom is and, to be honest, I do not think I want to. At least, if I don't know, I cannot be compromised. And yet Raidan...."

"Yes. Raidan. I'll see what I can find out about the Morenians. As for the other, well, there are a lot of people who would like to know the whereabouts of Robstrom. You see, Robstrom claims direct lineage from Prince Lensen, through Lensen's eldest daughter. And one of the stories being whispered in back rooms of taverns and other unlikely places suggests that proof of his claim exists. Conversely, a more dependable source suggests that proof *did* exist but was long since destroyed. The whole debate is, however, somewhat academic, as there have been no reliable sightings of Robstrom for, oh, three years."

"Three years! Then why does the Townmaster insist I am in league with him? He could be dead by now."

Pob shook his head. "It is believed, in certain circles, that Robstrom is behind the attempt to overthrow the government. It wouldn't take a huge mental effort to associate such a one with the ruling families in a neighbouring land, with whom Gerik has less than cordial relations. If you understand me."

"I understand what you mean, but the idea is nonsense! And it does not help me either. They will be looking for me tonight, in the Gull."

"Then you'd best not be there. In fact, I think you'd better not be anywhere you've been before. As soon as it begins to get dark, go to see Sirsha – the young woman we met yesterday – she keeps an apartment above the bakery on Half Hill. I'll join you as soon as I can."

Half Hill was exactly that, a slight incline leading from the bridge to the main residential area on the north side of the river. It was lined with businesses but, Lesandor was relieved to discover, only one of them was a bakery. Beside the bakery a stairway led to a balcony and a door.

At his knock, Sirsha opened the door and beckoned him inside. She seemed unsurprised to see him. Her smile was genuine and welcoming and, once again, he found himself barely able to take his eyes off her. Despite that, he did notice how the apartment, which was clean and cosy if a little shabby, had a rather temporary feel, as if it was not actually anyone's home.

He paused at the threshold and glanced around for a basin of water where he might rinse his hands, but there was nothing. There was, however, bread and soft cheese and a flask of wine on a side table beside the hearth. Sirsha told him to help himself. There appeared to be no one else there, a fact that rather pleased him. He poured himself a cup of weak wine and one for her also, and found himself deep in conversation within moments of sitting down beside her. She was easy to talk to and hungry for knowledge and he was only too glad to tell her about his homeland, for – as he had discovered whilst walking with Pob – doing so was the only thing that alleviated the despair Gerik engendered in him. Her eyes sparkled with a gold light as he spoke of the cities and towns built of stone and set among the forests of his native country, of the customs of his people and of the two great festivals of Morene that marked the greening and the turning of the trees; festivals which had long since ceased to be observed in Gerik.

After some time, she sighed. "It all sounds wonderful, Lesandor. I would hear more, but I have to go out for a while. You will be all right, won't you? I'll be back shortly and we can talk again. Maybe you will tell me more about the forests of Morene? You can stay here with me until morning, and then we'll find you somewhere further out of town."

She threw a woollen shawl over her head, tossing one end over her shoulder, then, with a brief touch on his hand and a lingering smile, left him alone to eat, and think. He experienced an unsettling mixture of disappointment that she had gone and anticipation of her return, followed immediately by the realisation that he had given Mysha hardly a moment's thought since he had arrived in Gerik. The two combined to make him feel tremendously guilty and he found himself looking around the room to try to divert his mind. It was not easy, for though the apartment was poorly furnished, every small detail bore witness to Sirsha's touch, and her scent was everywhere.

On the mantle over the fire was a collection of polished stones, the only ornaments in the room. He picked each up in turn, attracted especially to a smoky grey one with a golden line running through it. He wondered if Sirsha had collected the stones herself, finding them on the river bank maybe, washed ashore by the Prosperous – as he had been. As he turned the grey stone over and over in his hand, letting the gold band through its heart catch the glow of the fire and reflect it into the dark corners of the room, it occurred to him that he had never actually been attracted to a woman before. At home he had met girls whom he had considered pretty, but none who had made him feel the way Sirsha did. He had grown up in a world of Silvanii and woodmaids and accepted them as part of his life. As for Mysha, she would never have caught his eye let alone won his heart. But she was his wife and he should not be entertaining such thoughts about another woman whom he hardly knew. Despite telling himself that, he found himself wondering what it would be like if he had the choice, if she could be persuaded to leave Gerik and come back to Morene with him, to live in Deepvale among the trees of his childhood. He would not regret his mother's prohibition if one such as Sirsha were with him.

For the first time he began to feel bitter towards Yasdon, ignorant of even the most basic Treelaw, and his miserable, fever-prone holding, with its too often rain-spoilt crops and generations of poor management. Uncharitably, he decided that Petron would make an ideal successor to Yasdon when his time came, though he doubted Yasdon thought so. With that, a ghastly suspicion began to take shape in his mind: perhaps Yasdon had a reason to keep him in Windwood, other than his unwillingness to let his adored daughter out of his house – which was what Lesandor had, up to then, assumed was behind the holder's reluctance to even speak about their going to Deepvale. It would certainly explain why Petron was being trained so badly, allowed, almost encouraged, to be completely dissolute. Lesandor found his hands gripping the back of the chair in front of him, digging his fingers into the padded fabric. Well, he certainly had succeeded in taking his mind off his present predicament, his worries about Raidan's safety *and* his undisciplined fantasies about Sirsha – and felt worse for it.

The nausea and pounding headache were returning. He must focus, yet he knew it would do him no good to think about home, for the longing to be there would only make the current situation unbearable. Talking about the Silvanii and his homeland with an interested stranger was different to dwelling on such things alone. Instead, he chose to consider all he knew about Gerish politics. Much of his education had dealt with the subject, and Masgor was acknowledged as an expert.

Greedy and short-sighted, that was the general view Morenians held about their neighbours, but that was only a small part of it. Since the death of Prince Lensen's daughters, no particular family or group had held sway in Gerik for any length of time. Even when a core of government had remained, those in key positions had come and gone with such regularity as to make the study of Gerish history something of a nightmare for a boy who had very little interest in names and'dates. 'Unstable', was how Masgor described Gerik – and many of her rulers – being of the opinion that they were not so much short-sighted as resigned to the fact that they would not stay in power long enough to make it worthwhile instigating any long-term plans or projects, including a full scale offensive against Morene.

But this latest episode in Gerik's troubled history was different from anything that had gone before. The whispers and rumours suggested the current crisis had nothing to do with dislodging a few individuals or ousting a family that was gaining too much influence. This promised to be much bigger than anything Gerik had previously known. A new order. And, depending on the outcome, Morene could well find herself with a lethal enemy at her door, or else a better neighbour than she had ever known. For some reason, Lesandor believed that Robstrom, whoever he was, had to be protected. He wondered how much Sirsha knew and how much she would tell him if he asked.

He ate some bread and a little cheese and waited for her to return. Time passed slowly, for the sparsely-furnished room offered few diversions. He was not used to being bored and it was a peculiar sensation, especially at that time when he was in hiding from a strange authority, who had threatened his life and who may well be holding his friends captive.

The door latch rattled. Lesandor blinked and yawned; he had made himself as comfortable as possible and had been half asleep on the lumpy settle. The oil lamp had burnt out and the room was in darkness. He got to his feet and groped about for the tinder box, which earlier he had seen lying on a shelf near the hearth. The door creaked on its hinges and a shaft of pale light from the building across the road illuminated a narrow strip of the room and outlined the figure standing in the doorway.

"I am sorry," Lesandor apologised, "I seem to have let the fire go out, the lamp as well." He struck a light and set fire to a taper and, holding the flame aloft, he turned. In the doorway stood three heavy-set men, and just inside the room was an officer whom Lesandor had seen at the

Townmaster's offices when he had gone for help in locating Raidan and the other Morenians.

"We grew tired of waiting at the Gull. Tedious place. You won't need a lantern, the streets between here and the Townmaster's offices are well lit."

The three men in the doorway stepped into the room; two of them drew short swords. Lesandor let the taper drop into the hearth where it flared briefly and died.

Lesandor had wrestled with other boys and not always come away unbloodied, and had – very briefly – been sent to a tutor who could not tolerate his hesitancy with reading and writing and thought to cure him with a hazel switch. But he had never been beaten in anger, and neither Fabiom nor Casandrina had ever raised a hand to him.

Blood, metallic tasting and bitter, oozed from a split lip as Townmaster Florim questioned him at length, the same questions, over and over. Why had they really come to Gerik? What role were they playing in the uprising? Where was Robstrom? And over and over Lesandor begged the Townmaster to believe him that they had come to widen their trade links, that they had nothing to do with the uprising, and that he did not know who Robstrom was. He admitted they were interested in what was happening in Gerik, of course they were, but they were not involved. Each time he said so, the Townmaster would repeat the litany of questions and the officer who had brought him there would strike him across the face and he could do nothing to protect himself for they had bound him wrist and ankle to a chair carved from a solid piece of ash wood.

A vicious slap started his nose bleeding; the blood ran down his chin, dripping onto his chest. Questions and blows became his whole world so that he was surprised to see the first glimmer of morning light creep through the ebony-framed windows.

"You are beginning to vex me," the Townmaster said with a sigh. "And you surely realise you are being foolish. An open hand is but mild coercion. If you persist, I shall have to become more persuasive. In the end you will beg to tell me what I want to know."

Lesandor rested the side of his head against the high back of the chair and let the morning sun soothe him, trying to believe that the familiar grain against his bruised and bloodied face was a living tree, his mother's tree. Savouring every moment of respite, knowing they had not finished with him yet.

When the door opened, he raised his head groggily. The man who stood in the doorway was a stranger and yet he was also familiar. Like stormy waves, the wide purple borders of his robes undulated as he crossed the floor and came to stand directly before Lesandor's chair. The scent of expensive oils floated towards Lesandor and stirred him to full awareness.

From behind, the officer took a fistful of his hair and jerked his head around. He raised his hand –

"Enough!" the stranger said. "There are other ways to deal with this one."

"Every man has his weaknesses, eh, Delegate?" The Townmaster chortled, then turned back to Lesandor, "And we shall find yours, Lesandor, believe me."

"No need, Townmaster, I already know about this young man." The stranger spoke in rich, cultured tones. "All about him. And I know exactly what holds the most terror for him."

He smiled, and Lesandor recoiled as far as the bonds that held him would allow. The stranger before him was Pob, as he had never seen him before, and Pob did indeed know his hidden fears.

Pob nodded, reading Lesandor's thoughts. "Gerik itself – every treeless vista. That is what terrifies you, isn't it, Lesandor? The thought that you might never go back to Morene; the thought that the blood of the Silvanii that flows through your veins might never again be stirred by the sound of whispering leaves in the forest, or the sight of quickening buds in springtime; that the dances and the songs of your mother's people will only be a memory and, as time passes, you will eventually forget just how the songs went, or what her face looked like."

Lesandor clenched his teeth to stifle the sound threatening to erupt from his throat. He closed his eyes against the vision of Pob's leering smile but he could not block out the sound of Pob's voice.

"Silvanii don't dance in the dark, eh? But for you that's the only time they'll dance, in your sleep, in your dreams. And they haven't been pleasant dreams since you arrived in Gerik, have they? Forever is a long time, Lesandor. Think about it."

The Townmaster laughed coldly. "Silvana born, eh? Well, that's a turn up. Give him a day or two to think on it shall we, Delegate?"

"Why not? And let's say every day you keep us waiting after that will cost you a year before you leave here."

"I don't know anything! I don't know who Robstrom is!" Lesandor screamed. And his voice echoed off the walls of oak and satinwood, kauri and teak.

Chapter Four

PRINCE RAIDAN PACED the length of his room and indeed it was a fine long room, ideal for striding out frustrated steps over and over again. Somehow the traders had managed to lose them as soon as they were inside Stonehaven's perimeter. Appointments to meet up later were not kept, neither were promises to have word sent of where Lesandor was staying. By the time Raidan realised they had been duped, it was too late. Troi had disappeared into the teeming population of the town and was impossible to find. So, it seemed, was Lesandor.

Raidan had sent out all nine of his company to inquire, at the Townmaster's offices, at the main boarding establishments, at the town's infirmary. All to no avail. Now they were out and about, inquiring at smaller places, private houses that took in lodgers, inns and eating rooms. Raidan was left waiting, with only Tegun and his music for company.

Not that he had nothing to do. Through all the worry and frustration of the past days he had not quite forgotten why they were in Gerik in the first place and he knew Cousin Larse would be expecting a detailed account of all that had happened since they set out. In truth, he did have a lot to report, though not to Larse. They may have failed to find Lesandor thus far, but they had made certain other discoveries that were extremely interesting. He could not help feeling proud, knowing his father would be pleased with the intelligence he had managed to gather. One document, now safely inside his leather satchel, was certainly worth the yew bow it had cost.

"Well, that's two reports finished and still no one's come back."

Tegun stopped playing and regarded him seriously. "You should have let me go too, I could have looked."

"I know, Tegun. It's just that I think there's more to Lesandor's disappearance than we understand, and I don't know how dangerous Gerik really is. I couldn't risk anything happening to you as well. Anyway, I'm glad of your company."

"You're worried about him, aren't you? Don't be, I'm sure they'll find him."

"They have to," Raidan replied, more in hope than conviction.

The night sky had not been overly revealing, clouded and foggy in turn, with only brief glimpses of the stars' dance in the heavens. But there was something sinister coming, that much he was sure of. He wished his mother was there. He did not have her clarity of vision – no man did, such perception was a woman's gift – yet there was a foreboding that determined him to keep Tegun close, that warned him the boy could be in danger. As for Lesandor – he had no clear notion. But last night, when the stars briefly cast off their shroud, a cold dread had clutched at Raidan's heart. Time was running out.

Guidance would not be forthcoming from the skies, but from more mundane sources. If this latest search produced no more than the last, he would have to go back to some of the places himself, exert a bit of authority and hope it paid off. Yet this mission was supposed to be very low key. He stopped pacing and stared out of the window at the busy main thoroughfare and wondered what his father would do.

❦

The young woman opened the door and smiled warily.

"Can I help you?"

She reminded Raidan of another girl, somewhat younger, whom he longed to see again. Something about the way she smiled, and the colour of her eyes.

"I'm looking for my friend, Lesandor. I was told I might find him here."

"Here?" She looked surprised.

"Yes, here."

Her eyes became wary.

He took a step towards her, speaking quietly. "I don't know what's going on, or why. I just know that I've been separated from one of my companions and, to be honest, I fear for him. Can you help me?"

After a moment's hesitation she invited him inside. Much to his surprise, there was a chipped bowl filled with clean water on a rickety stand just inside the door, something he had come across nowhere else in this land. The young woman smiled as he rinsed his hands. Then, as he dried them on a small piece of nubbed cloth, she indicated an overstuffed and rather lumpy couch where he could sit.

He felt a little uneasy as she bolted the door behind him and more so when she disappeared into a room beyond. The apartment was filled with the aroma of baking bread wafting up from the bakery below and Raidan was reminded that he had not eaten for a full day. He pushed the craving aside, though he was pleased when she returned with a tray of food and relieved that was all she seemed to have gone for. She sat down opposite and offered him a plate of fresh bread spread thickly with sweet marrow jelly, and a steaming cup of hot milk with cloves and honey.

"You speak truly." It was a statement, not a question. "You are his friend and you are afraid for him – why?"

"Should I not be?" Raidan answered shortly, loath to express his true cause of concern to a Gerish native, even a hospitable one. "This is a troubled country. He is a stranger here and alone, and missing."

She shook her head. "All true, yet not true. There is more than that. You ask for my help but do you not dare to trust me? And another thing," she added, before he could think of a reply to her first question, "how did you find this house; what brought you inquiring for your friend here?"

"It took me three days. I asked a lot of questions, I followed some very unlikely leads, I also followed some rather unlikely people. Some said, 'I know nothing,' but their eyes said they were lying. Others pretended to be helpful – for a financial consideration – their eyes also betrayed them."

"You are wise then," she murmured. "To read enough in a face to find this house. I should be glad you are not an enemy, though you are a Morenian; some would say that was the same thing."

"I am no enemy, except to any who would harm those I care about.

And I will trust you, for I have no choice it seems. Lesandor should never have come to Gerik. It was a mistake. Even on the journey, before we were separated, he was suffering, eating little, sleeping less."

"Why? What ails him?" She was insistent, but Raidan shook his head and so she shrugged and replied, "No matter. I did see him, the day before yesterday, around noon. He had only arrived then – you were searching prematurely. He apparently had a close escape from the Prosperous, but he seemed little the worse for that." Her gaze clouded over. "I saw him again, last night. Whatever dangers you fancy Gerik holds for him, that cause you to worry so over him, I think they are less than the real danger he faces. He really is missing now."

Raidan noticed the collection of polished stones on the mantle over the fire. Soft sea greens and deepest black, side by side with mottled browns and rose pink. He reached up from his seat and took down a grey orb, bisected with a golden yellow band. It felt good, solid, cold. Her voice sounded unreal, her words – senseless. Why would anyone abduct Lesandor?

"I don't know your name." Her words cut through his thoughts, like the bright band through the greyness of the stone he held. They, at least, he could comprehend.

"Raidan. My father is Ravik, Ruling Prince of Morene." He did not have to tell her, but he felt he owed her that little honesty. If Lesandor was in danger she must surely be endangering herself now. "And I do not know your name either," he pointed out.

"Sirsha – and *my* father is Delegate Posseban. Maybe he can help you."

This would be Raidan's fourth visit to the administration buildings, but at least he had someone to ask for, a name, a lead. Townmaster Florim was worse than useless, though Raidan sensed a harder man beneath the soft and facile exterior: a man he was not inclined to trust.

"Delegate Posseban will not be available until later this afternoon and you'll need an appointment." The clerk behind the desk did not look up.

"Then I'll wait."

"You can't." The man raised his head and in his eyes Raidan caught a flicker of surprise. This was not the same clerk who had been there on

Raidan's previous visits, this one's expression suggested he recognised something about him. Maybe it was the travelling clothes, or the unmistakable accent of Morene, either way there was no longer any doubt in Raidan's mind that Lesandor had been there and this man had seen him.

"I will send a messenger to see if the Delegate can accommodate you. If he cannot, you will have to come back" – he flicked through a large hide-bound book – "in three days time. I can make an appointment for you for that morning."

Raidan studied the pictures in the wood veneer and did not reply. It seemed as if there was a door in the wall opposite, though it was hard to be certain. Meanwhile the clerk beckoned a young lad over and gave him whispered instructions, after which he paid Raidan no more heed but went back to his forms and documents.

After what seemed like an eternity of waiting, Raidan was shown into a small office lavishly hung with tapestries of seascapes and lined with alternate panels of golden-grained yew and red mahogany. Amid all this splendour, Delegate Posseban sat behind a large ebony desk from where he dominated the room.

Raidan was not easily impressed. Delegate Posseban impressed him. He also surprised him. The hand that clasped his arm, as the Delegate rose from his carved black chair to greet him, was rougher than the white and purple robes would have suggested, and the easy smile creased a scarred face that was more rugged than Raidan expected. Posseban's eyes narrowed and his smile took on a hint of amusement as he invited the young prince to be seated.

"I know who you are and your errand." Posseban's smile had faded. "I don't know that I can help you, personally." He spread his hands in a gesture of helplessness. "But, I do have contacts...."

"You must have heard something, Delegate," Raidan interrupted impatiently.

Posseban shrugged. "I hear things all the time. The town is alive with rumour. Foreigners from all over – friends, enemies, who knows? We are divided, so friends to some must mean the enemies to others, no? People appear, people go missing. What to believe, that is a hard question. Who to believe, that is harder still. There is a place where truth gets sorted quicker than here: the Gull. It is an inn near the harbour."

The peat fire gave off billows of dense smoke, which penetrated every nook and corner of the Gull so that Raidan was hard-pressed to see who was coming or going. He had only brought two of his ten travelling companions, more might have been too conspicuous.

The Gull was not new to any of them, many false trails had led here already but Raidan had no choice but to do as Delegate Posseban suggested and come back. Posseban had promised to send someone to meet him, someone 'in the know'. Raidan toyed with a beaker of colourless wine and thought about the Delegate, a bureaucrat of Gerik. If there was one category of people Raidan had been taught to distrust, that was it. Yet Posseban was not a high-ranking clerk, that much was clear, nor did he speak like a politician. Raidan found it hard to know what he really was, or to know whether he should trust him. Then there was Sirsha. Raidan had found himself inclined towards trusting the Delegate's daughter straight away; he probably would have doubted every word of Posseban's had he not met Sirsha first. Having met her, he wanted to trust Posseban for her sake; not a particularly good reason, he would readily admit.

"Is this seat taken, laddie?" The voice was unfamiliar yet Raidan recognised something in its tone. The newcomer's face was muffled by a wide scarf, only his eyes and the edge of a scar showing for a moment in the flickering light of a fat tallow candle before he settled back into the shadows. Nevertheless, Raidan knew him.

"You're welcome," he said with a half smile, wondering at the disguise.

"Pob's the name," the other replied, holding out his hand which would have revealed him as the Delegate, had Raidan needed any other confirmation of his identity. "We're among friends here – don't get any official types in the Gull." And he laughed.

Raidan's two companions had no idea that the man was no stranger, and from Posseban's last comment Raidan realised he could hardly let them know otherwise without giving 'Pob' away, though to whom he could not guess.

"You know where Lesandor is, don't you?" Raidan's voice was low but tinged with anger at the sudden realisation.

"I do, and I can help. I, Pob. No Delegate can help – you understand?"

Raidan nodded, his anger subsiding. If Posseban, or Pob, was playing both sides it was a dangerous game, but they would have to play along – for Lesandor's sake.

"In a little while you must leave here and go to the house above the bakery. A friend will go with you. Wait here until he comes over. He will invite you to supper. Vali is his name. I will meet you at the house when I know it is safe. I have good hopes of not being alone."

Raidan could not help the sigh of relief that escaped him.

"But is he all right?"

Pob nodded once. "As well as can be expected."

Two guards dragged Lesandor, dazed and disorientated, to what he presumed was a cell. A flask, a small loaf and a slop bucket were pushed in after him. And then nothing; he was left alone.

Some time later, when he had recovered his wit sufficiently, and the horror had subsided enough to allow him to think, he discovered he was in some sort of storage space, lined with divided shelves all stacked with scrolls. He had no notion why they had put him there, unless it was that he was being held unofficially. Maybe in this land of paperwork there was no record he was there, that he even existed.

Lesandor could not help but reflect on the irony of being surrounded by all this potential information: on the day they set out from Westmouth, Raidan had said that, given the circumstances, he was more interested in information than trade. But even had there been enough light to see by, Lesandor knew he was too stressed to be able to read: the ability left him unless he was relaxed, for it was not a talent that came naturally to him.

With nothing to do but wait, he slumped down in a corner.

Finally, exhausted, he slept.

He woke, shivering, from a fitful sleep. Cold and anxious, he made use of the bucket before turning his attention to the other items he had been given. The clay flask was plugged with a straw bung. He hoped it was filled with wine but, as he unstoppered the flask, the brackish smell told him the contents was what passed for water in Gerik. Reluctant to drink, he rinsed his face, wincing as he dabbed at the dried blood. He could not face the bread.

Time passed until thirst eventually demanded he drank. As expected, the water was rank, and he gagged trying to force it down. He had only managed one mouthful and was trying to swallow another when voices sounded from the other side of the wall. He spat out the water as he scrambled to his feet, torn between terror of being forgotten and fear of being taken back out and beaten again. When no footsteps came close he stretched, wincing as stiff muscles protested. The voices were indistinct, though Lesandor thought he recognised the Townmaster's deep guffaw. He moved cautiously towards the door and tried to listen.

When, at last, the conversation ceased and the absolute silence from beyond the door told Lesandor that no one was there any more, he leant his head back against the wall. He had heard very little, though the name of Robstrom had been mentioned more than once. 'The net is closing at last,' was the one phrase he had heard distinctly and he wondered why that disturbed him, why he should care.

Three days, three years – it seemed like that already. It would be that in fact – and more – if they carried out their threats against him. Yet if what he had overheard was true, if they found this Robstrom, what then? Having no need of information from Lesandor, would they keep their word and release him?

Before he could think of an answer, other than the first awful and unbidden one that came to his mind, he heard the sound of bolts being drawn. The closet was filled with sudden light, not from the door where he had been listening but from beyond the shelves. He shielded his eyes and his vision adjusted in time to see a portion of the shelving being pulled out of the way. A second door was revealed, one that led into the Townmaster's own office.

Townmaster Florim regarded Lesandor with anxious eyes, uncertainty written across every feature. Two paces behind him stood a comely, fair man whose short yellow beard and costume of leggings, loose shirt and embroidered over-tunic spoke of distant lands. The stranger smiled cautiously. Lesandor looked from one to the other, wondering if he should speak, should plead for aid.

"Lord Jowan of Malandel has persuaded me that he should have charge of you; that you can be of no more service to us. I am inclined to agree." The Townmaster spoke quickly.

His words made little sense to Lesandor who, at the same time was casting back in his mind for a memory of that name, Jowan of Malandel. It would not come but he was certain he had heard it before.

"Come, Lesandor, I am sorry to rush you but I have people waiting." Jowan indicated towards the door on the far side of the room.

Lesandor was only too willing to go, no matter what might lie ahead. Anything to get out of Florim's clutches – and away from the chance of meeting Pob again.

"Townmaster." Jowan nodded politely towards Florim, who stepped aside to let Lesandor pass. Near the door stood the ash chair. As he passed, Lesandor touched it wistfully.

"I have a ship in the harbour. You will be safe there." Jowan walked quickly out of the building into the wide square, paused for a moment to get his bearings and headed off in the right direction. He did not check to see that Lesandor was with him and so Lesandor followed.

They were half-way to the harbour before Lesandor asked, "What is happening?"

"I honestly do not know," Jowan admitted. He stopped speaking as they came across a group of young men blocking the street who looked at them somewhat askance but stepped aside to let them through.

"There is going to be a full-scale civil war here, unless I'm much mistaken, and our friend Florim back there will probably be on the losing side. Neither Malandel nor Morene needs to be in the middle of it. I came as an observer, we have interests here – but nothing worth taking sides over. If war could be prevented it might be a different matter...."

His accent was strange, very cultured, very foreign. Lesandor had to strain to understand every word Jowan said. He had looked older in the

Townmaster's office, now, walking beside him, Lesandor realised Jowan was no more than twenty-five, if that.

"And what if Robstrom shows up?" Lesandor asked.

Jowan glanced at him and raised his brows. "Does he even exist?"

Lesandor shrugged. "Townmaster Florim seems to think so. I had not heard of him before a few days ago."

"No, I did not think you had. I managed to convince Florim of that too. Robstrom may exist – who knows? His name comes up now and again; some say he is of royal descent, that he has a legitimate claim to Gerik, that, way back, he is related to your Prince Ravik." Jowan lowered his voice as they passed another group of armed men. "Should he exist – and should he make himself known – war might be avoided. For it is also said, rumoured, that he could gather the people's support – the government would fall and a new order would be established...."

"Surely then, his absence is proof he does not exist," Lesandor suggested. "Or do you think he is biding his time?"

"There is my ship." Jowan pointed to a fair-sized vessel moored out in the harbour, its gilded prow as strange to Lesandor's eyes as the Malandelian's costume. "We shall have to be rowed out to her. Sometimes I wonder if Robstrom is not someone well known, another name, another identity, waiting, testing people. What do you think, Lesandor, is that far too fanciful?"

Lesandor did not reply. They were near the water and there were too many people about to make the conversation safe to pursue. He was not sorry for that, for it reminded him too strongly of his most recent betrayal. He had trusted Pob with his life's story, revealed his innermost feelings and fears. He wanted to trust Jowan but he did not dare. He realised that if he went out to the ship he would be trapped again, if Jowan was not all he seemed. It was a risk he could not take.

There was nowhere to go. Lesandor realised that as soon as he ducked into a narrow side alley while Jowan's attention was elsewhere. Nowhere except places Pob had shown him: the room they had shared, the Gull, the diner, the house above the bakery – Sirsha's house. Even more than he wanted to trust Jowan, he desperately wanted to trust Sirsha. Yet could he really believe it was pure coincidence the soldiers had come while she was out on her secret errand? She was in league with Pob and Pob had betrayed him; Troi and his fellow traders had abandoned him; he had no more idea about Raidan's whereabouts than he had when he first went to the Townmaster's offices.

Back on the main thoroughfare he could just make out the harbour below, between rows of buildings. There were the twin masts of Jowan's ship, yellow sails tightly furled, waiting. Nearby, gulls squabbled over scraps of food. Children ran, shouting after each other, the birds flapped away. Lesandor stood, irresolute. The Gull was his only hope. He would sit, listen, watch and wait, until he had more idea about what was going on in Stonehaven. It was the nearest thing to a plan he could think of. As he retraced his steps, he noticed that groups of people were gathering on almost every corner, and then the familiar white walls of the inn were before him.

"We have wine on the ship, and better than you are drinking."

Lesandor froze as Jowan's voice cut through the hum of conversation around him. Then, with a wry smile, he lowered the beaker. He had nothing to fear from Jowan here. They were two foreigners in a crowded room; they both had to act normally, civilly.

"It is mostly water, the wine is just to mask the taste," Lesandor replied, then added, "I had some unfinished business."

Jowan sat down opposite him, uninvited. Lesandor called over a serving man and asked for another beaker.

"I too," Jowan said after a while. "Some of it the same business as yours, I would imagine, though I think you are unwise to travel through Stonehaven alone – however concerned you are for Prince Raidan's safety. For some reason I cannot ascertain, Townmaster Florim distrusts you. My offer of protection stands, help too, if I can provide any. You know where my ship is; she is called 'Sunbow' should you need to ask anyone to take you out to her. But if you wish to avail yourself of that today, it seems you will have to decide before the sun goes down. They've decreed a curfew and something tells me that it will be enforced rigorously."

Lesandor rubbed his temples. The headache and the nausea had returned in full. He did not know how much longer he could keep functioning. "I think Florim distrusts me simply because I am Morenian, maybe especially so because I travel with Prince Raidan. A fact I would have kept from him, but that he discovered. Raidan and I were separated, I had to go to Florim, I had no other means of locating the others."

Jowan inclined his head in gratitude for the confidence. "There may be more behind his distrust than you suspect. Then again, maybe not. I know Prince Raidan, not very well, but we have met in his father's court on, oh, two occasions at least. Last year I was appointed envoy to these lands by my king and kinsman – Feeard of Malandel. But you are my present concern; I understand Gerik is not a country conducive to your wellbeing."

"You seem to know a lot about me, Lord Jowan," Lesandor ventured.

"I do. Lord Fabiom told me much; we had plenty of time to talk on the voyage to Gerik and in the days we wasted in Westmouth looking for you."

"My father is here!"

"Hush. Not *here* precisely. He was headed for a place called Bridgetown when we parted company. I came around the coast by ship, he is travelling across land."

Lesandor shook his head in delighted disbelief, then he met Jowan's gaze. "I apologise for my action earlier, it was cowardly."

"No, it was circumspect. I had no right to expect your trust, and it seems you have fared ill at the hands of those you have turned to recently. I should have told you I had met your father. Finding Prince Raidan must be our main purpose now though. My other business can wait but my contact may be able to assist us. Have you heard the name 'Pob' since you came here? He will be joining us shortly."

❧

Raidan, his two companions and their escort walked unhurriedly through the winding roads of Stonehaven, seemingly a group of friends off home. Vali chatted with the three Morenians but his eyes darted everywhere and occasionally he would make an excuse to stop walking, to refasten his sandal strap or to examine something of interest on the ground, listening and checking all the while. They were accompanied up to the house by the smells of baking as the first of the evening batches of bread were taken from the ovens.

"There'll be some of that on the table shortly," Vali said as he knocked on the door and stepped back.

Sirsha greeted them all warmly, though she looked tired. Vali frowned at her, a question evident in his eyes.

"Things are coming to a head," she murmured. "There'll be trouble before the night is out – I hope Father gets here quickly and you can all leave. Prince Raidan, the rest of your companions must come here at once; you must stay together, and leave together. Vali, you go and fetch them."

As soon as Vali had gone, Sirsha bolted the door. She turned to Raidan. "Go back to Morene. There will be a new order in Gerik soon and we can be partners, not rivals. But until then ... well, there's no business to be done in Gerik at present."

"I can't go without Lesandor. No, listen to me." He took hold of her arm and held her as she opened her mouth to object. "You asked me before what ailed him. I'll tell you. This land – just being here is so painful for him. The curse that is on the soil, the poison that flows in the water, is the curse and the poison of death, the death of countless Silvanii."

"I know that," she whispered. "But why should he feel it so deeply?"

"Lesandor's mother is a Silvana."

Sirsha stared at him with wide eyes. "But he looked so – normal. I thought, no, I didn't. I never considered it before. Oh, Lesandor.... Prince Raidan – you won't be able to help him now. I give you my word, if he can be found I will find him and I will see him safely away from here. But you have to go. Tonight."

"Why tonight?" Raidan asked uneasily. He found himself again standing before the mantle looking at the stones arranged there.

"It had to happen one day, one night. There have been crowds gathering all day and the Townmaster has issued orders for a curfew at dusk. They won't like that."

She took down the grey and gold stone. "This one is my favourite, such stones are meant to be lucky. I wanted to give it to Lesandor. I didn't get the chance. Will you take it for him?"

Pob sat down at the table. Lesandor poured a beaker of wine and handed it to him. Their hands touched briefly and, at the contact, Lesandor looked him straight in the face until Pob looked away.

"You have a disconcerting look, my young friend, must be the sap that runs in your veins."

"Blood," Lesandor said curtly. "When I am hit hard enough – I bleed. In case you did not notice."

Pob glanced at Jowan. "I thought you'd have talked him round," he said warily.

"He has," Lesandor said, before Jowan could reply. "More or less, but the bruises still hurt."

"Believe me, I never meant things to happen as they did. Still, I'll accept the blame – I was naive to think you would be safe anywhere in Stonehaven. They must have been following you, to find you at Half Hill. Fortunately Jowan came along and I realised he could get you out. There was no one else I could turn to if I wasn't to reveal myself to Florim before time."

Lesandor looked from one to the other. "I am confused. You, Lord Jowan, say you came here with my father, but you two are obviously no stranger to each other. And Townmaster Florim was persuaded by some argument of yours that I should be released...."

"As for the last, well the 'argument' was a particularly convincing one, that's all," Pob answered. "Those two baskets of amber you dumped in the middle of nowhere. The fact that they did actually belong to Florim is a fact he's probably not yet aware of. I think his courier has been avoiding him, due to having misplaced his employer's most precious merchandise."

Jowan chuckled at that revelation, then explained to Lesandor, "As for the rest – I met your father by chance, Lesandor. I have been acquainted with Pob here for some months. He was the most obvious person I would go to if I was looking for someone, and he had already found you...."

Pob grinned. "It's over now. Prince Raidan is waiting for you. All of your people will be with Sirsha on Half Hill by now; Vali passed me in the street with the last of them just before I came here. As soon as you are all together we'll get you out of Stonehaven, out of Gerik if possible." He turned to Jowan. "Any chance of your ship taking them away from here?"

"Consider it done," Jowan agreed. "I have no desire to stay any longer. I must return to Feeard soon and let him know what's afoot; but we'll not intervene, whatever Florim and his ilk think."

"No, this is a situation the people of Gerik must resolve. They've waited long enough."

Lesandor raised his beaker of wine. "Thank you – both of you. I owe you my life twice over, Pob."

"And you can repay me one day. I'd visit Morene and see your wildwood tomorrow, after listening to your stories. It'll have to wait longer than that, but come I will, and you can tell me more tales. Sirsha informs me she has a hankering to visit too; I think you stirred her imagination. And she'll be glad to know you're safe. I wish I knew *she* was, but she'll not leave. Children, what would you do with them?"

So, Sirsha was Pob's daughter; Lesandor had wondered at the relationship between the two. And she wanted to visit Morene. More importantly, she had not betrayed him. Very firmly, he quashed the thoughts forming in his mind.

"You said you would not choose to reveal yourself to Townmaster Florim before time, what did you mean 'before time'? What time?"

Pob sighed. "Soon, very soon. This curfew was a mistake. People are angry. He has made them out to be the enemy. Even those who were undecided are turned against the establishment now."

Lesandor smiled, though he tried to hide his amusement by raising his beaker to his lips. "Had we not better be going then?"

Pob raised his brows. "We could do with sharing a joke in these troubled times," he suggested.

"Hardly a joke! It just occurred to me that Florim was far nearer to both the answer to his question and his quarry than he ever could have realised." Lesandor's face became serious then. "Though I am glad I did not know it at the time. I was not thinking rationally. I might have said anything to get out of there."

"I know," Pob said quietly. "It was a chance I had to take."

The day was further progressed than they had realised, and the western sky was tinged with the gold and orange of a glorious sunset as they made their way towards the bridge, and the bakery on the far side. Guards were much in evidence, so were clusters of townspeople. Only a few older folk, hurrying to their homes, went in ones or twos. There were no children to be seen.

"We must hurry. I meant to have you away before dusk." Pob's voice was low, anxious.

Jowan left them, striding down to the quay to ready a couple of small landing craft to ferry the Morenians out to *Sunbow*. The sea was tinged with red fire.

Before they reached the bottom of Half Hill, four great horns sounded, deep and discordant. Lesandor hardly needed Pob to tell him they signalled the start of curfew.

"We'll get into the house all right. The problem will be getting out again," Pob muttered.

Observing the huge crowd blocking their passage up the road, Lesandor was not even sure he shared Pob's confidence regarding getting in. Some of the people were armed with rocks and sticks, there even appeared to be a glint of metal here and there.

Pob tapped him on the arm – "This way" – and headed away, around the back of one of the buildings.

Suddenly a cry went up from the crowd, a roar of anger to match the horns blown moments before. The sound of many scuffling feet followed. Lesandor felt a return of the fear that had gripped him as he was bound helplessly as Florim's prisoner, the fear that he would never escape this accursed land.

Pob had disappeared down a narrow alleyway that would lead them out higher up the road and, with luck, bypass the crowd. Luck was not with them. As they reached the end, they were faced with another mass of bodies, for the people had surged forwards and were blocking their way again. Then the crowd parted momentarily and they could see that the orange glow which illuminated the evening no longer came from the setting sun but from the inferno that had been the bakery.

Chapter Five

LESANDOR AND POB both started towards the blazing building, pushing through the massed bodies as if they were not there. They were near enough to feel the heat, to hear the roar of the flames and the dull thunder of falling timbers, before they were stopped in their tracks, held back by strong arms as voices shouted in their ears above the sickening sounds of destruction.

"There's nothing you can do. It's too late. Too late!"

Lesandor forced his gaze to focus on the face close by his own, rather than the consuming fire before him. He recognised the man as a friend of Pob's, whom he had met on his first night. Beside him, Vali was holding Pob's right arm, another man, a stranger to Lesandor, was holding his left. Pob's face was contorted with horror as his lips shaped his daughter's name. Lesandor fancied he heard that same name in the maniacal cackle of the flames.

Suddenly Pob relaxed, his body almost slumping as his head fell towards his chest. A moment later he straightened. Cautiously, Vali and the other loosened their grip.

With a nod, Pob said, "There are guards coming. Vali, get Lesandor out of here, now! To the nearest safe house, no, that's too close – the fire might spread. Go to the rooms beneath the theatre. Wait for us there."

"But where's Raidan?" Lesandor asked.

"You go with Vali, I'll find Raidan."

"Let me stay! Let me help!" Lesandor pleaded.

"You are in no condition to help. And if they arrest you again..." He did not finish the sentence and indeed, there was no need. "I'll get Raidan to you as soon as I can," Pob promised.

"No." Vali shook his head and his eyes filled with the horror of the night. "I'm sorry, but Prince Raidan was – he went back inside the building. And there are four others of your party unaccounted for."

Lesandor said nothing. He heard, as if from a long way away, Pob giving Vali further instructions and then Vali's hand was on his arm, leading him through the crowds, away from the burning building and whatever lay within.

Away from the searing heat of the fire the air felt cool. Neither of them spoke. They seemed to walk for a long time. Eventually they arrived at a rough wooden door and went through, down a long stairway, along dark passages lit only by Vali's hand-held torch of burning rags and reeds.

"Here we are," Vali said gruffly.

The room beyond the low doorway was hollowed out of the rocks, cold and quiet. Vali looked at Lesandor oddly, hesitated, then lit an oil lamp and extinguished his torch. "I can't stay, I have to leave you and go back. Wait here, you'll be safe. I'm sorry about your friends – Prince Raidan gave his life to save some of the others, if there's any consolation in that. Those who are unharmed will join you as soon as it's possible. There's wine and water over there and basic supplies in that press behind you. I must go."

"Thank you," Lesandor whispered.

Vali had already gone.

The glimmering light of the oil lamp did little to dispel the gloom, which suited Lesandor only too well. Raidan was in the house over the bakery. Raidan was dead. All those frustrated days of searching and questioning and lies and imprisonment and he was dead. And Sirsha was dead and four others of their party, and he was still in Gerik, entombed in a cavern beneath a town built out of death and destruction. And he would never leave, never get out, never go home.

His animal scream of pain and fear filled the room, reverberating off the rock walls, echoing from the corners, to fall back around his head as he crumpled onto the cold floor and hugged his knees to his chest, sobbing breathlessly.

Time passed and no one came. Lesandor fell into a brief, exhausted sleep.

When he awoke he felt quite calm. He sat with his back against the press and thought of his sister. It was less painful than thinking about his mother, for Casandrina had been a part of the world beyond the wildwood for too long now, so that she understood too much. She would be worried and fearful for his safety and he did not want to think of her so. Though she would be missing him, Elzandria would not really comprehend what had befallen him. That was easier for him to cope with. As for his father: it would be far too easy to start believing Fabiom was close by, even now, and would walk through the door at any moment. If he was to hold on to any shred of sanity, Lesandor did not dare think about him. And Mysha, he could not think about Mysha. He had betrayed her in his heart and yet to think of her now would be a betrayal of the woman he believed he could have loved, the woman who had died alongside his dearest friend. And so he filled his mind with an image of Elzandria dancing and he wept for everything and everyone but no longer for himself.

Thirst roused him from his reverie. Lesandor guessed that the twenty or more tall clay amphoras in a rack were filled with wine, but there were no drinking vessels in the press. At the far side of the cavern was a natural water supply, bubbling up from the ground, disappearing through a small fissure. He had no choice but to drink from that.

To his surprise, the water was sweeter than any he had tasted before in this land. Untainted water – the first and only blessing of this terrible night.

The hardest thing was not to conjecture who among their group had survived and who had perished in the blaze beside Raidan and Sirsha. Vali had said four others were in the building, so he could hope that the other six of his fellow travellers were unharmed. But which six? And where were they now?

When, shortly afterwards, the door opened, Lesandor thought that question was about to be answered, for although he could see nothing at first, it was quite apparent that a number of people had arrived.

"Lesandor?" Pob's voice sounded strangely hollow in the cavern. "Ah, good. Are you all right?" Pob had aged ten years. His hair was grey with ash and his clothes were singed. "Prince Raidan *is* dead, I'm sorry, I had hoped they were wrong." His voice was barely steady. "Two others of your party also died and one other – the young boy – was badly hurt, but lives. A healer has been tending him; she says he should survive."

That, at least, was better than they had first thought, Lesandor realised, as Tegun was carried past on a makeshift stretcher. The boy was taken through to the far end of the cavern and beyond, to a room Lesandor had not known was there. Another stretcher followed. Lesandor looked at Pob questioningly.

"Sirsha," Pob whispered. But no hope surged in Lesandor's heart, for there was none in her father's face.

They followed the stretcher-bearers through to a small room, comfortably furnished and with a smoke hole that allowed for a fire to be lit and the place warmed. Lesandor shivered, realising for the first time how cold he was.

"It was petty of Vali not to let you in here. He had a key." Pob's voice was low, weary. "From what I can gather, Vali led some of your group, and some others who were there, to safety. Others, including Sirsha and the boy, were trapped. Raidan managed to free the boy and carry him out, then he went back inside, but it was too late. That was the last time he was seen. Vali also went back. He got Sirsha out. He had hoped to marry her."

Lesandor looked around for Vali. He was not there. Pob shook his head.

"It was you she called for."

"Pob, I...."

Whatever he might have thought to say was made unnecessary by Sirsha's weak, "Father?"

"I'm here, child," Pob murmured, leaning over the couch where she lay burnt and damaged.

"What's happening?" she asked, coughing as she spoke and crying out with the pain the movement cost her.

"Shush, shush," Pob admonished. "All is going well, the people have rallied to our side. By now the Townmaster's offices should be ours."

"So why are you here?" she asked. "Go to them, Father."

"No, I can't. I can't leave you."

"You've been waiting for this all your life. All those people are counting on you. You can't let them down now. They need you. Everyone who is lost tonight will have given their life for the cause, your cause. Everyone."

"Sirsha...."

"Please, Father, go! My love will go with you."

Pob looked helplessly at Lesandor. "I should go." He sighed. "Yet how can I?" He tapped a pouch at his hip. "Prince Raidan may not have found you, but in his searching he discovered some papers that I believed destroyed. Papers that will make all the difference to Gerik should we succeed tonight, and we will."

"Only if you are there," Sirsha whispered urgently. "Tegun stayed inside the house to save those papers. He risked his life, and Raidan gave his, that we might have a future. For their sake, too, you must go."

"Lord Robstrom?"

Lesandor glanced at Pob who managed a slight smile. "The time for subterfuge is past. What is it, Gantor?"

"The Malandelian ship is ready to sail and there is clear passage to the dock. We can get anyone down there who needs to go."

"Very well. That's you, Lesandor. The others are waiting in a room in the building above us."

"Can Tegun be moved?" Lesandor asked the healer who was tending the injured boy.

Tegun had been caught under a burning beam, his legs crushed and burnt, yet he managed a shaky smile as Lesandor leant over the stretcher and took his hand.

"It would not be my first choice but if he must travel then yes, he can." She continued to dress the wounds with damp moss, and Lesandor squeezed Tegun's hand as he jerked under the healer's ministrations.

"Raidan's dead, isn't he? He told me to look after his papers, they were important. They were in a satchel. I'd put it down and then the fire started and people were shouting and running everywhere. I had to find the satchel, Lesandor, but it was so smoky, it took me a long time. He came to look for me and then the ceiling fell and I was trapped. But I'd found the papers, and I gave them to him, and he passed them to someone – so I didn't lose them. He said they were important. I didn't want to let him down."

"Tegun, you did not let him down. The papers are safe."

Tegun did not seem to hear him. "The lady – Sirsha – she was still inside, she helped me, but she was hurt too, and Raidan carried me out. Then he went back...."

Lesandor forced himself to smile as he said, "You did well, Tegun. Lie still now; you will be on your way home soon." He took a deep breath and turned to face Pob, Robstrom.

"You have a people to lead into a new day. Lord Jowan wants to set sail as soon as possible; he too has his own people to worry about. Tegun can be moved. I will stay here with Sirsha, at least until you return. Send the others on."

"By the time I return, Jowan will be gone."

"I know that. Please do not argue. Sirsha is right, you must go. So I shall stay."

They looked at each other a long moment, then Robstrom nodded, leant over and kissed his daughter very gently on the brow and left without a word.

Tegun was carried out soon after, with the healer tending him. She touched Lesandor's shoulder as she passed.

"I have given the lady a draught of nightshade and thyme to ease her discomfort. I can do no more."

Then they were alone.

Sirsha turned her face towards him and smiled, though her eyes were filled with pain. "You were to tell me more about your forests," she reminded him. "Talk to me, Lesandor."

"No." He took a deep breath and tried to steady his voice. "I will not talk to you. Rest, my sweet, and I will sing you the songs the breezes sing in the canopies of trees, amid the flowers that blossom in the springtime."

"Oh, yes," she murmured. "I have dreamt of hearing the songs of the wildwood."

"And I dreamt of hearing them with you," he confessed, stroking strands of fire-dulled hair from the undamaged side of her face. Dreams that would not come true, for never would she walk the pathways that meandered between the trees of Deepvale, nor rest upon the soft lawns of the groves and glades there. Instead he would share with her the music and the beauty of those places even where they were, deep beneath the barren soil of Gerik. In that firelit night he would sing to her of the sun rising on the trees and the Dancing Glades, and of the wildwood awakening to another new day.

Never would she see the places he had hoped to teach her to love, but maybe she would remain long enough to see her father one more time. That gift he just might be able to give. His songs changed to evening chants, of darkness that settled softly in the secret places of the forest, of flowers closing their heads and birds nestled close on dusk-dusted branches, and his voice lulled her to a gentle sleep.

He sang on even as she slept.

His song became a song of mourning – a lament and eulogy for Raidan – until his voice faltered and cracked and all he could do was whisper, "Just one last time. If only we had got there sooner. Even if I could not have saved you, just to have tried, to have seen you one last time." But he could not help thinking he would have been able to do something, that things would have been different had he made different choices, different decisions.

Under the influence of his songs, Sirsha slept quite peacefully, though each breath rasped in her lungs. As he looked at her, thinking still of Raidan, Lesandor suddenly thought of another young woman, one who would be awaiting Raidan's return. Yet what had Raidan told him about her? Her name, her holding, and a very vague and rather biased description. Finding her was the only service Lesandor could do his friend and he vowed he would succeed, though he had no idea even how he might begin.

Sirsha stirred and moaned and Lesandor sang again, his voice husky now, a song of autumn and the Turning, when the leaves are painted from the palette of sunset before they fall to carpet the ground. The year dies, that life may come again with the spring.

Yet life and death do not always follow in their allotted cycle. Vivid images from his nightmares of falling Silvanan trees sprang into his mind. Death without any hope of rebirth. The bakery on fire, the trees cut down. Flames lapping at the sky, amber pouring like rain. Destruction and pointless, senseless waste.

"Lesandor, you're crying. Please, don't."

She tried to reach her hand towards his face but she could not manage and she bit back on a little cry, of fear more than pain. He held her hand tightly in his and tried to smile. What had her father said? 'The time for subterfuge is past'. Indeed it was. With that thought in mind he recited some of the most poignant and intimate love poems his father had written for his mother over the years and, when they were both crying and no more words would come, he sang her the songs his mother had lulled him with when he was a child. She fell back into a light sleep and still he sang on, exhausted. Noise came from the big cavern room and voices sounded outside the door. Lesandor slipped off his chair, to kneel beside the couch and kiss her lips.

"Goodbye, my Sirsha. My love will go with you."

He was standing again by the time the door opened. Robstrom looked towards the couch, almost reluctantly, as Lesandor walked over to him. Lesandor put his hand on the older man's shoulder. There were no words left. At the door, he paused and turned, to see Sirsha open her eyes and smile up at her father and hear Robstrom catch his breath in astonishment.

The man whom Robstrom had called Gantor was waiting just outside the doorway. He clasped Lesandor's arm and drew him aside.

"Your kindness tonight will be remembered. And the price is not as high as you may have thought. Lord Jowan had to move his ship out of the harbour, but he is standing off the coast a little way and we can get you out to him."

"I would not have you take men from where they are needed for my sake," Lesandor protested, though out of politeness rather than conviction. Gantor grinned.

"No, there'll be no need to do that. Things are pretty much under control. The Townmaster fled, and with 'Delegate Posseban' suddenly vanished, the rest of the town officers have surrendered without much resistance. The guards don't care to be leaderless, and a lot had already come over of their own accord anyway. Stonehaven is Lord Robstrom's. It's only one town, but it's defensible and it's influential."

Lesandor glanced back through the doorway but Robstrom's back was obscuring his view of Sirsha.

"In that case, we had better not keep Lord Jowan and his *Sunbow* waiting any longer."

To his surprise, his pack was beside the press, along with his ash bow and his quiver of arrows. He picked them up, then laid the bow and quiver down again.

"Gantor, would you see that Lord Robstrom gets these. Say they are a token for the future, against the day when trees grow here once more." He touched the wood of the bow. Soon he would feel the wood of living trees. It could not be soon enough.

They climbed the two long flights of steps, stone then wood, coming out into the deep black street where night lay heavy still. Lesandor blinked in unseeing surprise, he had thought it later, expecting the cold light of morning to greet them through the doorway at the stairhead.

"This way," Gantor said, turning to the left. Despite his earlier assurances that the night's work was done, he spoke quietly. He made his way unerringly through twisting side streets that cut through terraced houses, shuttered and barred against more than the darkness. Yet there was little obvious damage in this part of town.

"Are the fires out?" Lesandor asked.

"On Half Hill? Yes. The whole street fell, but it went no farther. The end houses were pulled down before the flames reached them, to widen the divide, and the flames were halted. The bakery was not the only target of the authority's wrath. Look to the bridge."

They had reached the end of a narrow street and were looking down on the River Prosperous and across it to the southside of Stonehaven. Dawn was tingeing the eastern sky with pastel shades of lemon and blue, though what was left of the swing bridge was illuminated not by the weak morning light but by torches set on tall posts at either end. The central span hung down into the dark waters, hacked asunder from the northside of the town to keep half of the population away from the Townmaster's offices and from joining with their rebel comrades.

Lesandor did not need to ask how they would cross – a fleet of small boats was lying just downstream from the broken bridge, ready to ferry anyone to or fro across the waters. With some caution they made their way down the steep slope that led to the riverbank. Even in the little light they had, the crossing looked perilous, for the river was laden with debris from the destruction that had preceded the dawn. For a brief moment, Lesandor thought he saw a girl looking for water-polished stones along the shore. He closed his eyes and on opening them again she had gone. Gantor was talking to him and did not notice Lesandor's momentary distraction.

"... will take you. Good speed, and thanks from all of us. And our deepest regret that our struggle should have cost Morene such a high price. Prince Raidan will be remembered here with honour."

"I will pass your message on to his father. He would wish you well, I think, as I do. Perhaps we shall meet again."

They clasped arms and Gantor left him with a small grizzled boatman whom Lesandor assumed had been introduced to him by name while his thoughts were elsewhere.

"Here, lad, climb on board. We'll soon have you to the Malandelian ship."

"But I thought...."

"That we'd just be crossing the Prosperous? Not at all. My boat may be old but she's seaworthy. You'll be with the Lord Jowan by noon, sooner if you're able to help row." He guffawed at Lesandor's bemused expression, his broad smile revealing much gum and a few worn teeth. "Not all the way, lad! We have sails to help us once we're out into the estuary proper."

And so the morning passed, in the steady sweep of oars and the erratic darting of the little boat under sail, until the pale yellow mainsail of *Sunbow* was clearly visible directly north of them. The boatman, whose name Lesandor had discovered was Gryf, steered them unerringly up to the ship, until the timbers of his boat were all but rubbing *Sunbow's* hull.

Lesandor clambered up the rope ladder thrown down to them, but Gryf would not accept the invitation to join him on board. As soon as Lesandor was safely over the deck rail he turned his boat into the wind to make his way back along the coast to Stonehaven.

Jowan was waiting at the deck rail and he helped Lesandor over, clasping his hand and elbow firmly.

"I feared for your safety, Lesandor. Tegun said he had seen you, but he's drugged and feverish and I was not sure whether to believe him. You look exhausted, come below and rest."

Lesandor went with him, hardly aware of where he was going. He *was* exhausted and so confused by all that had happened over the past days that he could barely comprehend that he was, at last, on his way home. Jowan glanced at him with some concern as they made their way down into the belly of the ship, then back towards the stern and into a luxurious cabin.

"There's water for washing and clothes to change into. Rest if you will, or come along to the galley and eat first, if you prefer. We'll reach Westmouth after dark so we'll disembark at dawn. With luck your father will be there. Word was sent overland yesterday afternoon that you would be returning by sea."

"And was word sent that Raidan and Yennow and Tiscollis would not be returning?" Lesandor asked quietly.

"No." Jowan poured a measure of strong wine into a cup for Lesandor.

"No, of course, they were alive then. Days are all merging into one in my head. They were all alive then." He leant against the ebony panels of the cabin walls and sighed. Jowan handed him the cup, saying nothing.

"I think I'd rather rest than eat," Lesandor decided. "I'm not hungry. I am tired."

Indeed he was so tired that when Jowan left him alone he barely had the energy to rinse his face and strip out of his damp, salt-stained travelling clothes into one of the fresh garments that had been left for him – a loose shirt such as Jowan wore – before curling up under a blanket on the comfortable berth. Sleep came at once.

He was sure he had not slept long, but when he woke and finished dressing in the clean, strange clothes and made his way back onto the deck, the sun was already setting, burnishing the western horizon. It was a wonderful sight, for to the west behind them and to the east before them was water, not land. They were well into the Straits of Morena now, Westmouth only a short distance away and then the crossing and home.

Jowan was leaning over the railings near the stern of his ship, watching the sun setting into the ocean. Lesandor remembered what Raidan had once told him about the people of Malandel: that they looked to the sun, that fire and gold were dear to them and the days of midsummer were their chief festival.

"Lord Jowan."

Jowan turned and smiled slowly. "Less formal, Lesandor, please," he suggested amiably. "We've been through too much for that."

"Thank you. I do not mean to disturb you –"

"You do not, I was just thinking. We had a visitor while you slept. A small ship caught up with us, from Pob – Robstrom, I should say. There is a letter for you. I'll send for it immediately. Will you eat now?"

Lesandor was still not hungry, or maybe he was past being hungry; he could not remember when he had last eaten. Jowan took the small satchel that was handed to him. "There's a letter for you and another for Prince Ravik, also all of Prince Raidan's reports and notes, which is a worthy gift for, I gather, they contain much intelligence, and may well have been appropriated by a lesser man than Robstrom. Some of the effects of those who died are there too; there's an odd assortment. If you can bear to do so, maybe you would go through them and sort them. You might know which are Raidan's – to pass over to his father. Here's your letter, I'll leave you alone for a while. I won't be far away."

Lesandor unfolded the letter and stared at it. Random symbols and absurd shapes combined into unintelligible patterns. "I cannot...." Lesandor swallowed. Jowan had not heard him. A memory came to him – his father, one arm around his shoulders, the other hand guiding his finger over and around the angles and curves of each letter as together they spelled out the names of Deepvale's great trees: ash, elm, beech, birch, oak ... patiently helping him shape those same words in sand and, later still, with a stylus on a waxed tablet. His mother watching all the while, smiling. The letters meant nothing to her, they were utterly meaningless, but she would watch her husband teach their child, as delighted as they with each tiny triumph.

Lesandor let his fingers trace the words on the scroll, imagining his father beside him, his mother smiling encouragement. Eventually the letters stopped dancing, took on form and meaning.

Sirsha was dead, as Lesandor had known she must be. She had slipped away shortly after dawn, peacefully. Besides that, the note was brief, though it contained the promise that, as soon as he could, Robstrom would visit Morene and would see the woodlands where the ash grew that had made his bow. Lesandor folded the letter and put it away in his belt pouch. He was aware that Jowan was watching him and he made himself open the satchel and remove the smaller objects that had been retrieved, to sort out which among them had been Raidan's. It was not a task he relished.

Among the items was a small grey stone, bisected by a band of gold. Lesandor held it in his clenched fist, feeling his nails digging into his palm. Slowly he relaxed his grip and carefully laid the stone on top of the satchel. Jowan came over to him.

"Are you all right?"

"Yes, thank you." Lesandor replied, sounding anything but.

"One of your party tells me Raidan was holding that stone when – when he died."

"It belonged to Robstrom's daughter, Sirsha. Perhaps she gave it to him. Anyway, I will give it to Prince Ravik. Strange, it is the one I chose. But then, we often liked the same things. Maybe that is why we got on so well." He felt his body begin to shake uncontrollably. "I am sorry," he gasped. "He was the best friend I could ever have had. And I did not get a chance to say goodbye."

The sun sank into the ocean and the land close off their starboard bow merged with the water, black into black. Clouds obscured the stars, still *Sunbow* sailed on.

Lesandor stood on the forecastle, leaning on the rail and waiting for the lights of Westmouth to appear before him. At last his vigil was rewarded, as flickering specks showed like so many pieces of amber against the darkness in the north-east.

Chapter Six

IN A HOSTELRY overlooking Westmouth harbour, Fabiom awoke from an uneasy sleep, opened the shutters of his room and discovered that during the night the *Sunbow* had anchored beside the Morenian ship already moored in the bay. Before he could finish dressing there was a knock on his door, too tentative to be Lesandor. He opened it to find Jowan there, the young foreign lord's grim expression alerting him to the fact that something was terribly wrong.

"Your son is safe," Jowan said at once. "I left him sleeping on my ship. He has been through a lot."

Fabiom beckoned him in, then closed the door. He indicated towards the one chair in the room, but Jowan went instead to the window and looked out over the harbour, the gilded prow and the furled sails of his ship bright in the morning sunlight.

He did not look at Fabiom as he said, "Prince Raidan is dead."

Fabiom covered his face with his hands and groaned. A hundred questions came to his mind and he could voice none of them. Jowan turned to him, and Fabiom managed to ask the only question that really mattered:

"Are you certain?"

"I'm sorry. Yes. There was a fire. The town of Stonehaven was a centre for the rebel forces and the authorities burnt out their headquarters. Prince Raidan was in one of their houses at the time."

Nothing he had heard during the days spent abroad in Gerik had prepared Fabiom for such tragedy, although he had heard all sorts of rumours during his time on the road and in Bridgetown – which was as far as he had reached before he was met by a courier from Stonehaven bearing an obscure written message about how pleasant it would be to meet old friends in Westmouth when the next ship docked. The letter had been sealed with Jowan's personal mark, that Fabiom would know it as true and trust the message. At once he had turned and retraced his steps to Westmouth, to await the arrival of Jowan's *Sunbow* and Lesandor. He had only arrived back in the coastal town late the previous evening, full of expectations of being able to head home quickly and be out of Gerik before any real danger threatened, and now this.

"Have you contacted the commander of the Morenian trade expedition?" he asked.

Jowan shook his head. "Larse, no. I thought it best to find you first."

They left the hostelry and made their way to the dock and the landing craft. As they went, Jowan told Fabiom what he knew of the final events that had transpired in Stonehaven.

"Lesandor will know better than I, for I was on board my ship that night, making ready to leave," Jowan finished.

They were being taken out to the *Sunbow* when they noticed that the Morenian vessel had moved close beside her. Jowan swore quietly and Fabiom glanced at him.

"It would seem word has spread to the rest of your countrymen. I would rather we had got here before that. Still, nothing can be done about it now."

"What matter?" Fabiom asked bleakly. "There is no good way to break the sort of news you brought me this morning."

"No, not for that reason –" Jowan began, pausing mid-sentence as his attention, and Fabiom's, was distracted by a strident voice that seemed, from its tone, to be asking questions and leaving no time for any reply: "So why had Raidan gone with them? You all need to get back to our ship. I'll have a full written report by noon," were the only words Fabiom heard clearly.

"For *that* reason," Jowan said quietly. "I had heard from the survivors of Prince Raidan's group that the commander of this expedition is somewhat officious."

"I filled in enough paperwork in Gerik to last a lifetime!" Fabiom heard Lesandor reply, though the words did not really register – Fabiom being too appalled at the sight of his son's gaunt face and unsteady stance to fully take in what he was saying.

Neither Lesandor nor Larse had noticed the arrival of the landing craft and its passengers and Larse was launching himself into another volley of questioning.

"Was his Highness searching for you when he lost his life, or was he not? I understand that he was, but if your account is otherwise then I would hear it."

"Prince Raidan was preparing to leave Stonehaven on board this very vessel," Jowan said smoothly, moving up beside Lesandor. "He was quite aware of Lesandor's whereabouts and of the fact that they were to be reunited as soon as they were on board."

"You, I presume, are the Malandelian. I do not understand your part in all this."

"I offered my services to your Ruling Prince, and they were accepted," Jowan returned, unperturbed.

"I see," Larse said stiffly. "That's as maybe, as is your account of events. None of it explains how Prince Raidan came to be in the company of the rebels in the first place. Were there no representatives of the proper authorities in Westmouth – the people with whom Morene signed a treaty?"

"Those authorities would have held us all to ransom!" Lesandor exclaimed. "It was the so-called *rebels* who saved us."

"Saved some of you," Larse reminded him, as if he needed reminding. "A coincidence? Or a convenience?"

"Their leader lost his daughter in the same fire!"

Fabiom had seen and heard enough. He stepped forward to face Larse, his hand briefly grasping Lesandor's shoulder as he passed him, almost able to feel his son's relief as he did so.

"Commander, there will be time for questions and answers and inquiries when we get home. And getting home must be our first priority. The unrest is spreading. Yesterday, word reached Westmouth of

Stonehaven's change of allegiance. This is no longer a safe harbour for Morenian vessels. We have lost too much already; let us debate the faults and failures of this expedition when we have a safer opportunity. We can be on our way the moment you make ready your vessel. It is not reports that you should be hoping to see by noon, but the coast of Morene on the horizon."

On his right hand the heavy bronze ring that marked him as a member of Morene's Assembly – and gave him the authority to usurp Larse's position – glinted in the morning sun as he crossed his arms over his chest. He could feel a dozen pairs of eyes on him but his gaze did not waver from Larse's face.

Larse returned his gaze uncertainly and with some antipathy. "Lord...?"

"Fabiom, of Deepvale," Fabiom supplied. "And you are?"

"Larse of Riverplain. Son of the late Lord Davin and the Princess Jaymna."

Fabiom's jaw tightened. "I see. Well, I suggest that we do not start apportioning blame for what has befallen here, not until we have all the facts, anyway," he said quietly, his look and tone dangerous. Larse did not argue.

They removed from *Sunbow* to the ship beside her, the Morenian *Galingale*. Lesandor helped move Tegun who, though drowsy with the pain-killing draughts he had been given, still felt each jolt and bump as he was lifted over the railings and down to the lower deck of *Galingale*. The two ships, which had been lashed together with hawsers, rubbed and groaned in protest.

Fabiom had not spoken with Lesandor, though he had longed to do so since the moment he had set eyes on him. Now was not the time. It was enough to know Lesandor was alive and would be away from Gerik soon. He watched surreptitiously as Tegun was taken below decks on *Galingale* and Lesandor returned to Jowan's vessel to take his leave of the Malandelian lord. Fabiom had already done so and was waiting on board when his son clambered back over onto the deck. He steadied Lesandor as he stumbled, then let go of his arm almost immediately as he saw Lesandor's expression stiffen and the grief he was bottling up inside threaten to overwhelm him.

"Come to my cabin as soon as you may," he instructed.

Sunbow set sail almost immediately and Fabiom wished they could do the same. Finally, however, they were on their way. He went below and sat in the small cabin that had previously served as Larse's office, and emptied out the satchel Jowan had given him. The contents looked pathetic spread out on the desk before him, just a few small objects and a rolled bundle of papers. There was a knock on the door. Fabiom did not bother to put the things away.

"Come in, Lesandor."

"The sea is getting rough, are you all right?" Lesandor sat down in the seat opposite his father.

Fabiom shrugged. "Bearing up," he said. "At least this vessel has capable officers and I don't have to watch the waves breaking over the deck."

"You still miss Grandfather, I know. It is hard to lose someone when you are not expecting to, is it not?" Lesandor asked, though the questions seemed to be directed more at himself than at his father. Fabiom answered him nevertheless.

"The pain eases, and the shock wears off. But, yes, it is hard."

"I wonder if, from now, I shall feel about fire as you do about stormy waters," Lesandor mused. "There is not much there to mark his going, is there?" he added, picking up the grey stone from the desk. "Take care of this; it is precious."

Fabiom did not ask why. "I want you to come home to Deepvale. Send for Mysha if you will, but spend some time with us."

"My service; it has hardly begun." Lesandor's objection was totally insincere as they both knew, and Fabiom smiled gently.

"And the remainder is temporarily suspended. It can resume as soon as you feel ready. Prince Ravik was appalled that you were included on this expedition. It had nothing to do with him."

Lesandor frowned. "I do not understand. Your letter said I was to join a ship of his. And Larse said his orders came from the prince, even though Lord Yasdon tried his hardest to keep me in Windwood."

"Oh yes." Fabiom sighed and began packing Raidan's things away, looking at the grey and gold stone curiously as he did so. "Ravik intended you to join one of his ships all right, the *Spikenard* which was bound for Varlass. She called by Windwood the day after you left. Your orders had been tampered with. I don't know if Larse knew."

Lesandor's jaw clenched and his eyes darkened. "And Raidan; was *he* tricked into going to Gerik?"

"That I can't say. Ravik told me Raidan was sent a message that you and he would be travelling together, but whether he was deliberately misinformed or simply made the wrong assumption I don't know."

"I do," Lesandor muttered. "He did *not* know that I was to go with him, in fact he was most surprised. They killed him, Father; they killed him as surely as if they had torched that building themselves." With that he buried his face in his hands.

"Lesandor, go and get some sleep," Fabiom said, moving around to sit on the desk close beside Lesandor's chair.

"I am afraid to," Lesandor said, so quietly that Fabiom barely heard him. "Maybe later, when I cannot see the coast of Gerik any more, maybe then. But there are flames in my head and people shouting and trees falling. No, that was a dream. I do not even know what is real any more."

"Something else happened." Fabiom kneaded the back of Lesandor's neck, trying to ease the knotted mass of tension there. "Jowan alluded to something about the townmaster in Stonehaven."

Lesandor looked down until Fabiom reached out to him and gently raised his face.

"Not now, Father. I'll tell you later, at home. I do not think I could bear to – anywhere else. But Larse is wrong about the rebels, their leader is a good man. He saved my life. Things will be different in Gerik if he succeeds. Tell Prince Ravik that, won't you?"

"I think it must be you who will do the telling."

"Yes, I suppose so. I was not thinking. Of course, I shall have to tell him everything."

A sobbing breath caught in Lesandor's throat and Fabiom pulled him into his arms and held him. An image of Jaymna dancing with green jewels flashing at her throat came to him, and Casandrina's words, 'She would be at home among the yews.'

For certain, the princess had taken her revenge in good measure.

Fairwater – attained at last, like an elusive prize. Yet what should have been a time of sweetest joy was as painful to Lesandor as the worst he had endured in Gerik. Ravik and Maedrim's sorrow heightened his own sense of loss, and he grieved for them also.

"I saw it," Maedrim whispered. "Yet I would not let myself believe it was so. My sweet boy – gone." She held Lesandor and kissed him and then excused herself, to go to her other sons and break the awful news to them herself.

Barely able to walk, she stumbled out of the room, two maidservants supporting her – the women almost as distraught as their mistress.

As his father had warned him, the prince wanted to know everything that had occurred in Gerik, in detail, and Lesandor had to relive each long, desperate day. He would have skimmed over his internment at the hands of Townmaster Florim for, apart from his absence for the three days, it was in no way pertinent to Raidan's tale, but Ravik stopped him and made him go back and tell all. And, once he began the telling, he could not stop until it was told in full. Both Ravik and his father listened aghast, for Fabiom too was hearing the story for the first time.

After the telling, when there was little left to say and Lesandor was given leave to defer the remainder of his service, Ravik offered him a choice of any item from among Raidan's effects. Lesandor took the grey and gold stone that had been Sirsha's, for there was nothing there that had been precious to Raidan.

Though Fabiom and Lesandor were offered accommodation at the palace they chose instead to stay with Yan in his rooms in the city for that one night. In the morning they would start on their journey home. They both longed to return to Deepvale as soon as possible.

Ravik made them promise to attend him first thing the following day, before they set off, and then took his leave of them, to retire to his own apartments with the remainder of his family and try to come to terms with the loss of his son.

The day was drawing to a close.

Lesandor took little persuading to go to bed soon after they reached Yan's lodgings. He slept fitfully, waking suddenly from one bad dream only to slip back into the clutches of another, while Fabiom and Yan sat up very late, talking quietly.

Dawn was colouring the sky, the light showing around the corner of the building across the road and through the narrow window. Lesandor sat up in his bed, suddenly wide awake and aware that he had heard something important in the final moments of his dreaming. As the flames had reduced the wooden building to ashes, Raidan had called out to him, something he almost remembered, something important.

Lesandor lay down again, though he was too frightened by the dreams that had haunted his night to want to sleep, despite the almost nauseating tiredness of his body. Nearby he could sense his father's presence, hear his steady breathing; there was some comfort in that at least, and in the presence of Sirsha's stone under his pillow. He took the stone out and held it, the last thing Raidan had touched. Somehow it bound the three of them together.

Besides his promise to Raidan, Lesandor wondered if what was troubling him was his father's assertion that Mysha should come to Deepvale. If she did, he would have to deal with his feelings for her and come to terms with having betrayed his marriage, at least in thought. Only then did he realise what it was that had woken him – not concern about his own marriage but the fact he had said nothing to Prince Ravik about Raidan's wife; nor did he know how he would do so, or even if he should. True, it had been a secret he had promised not to divulge, but that was when Raidan was returning to Morene, to a girl who was expecting his child and who knew nothing about her husband's royal connections. Exiled forever – would Ravik relent? And how would he tell Casandrina?

Lesandor rolled over onto his back, holding the stone against his chest, and tried to work out what he should do. Last night – on board the *Galingale* – he had gone to the cabin and had found her name etched in the wood and he had sworn to find her, to protect her. Now, back in Morene, that task seemed harder.

Of course – his cloak clasp! Lesandor realised what had been niggling at the edge of his mind. Before they left Windwood, Raidan had told him he had not brought the amber and silver clasp because he had not expected to see Lesandor on that trip. Instead, he left it behind – in Cuivah's care.

It was not much of a lead, but it was something. There were only two such clasps ever made. His mother had one, and Raidan's wife the other.

Eventually, against his own desire and with nothing resolved, he fell asleep again. At last too tired to dream.

When they returned to the palace in the morning they found Larse pacing up and down the long marble corridor, a look of deep anxiety on his face. They overheard him ask a court official if his uncle was ready to see him yet and be answered in the negative. Fabiom and Lesandor were admitted immediately.

"Raidan did well." Ravik indicated for them to be seated, and sat himself. "I've only gone briefly through the reports and papers he compiled." He shook his head in wonder. "He made some very interesting discoveries. He would have...." The prince stared at the ceiling, composed himself as well as he could. "I can't think of him in the past tense – I keep thinking he has a brilliant future. I love all my sons, but he was special; perhaps it was from sharing his mother's talent. She will miss him dreadfully." A deep breath stilled the tremor in his voice. "I've had other reports, besides yours, Lesandor, including one from those who were in this – bakery. They confirm what you were told, that he gave his life for his companions. I might wish he had not, yet I cannot be surprised, neither can I be anything but proud of him. I just wish there was more to show for his life."

Lesandor stared at the prince. *There is*, he thought. *Somewhere in Rushford is a girl who is carrying his child.* He said nothing.

Ravik reached over and took a sheaf of papers from a small table. "This is the report Raidan wrote for me. There's too much there for me to draw any immediate conclusions. I thought I would ask Yan to look at it. He has as much insight into and knowledge of Gerish history as anyone in the capital. Though there is another resident of Deepvale who might be able to assist, once more reports come in from Gerik."

"Masgor," Fabiom guessed.

Ravik nodded. "I'm sending people to Gerik. We must be apprised of how this uprising turns out, and whether the treaty remains intact, or not."

Lesandor shifted in his seat and Ravik looked at him curiously.

"Lord Robstrom signed no treaty with Morene, my lord. Yet, if I correctly understood what he told me, he is your distant kinsman and his claim on Gerik is valid. Proof of that fact was what Raidan discovered, the documents he was protecting, was it not?"

A sad smile touched Ravik's face. "Indeed. And Robstrom will possibly honour the treaty. Yet if he is defeated it is unlikely that those who were in power before the uprising will remain so; he has inflicted too much damage on the existing regime. That is where our danger lies. Despite all that was said about this being Gerik's struggle, I am inclined to offer him assistance. This morning I will send him word to that effect."

Lesandor was pleased at the news, pleased also with the gift Ravik presented to him – a shell and ox-horn lyre, inlaid with mother-of-pearl – one of Raidan's favourite possessions.

After that they took a little sweet wine together, in Raidan's memory, then parted, bonded by a mutual sorrow.

Part

III

Chapter One

DAYS IN DEEPVALE soothed, like spring water flowing over hands that had toiled too long. The child within the man responded to a mother's touch, a father's smile. Nights spent within stands of vital trees banished soul-rending nightmares.

Masgor's interest in the affairs of Gerik had not waned with age. He listened to all Lesandor had to say with great interest, quizzing him on details Lesandor had thought unimportant or had taken little notice of. Robstrom, especially, fascinated the old man, who consulted ancient scrolls and made copious notes, muttering to himself all the while. Lesandor was happy enough to talk about Robstrom. He also spoke of his journey through Gerik, even about his stay in Stonehaven, finding it easier to do so with the passing of each day, but he said nothing to Masgor or to his parents about Sirsha, other than that she had helped him and had died from the effects of the fire. Nevertheless, whenever her name was mentioned, Casandrina looked at him in a way that suggested she guessed more than he said.

Thoughts of Sirsha filled Lesandor's mind. Each time he walked in the woods, where life flourished in all the gorgeous splendour of the first month of summer, he found himself taking the paths he had planned to walk with her, visiting the grottoes and falls he had thought to show her, seeking out the burrows and nests of the woodland creatures she would never have seen in Gerik. He tried to tell himself that the feelings he had for her were imaginary, that only the desire to believe real happiness had nearly been his inspired his longing and sorrow, that they had not known each other well enough for it to be anything but illusion. With such thoughts in mind, he heeded his father's advice and sent a message to Windwood, a letter to Mysha telling her that he was safe and well and asking her to come to Deepvale, to spend some time there with him, and get to know his parents.

Early the next morning, he imparted Raidan's secret to Casandrina as they walked together through the bright garden, the grass springy and dew-damp beneath their bare feet.

"Cuivah? That is her name? And he said her background was somewhat tainted? Is that *all* he said?" she asked.

"Not all, no," he allowed.

"No." She regarded him solemnly and he looked away as she continued, "Well do I remember that name, Cuivah of Rushford: the woman who betrayed the trust of the Silvanii; the woman whose wickedness almost destroyed your father, almost cost me my life. Can it be a coincidence? If not, you were probably wise to say nothing to Ravik."

Lesandor drew a sharp breath. "Only because I did not know *what* to say." It was too late to turn back now. "I cannot just forget about her. She is waiting for Raidan to return even now. She will go on waiting. She doesn't know he is never coming back."

Casandrina, as she frequently did, surprised him. "Dear one, I am not suggesting you forget about her. Of course you must find her, and you must help her, however you can." Her eyes held his and she smiled. "Your father has commented how, each time Mysha's name is mentioned, you look somewhat preoccupied, concerned. So this is – part – of the reason? You were thinking of your friend's wife too."

He grinned and linked his arm through hers.

They continued walking.

Lesandor eventually broke the companionable silence. "Mother, do you think I dare take hope from the fact that you can accept Cuivah is in Morene? Might Prince Ravik do the same?"

"I cannot even try to guess. Your father would have far better insight."

"But if I tell him, it would put him in a dreadful position. He is a magistrate, and a member of the Assembly. 'No mercy' – that was Ravik's ruling. All her family, exiled for all time. That is why I said nothing when we were in Fairwater – to Father or Prince Ravik. Of course I wanted to – more than anything. But how could I?" He sighed. "What was Raidan thinking?"

Casandrina laughed. "Thinking? I doubt he was thinking at all. But I have been –" She stopped walking, unpinned her silver and amber clasp and gave it to Lesandor.

"Take this, wear it. It is the match to the one the girl has, as you know. It may not help you find her but it will be some way she might recognise you should you chance to meet – as you might recognise her in the same manner."

Lesandor fingered the delicate strands of silver and the smoothness of the amber held within the filigreed work.

"This was a gift to you from Father for your first wedding anniversary, I cannot take it."

"He gave both to me and I gave him back the other one so that we would have one each. At your leaving he gave his to you, that we might be with you wherever you were."

"I only loaned it to Raidan," he said contritely. "I did not think for one moment that it would not be returned."

She smiled, unconcerned. "No matter. You gave it out of your affection for your friend. So now I give you the second one, that you might find his wife, for the love you bore him and that he bore her. It is fitting. Amber was ever meant to be a gift of love."

Lesandor thought of the two baskets full of the stuff he had found on the donkey when he had been lost in Gerik, something else he had not told Casandrina.

"My life was ransomed with amber in Gerik," he said at last.

"That too is fitting," she replied, after the briefest pause.

And he knew she would have paid the price herself, had she been there.

Rose buds were opening on the trellised pergola, brilliant white against the deep greenness of their foliage.

"The garden will soon be at its best. Maybe we should celebrate Midsummer this year, in respect of your friend Jowan. He is from the Sunlands, is he not? It is their great festival, so your father tells me," Casandrina suggested. "Before then we still have to get you quite well," she added, suddenly more serious. "A visit to physician Nalio would be no harm."

"Being home is the only medicine I need," he protested.

Tenderly, she touched the fading bruises on his face, while deep in her eyes a glimmer of the anger she had sought to hide from him stirred.

"Mother, it is finished. I am safely returned," he told her, almost anxiously. "There will be changes in Gerik, a new order...."

"It is not Gerik that concerns me, not this time. It is closer to home that I am thinking of."

"Princess Jaymna?"

"Fool must she be that she thinks to thwart me! Ah no" – she laughed, unamused – "maybe she did not care about the consequences, sought only to prove a point. I still do not fully understand the ways of mankind." She looked at her son curiously. "For example, you, I think, forged some strong bonds in Gerik – despite all that happened to you there."

"No. *Because* of all that happened there."

"Yes," she said, though uncertainly. Then she sighed. "Maybe I do not have to worry too much about Jaymna. I suspect Prince Ravik may be inclined towards retribution himself. That will leave me only Windwood and Lord Yasdon to consider...."

"Mother!"

She glanced at him sideways with a hint of a smile and left him standing, bemused, as she moved away and began plucking sprigs of lavender until her arms were full of sweet-scented flowers.

Lesandor was more than reluctant to see a physician, even his father's close friend, Nalio. So, as a compromise, it was arranged that he should spend some time with cousin Kita and her husband, Nissus, and their three young children. The spirited pair were good company and devoted to each other, as they had been since they first met in Deepvale's hold-house beside Masgor's sickbed, when Kita was only twelve and Nissus a precocious thirteen.

Lesandor enjoyed the few days of his stay, revelling in the company of people whose livelihoods were bound up with the land and who talked knowledgeably and enthusiastically about all that grew. As ever, he admired the marvellous herbs Nissus was cultivating in his garden and conservatory, and tried to ignore the fact that most of his food was laced with such plants, with their various medicinal properties, based on Nissus's assessment of his health.

He would have stayed longer, had Fabiom not come to see him with the news that Yan had arrived at the hold-house, and that he had come to tell them something of what he had learnt from Raidan's papers.

Yan had been taking refreshments and talking with Casandrina; though she had left the hold-house by the time Lesandor and Fabiom returned, knowing what Yan had come to discuss with them and unwilling to join in a conversation regarding Gerik.

Masgor joined them in the day room, eager to learn more about the current situation, and especially about Robstrom. According to Yan, Robstrom had been in touch with Ravik personally, regarding Ravik's offer of help, which had been gratefully accepted.

"I have no precise details of what form that help will take," Yan apologised to Masgor. "However, I did discover something pertaining to a question of yours, Lesandor. You wanted to know what was behind your captivity in Stonehaven. Well, listen to this, I'm reading from Prince Raidan's report:

'There has apparently been talk, in certain circles, that if the curse the dying Silvanii put on Gerik could be lifted, the fortune of the land would be restored, and whoever could achieve that would have unassailable power. Two separate individuals who realised that I was Morenian, and who were not immediately hostile, put the notion to me. One actually said, "The links between our two lands are deeper than trade, for both lands are the Silvanii's, not man's." I see some sort of hope in that yet it makes me fearful for Lesandor and I trust no one finds out about his Silvanan heritage, for who can say how they might try to use him.'

"The Townmaster in Stonehaven was probably half-afraid of you, Lesandor, and half intent on manipulating you somehow, once he learnt the truth about you."

Masgor nodded in agreement. "Indeed, for that truth is potent. Gerik is completely barren because of the Silvanii. The curse they put upon the land was very powerful, their death poisoned the waters and the soil. A reversal of that would be of more value than any amount of amber, for they can produce so little of their own food that their coffers are almost empty; the country is impoverished."

"Townmaster Florim traded me for amber in the end," Lesandor reminded him.

"Thinking in the short term again. Their greatest fault, and possibly your salvation," Masgor replied.

"You sound exactly as you used to when I was a student with you," Fabiom said with a laugh.

Yan grinned. "Which brings us to the other reason why I've come home at this time. Prince Ravik was wondering if, by any chance, you might consider a sojourn in Fairwater, Masgor, as an advisor to his Highness while Gerik sorts out its internal conflicts?"

"He wondered that, did he? He does realise that I am eighty-eight years of age?"

"He does. And he said to apologise and say that ideally he would not ask you to travel. Indeed his first thought was that he would come to Deepvale, but he is loath to be away from the city – and his wife – at this time. He asked me to stress that this is nothing more than an inquiry."

"Of course I'll go! Why didn't you say so before?" Masgor exclaimed indignantly, delighted at the prospect, even more pleased that he had not been overlooked in favour of a younger generation of scholars.

During the next two days, Masgor gathered all the notes he had made, based on Lesandor's details and his own research, and declared himself fit and ready to travel. Fabiom was not so sure and asked Nalio to call, to check their old tutor.

After the physician had spent some time with Masgor he joined Fabiom, Lesandor and Yan in Fabiom's study, shaking his head in despair.

"Calling me was a mistake, Fabiom. You should have got my son in for this; Nissus has never been awed by Masgor, or anyone else, as far as I'm aware. If Masgor tells me he is determined to go to Fairwater, do you really think I will gainsay him? Would you?"

"Are you saying he shouldn't go?" Yan asked.

"No, I'm not saying that. I should, yet how can I? He's in moderately good health, considering his age, and the journey will do him less harm than not going and being bitterly disappointed. It's what he wants, and he can be of use to Prince Ravik. I have no grounds for standing in the way of *that*."

⬥

Days passed. Letters came to Lesandor from Rushford, less than helpful – there were seventeen registered stone carvers in the holding, none of whom acknowledged having a young mother-to-be in residence. Of the five retired magistrates, none had any recollection of performing a marriage ceremony in the period specified. However, a sixth had died recently, and another had left to live with his daughter's family in another holding.

Yan returned to Fairwater, accompanied by Masgor.

Lesandor waited for Mysha to come from Windwood, instead, all that arrived was a letter. It was from Yasdon and it informed him that they were delighted he was safely returned from his travels but, sadly, Mysha was afflicted with a mild ague and her physician did not recommend she make such a lengthy journey. Yasdon also made a light but unmistakable reference to the fact that Lesandor had not yet completed his full service in Windwood, and wrote that they were awaiting his return with great anticipation. Only vaguely did he allude to the possibility that they might visit Deepvale before the summer was over.

Lesandor's first reaction was one of angry indignation, followed swiftly by a huge sense of guilt regarding Mysha.

He knew he had no choice but to go back.

⬥

Chapter Two

TRAVELLING ALONE, APART from his pack donkey, and a foal that slowed him up considerably, Lesandor returned to Windwood via Rushford. Despite his hope that a stone carver who would not reveal a fugitive relative to the authorities might admit her existence to a friend of her husband's, his trip to Rushford was a waste of time. With Mysha unwell, he did not dare linger long. All he could do was leave discreet instructions with a number of people in the hope that Cuivah might be located before her child was born. Disheartened, he completed his journey.

Although he did not know it, Lesandor was seen by someone in Yasdon's employ almost as soon as he crossed into Windwood. He had only reached the outskirts of the municipal centre when the lord holder, accompanied by three servants, came to meet him.

"You do know we didn't expect you to travel alone. It really is unbecoming of your position, Lesandor," Yasdon reprimanded his son-by-marriage, organising the servants to take Lesandor's baggage and his beasts. "Look at that foal. That's very unusual – a white one. They're valuable, aren't they?"

"She is a gift for Mysha," Lesandor explained, concerned that she had not come to meet him. He feared she had not recovered from her sickness, but Yasdon reassured him – Mysha was quite well.

Mysha was unaware of Lesandor's arrival. Only by chance did one of her maids observe him coming into the hold-house with Yasdon, and ran to tell her mistress.

As they came through the door into the heart room, Mysha threw herself into Lesandor's arms, tears streaming down her cheek, thrilled at his return. He thought she looked as well as he had ever seen her, and wondered at her swift recovery.

He kissed her. "How are —"

"Come outside and see what Lesandor has brought you," Yasdon interrupted, catching her by the hand. She did her father's bidding, crying out in delight the moment she set eyes on the foal.

Seeing Mysha's reaction, Yasdon clapped Lesandor on the back, a wide grin splitting his face.

"That's a fine gift. You could not have chosen better! Now come inside, come inside. It's so good to have you home!"

Yasdon immediately began talking about celebrations. He was bound to throw one of his great parties.

"He is proud of you," Mysha told her husband when he complained at the prospect, Yasdon having at last left them alone together, though only briefly, in order to summon his house-steward to make the preparations. "He wants to show you off to his friends."

"I am not something he owns!" Lesandor replied with unaccustomed pique, though sometimes he wondered if that was not how Yasdon did regard him. Mysha looked worried.

"Don't be cross," she pleaded and, fearing she might cry, he said he was sorry and that he was not cross, and that he would perform for her father and his friends. She missed the irony of his words.

Although the day had been unseasonably damp, Mysha insisted on going outside again, to see that her donkey had been properly settled and fed. She stroked the velvet muzzle and pulled the long soft ears through her hands.

"She's lovely, Lesandor. So soft. Does she have a name?"

"My Aunt Marid named her Whisper. If you want to call her something else I am sure neither Marid nor the donkey will object."

"Oh, no, Whisper's a nice name. It suits her. Thank you for bringing her for me."

Her pleasure moved him and he was glad he had persuaded his great aunt to give him the precious foal to take back to Windwood.

"I hoped you would like her. Should we not go in? You ought to be taking care of yourself."

"Do you want to go in?" she asked in some surprise.

"Not particularly, I was thinking of you – if you have been unwell –"

"Unwell? No, what made you think that? I've been very well. I missed you of course, but that's not something a physician can cure, is it?"

The party was organised for the very next day, leaving Lesandor to surmise that it had been planned long before. The number of people who turned up only confirmed that fact, though Petron was noticeable by his absence. As on the day he had arrived in Windwood for the very first time, there were wrestlers and jugglers, magicians and contortionists, musicians and dancers, as well as food and drink in abundance.

Celebrations went on through the night and Yasdon accounted the party a great success. Lesandor was back in Windwood and there was little fear that Ravik would call upon him for some time, especially given the circumstances of the last venture. By the time the prince did require Lesandor's outstanding service, Yasdon presumed he would have a grandchild.

"I thought your family would have come back with you," Yasdon commented to Lesandor as, finally, the party wound to a close; thoughts of a grandchild having reminded him that he knew very little about any of his son-by-marriage's relations. "Since you first came here I have only once met your father, and then briefly. I really ought to know your mother, and your sister too. You said she was sickly." There was a touch of anxiety in his voice. "Nothing – er – serious, I trust."

"My sister, sickly?" Lesandor replied, totally nonplussed. He smiled at the image that conveyed. "Not at all."

He had completely forgotten a much earlier conversation that had given Yasdon such an impression.

"She will visit then?"

"Ah, no." Memory stirred. "She does not care to travel. Neither does my mother, unless she has to," he added quickly.

"Then I must visit Deepvale," Yasdon decided, pacing to the window to gaze out at his perfectly tended garden, still lit by huge candles, torches and oil lanterns. "Before the weather deteriorates."

Lesandor shook his head. He was tempted to remind Yasdon that he was Deepvale's heir, that his place, and his wife's, was there, not in Windwood. However, Fabiom had taught him the art of diplomacy; the hour of his arrival was not the ideal time to speak of his leaving, so he kept his counsel.

The final guests left. Mysha waved them off cheerfully. Away to the east, dawn was colouring the sky.

"That was fun!" Mysha declared, attempting to rearrange the shoulder of her gown. "Wasn't it fun, Lesandor?"

He wished she would not keep asking for his agreement and approval about everything; fortunately she rarely noticed when he did not reply directly.

He repinned the garment for her, letting his hand linger on her shoulder. "It certainly was a lively occasion." He could hardly tell her that he felt depressed after the party, or that he had seen himself like some grotesque exhibit. "I need some fresh air. Do you want to come for a walk?" He knew she would not.

"It's still the middle of the night!" she objected. "Anyway, I'm tired. Surely you are tired too?"

"Not so much," he told her. "And, after all that excitement, I doubt I would relax anyway – not without a walk. Will you excuse me?"

She would fall asleep quickly. She would not know how long he was gone. That suited him. He had no intention of returning until the morning was well advanced.

Five days after his return to Windwood, Lesandor came back to the hold-house early in the morning, after another night-time woodland excursion. The house was quiet; the only sounds came from the kitchens where the servants were preparing for another day's meals. Lesandor was thinking of breakfast with keen anticipation as he made his way back to the rooms he shared with Mysha and was startled by the sound of someone stepping out in the corridor close behind him.

"Master Lesandor, may I speak with you?" Petron's servant spoke urgently.

Lesandor could not bring himself to entirely trust Trisran, who was rarely out of Petron's sight, but he nodded casually, as if being approached thus was quite normal.

The servant glanced around. "My master watches you, sets me to spy on you. What can I do? I do not believe you betray your wife but he wants to believe it. He would see you discredited." Trisran seemed to run out of words with that.

Lesandor was painfully aware of the grey and gold stone he wore close to his heart, fastened around his neck on a bronze chain.

"Has he followed me?" he inquired, wary himself by then.

Trisran shook his head and would not meet Lesandor's gaze.

"But you have?"

"Some way. He sent me to do so, but I dared not enter the heart of the woods. I was afraid. I have heard strange tales. Even for my master I would not follow you there."

"Thank you for the warning, Trisran." Lesandor sighed. "I will keep mindful of it. You may rest easy tonight. I shall not be going out." *I shall go mad*, he added to himself.

"Tell me about Petron's servant," Lesandor suggested to Mysha, later that day.

She frowned slightly. "Trisran? I hardly notice him now. He's been around forever. He's nobody."

Lesandor tried one of Petron's old tutors.

"Ah, Trisran. An unfortunate boy. Bright enough, were he allowed to be. Always came to Master Petron's lessons. His shadow. No father, mother dead. If Lord Yasdon was not such a generous man, goodness knows what would have happened to him. He earns his keep by his work, seems happy enough, and loyal. Though he probably has little choice in the matter."

So, that was it: Trisran was Petron's fool because if he did not do as he was told he would not eat. He had no one, and nowhere to go. Suddenly Lesandor felt great sympathy for him.

"Least I could do," Yasdon explained, when Lesandor raised the subject of Trisran's employment with him. "Felt I owed it to him in a way. Petron's mother died when he was born. He and Trisran were the same age. Trisran's mother was a kitchen girl. She nursed both babies. When she died two years later I gave her son his keep."

Lesandor made a resolution not to feel too hard done by. Compared with Trisran he had little to complain about.

"I am going out tonight. Will Master Petron notice?" Lesandor asked Trisran, some days later.

"He need not," Trisran said, greatly daring.

Lesandor shook his head. "Yes, let him know and follow me, if you will. There is nothing to fear in the woods unless it is within yourself. Do you come with me?"

He could see Trisran struggling with the decision. Finally the desire simply to do something of his own, on his own, was too great for the boy.

"I will follow you," he said. "And I will disclose nothing you wish me to remain silent about."

Lesandor smiled slightly. "There will be little enough to tell."

Lesandor let Trisran catch up with him when they were well away from Yasdon's hold-house. They walked for a while in silence until Trisran found the courage to ask, "Where do you go in the woods?"

"Just to a quiet grove, to think, sometimes to sleep. It reminds me of Deepvale, of my childhood."

"The woods are dangerous."

"No," Lesandor said. "Do no harm there and no harm will befall you."

"A Tree Lady can steal a man's mind while he sleeps – yet you sleep there."

"They are not evil, though they *are* strong. They will not take what is not offered to them."

"I saw a man once, mad he was, he kept singing snatches of song. He never spoke. They said he was high born but he had slept in the woods and lost his mind. Heard the singing, could never forget it, never remember it either."

Lesandor sighed quietly in the darkness. He would never forget that singing either, yet it was not that particular loss that would drive him insane. They reached the wood edge.

"You may turn back now, if you wish."

They walked on together.

"I don't know what to tell my master."

The first birds of morning chirruped in the hedgerows, beside the path along which they strolled.

"Tell him the truth," Lesandor suggested. "Tell him I am enamoured of the woods and the Silvanii, and sleep beneath their trees. Tell him I am mad, if you will."

"I never heard anyone call them by that name before, their real name."

"You ought to meet my mother," Lesandor said.

Trisran regarded him quizzically, wondering if perhaps he was just a little mad after all.

Lesandor was left alone after that. He invited Trisran to accompany him again but Petron had grown tired of that pursuit and Trisran knew he could not get away. He would like to have gone.

Mysha never complained about Lesandor's wanderings. So long as he spent some time with her each night, she was not given to finding fault with him.

Summer ended. News from Rushford was vague, at best, so that Lesandor doubted if Cuivah was even in the holding anymore. Raidan had told him that she had little family left, and Lesandor imagined her alone with her new baby, wondering if her husband would ever return to her. He sent more money, more instructions, and went on waiting for some sort of lead he would actually be able to follow, determined to go to Rushford the moment he heard anything of substance.

Time hung heavy, despite Yasdon's insistence on giving him many responsibilities. Without the sanctuary of the woods, Lesandor had no idea what he would have done.

The worst thing, he decided, among the litany of things he disliked about Windwood's hold-house, was that the library was almost entirely devoid of decent books. It had taken him a while to work out what was wrong, for it was not a lack of numbers. There were plenty of books and papers in the library, some of them quite rare and valuable, but few were interesting. Four early-autumn days of blustering winds and unrelenting rain gave him ample time to really look, and he realised there was not one single reference to the Silvanii or to Treelaw to be found. The first omission was odd, the second was scandalous, for every holder swore at his inception to uphold that law, and his knowledge and comprehension of it gave him the right to his position, equally as much as his birth.

Lesandor learnt, from the same tutor he had inquired of regarding Trisran, that Yasdon's predecessor, Lord Herbis, had discouraged any interest in matters Silvanan – especially among members of his own family – after his son's disastrous attempt at wooing a Tree Lady on his seventeenth birth eve. That accounted for the library and for Yasdon and his family being entirely untutored, though how Yasdon had taken over the mantle and title of Holder in that state, Lesandor did not dare ask.

Throughout the remainder of the autumn there were at least the mulberry coppices in need of attention. Yasdon expressed delight with their progress and with the promise of the silkworm eggs from Fabiom that would be arriving soon. On a fine, chill morning they went to inspect the new mill that was nearing completion, in readiness for the anticipated harvests of future years.

"This is going well," Lesandor ventured as they left the building.

"It is indeed." Yasdon rubbed his hands together.

"Lord Yasdon, I need to go away for a short while. There is a matter I must deal with in Rushford, on behalf of a friend – a promise I made some time ago."

"Oh, I see." Yasdon hesitated. "This is not a good time, Lesandor. You see, I have another task for you, one that must be started immediately. You mustn't forget, despite the fact that you are my daughter's husband, your time of service with us is not complete. No, I can't let you go off now. I need you here," Yasdon said almost apologetically. Lesandor knew he was not as sorry as he sounded.

Yasdon liked to give him things to do and he liked Lesandor to do them well, so he could boast of his prowess afterwards. Lesandor considered that fact and said nothing as they made their way into the town and to

Yasdon's office in the municipal centre, to look at the Holder's next project.

"A new annex to the house. Accommodation for Petron when he wants more independence, or when he marries. I'm going to start building. I have plans here." Yasdon cleared the table and spread out two huge sheets of parchment. The plans were elaborate and detailed and meant little to Lesandor, though it seemed to him that the building was not so much an extension as a separate dwelling and he wondered at that. It was almost as if Yasdon was moving Petron out of the hold-house.

"I do not know how much help I will be," he said doubtfully. "I have never been involved in anything like this."

"Oh, it's easy. You'll pick it up. It's just overseeing. I have employed craftsmen and labourers of the highest calibre. Your task will be to see that they work together and present me with the finest new building in Morene."

Overseeing the craftsmen proved easier than satisfying Petron. Lesandor wished that Yasdon had not divulged his plans to his son, for Petron – who wanted no part in the work – insisted that he should have the final say in every step taken.

The carpenters were not used to being spoken to in the manner Petron addressed them, though fortunately the senior among the four was a mild-mannered man and the other three stayed out of Petron's way, so a sort of peace was maintained. Lesandor was amazed at how they were treated, even on occasion by Yasdon – who seemed to regard them as little more than menials. Anywhere else they would have been treated with great respect, for proper carpenters were highly trained, learned men, wise in Treelaw. Like the senior carpenter, the others had recognised Lesandor for what he was the moment they had been introduced to each other. He had seen it in their eyes and it was evident in the way they spoke to him and encouraged his involvement in their work. They liked to talk to him and he enjoyed their company.

Over the days, the second carpenter, the oldest among them and the only one native to Windwood, was pleased to explain to Lesandor about the suppression of Treelaw in the holding since Giar's loss of sensibility. One day he also volunteered the information that, at the time of Yasdon's

166

conferring, there had been a serious outbreak of fever in Windwood and Yasdon had not actually gone to Fairwater for some two years after Lord Herbis's death. Lesandor could only guess that Yasdon had not been tested at that point, the matter being treated as a formality. He was considering the implications when he was distracted by a conversation that had been going on for some time between Petron and the senior carpenter and was now getting rather heated.

"Oak would be best," the senior carpenter said patiently, for about the third time that morning. "We could get a licence for a little more oak."

"You are using oak in the roof beams. I want variety!"

Lesandor heard the carpenter ask what Petron had in mind for the columns if not oak. The man's patience was obviously wearing thin.

"Variety, I told you. One of this, one of that, one of something else." He looked smug.

Lesandor shivered, for Petron's words conjured shades of the Townmaster's offices in Stonehaven, even though, like all buildings in Morene, this one would be mostly stone, only the decor and framework being fashioned from timber.

Lesandor went over to see if he could help. "Some yew, perhaps? That has a pleasant grain and there should be no difficulty getting a licence for the amount we would need."

"Indeed," the carpenter agreed, his scowl turning to a smile as he acknowledged Lesandor. "Yew then."

"Not just yew!" Petron stormed. "Don't you listen?" He rounded on Lesandor. "You know the woods around here. What grows in those places you go to?"

Afterwards, Lesandor cursed himself for not having the sense to say nothing grew there they had not a good supply of already. He had felt the cold touch of fear and he had reacted irrationally. It was not the mocking laughter he minded, it was the real possibility that, by telling Petron the deepest wood was the haunt of the Silvanii and demonstrating, all too clearly, that he cared about the fate of the trees there, he had given his wife's brother a means of antagonising him, and sown the seeds of an idea that might see realisation in an appalling deed.

Petron did not believe him, and was delighted to have discovered that Lesandor, far from being perfect – as Yasdon would have everyone think – was superstitious and foolish; for only a fool believed every grove and coppice to be the demesne of the Tree Ladies. Fools like the toothless old man who helped with the planing, who had looked distinctly uncomfortable at Lesandor's outburst. Of course Petron knew the Silvanii existed, somewhere, but his education had made certain he would find it inconceivable that they should be part of his immediate environs, or that he would ever have any dealings with them. It seemed to him that Lesandor's imagination was under less restraint than was proper for a man in his position and that Yasdon ought to be told.

By the time Yasdon sent for Lesandor, the day was drawing to a close and Lesandor had his emotions under control. He had considered how he might minimise the damage he had already done. When he met Yasdon he made a point of being relaxed and cheerful, at least outwardly, a ruse he knew would pacify the older man.

"Petron is being a nuisance, I gather," Yasdon said.

"He wants his future quarters to be spectacular. Who can blame him?" Lesandor replied easily.

"He says he wants to embellish it with wood from the deep groves on the inland track –"

Lesandor wondered whether Petron had, in fact, told Yasdon what had transpired between them.

"– and you object."

"I do." Lesandor sat down as invited, still relaxed, still smiling. "For one thing there is no need to cut those trees; there is enough of the same timbers closer and more accessible. Petron has never been deep into the woodland, I believe, so it is not as if he has seen something he particularly wants to use."

Yasdon poured wine for them both. He too was smiling.

"That all makes sense and, though I don't mind spending the money, his plans would be most costly I think. But he told me you also objected on the grounds that you believe some of the groves there to be, um, Silvana haunts."

"That as well," Lesandor said, as casually as he was able. He took the wine offered to him. Yasdon was looking at him curiously.

"You *do* believe that, don't you?"

Lesandor did not reply but his faint smile answered the question.

"I suppose there is no harm in that," Yasdon said uncertainly. "Personally I have never heard mention of any of the Tree Ladies in this vicinity. Then I never go into the woods." He took a deep draught, a worried frown knotting his brow. Lesandor wondered if he should assure Yasdon that he was not given to imagining things, neither was he going to prove an embarrassment to him. But for once it was not Lesandor who was on Yasdon's mind.

"Leave them alone and they'll leave us alone, eh?"

"So you believe me?"

"To be honest, I'm not sure, Lesandor. I believe that you believe." He chuckled. "Nothing wrong with that, nothing at all. Just to be certain though; no harm in taking precautions."

Lesandor was unsure if he was merely being mollified or if Yasdon really was afraid. Probably a little of both, he decided. He was untroubled by Yasdon's motives. The trees would be saved, that was all that concerned him.

It was pure chance that made Lesandor return to the building site that evening. He had left papers behind in his agitation and he wanted to attempt to review them before work began the next morning. It was late and he did not expect many of the workmen to be about, yet he was surprised at how few were there. A stillness hung over the place, lights were quenched where normally the workers ate and rested after the day's toil. The chill tendrils of fear that had touched his mind, and had been brushed aside, returned as a freezing hand clutching his very heart.

"Petron!" he bellowed. There was no answer. "Petron!"

An elderly draughtsman came out of a dimly lit building and stared at him.

"Where is everyone?" Lesandor demanded.

"Some sort of party, I think. There were friends of the young master's here. He sent everyone else off early, then a crowd of them went off laughing and singing. Half drunk if you ask me."

"Trisran?" Lesandor muttered. He did not believe that Petron's servant would stand by and let the deep groves be destroyed, yet he could not be sure. Trisran had been brought up to do as Petron bid and that would be a hard habit to break. And what could Trisran do if he did oppose his master? What could Lesandor do? He knew what the Silvanii might do.

He ran to the woods through the deepening gloom. So far nothing had happened. He would know if it had. The woods spoke to him. Safe, all was still safe.

"We sense danger. Help us."

"We helped you once, aid us now."

Voices all around. Fearful, whispering voices of woodmaids, like leaves tumbling on fitful breezes. Lesandor could hear them. He heard other voices too, voices of men oblivious to the hidden life of the wildwood.

"Is this as deep as you can go?" said one.

"Any deeper and we'll be out the other side," replied another with a coarse guffaw.

"What about this tree? Good strong trunk."

"No, master. See – a fault line. That would be unfit for your building." Lesandor recognised Trisran's voice, speaking earnestly.

"Only the best! Only the best!" Petron was almost singing, clearly he was very drunk. "Let's try this path."

"You've been there, sir." Respectful but determined, Trisran was trying to steer them from the deep groves where Lesandor had taken him.

"Are y'sure?"

Lesandor watched from behind a massive ash tree. It was not Silvanan but it made him feel secure. As Trisran passed he dared to make a slight noise, a sound like a distant owl. Only the servant heard. Their eyes met briefly. Trisran seemed to be signalling for him to go back the way Petron's party had come and Lesandor nodded. He recognised some drinking friends of Petron's from the town and some of the younger workers from the site and noticed with relief that none of the men carried axes.

When they had all passed, he ventured out. He retraced their path. It was not hard to follow. He sensed two woodmaids travelling with him. There had been more and he guessed the others watched the intruders. Petron's party had clearly not reached the heart of the woods. Trisran had succeeded in misleading them sufficiently that they did not know which paths they had followed and which they had not.

Lesandor turned to his left.

"Not that way," gentle voices insisted, tugging him to the right with beckoning songs. *"This way."*

For a moment he almost forgot himself, following the songs and the singers, childhood overlapping the present, until he saw the red flag of material knotted onto a rope wound tightly around the trunk of the birch tree before him. It was no Silvanan tree. He laid his hand on the trunk to be certain. He turned and raised his lantern and saw another red rag. Moreover, the very air reverberated with a sense of huge outrage. Slowly, heart pounding, he walked to the elm and untied the rope, which he rolled up and passed through his belt. Beside the elm, a woodmaid's cherry tree was also marked, the rope so tightly knotted that he had to cut it through with his belt knife. The marked birch was too near the Silvana's elm and he untied that also. Cautiously, he walked along the tracks that led from that spot, fifty paces and return, two paces to the right and out again. No rest until the area was searched as thoroughly as he was able. He found another birch and another elm, neither Silvanan, which he untied anyway for they were too close. Still he sensed that he was not finished. The singers had fallen silent but a whisper of expectation lingered in the night-washed air. He would not ask for assistance. They had helped him once, now it was his turn to repay the favour. His lantern spluttered into blackness, his oil flask was empty. Leaning against an upright but long dead elm he closed his eyes and sighed deeply. Somewhere, someone else sighed. He opened his eyes and stared around but could see nothing, even the few stars that crept out from the cloud-swathed sky could not penetrate the intertwined branches.

Never before had he struggled through the wildwood, but anxiety overwhelmed his instincts. He grazed his shin on the broken branch of a fallen elm, scratched his face on a low bough that crossed his path, slithered down a rough dip. Nettles flicked at his legs, briefly hot, brambles clawed at his clothes, ripping, snagging. Nevertheless, he persevered. He was nearly there.

Not one but three ash trees had been roped and marked, chosen to support Petron's new abode. All three were Silvanan. One was hardly broader than Elzandria's; he could encircle it fully within his arms. His sweet sister – could any man ever threaten her so? He wept as he untied the trees, relief and anger vying for precedence, the emotional turmoil adding to his exhaustion.

The Silvanii knew him, knew who he was, knew his tears flowed from his heart. He heard a whisper of a song, not the woodmaids'. The Silvanii were singing. The song did not stop his tears though their source had changed. He slid down to the ground and pressed his bloodied cheek against the cool bark. They sang him to sleep.

Sun-spangled, green-dappled light – Lesandor stirred and groaned. Beside him on the damp grass, seven coils of rope lay like so many serpents. It was early, too early for men so drunk last night to be up and abroad. Lesandor pushed himself upright. He bowed formally towards the three trees and moved slowly away. The woodmaids were close now, they danced around him, barely visible. They wanted him to join in their merriment but he was too sore, too tired.

"It is not settled yet," he told them firmly.

They only laughed at him and danced faster.

Chapter Three

WHEN PETRON'S CHOSEN wood cutters did arrive, they were somewhat surprised at the trees that had been selected. Nevertheless, obediently, they spent the morning cutting and carting, watched for some while by Lesandor who, finally satisfied, returned to the hold-house. Petron was still abed, unlike Mysha who was up and waiting anxiously for her husband. He smiled a little sheepishly as her hands flew to her face at the sight of him.

Lesandor stretched out on the bed. He wanted to be back in the woods to make certain nothing untoward occurred, wanted, equally, to be around when Petron finally surfaced and saw what he had apparently chosen last night.

Yasdon solved the problem for him. He had seen Mysha carrying a bowl of warm water, and salves and had come to see for himself what was amiss.

"I tripped and fell, I had no lantern...." Lesandor sat up and propped himself on one elbow, wincing as he did so. "You made me a promise yesterday, but a promise is nothing if it cannot be upheld."

"The trees," Yasdon guessed. "Yes. A promise I will keep."

"Enforce," Lesandor insisted. "The trees have to be guarded or they will be cut. Already anger is roused, mutterings on the wind – listen to the branches groan...." He smiled as Yasdon stepped away from him.

"I will send men straightaway," Yasdon promised.

Lesandor lay down again, laughing softly.

"Go to sleep," Mysha told him. Her tone was unusually brusque.

"Oh no, I want word the moment Petron steps from his room."

He dozed anyway, until a light kiss on his brow woke him. He knew it was not Mysha. Disorientated for a moment, he thought it was his mother. There was no one in the room. Only a delicate fragrance hung in the air and a final note, as of a song left behind, lingered. A terrible sense of loss washed over him for all that might have been yet could not be, for all that he had lost yet never possessed. He wanted to go home.

"He's up," Mysha announced as she stepped into their room. "Why did you want to see him? He doesn't look well. I shouldn't think he's in a very pleasant mood." Her good humour had returned.

"Thank you," Lesandor replied. "I am sorry if I worried you."

"So you should be."

He followed Petron discreetly. And Mysha followed him. Trisran was out at the site already, a look of relief on his face that he was trying very hard to hide. The voice of the chief carpenter could be clearly heard from some distance.

"Idiots! Buffoons! Do you mean to make a fool of me? What is the meaning of this?"

"We cut the marked trees, as we were directed." Wheedling tones, but the craftsman's wrath, not easily roused, neither was so easily assuaged.

"Those who marked them are the greater idiots then, but you still cut them. Rotten! Look! Knotted! See! And this – what use is this except for firewood?"

Trisran seemed to be having a serious choking attack. Petron took no heed but continued on to see what the commotion was about. Shortly afterwards the chief carpenter and two of his assistants walked out.

"I think I could eat some breakfast," Lesandor decided. He smiled warmly at Mysha, who shook her head as she linked her arm through his.

———

The atmosphere in the house of Windwood's holder was uneasy. Yasdon, hearing the tale of the tree cutting, was almost convinced that the Silvanii had replaced the ropes on the selected trees themselves. Mysha told Petron that he and his party must have been so inebriated that they believed the trees they chose were good when really they were useless; Petron retorted that somebody had played an elaborate practical joke – at his expense.

Finally, when they would not stop discussing the matter, Lesandor admitted that he had been responsible. "I apologise. I was very angry. Had I been thinking clearly, I would have marked something suitable for use. You would have had your timber."

"Your foolishness made a fool of me!" Petron raged.

"No, you made a fool of yourself. I saved you. That is the second time. Once more and you will have a heavy debt to pay, brother."

"You two make me so cross!" Mysha complained. "You promised me you'd be friends."

Petron scowled but said nothing. He was unsure whether Lesandor was serious, yet if the roles were reversed, if Lesandor owed him his life, Petron would call in the debt: two years of service.

Petron did not believe Lesandor had saved his life. But what he believed would not be held in much account if the matter ever came before a tribunal. He knew he would have to tread carefully.

In the days that followed, thinking to humour Lesandor, Petron asked him about the Silvanii, bemoaning his lack of knowledge and listening with apparent interest to whatever Lesandor would tell him. Not that he learnt overmuch. Although Lesandor answered all of his questions he volunteered little besides. Nevertheless, Petron was genuinely impressed. He even read a copy of *The Chronicles of Lincius, Prince of Morene* that Lesandor had found in the bottom of an old chest hidden away in a storage room. In the chest had been many other books, including a copy of Fabiom's first published collection of poetry. The books had since been removed and now were all safely in the small study Yasdon had given Lesandor for his own use.

"*... So the prince forsook the bustling town of Southernport for the wildwood, and came to live among the beech trees with Sulmarita, exchanging the River Gallant for the Fairwater. Still, a prince must be there for his people and so, on the high hill overlooking the Fairwater estuary, Lincius had a marble palace built and there he held court.*" Petron read aloud. "What sort of prince would chose to leave a comfortable town and live in the woods?" he asked. "Is this made up?"

"No," Lesandor replied. "The woods are as fine a dwelling as any mankind has built, especially in the summer. And he did build himself a splendid palace at Fairwater. You have been there. You should know?"

"How do you know I've been there?"

Lesandor smiled sadly, remembering a whispered conversation between himself and Raidan, hidden behind a serving screen, watching Yasdon and wondering what kind of man he was. Lesandor was still not too sure of the answer, though he agreed wholeheartedly with Raidan's assessment of Petron. That seemed like a lifetime ago. They had been boys then, thinking they had their whole future before them, instead Raidan had barely seen manhood before his life was cut short.

"Lesandor, what's wrong?" Mysha asked. She had been spinning slub silk and listening to the conversation with some interest.

"Nothing. Sorry, I was just thinking."

"Fairwater," Mysha reminded him.

"Oh, yes. Before I came here I was in Fairwater and your family came up in conversation, not surprisingly. It was mentioned that you had been to the city, that was all."

Petron looked thoughtful. "It was a great place," he agreed. "Much more to do there than here, that's for sure. But I don't understand. Where did this Sulmarita live, after Prince Lincius built his palace on the hill?"

"In the palace, with him. Where else?"

"But she – how could she? I mean they're not *real* are they – not substantial?"

Wary of Petron's motives, Lesandor had been volunteering little information besides what was asked of him. Only with that question did he realise the full extent of Petron's ignorance. He had promised Prince Ravik that he would try to improve the knowledge of Treelaw in Yasdon's family; perhaps now was the time to keep that promise.

"They become substantial if they choose to marry," he explained. "Once they make that choice they lose their ability to regenerate after the natural death of their tree. That is why they are very particular when they do decide to take a husband. But, having done so, they can go where they will within Morene while their partner lives, though they prefer to remain near their tree. So long as Lincius built within, say, a quarter day's

176

walk of Sulmarita's tree, she would have had no problem living with him. That is why all hold-houses are built near woods. The first holders were all wed to Silvanii."

"Were they?" Mysha asked.

Petron looked disbelieving.

It might have been the perfect opportunity to reveal the truth about his heritage. The problem was, he wanted to tell Mysha, but not Petron, and certainly not Yasdon. He had to choose; there was no way Mysha could keep that secret, nor could he think how to explain why he wanted her to.

"That is how the land was colonised," Lesandor said instead. "Expeditions set out from Southernport, where the first settlement was, some of them went inland and every once in a while a man married a Silvana and found himself staying near her tree. He would make his home there, bring any relatives he had and, in time, the land would be allotted to him. It is basic Morenian history. Surely.... Never mind. If you read on, Petron, you will find a lot of it is in there."

"It's a bit heavy," Petron complained, and Lesandor had to agree. Nevertheless, Petron did not put the book down and continued reading. Lesandor was rereading another old history book and Mysha was looking through one of the poetry collections but she soon got bored and left to go and see her donkey.

At last, Petron put the book aside. "You seem to know a lot about the Silvanii. And I had presumed you spent all your time in Deepvale practising archery!"

Lesandor glanced up briefly from the faded text. "My family have lived close by a Silvanan wood for so long and have been responsible for its maintenance. Such knowledge is vital. In Deepvale, we consider Treelaw an integral part of the holder's duty."

His comment drew no reaction, not that he had really expected it would.

Yasdon relieved Lesandor of the responsibility of overseeing the rest of the construction work. The craftsmen had been persuaded to return to their labours and Petron, on Lesandor's insistence, was under strictest orders not to interfere. Lesandor's new task – for Yasdon would not leave him idle – was to inspect and map the woodlands. The Lord Holder claimed he needed to know what timbers were available and what state the woods were in. He did not quite dare ask Lesandor to discover where the Silvanii might dwell but left it to him to mark the maps with a symbol to show what areas were unsuitable for cutting, for any reason.

Lesandor asked for Trisran's assistance and Petron, annoyed but unwilling to display the fact, agreed. Petron was well occupied anyway. His seventeenth birth anniversary approached and he intended to celebrate the occasion in style.

Since their first conversation on the subject, Mysha had persuaded Lesandor to read her more extracts regarding Silvanii from the poetry books he had found hidden away with the *Chronicles of Lincius*. Lesandor had been glad to do so, eager to encourage any burgeoning interest she might have in the Silvanii and she, realising how enthralled he was by the subject, began to think that having a Silvana around the house would entertain him. Equally, she believed that Petron would be eminently suitable as a spouse for one of the Tree Ladies. With that thought in mind she had encouraged Petron to read the books that Lesandor had discovered, and Petron found himself agreeing with her, though not for Lesandor's sake.

As Lesandor was away from the hold-house a great deal during that period, and with so much else happening, the subject never came up in his presence. So it was a great and awful surprise to him when, halfway through the feast marking the last day of Petron's boyhood, Petron suddenly announced that he was going to follow Prince Lincius's example. Lesandor stared at him, open-mouthed.

A cascade of vivid wine spilt over the brim of Yasdon's cup. "Is that wise?"

"No," Lesandor said quickly. "It is *not* wise. You are not prepared. You have been drinking, eating."

"If you were married to anyone but my sister, I would say you were jealous," Petron told him. "And if you are so concerned about me, come along and see for yourself that no harm will come to me."

"You are mocking," Lesandor said coldly. "Mock me. That I can take.

It is your day, have your jests. If you choose not to believe that the Silvanii dwell in your woods, that is up to you. Yet do not mock them. If you rouse their ire no one will aid you. You must know the consequences. This House...."

Petron interrupted him angrily. "Do you say I am not man enough? Perhaps you think you would have succeeded had you taken this path, but I will fail?"

"I did not say so."

"Maybe you *did* try. After all, you returned home to your Silvanan woods for *your* seventeenth birth anniversary. *Did* you try – and fail?"

"You would know if I had."

"Maybe, maybe not. They say the madness takes all sorts of forms!" Petron laughed loudly.

Yasdon glowered, but Lesandor laid a hand on his father-by-marriage's arm and shook his head.

"It is of no account," he said quietly.

"Come if you will." Petron rose from his couch. "Trisran!"

Lesandor glanced anxiously at Yasdon, who shrugged, confused. Yet there was a strange look in his eyes. Lesandor wondered if Yasdon was remembering how it was he had come to be Lord Holder of Windwood.

"He has the right to try," Yasdon reasoned, rather unexpectedly. "Will you not go with him, Lesandor? See he comes to no harm?"

"I cannot promise that!"

"I will not ask you to. Just do your best."

Lesandor feared that Yasdon expected that his best would always suffice, yet saw he had no option. It was not his place to decide another man's fate. Instead he determined that if Petron risked his life or his sanity, and that somehow he managed to save him, then he would call in the debt Petron would owe him.

"He'll be all right," Mysha declared cheerfully, as Lesandor gathered up a cloak and a lantern. "I think it would be most pleasant to have a Silvana in the house. Don't you, Father?"

Lesandor gave her a quick kiss on the cheek and left.

He did not hear Yasdon tell Petron, "I don't know why I didn't think of this for you. It is a splendid idea. Splendid."

179

Lesandor let Petron lead them. His first hope, that Petron would not be able to find his way to the wood's heart, was soon disappointed. In the days since the idea was put to him, Petron had read and reread any account he could find that so much as mentioned the Silvanii. Furthermore, he had gone to the woods and searched out what he took to be a possible site for a Dancing Glade.

As they set foot on the short grass at the edge of the glade, Lesandor knew that Petron had judged correctly. He touched Trisran's shoulder, and extinguished his lantern. Trisran followed suit.

Even when he was searching for the trees that Petron had marked for the axe, Lesandor had skirted the open spaces. Petron did not share his sense of respect.

"Petron, if you are set in this folly, you go on alone from here. We may not wait in the glade with you."

"Scared?" Petron mocked. "You can make that choice, but Trisran is mine to command and I want him with me."

"No!" Lesandor snapped. "And quench your fire."

"Trisran, come with me," Petron ordered, seemingly ignoring Lesandor, though a moment later his lantern was dark. "Satisfied?"

Trisran made to follow Petron into the middle of the clearing but Lesandor stayed him. "All right. Go if you must, but be careful. Remove your shoes, make certain Petron does likewise, and both of you wash. As soon as he settles, move away to the edge of the glade, right out of it if possible. Whatever you do, try to stay awake."

Trisran nodded, wide-eyed.

Lesandor squeezed his arm before releasing him. "Stay awake."

Through the gloom, Lesandor could just make out Trisran indicating the stream, and Petron sauntering over to perform the ritual ablutions. A moment later Trisran did likewise.

Having no idea how the Silvanii might react to Trisran's presence, Lesandor determined not to sleep. He cared more about saving Petron's servant than he did about saving Petron; except that it had occurred to him that the consequences might be almost as dire for him personally as they would be for Petron if he failed. Yasdon had risen to ascendancy in Windwood because of Giar. Would he expect Lesandor to forego

Deepvale, in favour of Windwood, if Petron was not able to be holder there? He saw again the strange look that had come into Yasdon's eyes when Petron had made his announcement, and a sickening horror came over him with the certain knowledge that Yasdon actually wanted Petron to fail.

Soon no sound came from the glade. Lesandor supposed Petron slept and hoped Trisran had taken his advice and moved away. Night deepened. Lesandor's eyes became heavy. In an effort to fight off the sensation, he stood up and walked around. He stopped in his tracks when he heard the nearing sound of light laughter and could not help the smile that came to his lips. Leaning against the tree beside him, which he judged to be a silver birch from the texture of the peeling bark, he waited, sleep far from him. The laughter ceased abruptly. He wondered if he should intervene before anything happened or if he should wait longer and see what developed. He was loath to trespass into the glade.

The Silvanii were close. He caught the scent of them on the night air. He could hear the slight sounds of their moving.

"*Lesandor.*" They had come upon him and he had not known.

"Ladies." He bowed.

"*No danger tonight, son of the woods. What brings you to our Dancing Glade?*"

He turned his head. He could not be certain but it seemed as if most of the Silvanii and their attendant woodmaids were gathered around two sleeping forms. So, Trisran had not moved away.

"They do," he said quietly. "My brother and his servant. I did not prevent their coming here tonight...."

"*So you claim responsibility for them?*"

Lesandor felt a tremor of fear shake him. "Yes," he whispered, barely audibly.

"*Then we must be gentle with them.*"

He was alone. A shuddering breath escaped him. He could make out nothing in the glade and, all of a sudden, his legs were a great weight. He forced himself to step forwards, to find a hollow among the tree roots. It was an ash tree he found. He slept.

Great splattering drops of rain fell from the leaves onto Lesandor's face, waking him to a new day. For a moment he could not think where he was or why he was there. A gentle song lingered in his mind and he remembered.

"Petron." His throat was dry and his voice would not carry. He brushed a branch aside, disorientated. The Dancing Glade was not before him. He turned. A gap between two trees revealed the sparkle of water beyond. Still disorientated, he knew at least that the stream flowed through the glade. He walked to the water, drank and washed his face, then stepped through the shallow flow and past a tangle of ivy to blink in the sudden light of the open space. Petron was lying face upwards, snoring, rain falling on him, wet through. Lesandor pushed him with his foot and Petron stirred.

"What...?"

"It is morning," Lesandor told him, looking around for Trisran, of whom there was no sign.

"He must have been coward," Petron said scornfully as he followed Lesandor's gaze. "Fled back to the safety of the hold-house no doubt."

"You might have done well to follow his example in that case," Lesandor retorted. "By the way – pleasant birth anniversary."

"Huh!" Petron groaned as he stumbled to the stream to wash his face. "I'm so stiff and my head aches. And I'm soaked. Why didn't you wake me as soon as it began to rain?"

Lesandor smiled despite his annoyance. "I too slept. I too am wet."

Petron glanced at him. "So you are. Let's go home. That was a total waste of time."

"Did you hear nothing last night?" Lesandor queried.

Petron shrugged in reply. "Not that I recall. I had strange dreams I think. There was nothing to hear, was there? Maybe the wind in the trees, maybe the rain falling. Nothing else." He clapped Lesandor on the shoulder. "Never mind. You can't be right about everything all the time – it would be unfair on the rest of us. Coming?"

"I shall catch up with you," Lesandor told him. Petron shrugged again and pushed his way out of the glade, headed for the track back home. Lesandor cocked his head on one side. He was certain he had heard the sound of woodmaids' laughter some way distant. It seemed to have come from the direction of the grove whose trees he had discovered marked for cutting by Petron's rabble. He wanted to visit the Silvanan trees anyway. He owed them a great debt of gratitude.

The sound of giggling was unmistakable. Soon Lesandor was caught up in a merry dance. He did not resist.

"So lucky," one told him.

"I know," he replied.

At least they were leading him in the direction he wanted to go. Eventually they stopped and, as he recovered his breath, he realised they were not alone. Trisran was there too, sound asleep and quite oblivious to the presence of the woodmaids. Lesandor was puzzled. Petron's servant slept beneath the branches of a splendid elm – once marked by Petron for destruction.

"Two born on one day." The woodmaids seemed to find that rather funny.

"His birth anniversary too?" Lesandor muttered, then began to laugh a great laugh and Trisran stirred.

The woodmaids melted into the undergrowth as Trisran sat up, rubbing his eyes and yawning.

"A good night?" Lesandor inquired.

Trisran looked at him for a long moment as if he did not know him, then, recognition slowly dawning, he nodded. "Music, I heard the most incredible music." He touched his temples. "It is still with me." He looked around him, confused. "This is not where we slept last night. Master Petron...."

"Has gone home, disgruntled." Lesandor felt a stab of envy but managed to disregard it. "Unlike you, he was not chosen. Nevertheless, he is unharmed."

Trisran had not heard the last sentence. "Chosen?" he whispered. He looked up at the towering tree above him where a cloud-shaped mass of delicate, pale green leaves was breaking out from oval brown buds, between pink bud scales.

"I suggest you make her a girdle of greenery. It is usual," Lesandor said nonchalantly.

Panic took hold of Trisran momentarily. "I don't know what to do, the form. How can I?"

"Easily," Lesandor told him. "You are fortunate. Be grateful. I know the way. If you want me to, I will help you. You do want to go through with this?"

Trisran nodded. "More than anything in the world."

"Yes," Lesandor replied.

Later, leaving behind a tree decked with woven fern fronds, Trisran began to fret about his position, and Petron's reaction.

"You hardly need worry about that," Lesandor told him. "You can walk away from there now. You will have a new life, your own life."

"If he lets me."

"How can he prevent you? He does not own you. You do not need any of them any more, you shall see."

Trisran's stomach rumbled loudly, making them both laugh.

"I'd forgotten how hungry I was," Trisran said as he rubbed his belly. "Normally I get to eat something after Petron has feasted, but he dragged us out here before I got a chance last night – not that I'm complaining."

"Ah!" Lesandor clapped him on the shoulder. "Another factor in your favour – Petron had not fasted, while you had – albeit unintentionally. I was wondering, for it is required."

"How is it you know so much about the, the Silvanii?" Trisran asked, looking back at the green woods behind them.

"Family, mostly," Lesandor replied. "And, the difference between Deepvale and this holding, I suppose. The lore of the wildwood has been deliberately suppressed here for, how many years? Thirty? More maybe. It must be that since the late Lord Herbis's son tried to win a Silvana as bride, and failed. It was him you saw that time, was it not?"

"I wasn't meant to see him; they keep him away somewhere. How do you know about him?"

Lesandor fingered the spiral-decorated band on his right arm. "My service here is payment, did you not know? Giar met his fate in Deepvale whilst staying with my father."

Trisran was staring at him. "That's terrible." Then his look changed. "But surely *you* could have won a bride from among them? You seem so close to the woods." He shook his head. "I'm sorry. It's none of my business."

"It is no matter." Lesandor rubbed his face and laughed self-disparagingly. "If you must know, my mother would not let me."

"Your mother?" Trisran repeated. "Because of what happened to Giar?"

"No. She had her own reasons. I would have argued, but she knows too much about such things for me to do so effectively."

They had emerged from the woods and Trisran was prevented from pursuing the conversation by the arrival of Mysha, who had come looking for Lesandor.

By the time they got back to the hold-house, Petron had washed and changed his clothes, and was busy telling everyone who would listen how stupid the exercise had been.

"Would you rather they had taken your mind?" Lesandor asked. "You sound as if you would have been better pleased with that outcome. Does it not occur to you that you might have been spared, as the trees were spared?"

"Ah, I see. Now you will say that you saved me. Three times. Now I owe you. Is that it? Let me tell you, Lesandor, last night proved you false. There are no Silvanii in Windwood, therefore you did not save me from their wrath before. I owe you nothing, nothing! You, I think, owe me an apology."

"I am sorry," Lesandor complied easily.

"No, that won't do. Tonight, in public, when all my guests are gathered, I will accept your apology. After that I will have the timber I selected for my new building. I shall see you later, at the party then." He began to laugh. "I think I *shall* have a pleasant birth anniversary, after all."

Petron had reckoned without Yasdon's intervention. However he felt about the fact that Petron had not met with any mishap, the Lord Holder was certainly relieved that he had failed to secure a Silvana for his bride. In no way did he share Mysha's view that it would be a fine thing to have a Silvana in the family. Furthermore, while Yasdon had no objection to keeping Petron content, especially on such a day as his coming-to-manhood, he would not do so at the cost of antagonising Lesandor.

Gambling on just that, Lesandor had gone to Yasdon before Petron could. Although he had no intention of making any apology, he told his father-by-marriage that he would publicly acclaim himself foolish, providing that the trees were unharmed. As Lesandor knew he would be, Yasdon was appalled. He forbade Lesandor to go to the party, let alone make a spectacle of himself for Petron's gratification. Furthermore, he promised he would ensure the trees' protection. Lesandor suggested a compromise.

Ten days would bring them to the Greening, a festival barely observed in Windwood but always a time of great celebration elsewhere in Morene. Lesandor knew that it must be revived in the holding if there was any chance Treelaw would ever be respected in Windwood again. That it should be, he knew was vital; his sojourn in Gerik had made that painfully clear. He told Yasdon that Prince Ravik would be celebrating in Fairwater, and even forced himself to mention how it would be the perfect time for a party. As he had hoped, the combination of those two ideas was sufficient to start Yasdon planning a grand celebration for Windwood.

Pleased, Lesandor promised that, so long as the trees were left alone, over the ten days he would convince Petron the woods were Silvanan. If he failed, Petron could have both his timber and his apology at the Greening celebration.

"I shall not fail," he concluded, so assured that Yasdon agreed to persuade Petron to accept those terms.

❧

Over the next ten days Yasdon was busy, alternately making plans for Festival and lamenting the fact that he was not brought up to be a holder and, consequently, had received no proper guidance with regards to how these thing should be done. Lesandor did most of the actual work for him. It would be the last time. Apart from anything else, whilst he was in Windwood and under Yasdon's almost obsessive supervision, it was impossible for him to even think about looking for Cuivah and her child.

Resolutely he decided that he was not going to worry about anything over the next few days. Preparing for the Greening was something he had always enjoyed and he was determined that it should be no less fun in Windwood than it would have been at home. Among the preparations were many things he and Mysha could do together, which was a relief, for it eased the sense of guilt that still gnawed away at him.

The apple trees and cherry trees were in full flower, ready for the festival, as were many smaller shrubs. Mysha cut fragrant sprigs of lilac and wych hazel from the garden and filled the house with sweet scents, while Lesandor gathered anemones and wove the flowers into garlands for her hair, feeling closer to her than he had done before, and seeing some hope in that. In the town, the streets were wreathed with spring greenery and ribboned ivy, and elaborate floats were prepared and dressed for a parade to mark the fourth and final day of the festivities.

The morning of the Greening saw Petron rise early from his bed. He met Lesandor coming down the hallway from his quarters.

"As we are apparently going to celebrate the Spring Festival properly this year, I've invited some of my friends to stay for supper. I trust you are planning to join us?"

Lesandor promised that he would be there.

The day went marvellously well and the weather could not have been kinder. Mysha performed the duties of Lady of the holding with grace, bequeathing small gifts to the children and presenting laurel wreaths to athletes, wrestlers and race winners. However, much as she enjoyed those moments, she became increasingly agitated as the day progressed. She blamed herself for giving Petron the idea that he should go to the woods on his birth eve. The thought of Lesandor having to apologise upset her as much as it did her father. More so, possibly, because she knew Petron would not be satisfied with that. Somehow he would find a way to belittle Lesandor further.

Lesandor was unperturbed. He had made some major decisions of his own but all he would say was, "Do not worry."

To which she replied, "But you're not doing anything!"

And to that he made no answer at all.

As evening drew in, and their invited guests began to make their way up to the hold-house from the festivities in the market square below, Mysha suggested to Lesandor that they should go away for a few days, maybe even visit his parents. He agreed that they would do just that, though he did not tell her he had already written to Fabiom and Casandrina with word that they would be arriving very soon, and staying.

"We shall go as soon as Festival is celebrated," he said, as gently as he could.

She stepped back. "I hope you don't expect me to be at this gathering tonight!" she said, her eyes overflowing with angry tears.

"Oh, but I do, Mysha," he replied, wiping her cheek, pleased to see the spark of spirit she exhibited. "You *and* your father. You will not desert me now, surely?"

Early in the evening, Petron called for Trisran. His servant did not come. Petron cursed him for a lazy good-for-nothing, threatening harsh rewards if he did not show soon.

"He will be here," Lesandor promised. "He is busy at present."

Petron scowled but had no time to reply, with yet more guests arriving. Finally one of Petron's friends asked what was the special 'happening' that Petron had been mysteriously hinting at for the past few days.

Petron looked towards Lesandor, who replied, "Tonight you will witness something that no one in this house ever expected to see." At which Petron laughed.

"Spoken truly, Lesandor," he replied.

They had eaten and some, as usual, had drunk to excess when the gatekeeper entered and announced that the last light of day had faded. Petron rose from his place and raised his cup to Lesandor.

"Speech!" he called loudly.

Mysha clutched at Lesandor's arm. He patted her hand and unwound her fingers. On his other side Yasdon was attempting to get very drunk. Lesandor got to his feet.

"Friends," he began. He looked around the room from face to face, focussing on those whom he knew to be real friends. Some grinned at him encouragingly, others looked away nervously. "Tonight is an occasion for celebration: a wedding."

"What!" Petron spluttered.

"Your – foster brother – Trisran, is recently married. It is only right that we mark the event properly."

"Foster brother!"

Trisran walked through the doorway, though no one but the most intimate with the family would have recognised him as Petron's servant, dressed as he was in Lesandor's finest tunic. Even those who knew him hardly saw him. They had eyes only for the girl at his side. Lesandor stepped towards the couple.

"Congratulations," he murmured. She was truly lovely. For a moment he had to look away to compose himself.

"Lesandor, may I introduce my, uh, wife, Dulcissa," Trisran said formally. "Dulcissa, this is my good friend –"

She held out her hands. "I know Lesandor," she said softly. "He saved my tree."

Petron had stepped forwards and Yasdon had risen unsteadily to his feet.

"I believe Master Petron has something to say regarding the woods," Lesandor said, just loud enough for all to hear.

In contrast to most of the other revellers, Petron did not particularly enjoy the rest of the night. As for Yasdon, he was barely aware of what was going on.

Mysha was confused, and Lesandor promised to explain everything when they were alone. They would have plenty of time; it would be late the next day before either Yasdon or Petron was able to join in a sensible discussion.

A new dawn was already colouring the sky when Lesandor closed the door of their bedchamber. Mysha began to unbraid her hair. "She looked like a, like a – person. A woman. She is beautiful, of course, and graceful, but I wouldn't have known that she wasn't a real person – had I seen her elsewhere. Although the men all stared at her. I *did* notice that."

Taking her brush from her hand, Lesandor ignored his wife's final comment and began brushing her hair. "Of course she looks like a real woman –"

"She's exactly the same height as Trisran, did you notice that? How strange."

"Yes, yes it is." He had not realised that a corporeal Silvana's height was dependent upon her husband's, though he had been suspicious when he had met Prince Pharrell's Luthrina. That Dulcissa, like Luthrina, and like his own mother, was exactly the height of her husband confirmed his notion.

"Her hair is an unusual colour, I suppose," Mysha said, "Though not so strange that you would realise what she was. And her eyes, such a lovely shade of bright green. Are there others? Could I have met a Silvana without realising? What a strange thought."

As she gave him little chance to answer any of her questions, he did not feel too bad about not doing so.

"Mysha – there is something I have wanted to tell you for some time –"

"They won't live here with us, will they? I know I said it would be nice to have a Silvana in the family, but I'm not so sure now. I was actually a bit scared when I realised what she was. I'm sorry, what were you saying?"

He put the brush down. "Nothing. It can wait. It has been a long day. Come to bed."

As Lesandor had expected, the following day began late – closer to noon than to dawn. In the dining room, Petron paced up and down, refusing to look at Trisran or Dulcissa, especially Dulcissa. Lesandor had invited them to join the family for breakfast.

"What do you want from me?" Petron demanded at last.

Lesandor grinned and leant back on his couch.

Yasdon, nursing a serious headache, looked at his daughter's husband appealingly.

"This is a grave matter. If you claim him bound to you for thrice saving him, it would have to go before a tribunal. Think of the shame, Lesandor, think of me."

At Yasdon's words, Petron looked down at the ground. Heir to a grand holding, beholden for his life. His arrogance disappeared utterly.

Lesandor stared at Yasdon in amazement, and somehow managed to stop himself saying anything other than, "I came here bound in service. Are you suggesting *my* father is shamed by that?"

"Not at all. Of course not. But your situation is different."

"How so?"

"You know!" Yasdon said, not wanting to go into that matter in any detail. "It had nothing directly to do with *you*."

"But it had to do with Fabiom," Lesandor pointed out. "He was holder when Herbis's son took it into his head to present himself to the Silvanii on his birth eve, unprepared though he was." He glanced at Petron who was staring at him belligerently. Petron looked away as soon as Lesandor's eyes met his. "Giar's demise brought you and your family to the position you are in today; and me here in service. Can I not expect the same justice to apply, now that the circumstances are reversed?"

"Please, Lesandor, there must be an alternative. You know I will give you anything you desire, anything, but please not that."

Lesandor nodded, once. He guessed that Yasdon's concern was more for himself than for Petron. Two years in Deepvale would do Petron no harm at all; indeed, would probably achieve what Yasdon claimed he wanted for his son – that he should learn to conduct himself in a manner fitting his birth and position. But before that happened, Yasdon would have to go before the Assembly and explain how come he had let the matter get so far, how the Silvanii had been insulted, how he knew nothing of Treelaw and was holding Windwood on a pretence and bringing up his heir in ignorance.

"There is one thing I want, and that is freedom for Trisran. You have repaid him badly, Petron. You owed him much, he owed you nothing, yet he has been your virtual slave. Does it really surprise you that the Silvanii chose him and not you?"

Yasdon managed to look relieved and uneasy at once. "I am as much to blame. No, more so. I told myself we were generous with you, Trisran, when we were not. You have worked these years with no thanks, no wages. I will make that up to you. Lesandor?"

191

"On that matter I am satisfied. Providing you agree he owes you no formal service either. That has been more than discharged over the years. As for the other – there *is* one thing I would ask of you, Lord Yasdon...."

"Anything, anything," Yasdon agreed.

"Thank you. Then tomorrow Mysha and I leave for Deepvale."

Yasdon took a breath, as if to say something, then let it out again in a long sigh and simply nodded his head.

Mysha poured Lesandor a beaker of fruit juice and handed it to him, smiling at him adoringly, delighted with the way things had turned out.

Within moments, Yasdon had composed himself again. "Tell me, Lesandor, how is it you know so much about the woods?"

Dulcissa laughed merrily at the question. "Naturally Lesandor understands –" she began.

Almost imperceptibly he shook his head.

She laughed again and finished simply, "He is very perceptive."

Lesandor saw a startled realisation dawn in Trisran's eyes and knew that he understood what Dulcissa had not said.

It was not until Lesandor found Trisran and Dulcissa to say farewell, and no one else was within hearing, that Trisran said, "Once you suggested I should meet your mother. I'm sorry I can't on this occasion."

Lesandor clasped his shoulder. "So am I, especially as Lord Yasdon has decided that he will come to Deepvale with Mysha and me. That was not my intention. I could do with some support."

"I, too, am sorry to miss your mother's first meeting with Lord Yasdon." Dulcissa's eyes sparkled.

Lesandor grinned wryly. "Time has passed. I think she might be reconciled to my situation by now," he suggested.

"Are you?" the Silvana asked.

Lesandor shrugged.

"So what makes you think Casandrina will be?" she inquired.

Lesandor tried not to consider the question too hard. "Despite that problem, I am just pleased to be going home at last."

Home, with his parents and his sister, with the fading memory of dreams and the lingering images of a blissful childhood.

"Be happy," he told Trisran and Dulcissa, though they would hardly need any prompting. Yet, as he walked away, Dulcissa looked after him with sad eyes.

"His sorrow runs deep. If he were my son I would not easily forgive."

Chapter Four

YASDON NEVER WENT anywhere in anything but the grandest style, with curtain-draped litters and a large entourage of servants and guards. Lesandor remembered Yasdon's arrival in Fairwater, the first time he had seen him, the memory bittersweet.

For the journey to Deepvale, Yasdon took special pains. Consequently he was very put out when Lesandor blankly refused to ride in the splendid litter that had been prepared for him. He was more put out still when Mysha also chose to forgo her normal mode of transport for much of the journey. Mysha opted to ride one of the pack donkeys instead – having guessed, correctly, that Lesandor would prefer to walk, which he did, leading the donkey, pointing out any interesting plants and small creatures that they encountered and telling her about the places they passed through. When he wanted a rest, and if Yasdon was not looking, Lesandor would ride on one of the donkey carts laden with their luggage. In fact, apart from Yasdon, only Petron rode all the way in style, in a litter carried by four servants, though, being in a foul humour, he travelled for the most part with the curtains drawn.

All the way home, Lesandor was painfully aware how every step was taking him further from Rushford and the promise he had made to Raidan. The only consolation was that, if he could get Mysha settled in Deepvale, he would be able to return alone and take whatever time he needed to find Raidan's family. When not worrying about Cuivah, he brooded on how his mother might react to Yasdon. The nearer they got to Deepvale, the more convinced he became that he had made a terrible mistake in allowing his father-by-marriage to come. Not that Yasdon could have been prevented. He had been quite determined and, by the time they had actually left Windwood, he had seemed convinced that the visit was his own idea. The fact that it had taken them three days to prepare for the journey, rather than the one that Lesandor had intended, gave the holder plenty of time to come to that conclusion.

Petron's inclusion in the party had surprised Lesandor and Petron equally. Now that he had reached manhood, Petron should have remained in Windwood to deputise in his father's absence, and Lesandor guessed that was exactly the reason he had not been left. Such thoughts made him anxious to get home and discuss his fears about Yasdon with his own father. At the same time, he could not help wondering what was going to happen when Petron was called upon for service, for then it was certain to come out that he had received no tuition in Treelaw and was totally unprepared for the role he would eventually inherit.

Every worry went out of Lesandor's head the moment they crossed the boundary between Alderbridge and Deepvale, for all he could think about was being home.

They refreshed themselves at the hostelry in Watersmeet, where Yasdon suggested they stay for the night and continue their journey in the morning. When he saw how weary Mysha looked, Lesandor agreed, though he had been eager to press on. Without telling Yasdon, he sent a message on with one of the servants – to let his parents know they would be arriving on the morrow and that the party was considerably larger than had been expected.

Letter sent, Lesandor opened the shutters of the room they had been given in the hostelry. Outside the window, the trees were bursting into bloom. He could feel the wildwood calling him and realised that, had they left when he intended, there was a good chance that Fabiom and Casandrina would not have been home to greet them. The Greening brought out the wilder aspect of his mother and caused her to abandon the hold-house to spend several days and nights in the wildwood. But she and his father would be home by now. Lesandor knew he could no longer put off the inevitable. Tomorrow he would have to explain to Mysha what he had been keeping from her all this time.

Fabiom received Lesandor's message, and spent the remaining time it took Yasdon's party to reach the hold-house trying to elicit a promise from Casandrina that she would do nothing untoward to any of their visitors.

"While they are our guests," she eventually agreed. Her expression suggesting that as soon as circumstances altered in that regard she would be bound by no other restraints.

Fabiom could not argue with her, for even when she refused his requests she would smile at him gently, as if to ask his pardon, and he would be defeated.

When the travellers arrived, Casandrina met them at the door of the conservatory. She welcomed Yasdon cooly yet courteously and he, quite overcome, replied with equal grace.

Lesandor cautiously wondered if his fears might be unfounded. He introduced Mysha, and Casandrina greeted her with a kiss, then disconcerted her completely by taking Mysha's arm and holding out her other hand to Lesandor saying, "Come, children –" before leading them through to the heart room.

"Is that your sister?" Mysha asked, as Casandrina moved through to the courtyard beyond. "She's very tall, isn't she? She's very beautiful."

"Are your parents not at home?" Yasdon whispered to Lesandor at the same time.

They rinsed their hands in the basin. Lesandor acknowledged the four main doors of his home before nodding towards Calbrin – who was standing nearby with an armful of clean towels – and replying: "Our house-steward said Father had to go out briefly. He should be back shortly."

"And your mother?"

Calbrin grinned as Lesandor caught his eye.

While they were talking, Petron had gone through and was sitting with Casandrina. Lesandor could see his mother assessing the young man very carefully. She seemed in no way antagonistic towards him.

"I'd like to show you around the house, if you are not too tired," Lesandor said to Mysha.

"But when do we meet your mother?" she asked, echoing her father. "I hope she likes me," she added, before he had a chance to reply.

"Mother is waiting for us in the courtyard," Lesandor said. "Perhaps, Lord Yasdon, you would like to join her there. Calbrin will bring refreshments."

Petron was coming towards them, shaking his head. Lesandor could not read the expression on his face and presumed he was very angry, until Petron started to laugh.

"It seems I have been a greater fool than I thought," he admitted. "For what it's worth – I am truly sorry." Awkwardly he held out his hand and Lesandor grasped his arm without hesitation.

"Thank you, and welcome to my home." He turned to Yasdon and Mysha, to tell them what Petron had already discovered. "The Lady Casandrina is a Silvana, and my mother."

When Fabiom returned soon after, he found them discussing the bathing pools, which Mysha had seen with Lesandor and had been enthusing about to her father and Petron. Everyone seemed relaxed, and when Fabiom suggested they might spend the evening enjoying the water, the idea met with complete approval. Like Lesandor, he hoped his fears about this visit had been groundless, and that it might even go well. He tried to ignore the expressions on the faces of the various woodmaids around the house, who all seemed highly amused by the goings-on. A long time ago, Fabiom had learnt that this was not a good sign.

The day ended early, while the colours of the setting sun still tinted the sky, for the travellers were weary, Mysha especially. Yasdon was given the main guest room and Petron the tree-decorated room that had formerly been Lesandor's. Lesandor might have had some misgivings about that, until he discovered that Casandrina had decorated and furnished the second large suite of rooms for him and Mysha.

Illuminated with a multitude of beeswax candles, and strewn with scented flowers and herbs, the candle-bright, honey-perfumed chambers delighted Mysha, unlike the revelation about Lesandor's background. As she explored the rooms, she berated him for having kept such a secret, and repeatedly asked him why. He had no honest answer that would not have been hurtful, so he simply apologised and agreed that he should have told her. She was so tired, he doubted she had the energy to argue with him.

"You must promise to tell me everything, tomorrow," she insisted, as she settled down in the velvet-draped bed. She was asleep before he could do so.

Over the days that followed, Lesandor and Petron tentatively began to get to know each other as if anew. The bathing room proved helpful, for they both enjoyed the water and it was too early in the year to brave the river. They explored the holding, visiting family friends as they went, and, as Petron had once mocked, partook of daily archery sessions. They spent a fair amount of time in the library too, and Lesandor gave Petron a belated birth anniversary gift: a copy of *Tales of a Woodsman*, his own favourite book and one which he hoped would encourage the younger man to try to find out for himself what others had failed to teach him.

Meanwhile, Mysha became acquainted with her mother-by-marriage. Mysha had enjoyed very little female company before then and, to her own surprise, took a great liking to the Silvana, though she found it hard to accept that Casandrina was really old enough to be her husband's mother.

On the third day of the visit, Lesandor was summoned to his father's study. Casandrina was sitting on the window seat, her legs tucked beneath her, gazing down on the river shimmering in the valley below. She turned to smile at her son as he opened the door. Fabiom, who was propped on the edge of his desk, indicated that Lesandor should shut the door behind him.

"Prince Ravik is coming to stay awhile," Fabiom said, nodding towards a scroll on his desktop, marked with the royal seal. "He should arrive this evening."

"Today?" Lesandor said amazed. "Have you not just received that?"

He had seen a courier come from the direction of the town earlier, though he had taken little notice at the time.

"Apparently Ravik intended going to Windwood. When he heard that you were here he changed his plans."

"Perhaps he wants the remainder of my service, though he would hardly come in person to tell me so," Lesandor mused. "Does his letter give any indication?"

"Nothing," Fabiom replied, unrolling it again and reading through quickly. "Just that he is looking forward to seeing us, and hopes Masgor will be able to spare him some more time."

Lesandor chuckled at that. "Masgor will be more than pleased, I would guess."

"Don't say anything to him," Fabiom requested. "Nor to anyone else. I would have our prince's arrival come as a surprise to Yasdon, and see his reaction. I am not at all happy about what you have told me of his attitude towards you. And you are right about Petron – the boy is barely tutored, almost as if Yasdon never intended the holding should pass to him. It has to be more than some preference he has for his daughter over his son, for it would seem that Petron's faults are mainly of Yasdon's making."

"Yasdon told me that Petron's mother died at his birth. Perhaps he blames Petron for that," Lesandor conjectured.

"It's possible," Fabiom agreed, though doubtfully. "Yet if he really was intent on his inheritance passing through Mysha, it seems absurd that he should purposely contrive to marry her to the heir of another holding. A younger son of a High House would have been a far more sensible choice."

"I know," Lesandor said, with a deep sigh. "I keep thinking about it, but I have no answers, except that I am sure he means to disinherit Petron, if he can. It would make more sense if our two holdings were adjacent."

Fabiom grunted. "If that had been the case, it would have been through force, not marriage, that the matters between us were resolved."

Casandrina had been looking from her husband to her son quizzically.

"Petron is not Yasdon's son," she said at last. "Did neither of you know that?"

199

Prince Ravik arrived at sundown. His entourage was barely half that which had accompanied Yasdon, which was just as well, for accommodation was stretched as it was.

Fabiom was not disappointed by Yasdon's reaction to the royal visit. Windwood's holder appeared distinctly uncomfortable when the prince walked through the door of the day room, unannounced.

Only pleasantries and small talk followed, while they waited to go through to the dining room. Little by little, Yasdon relaxed, and was soon back in good humour, laughing easily, as was his wont.

His jollity did not last.

The woodmaids had spent most of the day preparing a banquet of all their own favourite foods. Yasdon, seeing what was being served, was appalled, and took Lesandor aside to say so.

"Your father can't treat the Ruling Prince this way. Where are the roast meats, where are the rare fruits from far-away places? He will expect the best."

"Prince Ravik has been visiting this house from long before I was born, Lord Yasdon. He has not complained yet. I think Father would know if his Highness was displeased, don't you?" He would also have said that if anyone, even the Ruling Prince, turned up at such short notice then what should they expect? Except he knew Yasdon's larders were always filled to overflowing with sumptuous and exotic foods.

At Ravik's request, the woodmaids sang and played for them while they ate. The food was plentiful and the meal went on for a long time. Heady wines and sweet morat flowed freely, and even Yasdon had to agree it was a great success – once he saw how the prince enjoyed himself.

When the main dishes had been cleared away and only soft cheeses and dainties were left to be passed around, Ravik stood up from his place and strolled over to one of the candle-lit alcoves where he had earlier left some papers. All eyes were on him as he leant against the wall and untied a scroll. He fastened his gaze on Lesandor's face for a long moment then he began to read.

"*Regarding the Grand Holding of Southernport. In this, the 40th year of the Rule of Ravik, son of Darseus, the holdership of Southernport has been confiscated from its previous Mistress, namely the Princess Jaymna,*

in view of her admitted culpability for the death of Prince Raidan. The
Grand Holding of Southernport will hereby be held vicariously on behalf
of Prince Raidan, until such time as it can be passed on to its new holder
– who will be the second heir of Lesandor of Deepvale, in recognition of his
friendship with Prince Raidan and of the harms done against his person
by said Princess Jaymna."

A stunned silence followed his reading, until Lesandor rose and went
to Ravik and bowed formally. Ravik handed him the scroll, then smiled
across the room at Mysha.

"Now you two need to produce two strong heirs: one for Deepvale
and a second for Southernport. Consider that a royal commission!" His
eyes had left Mysha's face and were focussed on Yasdon.

"We shall do our best, my lord," Lesandor replied with an easy laugh,
while Mysha blushed, terribly embarrassed until Casandrina took her
hand and squeezed it gently.

Lesandor knew this was definitely not the time to inform the prince
that Raidan had fathered a child – to whom Southernport could be
handed down if his or her mother's ancestry could be set aside. Rather,
he wished he had thought of a way to tell him before now, wished even
more fervently that he had managed to find Raidan's family. So far, every
trail had led him to a dead end.

"The details are not fully drawn up," Ravik was saying, bringing
Lesandor back to the moment. "However, there will not be one vice-
holder but several, and I will be asking you to be part of that curating
body, both on Raidan's behalf and for your unborn child. Should you
produce just one heir, then Southernport will be passed to his or her
second child." Briefly Ravik glanced again at Yasdon and frowned. "It's
poor compensation," he added, so that only Lesandor heard him. Still
speaking quietly he said, "It seems something he ate is not agreeing too
well with your father-by-marriage."

Lesandor glanced over his shoulder; Yasdon's face was a curious shade
of red and he was making a small, strange noise.

"Is he furious or delighted?" he wondered, equally quietly.

"I suspect we shall find out soon enough," Ravik replied. "Ah, Fabiom,
is that the very special wine that you have been keeping back from me

until now? I hear these things from Yan, you know."

Fabiom chuckled. "I shall have to have words with my cousin!" He poured the wine himself. "As this is the best Deepvale has yet produced, it seems fitting to drink it on such an occasion."

Petron waylaid Lesandor later, as Lesandor was leaving the hold-house for a nocturnal stroll.

"You never wanted Windwood, did you? That was a lie."

"I never said I did!" Lesandor protested. "All I want is to be here, at home. As far as I am concerned, my service with your ... with Windwood is finished, and Mysha and I will be staying in Deepvale."

"No, not your lie. His. He has gone to see Prince Ravik, you know. To protest. He will say that Deepvale owes Windwood an heir. Your first-born too, that's the least he'll settle for. He would have let you go home before now if you'd given him a grandson, not that he'd have let the child go with you."

"Petron. I do not know what you are talking about! Truly, I did not know about any of this. I have been trying to work out what is going on. Does Mysha know? Is she involved?"

"Mysha?" Petron snorted derisively. "She knows, I suppose, but she's not *involved*."

"Would she have left a child behind?"

"Would you?"

"No, of course not. But that is not relevant now is it? What about *your* claim to the holding?" Petron's look of bewilderment prompted Lesandor to take his arm and lead him back inside. "Let us get this sorted out, once and for all time," he suggested.

As Petron had guessed, Yasdon had demanded an immediate audience with Prince Ravik, claiming Lesandor and Mysha's first-born child to be heir to Windwood, citing Petron's intentions of damaging Silvanan woodlands and his recent insult-laden attempt to win a Silvana as wife, as proof positive that he was not fit to be considered for the position. He claimed he could no longer overlook the boy's failings just because of their blood ties. Ravik listened without comment, then asked Yasdon if he would mind Fabiom joining them, for this claim affected Fabiom as much as anyone.

Yasdon had no objection. He had been perturbed at Ravik's unexpected arrival, even more by the pronouncement made after the meal. Now it occurred to him that, with a little ingenuity, there was no reason why he should not achieve his aim of the past two years.

"It's quite simple," he said smoothly, the moment Fabiom entered the room and shut the door. "As I see it – you denied Windwood an heir, twice over. Now, I am not complaining for my own sake. I have done my duty by taking on the mantle of holder, and I do not deny that I have enjoyed the benefits. However, that does not change the facts. You were betrothed to the daughter of Windwood's holder. Had you honoured that, your son and hers would have inherited the holding."

"How can Fabiom be held responsible? It's not as if Herbis's daughter never married," Ravik pointed out. "What difference would it have made who she was married to? You have said that she was wed for thirteen years and in all that time she had no children."

"Oh, but she did have a child," Fabiom said. "Petron is Dala's son. Is that not so, Yasdon? By my calculations, he must have been born shortly after Lord Herbis died. Herbis may not have known he had a grandson but the boy is the true and just heir of Windwood nevertheless."

Ravik turned and looked at him, amazed. "Are you certain?"

"Casandrina is. She met Dala here once. It was a number of years ago but she recognised Petron as Dala's son immediately." Fabiom had no need to say more.

Yasdon spluttered a sharp denial, and Ravik was just considering the implications of Fabiom's words, when Lesandor knocked on the door of the study. Fabiom, the nearest, opened it and let him and Petron in. Yasdon looked away, scowling.

Petron did, at least, have enough manners to wait for permission to speak from the prince. When Ravik indicated that he should do so, Petron drew a deep breath.

"I don't understand a thing that's going on," he admitted. "I have just two questions: Who were my parents? And what happened to them?"

Ravik glanced at Fabiom, equally curious.

"Your father was a member of the Assembly. He was a lawyer and his name was Lambrose. Your mother was Lord Herbis's daughter, Dala. They were good people," Fabiom answered.

Petron turned to Yasdon. "Is this true?"

"Be careful, Yasdon," Ravik warned.

"Yes, yes, it's true!" he snarled. "Are you all satisfied now? It was mine. It was all mine. My uncle had said so on his deathbed. His daughter, Dala, wanted no part of it. She had a life of her own, away from the holding. Then her husband died in a stupid accident, a fall from a cliff, and she came back to see her mother with the news that after thirteen years, and having given up any hope of a child, she was pregnant. I was supposed to be going to my inauguration that very month. Instead she comes to see me with the news that she is not prepared to give up her claim after all. I accepted that. Not graciously I will admit, but what choice? Then there was another outbreak of fever. Dala took ill, so did my own wife who was also with child, both of them gave birth and both died – weakened by the birthing, the physician said. Dala's son was healthy and strong, unlike the boy my wife had. He died. No one else knew, and I realised how easy it would be to swap them in their cradles. So I did. There was a kitchen girl to nurse the child and no one asked any questions."

"And because of the fever and the loss of your wife you were excused from coming to Fairwater for quite some while. By the time you did, everyone accepted that Petron was your son," Ravik finished for him.

Petron stared at the man he had always believed was his father, but Yasdon would not meet his gaze.

"What now?" Lesandor asked.

"Now it is time for you to finish your service," Ravik said, unexpectedly. "Your debt to Windwood can be considered paid. As I understand it, there is only about one month outstanding anyway. As for you, Petron, I think it's time you began *your* service. For now, you can come to Fairwater with Lesandor. After that, we shall see."

He looked at Yasdon for a long moment. "I cannot take the holding from you, especially as there is no one who has been prepared to take it on. It was granted to you by my hand, and so it must remain – on one condition: you will come to Fairwater in exactly one half a year, and you will prove, before the Assembly, that you have a full and thorough knowledge of Treelaw and of the duties and responsibilities of a holder. Furthermore, once I am satisfied that he has the ability to take on the task when the time comes, you will formally declare Petron your heir."

Yasdon bowed his head. There was silence until, eventually, he looked up.

"I have no right to expect anything, from any of you, yet there is one thing I must ask...."

"Ask," Ravik said tersely.

"My daughter, Mysha, she does not have to be told any of this, does she? If I do your bidding, if I come to Fairwater and present myself to the Assembly."

"Of course she has to be told!" Petron snapped, but Lesandor shook his head.

"I would rather she was not, not yet anyway," he said carefully. "She would take it very hard. She is fond of you, Petron. She knows and loves you as her brother, and you know how much she cares for Yasdon. What would be gained by telling her in anger?"

Petron stood irresolute, his lips tight, until Fabiom touched his shoulder.

"This is the first opportunity you have been given to choose how you will act, knowing who you are and assured of your inheritance," he said gently.

Petron nodded. "Very well," he agreed. "I have no reason to wish her anything but good. I will say nothing, nor do anything that will make her suspect, until you deem it a fit time. You have my word."

Early on the evening of the sixth day, Yasdon, lounging over the remnants of dinner, sighed mournfully.

"I am more than sorry this sojourn cannot be prolonged, alas I have, um – business – I cannot put off, but I trust I may call upon you again."

"Whenever you wish, Lord Yasdon." Casandrina smiled sweetly. "I have a favour to ask of you meanwhile. You have had my son living in your house for quite some time, will you not return the gift and leave your daughter with me now?"

Mysha was delighted at the prospect. "May I stay, please, Father?" she implored. "I know you wanted me to come home with you, but Lesandor and Petron will be away, and you will be so busy, you said so yourself. I will be quite lonely in Windwood."

Yasdon was about to object until he felt Ravik's eyes on him. He glanced at the prince, who gave a slight nod and Yasdon sighed again.

"All of you leaving me! Ah, but you are right, Mysha, you will be lonely. And you, dear lady," he addressed Casandrina. "You speak truly. I have monopolised your son's time. I would be delighted that Mysha should get to know you better."

After the meal, Fabiom and Casandrina strolled arm in arm through the garden, leaving their guests to their own amusements. Casandrina sang quietly as she walked. For once her voice did little to soothe her husband.

"You are worried," she said reproachfully. "What do you think I would do to Mysha?"

"I – I don't know," he admitted. "I don't understand. What *are* you going to do?"

"Look after Lesandor's rather childish wife, for she needs looking after."

"And Yasdon?"

"Can go his way. He has been punished and now Mysha is more important." She watched Lesandor nock an arrow into his bow and aim at a distant target. "I wonder if he will ever again be truly happy."

Lesandor loosed the arrow but it flew far off its mark, for he had seen Elzandria at the edge of the woods, just across the bridge.

"Explain please," Fabiom asked, wrapping both arms around her. "You are not annoyed with me, are you? I did not really doubt you."

"You did. Yet I forgive you. Mysha is with child. She does not know it so, naturally, neither does Lesandor. She *should* know, but she had no mother to bring her up and Yasdon neglected much of her education." She kissed Fabiom's cheek. "Come midwinter, you will have a grandson and a new heir."

"A child that needs be kept out of Yasdon's clutches. Then it's well that her staying with us is settled. And maybe Lesandor will find happiness, after all," Fabiom mused, fondly watching his son and daughter laughing together.

Casandrina rested her head on his shoulder. "Not only that. I would keep Mysha here. Lesandor will be away and who would look after her in Windwood? Yasdon is hopeless. She is not strong. I would not have her travelling back that distance, even if her father *could* be trusted to give up both her and the babe upon Lesandor's return from Fairwater."

Chapter Five

AT BUNCHES OF grapes hung heavy on the vines which smothered the trellises, their dense foliage affording welcome shade from the afternoon sun. From their vantage point on the highest terrace of the vineyard, Mysha and Kita watched a liveried courier climb the hill to the hold-house. They saw him through the tunnel of leaves and fruit that looked out over the countryside and, as they ate honey-sweetened bread and soft cheese, they wondered indifferently what he brought. Kita's three children ran and played meanwhile, hiding from each other among the vines and calling out when they were discovered.

Mysha had flourished in the months she had lived in Deepvale, and had found an unlikely friend in Kita who also, and quite unexpectedly, was with child. The two women could hardly have been more different and yet they enjoyed each other's company in a quiet way and planned for the arrival of their babies, due in the depths of the winter.

"Maybe he brings word that Lesandor is coming home again," Kita suggested as the courier was lost from sight behind the white facade of the garden wall of Deepvale's hold-house. "He seems to manage to get leave often enough." And she laughed lightly, remembering Lesandor's last visit – when he seemed to think that Mysha should do nothing but sit with her feet up. "If he could see you now!"

"I've never felt healthier," Mysha agreed, gazing down along the path that wound through the terraces, the way they had come earlier.

"Mama, Mama! Tobi's fallen and cut his knee," shouted Tobias's twin, Tomis. "Mama, it's bleeding."

"This is what you have to look forward to!" Kita sighed. "I'm coming, sweetheart."

The damage was not great but it warranted packing away the picnic and making their way down the slope to the farm buildings, where clean water and salves were to be found. Darseus, the farm manager, and the seven-year-old twins' hero on account of his ability to wrestle anyone and win, dressed the wounded knee.

"That should see you all right, young man," Darseus said, then sat back on his heels and looked up at Mysha. "I was near forgetting, Mistress. Lady Casandrina sent word that, should anyone see you, would they ask you to go home. Seems there's a message come for you from your father."

The letter was short and vague, inquiring after Mysha's health, promising gifts for the baby, mentioning that he had heard from neither Lesandor nor Petron and trusted they were both well. Mysha read it twice, a frown creasing her brow all the while.

"There is something untoward?" Casandrina asked. "What does he say?"

"He doesn't – that's what's bothering me. This is very unlike Father." Mysha read the letter again, aloud this time, for Casandrina to hear.

"He's usually so full of schemes and plans and all sorts. He sounds sad, doesn't he? It's almost as if he's asking me to visit, but doesn't like to, because of me being the way I am." She smiled and rested her hands over her child. "Kita says all men are the same, even Nissus, and he's a physician! They worry so about women having babies. Lesandor's the worst though; he's such a fuss."

Casandrina laughed. "Fabiom was little better before Lesandor was born, even though he knew he had no cause to worry about me. It is in their nature, I suppose." She wished, yet again, there had been some way to keep the news of Mysha's child from Yasdon, though of course that would have been impossible. As soon as Mysha had known, she had written to her father to tell him, and now she was thinking of going to see him, Casandrina could see that in her eyes.

"Nissus says I am very well, and with nearly four months to go before the baby, I could make the journey, couldn't I? If I leave it any longer it will be too late, and Father seems so busy, he can't visit me here. He's doing some sort of report of the woodlands of the holding – it seems it needs to be finished before the Harvest Festival. He'll be sorely missing Lesandor for things like that, I suspect."

"Yes," Casandrina agreed. "You are probably right." She looked at Mysha for a long moment and could think of no way to talk her out of going. "Take someone with you," she suggested eventually. "Someone you can trust. It is a long way after all."

"Whom should I take?" Mysha asked.

Casandrina considered the possibilities.

"Calbrin," she decided, knowing their house-steward could be appraised of the situation and would say nothing, but would watch over Mysha and Deepvale's unborn heir with complete devotion.

The courier had come directly from Yasdon and he had not come alone. With him was an entourage of five guards and six servants – a fact that Mysha discovered when she went to the hostelry to tell him that there would be no reply, instead she and another companion would be travelling back to Windwood with him.

The man, whom she knew by sight, showed no sign of surprise, only answering that he would be pleased to wait if she needed a day or so to prepare.

"Yasdon knew," Fabiom muttered, two days later as he and Casandrina watched Mysha and her escort leave. "He sent enough men to carry her litter and to care for her in the manner he always travels himself. He knew she would go."

"Calbrin will take care of her," Casandrina said, more hopeful than certain. Then she laughed in amused dismay.

Fabiom looked at her and grinned. "I know, we are becoming paranoid! In just over a month, Yasdon has to present himself in Fairwater and prove that he possesses enough knowledge and understanding of Treelaw to continue as holder of Windwood. If Mysha is not home here by then, I shall simply send word to Lesandor to go and fetch her. The child is not due until midwinter, after all. Still, it's hard not to worry after what he tried with Lesandor."

"The house will seem empty," Casandrina murmured. "Even Calbrin is gone now."

"Ah my; what shall we do with ourselves?" Fabiom wondered as he enfolded her in his arms and kissed her. "Just you and me, and no responsibilities." He loosened his hold and stepped away half a pace, without releasing her. "Soon enough there'll be a new baby, who'll be the centre of attention. Even before then, there'll be Harvest Festival to think about. Yet for now there's nothing and no one, except we two. So lead me into the wildwood, my lady. No one will miss us for a day or two, or more."

Mysha arrived at Windwood's hold-house to find Yasdon in high spirits.

"You've come! I knew you'd come. You're my good girl!" He hugged her, though carefully, taking care not to crush her too hard against him. "Just look at you!"

"And look at you, Father – you've put on weight," Mysha told him crossly. "It's not good for you."

"I know, but what else was there for me to do? I've been so miserable here on my own. Now you're home I'll be much better, you'll see. Come and see what I've got for you. No, no, you must be tired. Rest first and have a little refreshment and then I'll show you. There's plenty of time."

She was glad of the rest but she had grown accustomed to simpler fare and did not really enjoy the heavy, overly-sweet food he provided. Not wanting to hurt his feelings, she ate a little of everything and put her poor appetite down to her condition. He was happy to accept that and glad enough that she did not take long over the meal, anxious to show her what he had been doing in her absence.

The nursery was furnished with everything a child could need, and more besides. An exquisite, silk-draped cradle took pride of place and toys galore vied with each other for space. As if in a dream, Mysha moved around the room, touching each object in turn, gazing at the decor. The mosaic floor was a riot of bright flowers and birds, the walls were adorned with murals of rainbows and dolphins and the ceiling was patterned with all the major star constellations, in leaf silver on deep blue.

"Do you like it, Mysha?"

"I do," she breathed. "But, Father – I can't stay."

"You can, you can. It's all arranged. I'm sending that Calbrin fellow back to Deepvale with word that you'll be staying, and that he's not needed anymore. You see, Lesandor is coming back here. That's my other surprise for you! We'll all be together again – here – in Windwood. As soon as he's finished his service in Fairwater, he'll be home."

Ignoring the incredulous look on her face, Yasdon took hold of her arm and steered her towards an alcove at the far side of the room.

"Look, here's the nursemaid's place. The little one will have someone to look after him night and day. You won't have to worry about a thing."

"But, he's my baby, I want to worry about him!" she said, turning back to the cradle and smoothing the pale green drapes with her hand. "I had a letter from Lesandor just a few days ago. He said nothing about coming here. He's looking forward to being in Deepvale, to the birth of our child there."

"He'll be here, you'll see," Yasdon said, all smiles.

Yasdon had tried to do the study he had been set, reading the books Lesandor had found and a few others he had been given by Fabiom. It had been little use. Having taken in the basic theory, he was then required to spend time in the woods to learn about the growing and the seasons of the trees and make certain that the details he had read about, regarding the identification of each species from the drawings on a piece of paper, could be applied to the living trees. And that he could not bring himself to do. Neither was that his only problem. In the court archives in the municipal centre were the records of cases of felling without licence or wilful damage to the woodland environs, and the penalties meted out. Yasdon had never dealt with any such case himself. They were rare enough and, when they had arisen, he had always made certain to pass them over to other magistrates. Looking through them, over the past few months, he discovered he could not follow the complex code of degree that made the felling of one tree perfectly acceptable and of another a heinous crime.

Besides all the details he had already tried to learn, factors such as distance from a Dancing Glade, or the proximity of smaller trees to larger trees that might be Silvanan had to be taken into account.

In the end he had given up trying. Instead, he formulated a plan, one that would buy him time if nothing else. If he was careful, and clever, time was all he would need.

Mysha still knew nothing about her father having to learn Treelaw to maintain his position, however, she was quite aware that something was seriously wrong. Calbrin was gone. He had not even said goodbye, which she thought strange. Yasdon claimed Deepvale's house-steward had returned to that holding.

Mysha wrote a long letter to Lesandor, in which she could not bring herself to ask him if he was really coming to Windwood. She knew full well he was not, that her father was lying. Instead she told him only that she was visiting Yasdon, and suggested he should ask for some leave and come and visit himself, they could then return to Deepvale together. She gave the letter to her maid, to deliver to the courier who would be going to Fairwater in three days' time, hoping an answer would come soon, and that it would come in the form of Lesandor himself, to take her away. Meanwhile, so as not to rouse Yasdon's suspicions, she picked up on her old routines of home life, decorating the hold-house with her favourite flowers, continuing with an unfinished tapestry and helping with the household organisation. She invited special friends for supper, consulted the family physician and commissioned the holding's best weavers to make her new gowns for the last months of her pregnancy. All the while she returned again and again to the nursery, making minor adjustments and telling her father how beautiful it was. Yasdon patted her hand and bought her expensive perfumes and paid handsomely for a famous flute player to come from a neighbouring holding to play at one of her dinner parties.

Her maid handed Yasdon the letter Mysha had written to Lesandor. Yasdon threw it onto the fire without opening it.

In Fairwater, Lesandor bought a toy ship and decided that, with Ravik's consent, he would name his son Raidan, which brought his thoughts back again to the problem of Raidan's missing wife, and the inheritance of Southernport. Eventually he confided in Yan who, amazed at the revelation, promised to assist him.

"Your sources in Rushford are obviously no help," Yan agreed, after Lesandor had told him about all the inquiries he had instigated, trying to locate either Cuivah or her family, and the mostly uninformative replies he had received.

"They were exiled after the silk scandal but I can find no record of where they settled. Of course there are rumours: Malandel, Decorta, even Gerik. Some say they went back to Varlass, which though unlikely is not impossible. Yet Raidan met Cuivah in Rushford...."

"The business with selling sericulture secrets to Varlass was what, thirty-five years ago?" Yan muttered, thinking aloud. "Maybe some of the family risked returning to Morene, changed their names even. Yet the girl told Raidan her lineage, despite the shame it carries."

"Which is why he did not tell her who *he* was," Lesandor agreed.

"And why you have said nothing to his father."

"Or to mine. I did not want to compromise him." He sighed. "I have never kept anything from him before; it does not sit well. And I am sorry to put you in this position – you are close to Prince Laurens, I know."

"That is of no matter. I will keep your confidence."

Lesandor wandered over to the balcony of Yan's study and stared down onto the street below, at the people moving by, some of them young mothers with infants. "How will I find her, Yan? How will I ever find her?"

"When you wrote to the holder in Rushford, what's his name – Ussenis? Did you mention Raidan's name at all?"

"No," Lesandor sighed. "How could I? Raidan had gone to the holding on official business, on his father's behalf. Under the circumstances I would imagine he would have been very discreet about his relationship with any girl, let alone the granddaughter of the chief perpetrator of the worst crime in Morene's history."

"A fact he was initially ignorant of anyway," Yan mused.

"As Raidan told me – by the time he discovered it they were quite in love and it did not matter to him."

"Nevertheless, it would certainly matter to Ussenis."

"And to Ravik, I would imagine. The family was banished for all generations – with no recourse to mercy. So it is written and sealed."

"Which brings us back to your dilemma," Yan agreed.

Lesandor grimaced at his cousin, over his shoulder. "Yet Raidan intended to tell his father."

Yan nodded. "But not until the child was born."

"Exactly. And that was the promise I made to him: to do what he had intended. But there has to be a living child, of Ravik's blood, of Starven and Lincius's blood. It is the only hope. If not...."

"Indeed." Yan considered their options. "Ravik is a good man, and just. And Raidan was much-loved. Ravik will not reject the child, I am certain. And for its sake, and Raidan's, he will try to find a way to offer sanctuary to the mother."

"That is my hope," Lesandor agreed.

Yan started searching through his library. "You have considered that she might have left Morene by now – returned to her family, wherever they are?"

"I have."

With a grunt of satisfaction, Yan picked out and unfurled a scroll which depicted a detailed map of the country. "Very well. I have some time. Show me where you have been and then fetch me the letters you have received. I will go to Rushford and see if I have more luck than you."

Before Lesandor could do more than open his mouth, Yan added, "Yes, I will be discreet."

Nine days later, Lesandor received a letter from Windwood. He weighed it in his hands without undoing the seal, which he recognised as Yasdon's. That Mysha had returned to Windwood he knew; that his parents were concerned he was equally aware, though none of his father's letters had mentioned the fact.

"Well, are you going to open it or just try to guess its contents?" Petron asked. He was supposed to be studying for a debate on conscience and morality that afternoon but his curiosity was piqued and he put aside the documents he had been reading. Lesandor raised his brows then snapped the seal impatiently.

"I think I can guess," he said, then stiffened as his mind began to register the meaning of the words he was seeing.

Petron was watching him. "What is it? What's wrong?"

"Fever. In Windwood. Mysha has fallen ill." His hand shook as he lay the scroll down. Petron immediately picked it up.

"Illness is spreading ... have taken steps to contain it ... centre of holding isolated ... some hope it might be contained to the coastal region."

Lesandor fiddled with some clay game pieces set up on a board. "Last time he told me Mysha was ill, it was a lie. Dare I believe that this time is also deception?"

Petron pursed his lips. "He might have reason to say so; an excuse for her staying there rather than returning to Deepvale."

"Staying or being kept?" Lesandor wondered. "Then again, maybe what he writes is the truth. I'm surprised there is anyone alive in Windwood, it seems to be plagued by sickness!"

Lesandor went to Ravik to request leave to go to Windwood. His request was refused.

"I can't take the chance," Ravik told him. "If there was an outbreak and it has been contained and the area has been properly isolated, then it must remain so for at least another month. You know that."

"Yes, my lord, I do. But surely I could go there? If I then cannot leave for a month, so be it. Last time he was supposed to come here to Fairwater, Yasdon could not do so because of sickness in Windwood. It seems too much of a coincidence that he should be prevented in the same way now. He is due here any day."

"I am well aware of that," Ravik said. "As I am equally aware that the last time he wanted you to go to Windwood, against your will, he informed you that Mysha was unwell. And you went – as you told me yourself. Has it not occurred to you, if indeed there is no fever, *that* might be what he hopes will happen again? I will send men, but you will not go. That is my final word."

Chapter Six

THE NOTICES WERE posted at the various crossroads and boundaries, isolating three separate parts of the holding each from the others, and from the rest of Windwood also. Ravik's agents, sent to verify the rumours, saw them and returned swiftly with that information. All the inhabitants believed the sickness was closing in towards them, that their neighbours across the valley, beyond the town, or over the hill, were already suffering. Food parcels were left here and there and were scavenged by wild pigs and kites, and everyone was relieved when it seemed that they would escape this time.

Mysha brooded in her father's house as winter set in. While the onset of cold weather would see the end of the sickness, it would also see the end of any chance she might have to leave Windwood. At least she could hope that Lesandor would arrive soon, once the central part of the holding had been released from isolation.

The physician fussed around her and told her terrible stories about fevers of years gone by, warning her against setting foot even beyond the garden walls.

"Are lots of people sick? Oh, I do hope no one dies," Mysha fretted. "Have you tended them?"

"No, Mistress! I would not come here, to you, from another's sickbed. But I've heard there are many, so you heed me!"

With the precious child she was carrying, she needed no warning to keep her isolated; there was no way she would put him at risk. Her efforts to arrange the nursery ceased to be pretence; it would be used after all.

That the town was off-limits was no hardship, Mysha had no desire to go there. What she missed most was walking in the woods, the way she had done in Deepvale.

The old arched door in the garden wall, set behind the winter-flowering wych-hazel, could barely be seen from the house. No one saw her leave. Windwood's forest no longer held the terrors for her it once had; she felt at ease there, and safe, even when she discovered she was being watched.

She recognised Dulcissa at once and was delighted to see the Silvana; she had missed Casandrina's friendship and care for the past three months.

Dulcissa regarded her strangely for a moment, then asked, "What brings you out to the woods on such a day?"

Mysha shrugged. "Lesandor always loved coming to the woods, I thought his child might appreciate being here. Is that silly?"

"Not at all," the Silvana replied. "Yet I am surprised...."

"It's safe, isn't it?" The colour drained from Mysha's face. "It's so cold, I thought the fever must be past. Oh, Dulcissa, have I done something terrible by coming out today?"

"No, hush!" Dulcissa took her arm, concern replacing amused interest. "There is no danger. Come, sit on this stump and relax. I meant only that you were not inclined to walk in the woods before, even in high summer."

"Oh." Mysha looked around at the winter trees. "No, I wasn't, was I? Well, I've learnt a lot. Casandrina has taught me many things." With her fingertips she traced the shape of a knot in the tree stump. "I knew she didn't want me to come back here, but I came anyway. I wish I hadn't." She made no effort to brush away the tears that rolled down her cheeks. "I miss her, Dulcissa. I wanted her to be there when my baby was born."

"Why did you come?" the Silvana asked.

"To visit Father. He wrote to me. He sounded sad. I thought I'd only be here a short while. But then, with the fever, I couldn't go back, and with no letters getting in or out I haven't even heard from Lesandor. Father says he heard that Prince Ravik sent him overseas to Varlass. So now I don't even know if he'll be back here by midwinter." She wiped her eyes.

Dulcissa gazed up at the sweeping boughs of the elm above them.

"Oh, Mysha," she whispered. "There has been no fever."

Mysha had loved them both. Now Yasdon was making her choose between himself and Lesandor and she made her choice. Through her tears she whispered her husband's name. She could not bear to think of him believing she had conspired against him with her father and, realising that, she knew she had to get away as soon as she could after their son was born.

❦

He came into the world on midwinter's day, with his father's dark hair and his mother's grey eyes. She called him Jarin and held him close and wished that Lesandor was with her.

The physician and the midwife fussed around and whispered outside her room but Mysha took no notice. Unless he really had gone to Varlass, Lesandor should have been back long before now. The holding was clear of fever and, while the weather was cold, it was not so bad as to make the roads impassable. If he had gone, she should have received word.

The midwife came back into the room and took the sleeping child from her arms. The woman's smile was wide but it was only on her mouth; her eyes were as bleak as the winter skies. Mysha was too tired to notice, annoyed when she was moved yet again for the bedding to be changed. She wondered why she was bleeding so much.

"She must be allowed to rest," the physician whispered. Mysha heard him quite clearly. "She is not strong and the birth was very hard."

"She will be all right though, won't she? She must be all right. She's all I have."

"We'll take the best care of her, my lord, you have my word."

She heard them as if they were talking about someone else, not about her. There were only two things clear in her mind: she had a tiny baby to care for and his father did not know he had been born. Nothing else seemed terribly important.

"Mysha?"

She turned her head and regarded Yasdon, seeing him as a total stranger, not part of her new special world at all. "Casandrina knows what to do. Where is she? Oh, I'm not…. Dulcissa, then. Please call Dulcissa."

"Hush, hush. Why would you want a Silvana around at this time? Silly girl. We're not planting trees – you've had a baby."

"Where's Lesandor?" she whispered. "You promised he'd be here before…." She shut her eyes and a tear squeezed through her pale lashes.

"Never mind about him," Yasdon said brightly, too brightly, his voice as insincere as the midwife's smile. Her eyes snapped open.

"Something has happened to him, that's why he's not here. Why haven't you told me? He's not coming, is he?" She tried to sit up. Yasdon's pudgy hands on her shoulders kept her pressed back against the pillows.

"Shush now! You're to rest. You can only worry about yourself now. But no, he's not coming. He can't."

"Why can't he?" She wept in frustration.

"Oh, Mysha, I'm so sorry. I didn't want to have to tell you this, but he – he was on a ship, there was a storm. I'm sorry." He finished with a sigh as she buried her head in the pillows and sobbed bitterly.

The physician said that she had been too weak to live, that he was sorry but he had done the best he could. The midwife told Yasdon of a young woman who copied manuscripts in the municipal library and whose birthing she had attended just four days before. She had lost her husband recently and had little money. For a small consideration the midwife was certain she would nurse Mysha's infant alongside her own.

"This is not how it should be," Yasdon muttered over and over. "I had it all worked out, but not like this. Not like this."

"My lord, are you all right?" the physician asked anxiously.

"No, I am not!" Yasdon snarled. "My fault, it's my fault. Mysha! I am so sorry."

The physician took his leave.

"I'll send for the woman and her child to come to the house," the midwife said as she, too, left.

Yasdon paid them no heed.

Yasdon was not a man to bear responsibility for a tragedy, even the death of his only child, for too long. He soon began to cast outwards, looking for others to blame, and in that searching he found Lesandor. Lesandor who had refused to stay in Windwood, who had taken Mysha away, even turned her against him. If Lesandor had not insisted on dragging her across the country and had let her stay at home, where she was properly looked after, Mysha would have been stronger, strong enough to survive.

Now they would claim the child for Deepvale and take him away. His grandson, his only grandson. Had things gone the way he had originally dreamt, and had she been allowed to live, Mysha's second child could have gone to Deepvale, or to Southernport. Three holdings, each with a child of Yasdon's line in control, that was how it should have been. A new dynasty.

He began to imagine a future with a new royal family of his descendants. A future that Lesandor had robbed him of; all because of his Silvanan blood, Yasdon realised. It was the Silvanii of Windwood who had turned Lesandor against him, the boy had been happy enough when he had first come. It was their fault. After all, he had always liked Lesandor. Maybe Lesandor was not entirely to blame. But the Silvanii, they had been waiting, angry with Yasdon and his family all these years, waiting to get their revenge. Well, they had it now. Mysha was dead, but he would not let it rest at that.

Yasdon had garnered enough information from his studying to have an idea about life in the woodland tracts. He would show them who was Lord Holder and who were the subjects. Later, he might still have to go to Fairwater, to prove to Ravik that he was fit to remain in his position. He would worry about that when the time came. Ravik was not blameless either, neither was Fabiom. Suddenly he snorted with vicious laughter. He could pay them all back at once. Once he had dealt with the Silvanii, he would pass Jarin off as his own son, the child's wet nurse, the young widow, as the boy's mother. It was perfect. The only remaining problem would be Petron.

Axe in hand, Yasdon made his way to the wildwood. He did not return to the hold-house. The woman hired to nurse Jarin came and found the baby gone too, his cradle empty save for a tiny, unseasonal sprig of pink flowers. She waited for three days. Eventually the house-steward gave her a small purse of coins for her trouble and she left.

<hr />

It was the not the first time Trisran had been to Fairwater and yet, alone in the capital, faced with the task of finding Lesandor, maybe even in the royal palace, he could not help but be nervous. He had gained a great deal of self-respect since his marriage to Dulcissa but his life had been confined to the woods since then and the shining city overawed him with its vast buildings and complex streets, its bustling thoroughfares and teeming citizens. It was a long while before he could bring himself to ask someone how he might go about finding Lesandor. The street trader he chose was unable to help, as was the young soldier and the shoemaker. Footsore and weary, he came upon a small square, planted with silver birch trees and set with benches. People passing through stopped to drink at the ornate fountain which adorned the centre of the square. Glad of the respite, Trisran did likewise, admiring the sculpted Silvanii poised around the basin rim, dipping their hands into the icy water.

"A superb work of art, is it not?" a middle-aged man commented as he wiped his damp chin with the edge of his cloak. Two bright rings sparkled on his hands.

"It, it's beautiful, yes," Trisran stuttered, wondering if he dare address one with such insignia of authority as this man wore.

The problem was resolved for him. "I think you are a stranger here," the man said casually. "And lost, perhaps?" Trisran nodded. "Seric, of Southernport is my name. Maybe I can be of service to you?"

Trisran could hardly believe his luck, that amongst all those people, he had not only found someone who would go out of their way to help him but someone who knew Lesandor personally.

"As the philosopher Merites reminds us: kindness to strangers and hospitality to travellers is due *to* all and the duty *of* all," Seric said, before sending various people off to make inquiries.

While waiting for their return, Seric took Trisran to a fine eating room overlooking the estuary, where he insisted on buying a meal for them both.

They had just finished when word came that Lesandor had been located.

Lesandor was in the great library, pouring over an obscure archery text. He looked up as Trisran's shadow fell across his book and a moment passed before recognition dawned in his eyes, then a tired smile curved his mouth.

"Trisran! You are well, that's good. I was concerned for you. Still, I suppose Dulcissa has been looking after you."

Trisran nodded and smiled himself. "She has. As she has been looking after your babe these past days."

Lesandor's eyes widened. "What do you mean? Trisran, what are you saying?" Indignant heads turned and Lesandor closed the book. "Let us get out of here," he muttered.

Out in the cold courtyard, Lesandor turned to Trisran impatiently.

"Are you saying I have a son? Yasdon wrote and told me his mother died two months ago, before he had a chance to be born. Was that a lie?"

Trisran bowed his head. "I wish I could tell you it was all untrue, but Mysha is dead. Not two months though, that *was* a lie. She died just twelve days ago, two days after giving birth to a fine boy. According to the midwife, the birth had been difficult but – well – the woman said that she might have lived, except that Lord Yasdon told her you had been drowned. The midwife thought maybe the news was more than Mysha could bear in her weakened state."

"Yasdon told her I was drowned? He lied to both of us? This time he has gone too far!"

"No, he went too far when he took an axe to a holly woodmaid's tree. Lord Yasdon will deceive no one again."

Lesandor shut his eyes. "I see." He let his breath out slowly, then laughed. "And I have a son! The baby is well, you say? We must find Petron and tell him everything. What is happening in Windwood now?"

Trisran looked at his feet. "Nothing, as far as I know. I'm afraid I just covered the body with stones. No, Lesandor, don't look at me like that! What could I do? There are enough people who might think I held a grudge against Yasdon. If I had gone to the magistrates – I don't know if they would have believed me. I don't know if I would have dared tell them the truth anyway. With so little respect for the Silvanii in Windwood, who knows what might happen if it was reported that the Lord Holder had met his death in the heart of the wildwood, even if he *was* found with an axe in his hands? At best, the people would be afraid, and fear results in irrational behaviour. I wanted to see you first, and Petron I suppose." The last he added reluctantly, and Lesandor had to smile.

The meeting between Trisran and Petron was strained from the start. It was the first time the two young men had met since Trisran had been released from Petron's service.

"Your father is dead. He...." Trisran began.

"We have learned that Yasdon was not Petron's father," Lesandor interrupted. Petron glared at him. Lesandor paid that no heed for, as he had hoped, some of Trisran's antipathy disappeared with those words. "Lord Yasdon was killed by the Silvanii when he tried to attack their trees with an axe," Lesandor continued, speaking to Petron now, less vehemently than Trisran had been going to explain.

"What do you mean, he's dead?" Petron muttered, the import of the first message only then making itself felt.

Trisran was more interested in the unexplained revelation that Petron was not Yasdon's son.

Lesandor turned back to Trisran, partly intent on letting Petron come to terms with what he had just heard, partly intrigued by the manner of Yasdon's death, which he had originally disregarded in the light of the news about Mysha and their child.

"Why did Yasdon turn against the Silvanii, Trisran? Surely not because of having to learn more about Treelaw to keep his status."

Trisran looked bemused. "I knew nothing about that."

"No, of course not," Lesandor apologised. "Maybe that was it. It would seem strange though. What could he hope to gain?"

"No, it was something else." Trisran swallowed hard. "Dulcissa said he was cursing and shouting. He blamed the Silvanii for Mysha's death."

"The Silvanii?" Petron repeated. "She died of fever. Whose fault was that?"

Lesandor shook his head. "She did not die of fever. That was another lie. And there is more –" He held up his hand to stop Petron commenting on that last revelation. "Before she died, Mysha gave birth to a son. And, Trisran tells me, he is quite well. Apparently, I am a father."

Petron's jaw dropped. "I don't understand."

"I don't know anything about the events that led up to this," Trisran admitted. "Except that, less than a month before the child was born, Dulcissa met Mysha in the woods, near her tree. Mysha was well herself but she had been convinced by Lord Yasdon that there was sickness in the holding and she had been trapped there when she really wanted to return to Deepvale. She also believed you were away, in Varlass."

"No," Lesandor muttered. "I have been here, and in Southernport, mourning her death and our child's, as I believed."

"Then she did die – after the child's birth – and Yasdon went berserk with an axe in the wildwood?" Petron asked doubtfully.

Trisran did not look at Petron. "He blamed you, Lesandor. That's what he was shouting. That you had taken her from him, made her go to Deepvale, that the child was his heir. But more than you, he blamed the Silvanii for turning you against him. He seemed to think they had been planning their revenge since Lord Herbis set aside the proper study of Treelaw, and because they no longer received the respect they might have thought their due. He was threatening to have the whole woodland razed."

"We had better speak with Prince Ravik," Lesandor decided.

After a number of audiences with Ravik, various of his advisers, and members of the Assembly, Petron was elevated to the position of Lord Holder and given a year's suspension in his service to the prince. Lesandor's final year of service was also to be delayed, though only briefly, while he made arrangements for his son's care. For a while at least, he too was going home.

Four days after Petron's elevation, Lesandor went to find him, to tell him they were ready to go. The young holder was in his room, sitting on the floor with his knees drawn up to his chest. The look on his face, when Lesandor came into the room, was one of total despair.

"I'm not ready," he whispered.

Lesandor knew he was not referring to packing his belongings for the trip home.

"I am coming with you, remember. I have a son to meet." *And a wife to mourn anew*, he added to himself.

"But then you'll be going back to Deepvale – as you should," Petron added hurriedly, in case Lesandor should think he was playing Yasdon's games.

Lesandor chuckled. "Yes, I will. But Prince Ravik has said that he will not leave you alone. You will have help. You have done well here – the holding will flourish, you shall see. It is yours by right anyway."

"I know. Somehow that doesn't make it any easier. Oh true, I've learnt a lot, but it's all book learning. Who's going to respect me in Windwood? They've all seen me drinking, womanising and gambling since I was what, thirteen?" He shook his head. "I remember my birth anniversary celebrations that year. Yasdon threw a party for me that, well, let's just say Mysha was not invited. Things got progressively worse from there on. No one will take me seriously."

Lesandor threw his bags at him. "They will, if you give them a chance! Maybe it won't be easy, just remember the holding deserves better than it has had. You can make a difference, a good difference. Do that and people will forget the past soon enough." He grinned. "And Trisran will be there to help, should you have any problems with the Silvanii or Treelaw."

Chapter Seven

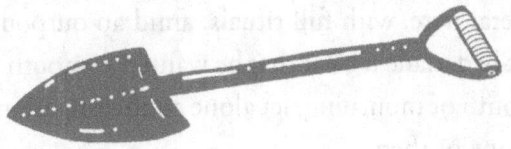

LESANDOR AND PETRON arrived in Windwood to find the holding in a state of disarray. Fortunately, Ravik had anticipated as much and had sent the new young holder back with a sizable escort.

Yasdon's absence had been noted, though his body had not been discovered. Petron was unsure whether that was a blessing or an added complication, until he found that Ravik had already sent a proclamation to the holding's elders that Yasdon had abdicated in Petron's favour; a fact that neither the prince nor Petron felt inclined to explain.

While the elders hurriedly convened a meeting, Lesandor made his way to the woods. Although he did not know where Trisran and Dulcissa dwelt, he was certain he would be able to find the place. Indeed, he had hardly set foot between the trees at the very edge of the woodland before he was met by two of Dulcissa's woodmaids who cavorted around him as they led him along the winter-bare paths to his desired destination.

The little house Trisran had built for himself and Dulcissa was snug and warm. Jarin lay sound asleep in a rush cradle near the hearth, swathed in soft velvet blankets, blissfully unaware of his father gazing down on him with tear-filled eyes.

Early the next day, Lesandor returned to the woods, this time with Petron. He would far rather have spent the time with baby Jarin but there was an urgent matter to attend to. The morning sun cast a pallid glow through the frosted branches of the alders and willows along the river bank, onto the rough heap of stones that marked the place where Trisran had found

Yasdon's body face down in the shallow waters at the edge of the river Grebe, an axe clutched in one cold hand.

Trisran was waiting for them, with three spades.

It had not been an easy decision. A holder's body would normally be burnt on a funeral pyre, with full rituals, amid an outpouring of public grief. But Ravik had made it clear that he wanted a smooth transition and the idea of a month of mourning, let alone an investigation into Yasdon's death, suited none of them.

As they dug a proper grave, Trisran told them how, with some difficulty, he had managed to pull the bloated corpse clear of the swift-running waters, rolling it over and recoiling in horror as he recognised the Lord Holder's face. Dulcissa had sent him. She had known what he would find, though not whom, for Yasdon had not been familiar to any of the other denizens of the wildwood. Only his anger and savage intent had been recognised – and had been met with their own reward.

With the late and unlamented holder safely buried, Lesandor spent some time with his infant son, after which began the task of unravelling the holding's convoluted finances.

Petron scanned the household accounts, barely able to believe what had been spent on the nursery refurbishments, while Lesandor looked through some of the productivity records. From time to time a mournful sigh escaped one or other.

"This is a waste of time. I'm only looking at the accounts because it seems marginally preferable to going to the magistrates' court and seeing what horrors await us there. As for these, I'm tempted simply to burn the whole lot and start afresh. There's nothing to be salvaged from here." With that, Petron slammed his ledger shut.

"I wish it were that simple," Lesandor agreed. They both knew it was not. Yasdon's records and accounts had so far revealed the holding to be deeply in debt to three others, besides Yasdon's own personal debts to numerous individuals. The late holder had kept his creditors at bay by claiming to borrow on behalf of others and borrowing afresh from new sources whenever it was impossible to hold out any longer.

"Lies! All I find are lies and more lies and deceptions and, and...."

"Examples of gross stupidity," Lesandor suggested, as his eye fell on an entry that showed a one year profit for part of the holding's fruit growing areas, achieved by selling the timber from the cherry trees there. He closed his book and put it aside. "There was no sickness, was there, none at all? Trisran was correct that the rumours of fever had been nothing but a ploy of Yasdon's."

"True, it was just another lie. Why?"

"Calbrin, our house-steward. He accompanied Mysha from Deepvale. Mother sent him. Father received word that he too had succumbed to the sickness and died. Yet there *was* no sickness. He was always my friend. Damn Yasdon!"

Petron was startled by Lesandor's vehemence. "Wait. You don't know that anything – I mean – until the incident in the woods, Yasdon never actually *did* anything to anyone. He was too weak. You knew him, Lesandor, whatever else he was, he was never a murderer. Listen to me: I hated him more than anyone and now I'm defending him!"

Lesandor thought of the dead holder as he remembered him before his schemes had been exposed. He knew Petron was right, Yasdon was weak. Not like Townmaster Florim in Stonehaven, who appeared soft and who, as Lesandor was only too aware, was capable of the harshest and cruelest actions. According to the information that had come out of Gerik in the past few months it was he who had ordered the bakery to be torched, knowing full well that there were people in the rooms above. He had paid with his life, for whatever good that would do Raidan and Sirsha and the others who had lost their lives that night. None of that helped explain Calbrin's disappearance, Yasdon had been no Florim.

The very next day, unable to put off the chore any longer, Petron went to the court chamber and Lesandor accompanied him.

"I've found something you need to see." Petron closed the ledger and rummaged through a collection of scrolls. "Here, this will be the one."

With utter disbelief, Lesandor saw Calbrin's name and an accusation of petty theft. "Six months' hard labour," Lesandor read aloud.

"And a beating, prior to his release," Petron noted.

"This is nonsense. Calbrin is the most honest man I know!" Then his indignation turned to delight and he laughed. "But he is alive. This means he is alive. But where? Where would they send him?"

Petron took Lesandor to the port to see if Calbrin's name was down as a rower on any of the galleys recently set out. When that produced no results they went to the town's garbage pit, then further afield to a small limestone quarry. Eventually they headed off to a clay pit, a quarter day's journey down the coast from the municipal centre. But, as elsewhere, there was no mention of Calbrin in the records.

"I don't know where else to suggest," Petron admitted.

Hope began to fade.

Petron scratched his jaw. "When we visited Valehead, to meet my great-aunt – *our* great-aunt –" he smiled at that memory and their mutual relationship to Tarison and Marid, "Tarison mentioned coloured clays. Do you remember? Mysha was very taken with those fine white bowls decorated with yellow and orange."

"I do remember," Lesandor said. "They were stained with ochre – from this holding – but the mine is disused."

"It was, but I saw something yesterday in the records – some income from a source I didn't recognise. 'Colour' – I wonder...."

They set out immediately, another half-day's journey, broken by an overnight stop so that they arrived at the mine the following dawn.

Lesandor's elation at spotting Calbrin turned briefly to horror – and then, as quickly, to relief as he realised that the bright red that besmirched his friend's skin was ochre dye, not blood.

Bruised, scraped and underweight, the house-steward was otherwise undamaged. Even as Petron signed the release papers and Lesandor embraced him, Calbrin was protesting his innocence. It took him some time to realise that his rescuers were already in no doubt about that.

That evening, Petron picked up the order for Calbrin's arrest. "What are you going to do now, Lesandor?" he asked, screwing up the paper and throwing it on the fire.

Calbrin had enjoyed a hot bath and a decent meal, his first for months, before collapsing, exhausted and emotional, into bed. Lesandor had stayed at his side until sleep finally overcame him.

Lesandor watched the paper burn. "I do not know. Take Jarin home, restore Calbrin to his family, finish my service, keep a promise I made to a friend. Beyond that I have no idea."

"You must have something in mind," Petron insisted. "You always seemed so – certain – I suppose. I know things have not gone as you hoped. You didn't want to marry Mysha, did you?"

Lesandor sighed and shut his eyes. "It seems terrible to say that now. But no, if you want the truth. Who knows, maybe if we'd had time, I think we could have been happy enough. Now I just feel guilty."

Petron gave a dismissive snort. "You're being too hard on yourself! I'm no expert, I've not yet had one relationship that meant anything at all, but I knew Mysha well enough. She *was* happy, Lesandor."

"Thank you." It was Lesandor's turn to laugh. "Did you really think I was having an affair, when you sent Trisran to follow me?" he asked.

Petron reddened. "How did you know?" Then he laughed. "I thought I was being so clever too!" He wiped his eyes. "Yes, yes I did. Though, to be honest, I wasn't sorry he discovered nothing. If you had been, and if I'd said anything, Mysha would have been heartbroken. I don't know if I could have done that to her, though I would have enjoyed having a hold over you. You weren't, were you?"

Lesandor felt the weight of Sirsha's stone around his neck.

"No. Even if I had wanted to, I am not that stupid. I'm afraid there *was* someone though. Not here. Not even in Deepvale. Nothing happened, but not because I did not want it to. Circumstances were against us, as was time. Guilt is a horrible thing, Petron. I would not recommend you ever do anything to burden yourself with such a load." He let out a half laugh. "It is odd. You are the first person I have said anything to. A few months ago I would have sworn you'd be the last I would confide in, about anything."

Petron nodded. "Things have changed in that time, in more ways than either of us could ever have imagined. I'm grateful for your confidence, but I have to admit to a certain voyeuristic curiosity, unbecoming in a lord holder I'm sure."

"What? Oh you mean, who was she? A young woman I met in Gerik, would you believe? Her name was Sirsha. She was very special. I even thought of trying to persuade her to come back with me, despite Mysha." He rubbed his hands over his face. "And I still have not resolved that tangle of emotions, not that it matters any more."

"And now? Could you not go back there? I know you hated it, but...."

"I would. For her I think I could go back. Except, she is not there anymore. She is somewhere else, with Raidan and Mysha."

"I see. I'm sorry." Petron hesitated. "But maybe not with Yasdon?" he suggested.

Lesandor managed to smile. "No, possibly not." He stood up. "Before we get into *that* philosophical quagmire, should we not remember that we have a very sick holding to restore to health and you must be the chief physician?"

Petron took the hint, though reluctantly, his curiosity still far from satisfied.

"I can write a pardon for Calbrin, though his 'crime' will still be on record, else I can overturn Yasdon's decision, even though he was supposedly the injured party."

Lesandor raised his brows. "Judge *and* chief witness? Very appropriate. Presumably he forgot the oath he took on becoming a magistrate, that is if he ever took the oath and did not simply appoint himself."

"*Friend and stranger, rich and poor, all are alike. It is an abomination towards all the Powers and all that is right and good to show partiality. The true mark of a ruler is to do justice,*" Petron quoted. "Hardly Yasdon's sentiments."

Lesandor chuckled, though without amusement. "Indeed. Write Calbrin a pardon for now. If he ever should need the crime cleared we will come back to you. Your work will be much easier if you do not have to expose Yasdon for the charlatan he was. If you ever find you have to do that, you will also have to make it clear that you are not his son and we have only my mother's word for that, which might not constitute proof positive in the eyes of most of the elders of this holding."

Very little snow had fallen on the mountain passes that year, and so, with Calbrin found, and baby Jarin deemed by the local physician fit and strong enough to travel, Lesandor made ready to leave Windwood. He purchased a long-eared goat with a young kid at foot, to provide milk for the infant and to carry their food and personal belongings, and loaded Mysha's white Whisper with the baby's cradle and warm blankets – she too was going home.

"I've made Trisran manager of the silk mill," Petron told Lesandor ruefully, checking all the harness straps one final time.

Lesandor grinned. "Good. Make the most of the resources you have and things will sort themselves out here. And I'll come back as soon as I can."

"Thank you. I appreciate it. Despite Prince Ravik's avowed faith in me, I am really not prepared for this responsibility."

"As I am not prepared to be a father, especially of a motherless child." Lesandor waved to Calbrin – who, with Windwood's house-steward, was bringing their belongings to the gatehouse – before turning his attention back to Petron. "Do you remember, you once asked me if I had presented myself in the wildwood on my seventeenth birth anniversary?"

"Another memory I am not proud of, but yes, I do," Petron admitted.

"Well, I did not, but it *is* what I had gone home to do. I had always intended to."

"Intended to? But I thought you told me it had been as much your idea as Yasdon's that you should do your two years' service here when you were sixteen."

"Yes. I thought I was being clever! I had presumed that, should I be successful, I might not have to return to Windwood, that Yasdon might release me, or Prince Ravik would force his hand, make him take some of the payment my father had previously offered, so I could stay home. That is another issue. The point is, one of the benefits of marriage to a Silvana – as I saw it – is that you get all the pleasure of having a lovely and loving wife from almost the day of your coming to manhood, but the responsibility of fatherhood is deferred until you are actually old enough to shoulder it. Thirty-four seems to me an ideal age, far more so than nineteen. Speaking of which, I see my son."

Dulcissa and Trisran had arrived, with baby Jarin wrapped in layers of soft blankets. With gentle care, Dulcissa placed the child in the cradle strapped to Whisper's harness.

Singing very softly, she stroked his fine hair. "Blessings, little one. All happiness," she whispered as she kissed the baby's forehead.

As Lesandor tucked a fine, waterproof deerskin over the cradle, Jarin's tiny fist closed about his thumb.

"Sometimes you just have to get on with things," Lesandor said, speaking still to Petron, but smiling at his son, "and pray your best is good enough. Because anything less will not suffice."

In the matter of childcare, Lesandor and Calbrin learnt as they went. Finding hospitality along the way, each day they set out late and found shelter early to keep the baby out of the worst of the cold. Lullabies Casandrina had once sung to Lesandor, now soothed Jarin, who each night slept soundly on his father's chest.

Keeping the baby clean was another matter. Dulcissa had instinctively known what Jarin needed in that regard. Lesandor was not so skilled. The weather was cold and keeping the baby dry and warm was paramount. Often the two seemed mutually exclusive and more than once they arrived at a house or hostelry with an uncomfortable, grizzling infant, to be scolded by the woman of the house, whereupon Jarin would be hurried off to be washed and wrapped in clean, fresh cloths.

At least Calbrin had milked a goat before, which was useful as Lesandor failed to master the skill. However, his voice could soothe not only his son but the animal, too, which meant the big speckled doe gave sufficient milk for the baby, the two men, and her own kid.

Just before noon on the sixth day they came around the final bend in the road and glimpsed the terra cotta roof tiles and white walls of Deepvale's hold-house, high on the hill before them. To their left the wildwood was the only thing visible, to their right were olive groves, bare vineyards and mulberry orchards.

With a word, Lesandor halted the donkey.

Calbrin let out a deep sigh. "Home – finally. I honestly thought I'd die in Windwood. That was the worst – thinking I'd never see home again. I'd rather be like Ramus – cared for by woodmaids and your lady mother at the end. That's the way to go, I reckon: very old, and very peaceful."

Lesandor, his chilled fingers struggling with the cradle's straps, chuckled. Briefly he lifted Jarin into the air – "Look, little one. Welcome home. Your many-times great grandfather, Laurus, came to this place generations ago and met his lady – the ash Silvana Sharaleima in those woods." He bundled the baby back into his cosy blankets and held him on his shoulder. "She taught him how to live off the land and how to make silk. Together they founded a settlement that grew to be the town Deepvale is today. You are of their line; you will learn to love this holding, its people and its wild places – as I do."

In response, Jarin gurgled and blew bubbles at his father. Lesandor adjusted his hold. "You are right. That is enough history – we will go to the house."

In the sheltered, sunlit courtyard of Deepvale's hold-house, Casandrina dropped her spindle and rose to her feet, her gaze unfocussed.

Fabiom – who had been fletching arrows close by as she spun her silk – jumped up and caught her by the wrist. "What is it? Casi, what's wrong?"

She cocked her head, a tiny frown lining her brow. "Nothing is wrong. I can feel … someone. I am not sure. Lesandor is close. He is coming home. But there is someone else, of our blood. I do not understand." Her frown deepened. "Unless your son has fathered a child we know nothing of."

"Oh, that would make him 'my son', would it?" Fabiom asked. He kissed her and picked up his cloak, throwing it over one shoulder.

Before he could even fasten it, his farm manager burst through the house into the courtyard, Kir'h and Lan'h beside him, all three talking at once.

"Hush!" Casandrina commanded her woodmaids. "Speak, Darseus, please."

"My lady! My lord! Wonderful news. I can scarce believe it…."

Casandrina ran through the house and down the road, away from the hold-house where the woodmaids were already busying themselves, preparing for Lesandor's return.

By chance, the first person to see the travellers had been Calbrin and Darseus's father, Kilm – Fabiom's erstwhile and supposedly retired farm manager – who was in the mulberry orchards beside the road, looking over some recently coppiced trees. The old man stood, mouth agape, as realisation slowly dawned. Then with a whoop of delight, and tears he did not bother to wipe away, he embraced his youngest son, whom he had been mourning for a full season.

Witnessing the scene, the orchard workers hurried over. There was much rejoicing that the house-steward had not perished in Windwood, as had been reported. There was even more amazement that Lesandor's son had been born and was home, safe and well – for the holding had mourned Mysha's death, like Calbrin's, months before he was due to enter the world. Word rapidly spread back to the hold-house of the homecoming.

Before the travellers and their ever-growing escort reached the hold-house, Fabiom had sent out a hunting party and set servants to prepare for a feast – inviting all the estate workers and farm families, as well as friends from far and near. Then he followed the path Casandrina had taken – to meet his grandson.

Celebrations went on for several days, with mornings spent hunting and afternoons and evenings spent feasting, drinking and dancing.

Eventually, the festivities wound down. Relieved and reluctant in equal measure, Lesandor let Jarin go home with Kita. His father's cousin was happy to nurse Jarin along with her own baby: a little girl, born three days after midwinter, whom she and Nissus had named after Mysha.

Lesandor was content, especially when his mother promised that she and Kita would care for Jarin for as long as necessary. His own childhood had been idyllic, he could want nothing less, or more, for his son.

Had he had a say in the matter, Lesandor would have named him Raidan, but he would not take away from him the only thing besides his life that Mysha had been able to give him. It was a fine name too, having been borne by a Silvana-born poet, who had long been one of his father's favourites and to whose writings Fabiom had introduced Mysha, much to her delight. As Lesandor had admitted to Petron, he would never have chosen to marry Mysha, yet somewhere in the time they had shared he had grown very fond of her and he found it hard to accept that she was dead, harder than he had ever found it to accept that they were married.

Winter still had a firm grip on the year when Lesandor returned to Fairwater to complete the final year of his service. It was a wrench to leave Jarin, and he was amazed how such a small person had become such a big part of his life. Now he was a father himself, he was even more anxious to keep his promise to Raidan, and offer whatever assistance he could to Cuivah and her child.

He had not long settled in when he received word from Yan – that, at last, the elderly, retired magistrate who had signed Raidan and Cuivah's betrothal validation had been found. With the magistrate's help, Yan had unearthed some actual facts about Raidan's wife, including that she had distant family in Shakenyew and that she had been in contact with other relatives about going there. Most importantly – she was travelling with a child.

"Shakenyew, in the north, that's where they're bound, it would seem," Yan told him when they managed to meet up – at the edge of the archery field where Lesandor was watching some young archers who would be leaving for Deepvale within a few days, to train with Fabiom for a season. "I'm still waiting for confirmation, but it looks as if that's where you'll have to go if you want to find them."

"And she has family, thank all that is sacred," Lesandor said. "I have been imagining her alone, maybe even homeless. It is bad enough that she has had to manage without her husband and no way of knowing what has become of him." He sighed as he handed back Yan's copy of the marriage papers. "I had thought the time had come that I must tell Ravik, though I have no idea how he would take the fact that I have known about Raidan's secret family for almost two years and have said nothing."

Yan unstoppered a flask of hot spiced wine he had brought out with him. "No idea, eh? Are you sure?"

Lesandor opened his mouth, but no words formed in his brain.

Yan nodded. "Well, with luck you won't have to find out."

"Exactly. And you will receive word when she has actually arrived, so that I can go and speak with her? Before I do say anything, I will need to confirm the age of her child. So much time has passed, she could feasibly have had another since." Lesandor took the cup of hot wine Yan offered him. "Shakenyew –" he paused, considering, "I have little knowledge of the place."

"It's small, not of any great significance, as far as I'm aware, politically or economically," Yan told him. "Noted for producing some good musicians and first class bowyers," he added, after some thought.

"I am happy enough with the bows I have; I shall settle for finding Cuivah and her child." Lesandor raised his cup to his cousin. "Thanks to you, Prince Ravik will hopefully soon have a new grandchild and, providing he can disregard Cuivah's heritage, Southernport will have a new holder-elect."

Chapter Eight

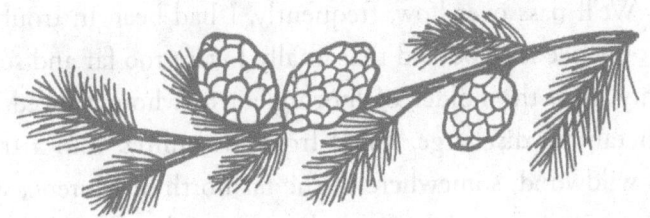

AS HE HAD received no further intelligence from Yan, as soon as his service was complete and he had paid a brief visit home, Lesandor returned to Windwood, where Petron pressed him to stay awhile – until after the Turning and Harvest Festival at least.

Now that there were positive things to do in the holding, as well as damage still to undo, Lesandor was kept occupied; a situation that suited him well. Beyond actually finding Cuivah and the child, his future seemed shrouded in uncertainty. Had she been well, he would have asked Princess Maedrim if she could enlighten him – if there was anything to be read in the night sky. But it was not just the secret he harboured that prevented him; since Raidan's death, Maedrim no longer consulted the heavens, neither did she take much interest in more mundane affairs. The loss of her youngest son had broken her spirit, and her heart.

Lesandor had been in Windwood some months when Trisran introduced him to Cavan, a forlorn old labourer with neither family nor home who occasionally helped him at the silk mill. Lesandor vaguely remembered Cavan from earlier days in Windwood, when – if he recalled correctly – the toothless old man had assisted around various building sites.

Dulcissa had come across Cavan wandering through the depths of Windwood's forests and, recognising his sorrow, had invited him home for a meal. Since then, Trisran had given him whatever employment he could and brought him home on occasion, to share both food and company.

Cavan's tale was a sad one, and one he was reluctant to tell in full until the day when both he and Lesandor were in Trisran's house and Trisran happened to mention Lesandor's ancestry, then the old man shared his story willingly enough.

"Pour me another cup of wine and I'll tell you as cruel a tale as you will hear. We'll pass over how, frequently, I had been in trouble as a youth. It only needs to be said that finally I went too far and seriously angered my lord, the holder of Stormglen, to whom I owed service I was reluctant to discharge. I fled from his militia, into a trackless stretch of wildwood, somewhere in the far north of Morene, where I hid for many days and nights including the night of my birth eve. I had known little of the Silvanii until then yet, despite my ignorance, I won a bride from among their number. Undiscovered by my pursuers, I settled in that area with my wife and there we lived" – he took a deep draught of his wine and stared into the cup for a long moment – "until her tree was felled."

"Felled! No –" Lesandor closed his eyes, reliving the horror of the nightmares he had endured in Gerik.

Lesandor heard Trisran whisper, "Cavan, I'm so sorry." In his friend's voice he heard the fear that something or somebody might one day threaten Dulcissa.

For fifty years – Cavan told them – he had wandered broken-hearted and disconsolate. It had taken him ten of those years to discover that the pain eased, somewhat, when he stayed close to the woods or mixed with people who knew the Silvanii. He was only glad to have found Trisran and Dulcissa, even though their togetherness brought all his own memories flooding back.

Lesandor wondered which was worse, to have shared such a union even for a short while and then to have lost it, or to have been denied it altogether. Cavan's face was marked with an emptiness and despair he could never know, yet the yearning within his own heart was something Cavan may not comprehend.

The old man understood more than Lesandor realised. He saw Lesandor's pain and asked him for his story. Until then, Lesandor had said little to Trisran, other than the fact that Casandrina had forbidden him to seek a Silvanan wife. Inspired by Cavan's tale, he told them about his thwarted dreams, about Mysha, even about Sirsha. When he was done,

240

Cavan looked thoughtful, though he said little. However, the next day he suggested that, once Lesandor was free to leave Windwood, they should travel together for a while, that it might do them both some good.

"I shall be finished here soon," Lesandor said, agreeing with Cavan's suggestion.

The time of the Turning had passed and Windwood had celebrated Harvest Festival in style, as was fitting given the progress Petron had made and all that had been achieved in the year and a half he had been holder.

Happy the holding was prospering and Petron was coping, and eager to see his son, Lesandor planned to go home for his birth anniversary, immediately after which he would set out for Shakenyew and not leave until Cuivah was found. Meanwhile, he invited Cavan to accompany him to Deepvale. Cavan willingly accepted the invitation.

"How old are you?" Cavan asked, a few days later, as they began their journey.

"Twenty," Lesandor replied, feeling twice that many years weighing on him.

Cavan looked him over. "And you are confident that at seventeen you could have won a Tree Lady for your wife, had you tried?"

Lesandor chuckled lightly. "As confident as any man dare be," he replied. "It is easy enough to be certain when you do not have to face the risks."

"Yet you could, still...."

Lesandor stopped walking and stared at his companion. "What are you saying?"

Cavan, glad of the respite, found a sheltered bank upon which he spread his cape and sat down. He indicated to Lesandor to join him there. "Why seventeen?" he asked.

"The trees mature at that age. You know that as well as I."

"Better," Cavan told him. "Whatever age their trees mature, Silvanii must seek a partner of the same age in order that their cycle of rebirth may be effective. That way, though they sacrifice their own ability to regenerate, they do at least ensure that a new Silvana will be engendered to take their place. Ash trees, elm trees, they mature at seventeen and their Silvanii will only take a husband of that age. But ash and elm are not the only trees in our woods."

Lesandor stretched back on the bank and watched the clouds scudding overhead. "I know that," he said. "The trees of the woodmaids all mature early, hazel and whitethorn, holly and elder...."

"Early, yes," Cavan interrupted. "What of those that mature later, twenty years or more?"

Lesandor sat up again. "Such as?"

"The great pines, cedars, larch, yew."

Lesandor studied his hands. "I gave her my word."

"Your mother? You gave her your word to forsake the ash groves. The Silvanii of these other trees are quite different. Sometimes I wish I'd had the chance to seek another wife. You take the chance for me. My life is all but over, yours is still ahead of you. You cannot give up at twenty; it is a long time to live in despair, I know."

Lesandor looked at the old man, wondering if Cavan foretold the future truly. Would he end up in the same straits?

He was tempted, sorely tempted. Maybe his dreams could come true after all. Casandrina hardly spoke of Silvanii beyond those who dwelt in the wildwood of Deepvale. Silvanii travelled little, they shared little. It was hardly surprising she had not considered the possibility Cavan laid before him.

"When are you twenty-one?" Cavan asked.

It would not be long, another birth anniversary, another year.

"Soon."

"I have done a lot of study, a lot of thinking. I had little else to do, after all. Trust me on this."

"Thank you," Lesandor said. He found himself scanning the horizon for trees and stopped himself immediately.

"I think I'll not travel with you, Lesandor. I'll go back to Windwood instead. I can always visit Deepvale at some later date. You have things to think about, things to do. Best you travel alone for a while."

Lesandor got to his feet and helped Cavan to his. "I shall not be staying in Deepvale long. I have got to go to one of the northern holdings to see someone. It may be some while before I am home again."

"No matter," Cavan replied indifferently. "Time is nothing, as the Silvanii know. Where are you bound?"

"Shakenyew." The trail had gone cold again, yet where else could he go to look for her?

"Shakenyew? Indeed. Where better to spend your twenty-first birth eve –"

Without another word, Cavan started back the way they had come. Whatever choice was to be made, it had been left to Lesandor.

Lesandor sat back down and watched the clouds for a while longer. There were no answers to be found in their shifting patterns. Eventually, he stood up again. He glanced back in the direction of Windwood, where he could still see the figure of Cavan shambling along the road, then turned towards home. It occurred to him that he had never found a Silvanan larch or yew in Deepvale, nor had he come across one in Windwood.

The day of his birth anniversary loomed close, yet he tried to dismiss the idea of looking elsewhere. His responsibilities lay in Deepvale; how could he think about searching outside his own holding?

Shortly before nightfall, he came to a junction in the road. After a moment's hesitation, he turned away from the familiar path and headed northwards instead.

Part IV

Chapter One

SHAKENYEW WAS A minor holding, consisting of one mid-sized town, some outlying villages, four stone quarries, and a few dozen sprawling hill farms. Besides bowery, as Yan had mentioned, wool, mutton and building materials – especially a much sought-after yellow limestone, with shades of pink and veins of red and grey – were the mainstay of the economy.

The town boasted only two hostelries, one on the outskirts, the other in the centre. Lesandor found lodgings in the latter. Shakenyew's hold-house would have been more comfortable and he could have expected to be welcomed and entertained there, had he not been reluctant to reveal his identity while he searched for clues as to the whereabouts of Prince Raidan's wife and child. The matter was too delicate to jeopardise simply so that he could have a softer bed and better food.

He could think of no good reason to be in Shakenyew as either a silk or wine producer, for neither mulberries nor grape vines grew in the northern holdings, so he chose instead to make use of his innate understanding of plants, along with the knowledge Nissus had imparted to him over the years, and passed himself off as a herbalist seeking new plants or new uses for those he was already familiar with. It was a subject that encouraged many people in the hostelry to speak with him and those who began by asking him questions were more than willing to answer some of his, for it was ever in such places that the best information could be uncovered.

It was not until the evening of the fourth day of his sojourn in Shakenyew that Lesandor came across the great yew woods. Initially he had assumed the holding took its name from the small clusters of the trees on its southern border, but the keeper of the hostelry had told him of the ancient woods farther in and spoke of them with dread. No one went there; Lesandor would be well advised to keep away. Lesandor thanked him for the information and the advice, accepted the one and rejected the other. Yasdon had spoken of the woods of his holding in the same way; it was not inconceivable that even in Deepvale some people felt similarly about the woods where his mother's and sister's trees grew, though he could not imagine it.

The vast yew woods were far less welcoming than those forests where Lesandor had grown up. Nothing grew in the shadow of the sombre trees. Beneath his feet, fallen needles rustled; beyond that there was no other sound to be heard. The sunlight found only narrow ways in. Shafts of golden light glinted off of blood-red berries and contrasted sharply with the dark green mantle of the woods. It was very beautiful in its own, aloof way.

By the time Lesandor returned to his room that night, it was very late. There was no question in his mind that the woods were a Silvanii haunt. He had found something he would have refused to admit he had even been looking for, though he was no closer to making a decision. There were still six days before his birth eve.

For the next six days he asked after Cuivah and followed leads that led him nowhere; he became acquainted with Ussenis, the Lord Holder, who believed him to be a herbalist and a distant cousin of the young woman he was looking for. He acquired some wood-sanicle seeds that he sent on to Nissus in Deepvale – discovering the plant to be well-regarded in the area, where it was commonly known as 'heal-all' – but no information about Raidan's missing wife. Mornings and evenings, he wandered in the woods, searching for his own inspiration, and found none. The morning of his birth eve dawned and he stayed in the hostelry. The rest of his life spread before him.

He thought of his parents and their happiness, and of Trisran and Dulcissa. He felt no anxiety about Jarin; Casandrina and Kita would take good care of him for as long as necessary, and if Lesandor had a wife she would surely raise the child as her own once he was weaned. Fabiom was fit and well; it should be many years before Lesandor was needed in Deepvale, by which time Jarin would be old enough to take on the day-to-day responsibility for the holding.

All his thoughts seemed to be in favour of Cavan's suggestion, except one: again and again he saw his mother's face, and he recalled her concern when he expressed his desire to seek a Silvanan wife. He heard her tell him that such a course would not bring him the happiness he was seeking, that he had to find it within himself. Yet he *had* sought and he had not found it. He believed he had left it behind in the woods of his childhood, and if he was to discover it again it was in the woods he would have to look.

His mind was made up.

As dusk settled around him and the trunks of the trees became one with the shadows, Lesandor could not help but wonder if he would have felt so afraid had he gone to the Dancing Glade in Deepvale's wildwood when he was turning seventeen. He looked about uneasily, but there was nothing to see. All during the six days he had been visiting, he had hoped that he might have seen or heard something of the Silvanii, yet there had been nothing. Nevertheless, the sense of their presence was very real to him. He settled down as well as he was able. A cold wind was blowing and he pulled his cloak closer about his body. Nearby the river flowed silently. He waited. He slept.

They were not long in coming. He could hear the whisper of voices in his dreaming. No laughter. He was not surprised. The dark yew trees did not suggest merriment; they were stately and proud and he guessed their denizens to be likewise.

"He is bold."

"Too bold, I would say."

Fear, push it aside. He knew from his father what to expect, still he was afraid.

"Much too venturesome. What to do with such a one?"

There was a ripple of quiet laughter then and Lesandor grew more afraid. He wanted to wake up, but his body would not move, his eyes refused to open.

A voice began to sing and his fear subsided. The song was strange, unlike anything he had heard before. He could find no beauty in it but it could not harm him. It stopped.

"More bold than I thought," said the first speaker.

"How stays he unmoved?" the second inquired.

None replied.

He could hear whispers, conferring maybe. Silence fell, a long brooding silence during which he slipped into a deeper sleep. Movement, still Lesandor could not wake but he was aware again. More voices, new voices, the number of the Silvanii had increased. They seemed to be disagreeing. He tried to listen but his mind wandered; he pictured his sister dancing with garlands of flowers he had woven for her, remembered his mother singing the great songs of the forest. Peace filled his mind.

"He smiles!"

He stirred at the voice, the surprise he heard.

"You say he was unmoved by your song? Who is he?"

He tried to answer but only a low moan escaped his lips.

Another voice, another song. His mother's voice was sweeter, her theme lighter. Maybe he smiled again. The singing stopped.

"Silvana son — he must be."

"Then I claim my right." He had heard that voice first, he recalled.

"And I claim seniority, Taxiana," replied another.

And suddenly he really was afraid and his fear was such as he had never known, even held prisoner in Gerik.

Chapter Two

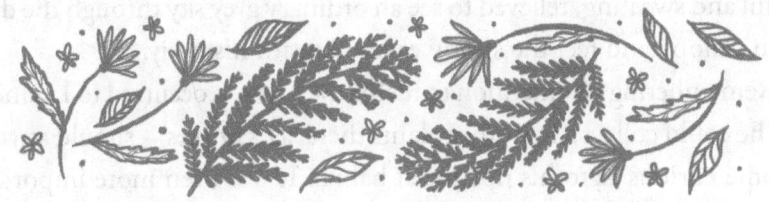

THERE FOLLOWED THE most awful nightmare, of terrible sounds like a storm, and voices chanting. However, when Lesandor opened his eyes in the early dawn he had very little waking recollection of the night's events. The yew under which he slept was very large, very old.

"I am flattered," he said, wincing as he eased himself upright. He was lost, and found it hard to get his bearings. One part of the yew woods looked much like any other; somehow he had to find his way to her tree again. As there was nothing growing nearby with which to make a garland, he tied his belt sash around a low branch, promising to return with something more suitable.

Walking slowly, he noted the features that would help him find his way back. His heart was light and he sang, not the songs he had heard last night, rather songs his mother's woodmaids had taught him as a child, songs filled with pleasure and hope. Then he laughed.

Out of the woods, he collected grasses and leaves from the riverbank and made a green garland for the lady of his tree. He brought it to her straightaway, as much to make certain he could find his way back as anything, for he did not wish to get lost that night. He made only one false turn and arrived without further incident at the grove where her tree grew. There he swapped his sash for the garland and left again, still singing.

When he returned that evening, the garland was dead.

The sight was disquieting but he would not be discouraged. In his wanderings he had come across some caves, one of which had a small spring and pond within, where all sorts of plants were growing out of season. He would go there on the morrow and collect beautiful things to make her a new garland. Having made that decision, he settled down beneath her tree and soon fell asleep, to dream of creaking timbers and howling winds, groaning hawsers and chanting voices, until he awoke fearful and sweating, relieved to see an ordinary grey sky through the dark green canopy and feel the steady earth beneath his body.

Remembering his intention to revisit the caves, it occurred to Lesandor that he could collect a few other plants there, as 'samples' – should anyone become curious as to his nocturnal habits. It was even more important to him that the good people of Shakenyew were ignorant of his quest for a Silvanan wife than that they were unaware of his search for Cuivah and the child. He could easily make them think that he had spent the night in the caves, dusk having fallen while he was engrossed in the plant life there. Hopefully no one would have noticed his absence or his early morning arrival anyway, and he would not have to explain.

While he was collecting more materials for a garland, it started to rain and he sheltered in the caves. The rain persisted and he settled down to wait it out. There were many caves amid the rocky outcrop, some mere indents in the rocks, others seemingly vast cavern complexes, and he was tempted to go exploring until he decided that the time could be better spent considering some practical matters, such as where and how they would live should he succeed in his venture.

There were no dwelling places nearby the woods at all, and he had also to consider that he would need to support himself. It occurred to him that his story about being a herbalist might continue to stand him in good stead. Thanks to Nissus, he did have a fair knowledge of the practical aspects of herbology and, luckily, he had not claimed to be a physician, although the two often went together. A commercial medicinal garden out of the shade of the yew woods might well provide for them. He thought of Trisran and Dulcissa's house and imagined himself building something similar, a home for himself, for his wife, and Jarin and, in due course, for another child; a place where a Silvanan daughter could come and be close to them.

Deep in thought, he left the caves and started to make his way back to the town. Only when he came to a deep gorge did he realise he had mistaken his route and he stood, disorientated. There was nothing for it but to go back into the woods and cut through. After a while he thought he had got his bearings, even though he was not familiar with his surroundings. He paused for a moment to be certain and then cocked his head, listening to a mournful sound that echoed through the trees, a noise he did not recognise and felt he should.

Curious, he made his way in the direction it seemed to come from; but sound is deceptive in a wood and it faded even as he thought he neared its source. He stood again, irresolute, and again heard it. This time there was no mistaking the direction whence it came, or the anguish it conveyed.

As he neared the place, his heart began to pound and his palms became clammy. Cautiously he proceeded, disregarding obstacles in his path. Though wary, he was determined to discover the source of the noise. When he did, he could only wish he had not – for nothing in his life had prepared him for the sight before him.

The yew tree was large, almost as broad as his own lady's, but it reached only half as high. Its three main boughs had been ripped from the trunk, two completely, the third almost so, while a viscous trail of amber seeped from the sundered wood. The tree was dying and, with it, a Silvana. It was her voice he had heard, for she had not yet gone. He knew she must linger with her tree.

His dream – the sound of breaking wood and rushing winds – he had thought it a nightmare, obviously it had not been. He could only think that he had slept through a violent storm.

"*Help me.*"

"I.... How can I?" He covered his face with his hands. There was nothing he could do, save take an axe to finish what the storm had begun and shorten her anguish. In his heart he knew he could not do that.

"*Stay with me then.*"

How could he comply, and yet, how could he refuse?

"I will sit with you, Lady," he whispered, brushing a tear from his cheek. "For a while."

Time meant nothing to them. She would not count the days, nor feel the lonely watches of the passing nights, as she waited for her final dawn.

"*Closer,*" she told him. But he could not bear to be nearer, so he sat some way away from the dying tree and sang to her as he had sung to

Sirsha; and he mourned for Sirsha and for Mysha, and for the dying Silvana. When the sun reached its zenith he left, promising to return.

Each day, on his way to the caves to collect materials to make garlands for Taxiana, he spent time sitting by the damaged yew. Never on his way back. He could not bring himself to pass by the dying tree with an armful of greenery that was a courtship token and represented a lifetime stretching ahead; neither could he go to Taxiana straight from the dying tree but needed the cool, dark peace of the caves to clear his mind, the careful choosing of ferns and flowers and the joyful weaving of the garland to salve the aching helplessness, and prepare him for the night ahead – when his own lady might come to him even though he slept.

Each day he brought Taxiana wreaths of flowers and ferns to hang about the branches of her tree and each evening they were withered. On the final day he abandoned the growing things and brought her bright ribbons. Then he sat down and waited.

She was as dark as his mother was bright, with amber-gold skin, and night-black hair that fell to her knees; as beautiful as her tree was beautiful, stately and sombre. She did not smile easily nor was there laughter in her eyes. She regarded the ribbons with disdain, yet her voice when she spoke his name was soft enough.

"Lesandor, Silvana-son, rarely do men venture into our woods."

"Rarely do men understand the yearnings of their hearts, my lady," he replied.

She did smile then, her red lips curving into a smile that, though slight, promised everything he had ever desired.

Before he could take even a step towards her, once again her attention shifted to the ribbons. They seemed out of place in the dim, dark grove. "I have no need for such things," she told him.

"I shall take them away, I knew not what to bring for you."

"I am content, for now. Later, maybe, I will ask a gift of you," she replied, looking at him searchingly. "You know my name?"

"Taxiana," he said. He had heard it spoken. She smiled in earnest then.

Lesandor lost count of the days he spent in the yew woods. Taxiana would not willingly venture out nor would she see him leave, though he needed to find food, for there was little enough to be gleaned in those barren groves. For the first few days – with his passions, senses and thoughts focussed solely on Taxiana – he forgot about the dying Silvana, except in his dreaming, which was nightly haunted by the sounds of the storm. It was almost by chance that he came once more into her part of the woods. He was making his way to the deeper section of the river, to try to do some fishing, when he heard the sound of her sighing. For a while he sat near the damaged tree, unable to go close, despite her imploring him to do so. She moaned and called to him, then fell silent as Taxiana appeared.

"Lesandor?"

"I feel so helpless," he whispered. "Is there nothing we can do?"

"And what would you do?" Taxiana inquired.

He glanced around, surprised at the coldness he heard in her voice.

"She is suffering so."

"And she wants you to go to her. You must not listen, Lesandor, promise me. No, promise me you will not come here again. Amber such as hers could hold fast more than an unwary insect."

He rose to his feet, looking uncertainly from the dying tree to his wife.

"Come away," Taxiana said quietly.

He went with her. He did not look back.

There was no singing in the yew woods, no dancing. The Silvanii of the yew trees met quietly when they met at all. They preferred to remain solitary, and there were no woodmaids for there were no other smaller trees able to grow among the yews.

Lesandor began to feel lonely for the sound of laughter, for the brightness of a clear sky, for his family. He had no wish to take Jarin from the bright, vibrant places in Deepvale, nor did he think Taxiana would care to have the child there for, though she knew he had a son, she expressed little interest in him. Lesandor found himself saying less and less about his past life or his friends and family. He was not unhappy, yet he was not truly happy either. He feared he would become restless in time but that time had not yet come and he put the thought aside.

His search for Cuivah was set aside also.

"In the spring," he told Taxiana.

To which she replied, "Let it be. If she had wanted to be found, you would have found her before now." And he thought she was probably right and wondered why that had not occurred to him before. He put his mother's amber cloak clasp into his belt pouch for safe keeping, beside Sirsha's stone.

The little house he had planned held no appeal for Taxiana. They made a home in the caves instead.

"For now, for the winter," he said.

"*Now* is a very long time," she answered.

The damaged yew tree was dead, its berries withered, the Silvana gone. Unable to stay away, Lesandor had returned once more and had been relieved at what he had found though surprised also, for he would have expected her to stay longer.

❦

Shortly after midwinter, Lesandor needed to visit the town to purchase supplies. He went to the hostelry where he had stayed before and bought himself a good meal of hot food. It was pleasant to sit among the patrons of the place and listen to the chatter, banter and occasional songs, though he had no desire to stay. It occurred to him that he also had little real desire to leave. He leant his head against the rough stone wall and realised that he felt nothing. All his hopes, ambitions, memories even, had faded. It was as if they had never been.

Because he had to, he sent a letter to his parents. There was little real warmth in the words he wrote. More out of a feeling of duty than affection, he asked after his son – whose second birth anniversary had been and gone – and, having sealed the letter, he could not recall if he had even mentioned Elzandria's name. Possibly he was tired, he thought, too tired, yet he did not feel especially so. He felt empty and that did not worry him, though he thought perhaps it should. He listened to the conversation and felt no need to join in. Even when he was included he merely smiled politely, offering no comment unless he had no choice.

"You wouldn't be looking for a job?" The man who asked was stout and well dressed, prosperous looking.

Lesandor was surprised by the question; no one had ever asked him anything like that before. It occurred to him that his clothing was no longer quite as good as it had been and his whole appearance was unkempt; perhaps he looked as if he needed work. He shook his head.

Someone across the room asked what sort of work was on offer and the stout man told him there was need of labourers to help with the construction of the library extension for Shakenyew's municipal buildings. A tall, solid man offered his services as an accredited feller, and was taken on. Lesandor took little notice. He finished his meal and left.

Timber from the yew trees contrasted sharply with the black bark – bright, golden wood with grain like laughter lines. The little that was licenced to be felled was in great demand in the town, and far beyond, for furniture and for finishing buildings. The Silvanii took little notice, they inhabited the deepest parts of the woods where no one walked, let alone came to cut the trees. Or so it had been supposed.

Lesandor was standing beside the dark river that ran through the woods, armed with a short bow and searching for fish, when he felt the ripple of fury and heard the drawn-out cry of anguish as a Silvana met her death. Instinctively he knew Taxiana's tree was secure yet his first impulse was to run back to her grove to make certain. Stopping himself, he turned instead towards the area being cut – a lifetime of caring overriding three months of indifference and compelling him to act to prevent any more harm.

They knew what they had done. He could see it in the appalled glance of the overseer, who had arrived just moments before, more so in the hunched and sobbing bulk of the tree feller, his axe flung far from him, shards of golden-grained wood clinging to its blade.

The tree was not large, it lay on its side in a widening pool of congealing amber.

"That will have to be guarded, can't trust all folks. Must notify his Lordship up at the hold-house. That amber will have to be taken to Fairwater. There'll be trouble. There'll be big trouble." The overseer, mumbling to himself, looked up sharply when he caught sight of Lesandor. "What d'you want?"

"The same as you. To see that all is done here as it ought to be, and then to make certain you go as far away from this place as possible." Lesandor spoke quietly, turning away from the sight of the felled tree. "I heard her dying," he added to himself, then asked, "Is he all right?" nodding towards the man on the ground, whom he recognised from the hostelry.

"Hard to say. I've only once heard of the like before. That time they reckoned the man who cut the tree went mad within a halfyear. But then they said he stayed in the woods, seeking forgiveness, and the Silvanii sang to him. That was what finished him. Guilt and Silvana song, a potent combination, I'll warrant."

"Yes," Lesandor agreed.

For the first time since he had met Taxiana, he thought of the old man, Cavan, who had lost his Silvanan wife in such a manner, and he shuddered.

Taxiana's tree was far from the area being felled. She was quite safe. No axe would ever fall in that part of the wood. Lesandor offered to go to the townsmen, talk to the holder and persuade him to stop the felling altogether. Taxiana was not interested.

"They must be punished," she said for the fourth time. "They cannot be asked, they must be made to understand. It has been hard in the past. It will be easier now."

"How, easier?" he asked suspiciously. She smiled, her lips as red as the berries of her tree, as red as blood. It was rare that she smiled, now to see her do so gave him no pleasure. Her eyes were cold.

"You will exact revenge for us," she whispered. "You already know who cut the tree; now you must discover who ordered the felling and for whom the timber was intended. They must die. All of them must die."

"You are asking me to kill at least three men! It was an accident. Had they known the tree was Silvanan they would not have done such a thing. Taxiana, it was a horrible accident."

She shrugged. "Possibly. That is not your concern, nor mine." She looked up at the tangled branches of her great tree and then back at his face. "There is death for men in the yew tree. Fitting punishment, I think."

She wanted him to poison them. He refused. She insisted. Finally she told him that he had no option. Just as it was on his tongue to say he would do nothing of the sort, he realised she was right; he had no option. She was far stronger than he, far more powerful. He could not stand against her. If he chose to resist, it would be at the cost of his own life and there was not that much fight left in him. Somewhere, his will had drained away, along with everything else. He was an empty vessel waiting to be filled with the poison that flowed through the yew trees that were his world.

"No," he said and walked away. She did not follow him.

'No'. It was just a word. It meant nothing, as Taxiana well knew. He would do what she asked, that she also knew. And Lesandor knew it as well as she. Perhaps he would not do it as swiftly as she would like but he would comply eventually. A few days made no difference. Time was nothing, death was death, she could wait.

He went back to the town, as he had suggested, to speak with the works overseer and Lord Ussenis, the holder, and secure a promise that the inner trees would be left unmolested.

If they were surprised at his interest they did not say so, too shocked, maybe, at what had transpired. The cutting of a Silvanan tree had been a terrible mistake: fellers from beyond the holding misunderstanding their orders.

Lesandor returned to his cave home, satisfied, to find Taxiana no less adamant. She cared nothing for their excuses or for their lives, and she would give Lesandor no peace until he agreed to do as she asked.

Days and nights went by until one morning he stepped out of the cave, knowing that late in the night just passed he had agreed to carry out her wishes. Within, he felt little resistance to the idea. He recalled her saying that he had tried to give her a gift and she had wanted neither his flowers nor his ribbons; would he refuse her the one thing she really wanted?

Unshaven, with matted hair, and eyes dark from lack of sleep, he started towards the town, attracting strange looks from passers-by on the way. He took little notice of the stares, just as he took little notice of anything else. He nearly walked into the woman and child coming the opposite way along the wide road. The woman looked offended and her eyes, like pools of dark honey, rekindled a memory he had thought lost forever. He stammered an apology and when she heard his voice, which contrasted sharply with his look, her expression softened. Instead of whatever angry words she might have said, she asked the way to the house of the lord holder instead.

Lesandor indicated the road she must take, a slight hill she must climb. He pointed to the hold-house, its terra cotta roof tiles just visible beyond the trees.

"Turn at the junction up ahead. You will not get lost," he finished.

Distractedly pushing strands of pale brown hair from her face, the woman looked back.

"We came that way," she sighed, her voice weary. "We must have gone straight past. There is an ash tree there; is that it?"

Lesandor had forgotten.

"I will walk with you part of the way," he offered.

She was right. At the junction, an ash tree was indeed growing. He rested his head against it and felt hot tears wet his cheeks. The child looked up into his face, her great hazel eyes staring into his as, tentatively, she reached for his hand. And he held onto her as if his life depended on it, as surely it did.

Chapter Three

AELINN HAD NEVER been to Deepvale, she was not even sure
where the holding was. Nevertheless, she had found herself promising
to go there. There would be little help for Lesandor in Shakenyew, where
his story would terrify the holder and his council, and the best they could
do would be to throw him into prison and risk bringing the wrath of the
Silvanii on themselves.

He had told her his mother was a Silvana. Aelinn was not at all happy
at the prospect of meeting a Silvana – she had her own reasons for staying
clear of the Tree Ladies – yet if anyone knew what to do, it would be
Casandrina. And so Aelinn was getting ready to go to Deepvale.

"Deepvale? It's down the east coast. A goodways. Should take you
four or five days if you travel fast, and you could, for the roads are well
made and there are always passing trade carts if you need a ride." The
storekeeper glanced at the small, red-haired girl playing with her rag doll
on the floor by her mother's feet. "You'll need a ride, won't you?" He
smiled sympathetically.

Aelinn sighed. "I have to get there as soon as possible, but I've little
money left. I was hoping to find employment; there's no time for that
now." She packed up the bread and ewes' cheese she had purchased.

"That's a pretty brooch you're wearing, I know someone who'd pay
well for something that fine."

Aelinn stiffened, her hand going to her shoulder to pull her cloak
back over the clasp. Her mouth quivered. "No, I couldn't. He gave it into
my care for safekeeping and I have nothing else to remember him by."

"Up to you, of course," the storekeeper replied. "Just a thought."

She sold the brooch for less than a quarter its value, in the process getting sufficient funds to secure passage for herself and Lyrra to Deepvale, along with shelter, and food for them on the way. She had the child, she told herself, that was enough to remember him by. As if she would ever forget.

Fabiom was sitting in his conservatory, looking over the latest legislation from Fairwater, the details of which his old friend, Seric, now a fellow member of the Assembly, had brought him. The paperwork was not urgent and had been merely an excuse to visit Deepvale, after Seric had chanced to meet up with Philon and they had bemoaned the fact that it was well over a year since they had enjoyed the hospitality of Deepvale's hold-house. Yan and Masgor were also there, discussing the legislation, when Aelinn arrived, having carried her daughter up the final part of the hill.

Dusty and exhausted, she nearly dropped the little girl as she neared the entrance. Fabiom went out to her immediately.

"Lord Fabiom?" she asked breathlessly, as the child hid her face against her mother's shoulder. He indicated that he was, and brought her into the conservatory to sit and rest.

"What can I do for you, lady?" he asked, concerned.

Before Aelinn could reply, Lan'h, who had been summoned by Yan, appeared with a jug of berry juice and offered the visitors a drink. Rag doll in hand, the little girl climbed down from her mother's lap and went to the woodmaid, giggling as she did so.

Aelinn looked on, surprised. "Lyrra! She is usually so shy. The only other person she has ever taken to so quickly is your son."

"You have seen Lesandor," Fabiom realised. "Did he send you? We have only received one letter from him in almost half a year – and that was barely legible and made no sense. I have had people searching for him, but no one seems to know where he is. Is he all right?"

"No," Aelinn replied, answering Fabiom's last question only. "And he needs help. Though what help, I cannot imagine."

She told how Lesandor had asked her to take word to Deepvale, how he had poured out his heart, leaning against the ash tree that marked the turning to the holder's house. She was afraid for him, afraid of what he might do; she had tried to persuade him to travel with her but he would not leave. That had been five days ago.

Lyrra jumped down from her mother's knee again, smiling. "Hello," she said to Casandrina, who was standing in the doorway.

"I misheard," Casandrina whispered, her hand smoothing the child's bright hair. "Not a yew. He could not."

But Aelinn told her it was so.

"I cannot believe I never told him, never warned him. Did I fail him so utterly?"

"You did not fail him, Casi. We did not fail him. How could we have foreseen this?" Fabiom reasoned.

"They are death," Casandrina murmured. "Always. How could he not know, not understand?"

"He understands now, only too well," Aelinn said quietly.

With a gentle touch to Lyrra's cheek, Casandrina turned away. Something dire in her expression made Fabiom follow her.

He lost her for a few moments and found her again just outside the boundary edge of the garden. There had been a yew tree there, small enough, granted, yet still the height and more of a grown man, which now was ripped from the ground by its very roots. Fabiom had never seen such a look on his wife's face and he approached her cautiously, fearing the rage that gripped her, yet she let him take her torn hands in his and kiss them tenderly.

"Casandrina." He whispered her name as he enfolded her into his arms, feeling her shake with grief and anger both. Holding her and stroking her hair, he gazed in horrified fascination at the ruin of the tree behind her.

Wordlessly, she extricated herself from his embrace and walked away, across the garden, Lan'h following. This time Fabiom did not go after her. He knew she went to seek counsel among the other Silvanii, though what advice they could offer, he could not guess.

He returned to the conservatory where, Masgor's hearing not being all it had been, Yan was repeating what Aelinn had said.

After Yan had explained, Masgor shook his head. "It's a pity he can't simply cut her tree down."

Seric looked in shocked surprise from the old tutor to Fabiom, but Fabiom's expression gave nothing away.

"The legal consequences would be severe," Fabiom replied at last, at which Masgor snorted.

"Fabiom! It's not a matter for jokes," Seric said.

"Do I laugh?" Fabiom retorted.

"Take no notice of me," Masgor said. "Old age is a wonderful excuse for blatant disregard of the law. What could they do to me? It's only a pity I no longer have the strength to wield an axe."

"Not so old that you don't know what you're saying," Philon told him.

"The consequences for murdering three men would be severe too," Fabiom muttered, seemingly to himself.

"Speaking as a magistrate?" Yan asked.

"Speaking as his father."

"Surely you're not weighing the matter in legal terms?" Seric asked, bemused. "Neither is a viable option. Can you not get him away from there, and keep him away?"

Fabiom looked towards the woods. "I can only speak for myself, but I can tell you that there is no power, no law, no man who could keep me away from here and from Casandrina."

"You cannot compare Casandrina with this Taxiana!" Yan said, aghast.

"She too is a Silvana."

Aelinn looked from one man to the next until Fabiom felt her eyes on him and turned, smiling, towards her. The others went on arguing among themselves as to what could or should be done.

"You have done us a great service. Please, be our guests, you and your daughter. Have some refreshments, bathe and rest. You must be exhausted. I must go to my son."

Aware of Kir'h watching him, he turned his head to see her beckon to him. He excused himself from the company and went to her, out of sight of the others. Zin'h was with her. He hoped they had not come up with some outlandish plan to help.

"Casandrina told us we must stay here. But we want to come

too," Zin'h whispered. "It is important, Fabiom. Away from her tree, Casandrina will be at a disadvantage. We can help. The more of us that are there, the better chance she will have against Lesandor's.... Against *her*."

"What are you saying, Zin'h? What is Casandrina going to do?"

"Casandrina will challenge her. What else can be done?"

"No! I could lose them both." He turned to face the woods, a look of panic fleeting across his face. "Where is she now?" he demanded. Then he took a deep breath. "No, she cannot go that far alone, can she?"

Kir'h took his hands in hers. "She can only go if you show her the way."

"Very well, then I must deal with this by myself."

The recollection of what the Silvanii of his own woods had once done to him, years ago, came to his mind. Stripped of his memories, unable to tell dreams from reality, he had endured a nightmare period of confusion and loss – and *they*, though acting out of self-preservation, had borne him no ill will. He could not dwell on that, Lesandor was too precious. "I must go quickly. Whatever solution there may be, it cannot involve anyone else, especially Casandrina."

The rowan woodmaid's grip tightened. "But you might.... If something dire befell you...."

"Kir'h, I shall be careful. I promise. I shall go and see what the situation is, that is all. That has to be better than Casandrina going to challenge a yew Silvana in her own forest, doesn't it?"

Zin'h, who had briefly run off, returned with a small package. "Beeswax," she told Fabiom. "To block your ears."

Fabiom shook his head. "I shall need to speak with her, to hear what she has to say."

The petite whitethorn woodmaid glowered up at him. "If she sings to you, you will not return to us. If you are lost, Casandrina will return to her tree, unable to travel anywhere. Lesandor will be alone forever – with *her*."

Fabiom took the package. "You are right. Whatever else happens, *that* cannot be."

Despite her weariness, Aelinn offered to act as his guide back to Shakenyew. Fabiom declined, certain he could find the way, though he had never been to the holding. Instead, he asked her to wait with Casandrina, if she was in no hurry to return to her own home.

Aelinn was in no hurry to go anywhere. She had been calling on her cousin in Shakenyew in desperation, having nowhere else to go.

Though he was anxious to set out as soon as possible, there was one person Fabiom needed to see before he left. He made his way to the nursery where Kita was untangling a hank of silk waste while her daughter and Lesandor's son, just woken from a nap, tumbled together at her feet.

"Where's Casandrina?" Kita asked. "I hate spinning. It's bad enough doing it with friends, I'll not sit here alone with a spindle when I could be in the garden."

"She had to go to the woods," Fabiom said, dropping to his knees beside the little ones. "I swear Jarin is twice the size Lesandor was at his age. You fed him too well!"

"Don't blame me – he's much bigger than my Mysha. He's going to be a sturdy lad, that's for certain," Kita agreed.

Fabiom lifted Jarin onto his lap. "I've got to go and get your papa. I'll send him home to you, I promise."

Kita abandoned any pretence of spinning. "What's wrong?"

Fabiom kissed Jarin's head and looked up at his cousin. "Lesandor seems to have got himself into a spot of trouble. I've got to go north. Can you do me a favour?"

"Of course, anything."

"Tell Casandrina that I've gone, that—"

"Wait! Since when have you not communicated with your wife?"

Mysha trotted over to Fabiom and grasped at Jarin's feet; both children laughed gleefully.

"She is busy and I'm anxious to go and – she's going to be less than happy that I haven't taken her with me."

Kita frowned. "He's in that much trouble?" A squeal interrupted her. "Mysha! No. Not nice. She adores Jarin but she will bite him."

Fabiom swung the little boy up out of harm's way. "In that case, perhaps I should sort out betrothal papers for them before I go. What do you think, Jarin? Would Mysha keep you in line and stop you making very, very silly mistakes?"

Kita cocked her head. "I don't like the sound of this, Fabiom."

"Your daughter and my grandson? You just said she adores him. True, they are close in age, and it makes sense for a girl to marry a man who is established and settled, but you and Nissus are of an age and married young and seem to have done all right. It's not as if Jarin's future is in doubt: he'll be raised to be a holder, after all." He sighed. "Let's hope his father can fulfil that role first."

"No. Not that." Kita joined him on the floor where she bundled her daughter onto her lap. "How long are you planning to go away for? How much trouble is Lesandor in? I don't think these two will be considering marriage for a good while yet, after all."

Fabiom handed Jarin over. "Just tell Casandrina that I'll get Lesandor home. Oh, and we have a house-guest. Can I leave her and her little one in your care also? I'll be back as soon as I can." He kissed all three, then left before Kita could ask any more questions.

By the time Fabiom left the nursery, the woodmaids, with more practical help from Yan, had made up a pack of clothing and food for the journey ahead. Of the many offers of help he received, he accepted only one – that of Ralfus, Philon's aide and a one-time archer under his own command in Gerik.

Leaving Casandrina was the hardest thing Fabiom had ever done. And when, just before they reached Valehead, he felt her call to him as she tried to follow, it was all he could do not to go back. As night crept over the eastern horizon and the sun descended into the distant hills to the west, Fabiom sat hunched over the fire Ralfus had built, unable to eat anything, watching the road, fearful that she would catch up with him.

"We'll head on, Commander," Ralfus said, packing the food away and looking at Fabiom with concern.

They travelled through the night, moving swiftly, and her call faded from Fabiom's mind before the dawn broke. The emptiness was worse than the worrying.

'Casi!' His mind cried out her name. There was no reply.

She could not hear him for she was too far away, weeping with despair, lost.

Aided by her woodmaids, Calbrin found her and brought her home.

Chapter Four

SOON AFTER AELINN set out for Deepvale, Lesandor took a room in the town-centre hostelry, where his sleep was tortured by Taxiana's voice, nagging and goading him to go through with what he had promised. He knew the dreams were not just of his imagination, she was close enough to exert her will over him when his mind was not alert, especially regarding something he had already given his word on. More than that, he missed her with a terrible longing. The worst part was the realisation that he could not go back to her until he had done what she wanted. He did not know how he would live with the consequences of her demands, or with the consequences of denying her.

His only hope was that he might be strong enough to withstand those demands for a few days more, for he had to hold onto the belief that help – in some form – would be forthcoming, and soon, before the situation deteriorated. The second day proved him wrong.

The death of a Silvanan tree was not something that would be easily forgotten and the subject came up in conversation over and over. Blame was laid, first here and then there, and feelings were already running high by the middle of the afternoon when a swarthy man came through the hostelry doors.

"You still out and about, Bathis? Thought his Lordship would have had you locked away by now," one of the patrons shouted.

The newcomer scowled and muttered something inaudible.

"Who is that?" Lesandor asked another customer.

"Bathis. He was in charge of the tree fellers. It was he who gave the orders for where and what to cut."

"They were misread, mind you, not deliberate, but he never was very precise," another volunteered. "The tree feller was not to blame for misreading his instructions. Bathis should learn to tell his right from his left."

Lesandor felt a rage in him such as he had never known. All he could think was that it could have been Taxiana's tree broken and bleeding amber; it could have been his lady's voice crying out in agony as Bathis's axe struck. Somewhere, among his few belongings in his room, was the poison she had prepared. He gave that no heed. His knife was nearer to hand. Only the long, bloody line drawn across the man's left arm made Lesandor hesitate and, by then, others had come to their wits and managed to overpower him. It took four of them.

"There'll be none of that here!" the innkeep bellowed, only annoyed that his tables had been overturned.

Lesandor was thrown out without a chance to retrieve his few possessions, including his purse and cloak.

Unseeing and uncaring, he stumbled to the outskirts of the town and into the hostelry there, where he purchased a pitcher of cheap wine, which was all he could afford with the small coinage he carried in his belt pouch. Afternoon passed into evening.

He was sitting alone on a hard bench, staring at the cup full of golden liquid, which reminded him painfully of yew heartwood, wondering if getting very drunk and remaining so would be expedient, in as much as it might prevent him from taking any irreversible steps, when two men sat down beside him.

"Misery makes a poor drinking companion, friend," one commented, and Lesandor pushed the half-empty pitcher towards him.

"Help yourself." He rose as if to leave but the other stopped him.

"Sorry, didn't mean to intrude if you'd rather be alone. Just that me and Berri here thought you looked like you could do with some company, or some sport."

Lesandor retook his seat. "I could do with a diversion."

Unwilling though he was to get involved with any of the locals, he had just discovered that even two cups of wine, undiluted and taken on an empty stomach, had made him unsteady on his feet. Sitting was therefore preferable to standing. The one called Berri grinned, though whether at his answer or his barely concealed shakiness Lesandor was unsure.

The other poured a small quantity of Lesandor's wine into his own cup. "Where's the water?"

Lesandor shrugged. "No one brought any over."

Berri laughed and raised his hand to call over a serving boy. "Out-towners, that's us," he told Lesandor. Come up from Greendell yesterday. Local lads want an archery contest. They've a team of three and they pointed you out as another blow-in. There's not much on it except a few drinks for providing the entertainment. Still, it's better than dying of boredom."

The bows were made of yew, their flexibility belying the nature of their origins, or their denizens. Lesandor tried not to think of that, despite how the feel of the wood beneath his hands made them tremble. He laid down the bow and tightened the straps of the leather bracer until his arm ached. Across the courtyard, Gelbin, the innkeep's youngest son, was setting up a row of six oval targets with barely perceivable centres.

"One point for the outer edge, five for the middle, eight for dead centre, lose a point for hitting the wrong target!" Much laughter greeted the lad's comments.

Lesandor did not hear. He was aware only of the throbbing pain in his left arm, the focus of his concentration.

"I'd loosen those bindings if I were you, young man," said the mistress of the house, portly, jolly, but concerned.

Lesandor made no move, so she deftly did the task herself. He did not object. The rush of blood to his lower arm surprised him and the colour returned to his hand.

"Much better," she muttered and walked away to fetch refreshments.

In the event the 'out-towners' did not win, but they lost with a respectable score and Lesandor acquitted himself well enough for more than one of the spectators to offer him an individual challenge. The wine flowed, the shooting was not of the highest standard, and, by the end of the day, Lesandor had enough money to take a room in the hostelry and pay for a meal. The food was good and plentiful and the company merry.

Lesandor was reluctant to leave the bustling common room to retire to his small bedchamber. If his dreams had been disturbing the previous night, he dreaded what this night's might bring since he had tried to take another man's life. Eventually the fire burnt down in the hearth and he had no choice but to retire. He was aware of the inn mistress's eyes on him, the look of solicitude on her face as he wished her a peaceful night and made his way up the narrow stairway. Only moments after he had shut the door behind him there was a knock and he opened it to find her standing there, with an armful of blankets.

"It's a chill enough night, thought you'd better have an extra cover," she explained, wishing him a safe passage through the dark watches ahead.

At breakfast the next morning she served him herself, piling his plate high with scrambled eggs and fresh baked bread.

"If you'll give me that tunic I'll wash and mend it for you," she offered. "If you're planning to stay."

He was, and he thanked her for her kindness.

"Nonsense, anyone would think I didn't look after my customers properly, seeing you like that. Why don't you shave, too? You look like a foreigner."

He grinned sheepishly and took her advice. Later, after she mended his clothes, he let her cut his hair.

"That's better, you look like a man of standing now." She folded her arms across her ample bosom and regarded him seriously. "More than that, in fact. You're younger than I thought, too; and in some sort of trouble, I'll warrant. I'll not pry. It's none of my business, but if you need a friend, come and talk to me. I've four sons of my own so I know how to take care of lads such as yourself."

For the next five days Lesandor financed his keep, and enough wine to keep his mind sufficiently numb for his purposes, by wagering his skills as an archer. Given the condition he was in, many fellow patrons of the hostelry were willing to test their skills against his, yet he won more than he lost overall.

The inn mistress watched him meanwhile, feeding him well and caring for him as much as she was able, more and more convinced that something was very wrong. Her eldest son told her she was being foolish and her husband told her it was none of their business. Still she could not let it go and eventually sent her youngest boy out and about to make inquiries.

Not quite sure what it was he was trying to discover, Gelbin made his way to the town-centre hostelry. There he saw two men sitting, talking with the innkeep. One was a soldier and rather unremarkable, the other by contrast was quite striking: he was a handsome man, sparsely built, with dark curls touched at the temples with grey, and large blue eyes edged with numerous laughter lines, though he was not smiling at present. Gelbin had never seen such fine clothes or such expensive jewellery and accoutrements. Apparently similarly impressed, the innkeep was giving his customer his undivided attention, though he was shaking his head.

"No, I'm sorry, my lord, I've not seen your son here. Surely he will be up at the hold-house?"

While they were not entirely alike, there was enough about the young man at his parents' hostelry and this strange lord sitting before him, to convince Gelbin that he knew where the lord's son was.

"Sir," he ventured.

The innkeep glared at him with startled annoyance. "Gelbin, what are you doing here? I'm busy," he hissed.

"Sir," Gelbin repeated, ignoring the innkeep.

Fabiom smiled kindly, putting him at ease.

"I think I know where your son is. He would be twenty years maybe, tall, with blue eyes, and hair dark, like your own, though finer and straighter?"

"That's Lesandor," Fabiom agreed. "You say you know where he is?"

"Yes, my lord. He's staying at my parents' house. It's a boarding house and inn on the outskirts of town."

The innkeep scowled as Fabiom rose to his feet. Gelbin noticed that Fabiom, like his son, was tall.

"Thank you. Will you take me there?"

Gelbin nodded as Fabiom turned to his erstwhile host. "And thank you for your trouble." His travelling companion put a handful of coins on to the table.

"Thank *you*, sir," the innkeeper replied, his good humour somewhat restored.

A newcomer, a brawny, balding soldier, shot against Berri and won by a single point. Lesandor took on a local glass blower. It was another close match, which Lesandor won with his last arrow – a straight shot into the centre of the target.

"Name your stakes, lad!" the soldier challenged. "I'll take you on."

"Whatever you like," Lesandor replied, confident from his last victory.

"How if we make it worthwhile then? Say a half year's service of the loser to the winner, beginning immediately."

Lesandor laughed loudly at the proposal. Having seen his new opponent shoot, he was in no doubt that good though he was the soldier's ability did not match his own. A half year's service – there might be some benefit in that too, given the straits he was in. So thinking, he accepted the wager.

The lot fell to Lesandor and he opted to begin. His first shot struck just short of the centre, the next wider still, though within the second ring, the three that followed all hit home and he glanced with satisfaction at the little cluster of arrows embedded in the centre of the target. The murmurs grew louder. Those who had backed him cheered wildly.

There was hardly room for more than three arrows in the target's heart, hardly room to better Lesandor's total, yet moments later five eagle-flighted arrows crowded into that space for a perfect score.

Lesandor stared at the target, suddenly horribly sober, then turned to face his opponent.

"Father!"

Nearby, the soldier who had challenged him stood with his arms folded across his chest, grinning broadly.

"Good shooting, Commander," Ralfus acknowledged quietly, as he took Fabiom's bow and quiver.

Mind racing, Lesandor retrieved the jasper-tipped arrows then let his father usher him into the relative privacy of the hostelry, away from the spectators, who were still acclaiming Fabiom's prowess.

Their hostess showed them into a side-room, where she served them herself.

"I'm so glad someone has come for him," she confided to Fabiom, setting down a platter of mutton, beans and flat bread.

They talked late into the night and, in the course of their talking, Fabiom learnt the whereabouts of Taxiana's tree.

"Everything will be resolved," he promised.

Lesandor was doubtful. He felt powerless against the hold Taxiana had over him, certain his father would fare no better than he with pleas and arguments.

"You cannot reason with her. She will not listen," he told Fabiom. "I have tried, believe me."

"I do. Yet there are more ways than one to achieve any purpose." Fabiom leant across the table and grasped Lesandor's arm. "You look dreadful" – he shook his head – "I intend to secure your release from her awful demands, no matter what I have to do."

Lesandor picked over the remains of food, long since gone cold.

"The wager in the yard – there was a purpose behind that, I presume?" He did not look at his father.

"Uh huh. You made a bet. You lost. I collect. Tomorrow morning, at dawn, start for Deepvale with Ralfus and go home to your mother – and your son."

Lesandor looked up. "No, I, I cannot leave her. Father, you cannot ask that...."

Fabiom's expression silenced his arguments. "Service contracts are binding, as you well know. Were they not, you would never have gone to Windwood. So yes, I *can* ask it of you. And I have. Stay with your mother, and tell her ... tell her I'm sorry for leaving the way I did." He scooped some of the leftover mashed beans onto a morsel of bread. After a lengthy silence, he added, "From what you have told me, Taxiana sounds to be of high status, yet, however senior she might be, Silvanii cannot travel far from their home woods without great effort."

"Mother went all the way to Southernport with you," Lesandor reminded him.

"Yes, she did, but 'with me' as you say. That's the point. I've never read nor heard tell of a Silvana travelling without her partner. They have only one focus of direction – their tree. Yet even if I am wrong about that, still I think you will be safe in Deepvale. Your mother would not let any harm come to you there."

In his mind, Lesandor saw again the expression in Taxiana's eyes as he pleaded for the lives of the three men she wanted dead, the cold glimmer of triumph as he took the flask filled with poison distilled from bark and berries. Yet he knew his father was right; Casandrina would be even more dangerous if her anger was roused on his behalf. As for feeling safe, he had no real opinion about that. Walking away from Taxiana, if only for half a year – that would be hard, though the thought of going home was appealing. Not that he had any choice. As Fabiom had reminded him: he had gambled and lost. Twice now.

They parted the next morning, at the junction where the ash tree grew.

"Father, I am truly sorry," Lesandor said. "I was foolish." He shrugged; shame, relief, fear and gratitude warring within him.

Fabiom embraced him. "Go quickly."

After a moment's hesitation, Lesandor turned his face towards home.

Fabiom breathed a quiet sigh of relief. That part, at least, had been far easier than he had anticipated .

"Take care of him, Ralfus, I want him as far away from here as possible by nightfall."

"Be careful, Commander," Ralfus warned.

Chapter Five

FABIOM HAD NO intention of being anything but careful; being married to Casandrina for almost forty years had not lessened his respect for the Silvanii.

He went immediately back to the hostelry and collected his pack, speaking to no one, determined he should be left alone. No one else would bear any responsibility for his actions.

The outbuildings at the back of the hostelry were kept unlocked. In one, among the tools, there were several stone axes, and one with a bronze blade and a short wooden handle – easy to conceal.

Fabiom stood, barely breathing, staring at the axe.

Though he had gone to Shakenyew with the intention of talking to Lesandor's wife, that had been before he had actually seen his son. Nothing Aelinn had said had prepared him for the despair in Lesandor's expression, the deadness in his voice, his stumbling gait. Casandrina's beautiful, graceful boy had been broken.

He reached out his hand, testing the bronze blade; it was honed, ready to use. On the day Lesandor was born, Fabiom – with help from his childhood friend Nalio – had felled the only yew tree in the garden of the hold-house. He had cut it, thinking to protect his new baby from the temptation of the bright berries in the years ahead. It was a decision he now bitterly regretted.

"I am sorry," he whispered. "I made the wrong decision: I should have taught you about the danger, not tried to protect you by removing it." He leant his head against the doorframe. As a child he had learnt that lesson the hard way, nearly poisoning himself with berries from that same tree, saved – and punished – by his own father. He took a deep breath, and the axe. There were no choices left.

The yew woods blurred the horizon, lying between the familiar sky and earth as something unknown, the place where he was bound. Their green was not a shade that was known to him, neither was their shape familiar. Strangest of all were his feelings towards them, the antipathy and anger. All of a sudden he was reminded of his own mother, her fury the day he told her he had gone to the woods on his seventeenth birth eve, and her expression when he and Casandrina had returned to the hold-house ten days later. Remembering that, he walked past the man leaning against the road-stone that marked the municipal boundary.

"You've left your quiver behind this morning, I see."

Cursing under his breath, Fabiom paused, turned and nodded amiably.

"So you might. There's nothing living in those woods. Nothing that an arrow would be use against anyway, even one flighted with the wing feather of a golden eagle. But I'll warrant you're out hunting nonetheless." The man pushed himself upright, away from the stone. "Bathis is the name," he added thrusting out his hand. His eyes did not quite meet Fabiom's, flickering instead from Fabiom's pack to the horizon and back again, his calloused hand clammy as it gripped Fabiom's upper arm. "You didn't go off with the boy then? It was a clever move, winning his obedience like that. I'd guess he hadn't intended to leave Shakenyew just yet."

"He had some unfinished business, but I can deal with that for him."

"Friend, I am his unfinished business. I have the scar to prove it." He tossed his cloak back over his shoulders and held out his left arm. An ugly red line ran from his elbow almost to his hand. "And it's only there because I was quick enough to get my arm between your lad's blade and my throat. I trust the contents of that pack are not for me."

"I am sorry about your arm, and your troubles, friend Bathis. If it's of any consolation, I can assure you there's nothing in this pack to concern you."

"Other than a sharp axe," Bathis suggested. Before Fabiom could react, Bathis nodded towards his own pack. "Likewise."

278

Bathis was insistent, claiming he was already in as much trouble as he could be. As he saw it, Fabiom was doing him great service, for the Silvanii would have had his life already, by choice.

"All I want is to be of help. But tell me, before you say no again, what will you do alone? In their eyes I am doomed. How much more guilty can I be?" Bathis laughed hollowly.

At that, Fabiom reluctantly agreed. "Very well. And thank you. It's not that I'm ungrateful, just that this is something I have no right to involve another in. There is one stipulation though – if it comes to ... if we have no other choice – both the first and final blow must be mine. It will make no difference as far as the Silvanii are concerned, but legally the responsibility will be mine. I'll not have another carrying that burden for me."

Bathis shook his head emphatically. "Final yes, I'll grant you that, willingly, but the first, no. That will be my strike. I'll take my chances with his Lordship and the magistrates. I'll wield the axe. You must deal with *her*. I worked it out – why he was so messed up – she's corporeal, isn't she? I couldn't face that."

Once within the boundary of the yew woods, they slowed their pace to what would have been a stroll – under different circumstances. Fabiom wanted to appear nonchalant. It was difficult. Never before had he been in a forest that made him feel uneasy and, knowing his purpose, he felt more apprehensive still. He should have come at night, a late autumn night; as if there could be a right time, a right season for what he was about to do. Yet to face her in the early springtime, when she would be most potent, he was reducing his already slim chances of success.

He glanced over his shoulder. Bathis walked behind him, treading carefully. That there were two of them would probably make all the difference, Fabiom realised.

Other than the sound of their breathing, shallow and fast, and of their footfalls, the forest was quiet – too quiet for Fabiom's tastes – and dark. Little light filtered through the heavy canopy.

Lesandor's directions were clear in Fabiom's mind and he led Bathis unerringly towards their destination until they arrived in a glade where a broken yew stood.

"We'll wait here." Fabiom lowered himself to the ground, his back against a mossy rock.

"Wait? For what?" Bathis scowled and looked urgently around. "Come on. We can't wait here. I can't stay here!"

"We wait for evening. Silvanii don't sleep, but they do rest. They are creatures of the day, of the sunlight."

Bathis, with another anxious look around, sat down. Like Fabiom, he chose to lean against a rock rather than a tree trunk. "So why did you come so early?"

"To make sure I could find where her grove was. I thought I could find it, but I was not certain."

"And you are now – we're close?"

"Close enough. Not too close." Fabiom took out a flask. "It's just water –"

"I've some bread," Bathis volunteered.

As evening fell – a quiet evening with few birds – Fabiom offered Bathis some beeswax to stop up his ears. Bathis shook his head.

"I thought of that – believe me. I packed that even before my axe."

Fabiom softened the wax between his fingers, but when it came to inserting it, he only put one piece in, keeping the other in his hand. Then he led Bathis on the final part of their journey.

At a signal from Fabiom, Bathis pressed himself against the trunk of a tree at the edge of the grove. Fabiom stepped forward, alone. From years of experience, he sensed which tree was inhabited and therefore had to be Taxiana's. As he had told Bathis he would, he dropped his pack beside it to mark it.

"Lesandor has gone away," he said, finding himself unable to call her by name. "He is not coming back."

"He will be back."

"No." His voice faltered for an instant. She was beautiful and he was surprised. Worse, she looked young, almost vulnerable. Had he not been so appalled at Lesandor's condition he would have turned and fled from that dark place. As it was, he would not forget what she had done to his son. "No. He will not set foot in these woods again."

She moved closer to him. He could feel her breath on his face, smell the scent of her, unfamiliar.

"I can feel him. He is not too far away. I will call to him and he will return to me. He has no choice."

He forced himself to look beyond her, at her tree, rather than at her face. The sight was scarcely less intimidating for the girth of the yew was massive, larger by far than he had expected, and he regarded it with dismay. He knew he was strong still, the years had not yet taken that from him, but even with Bathis's help the task he had set himself seemed as daunting physically as it did to his sensibilities. As the enormity of what he was about to do finally registered in his mind, the world beyond the woods suddenly seemed a long way away. He could sense Taxiana's eyes on him. He would not meet her gaze.

"You think to bargain maybe?" she mocked. "What could you give me in exchange for him? There is nothing I desire. No. He is mine. He came to me of his own volition and I will not give him up. I will not give him up, Lord Fabiom."

A shudder ran through him as she spoke his name, another as the first notes of a song vibrated through the silence of the evening. Dismayed, he fumbled with the ball of beeswax but it slipped from his fingers – and from his thoughts. She sang of emptiness, a long sleep, the allure of nothingness. As if in a dream, he watched Bathis open his pack and take out a heavy, stone-sharpened axe, and wondered why they were there.

Taxiana's song was cut short by a scream of anguished rage as Bathis's first blow fell untrue, slicing only through the bark and glancing off the hard wood within. Freed from her thrall, Fabiom dropped to his knees, scrabbling about in the debris of years past, finding a pebble and some dried berries before his fingers came into contact with the yielding texture of the beeswax ball. Ramming it into his ear, he watched with horror as the cut inflicted on her tree appeared on her body: a gaping wound across her belly. Momentarily paralysed by the sight, he did not realise she had closed the gap between them until he felt her hands claw at his neck even as the next blow struck. He lunged sideways and she missed his throat, her nails raking the skin of his right shoulder and half way down his arm instead. In the instant before she vanished from his sight, searing pain shut out the sounds of dying.

It was well gone midnight when Fabiom dropped his axe from his raw hands and surveyed the wreckage of the yew tree. He was shaking with the exertion he had expended and with suppressed fear, mingled with anger. His wounded shoulder felt as if it was on fire.

Bathis sank to his knees beside the stump, placing his hands on the ground on either side to support his drooping shoulders. He was about to speak when he pulled his left hand from the ground and froze, an expression of fascinated horror on his face as viscous strands oozed from his fingers back to the ground. He wiped his hand on his clothing, only succeeding in making the situation worse.

"Leave it for a few moments," Fabiom rasped. "It will harden in the air. Then we must get out of here."

"I can see why things happened in Gerik as they did," Bathis murmured, rolling the drying amber between his fingers.

Fabiom was almost more shocked by Bathis's words than by what they had just done and in a way it frightened him more too, for Bathis had nothing to lose now. However, he said nothing other than, "Come on, we must go."

It had taken far longer than Fabiom had expected to destroy the huge tree. Now, though his legs could hardly support him, he knew they dare not remain in the woods a moment longer than necessary. They had to find a way out, for they could not risk spending the night, lost, in the dark tracts of the yew wood.

It was as much as he could do to pick up his axe but he would not leave it behind, beside the felled tree. Still shaking, soaked with perspiration and barely able to hold his lantern aloft, he stumbled in what he hoped was the direction of town. Bathis followed.

Knowing the fate that had befallen Yasdon, Fabiom was careful to avoid any trees he felt might be sentient. It was never easy to be certain, but their anger was such that, on this occasion, it was more obvious than usual. If they were to make it out alive, Fabiom knew he dare not make a mistake – one sweep from a bough was all it would take. With care, and glancing upwards as much as at the barely illuminated path, Fabiom guided Bathis to safety. Neither spoke.

There was no point in asking for the Silvanii's forgiveness; Fabiom knew neither condonation nor understanding would be forthcoming. Ideally he would have kept his identity hidden from them, but Taxiana had known immediately who he was. How many others recognised him as Lesandor's father, he could not guess.

The woods seemed endless. Paths twisted where he thought they should be straight, turnings appeared where he thought there were none. The light from the lantern gave him no help, casting deceptive and distorting shadows across his path while, about their heads, huge branches thrashed in a rising wind that emanated from no source outside the woods. Trying to block out the pain in his shoulder and the noises closing in, Fabiom quickened his pace. The Silvanii did not speak, though Fabiom sensed they were close, shadowing them, watching them. His tiredness vanished. His only thought was to get back to the open road as rapidly as he could.

The first grey smudge of the dawn showed on the horizon, the most wonderful sight to Fabiom's eyes. The woods were behind him, the town ahead. He refused to think about what he had just done. He needed a bath and a meal and, most of all, sleep.

Bathis left him at the marker stone where they had met, headed for home. Theirs was not an association either wished to continue any longer than necessary, though, in their own way each was grateful to the other.

Fabiom went on to the hostelry, to the room Lesandor had been renting, glad of the brief time of solitude and a chance to wash the sweat and grime from his body. By the time he was done, breakfast was being served. He made his way to the dining room.

When the food arrived, he found he had no appetite and retired back to the room, where he tried to think of mundane matters, and failed. He turned his mind instead to the legislation he had been considering and discussing when Aelinn arrived, but such thoughts invariably led to the memory of her arrival and the news she brought. He lay on the bed. It was impossible to think of nothing at all. Sleep seemed far away, though his body ached and was weary to the very bones. He knew he was afraid to sleep, afraid of the dreams sleep might bring. Eventually the demands of his body overcame his resistance and he did sleep, though fitfully.

The sound of the noonday bell roused him, to squint at the sharp rays of sunlight knifing through the slits in the window shutter. Every muscle ached and complained, and the lacerations on his right shoulder and down his arm were inflamed. He fastened his tunic carefully, making certain his shoulder was not visible. The day loomed before him, as dark and foreboding as the damaged yew woods.

In the dining room, trying to appear unperturbed, Fabiom ordered a simple meal of bread and beans. Waiting for it to arrive, he finally allowed himself to really consider what he had done: more than murder, the felling of a Silvanan tree threatened the very essence of the relationship between the Silvanii and Morene's human inhabitants. The penalty was fixed. Only the manner in which it was carried out was open to speculation. He spent the time it took him to force down the food imagining what he would do to another holder who came to Deepvale and deliberately committed the same atrocity. For certain, he had no desire to suffer whatever penalty Ussenis might think fit to impose on him; yet now the deed was done it would have to be accounted for. His own feelings were of little consequence.

Having eaten all he could stomach, he paid his bill, along with what was outstanding on Lesandor's. He fancied he received some strange looks, which might well have been figments of his imagination and, even if they were not, probably had more to do with the archery contest than anything else.

Fabiom was preparing to leave the hostelry, to go to the duty magistrate in the municipal offices, when – in a voice that carried around the dining room – the innkeep began telling a few of his familiar customers how Bathis had been discovered in the yew woods beside a felled tree, quite dead, his hands encrusted with amber.

The room fell silent.

"Apparently, Bathis arrived home, late last evening, with a piece of amber, promising his family they were all going to be rich beyond their dreams," the innkeep informed his enthralled audience. "He told his youngest brother to go with him, back to the woods. But the lad balked at the last minute, so Bathis went alone. When morning came and he'd not come back, the brother sent for friends, and together they searched. They found him all right. Both hands caught fast in amber, and his skull cracked by a huge branch that must have swept down and killed him."

"He cut another Silvanan tree? He must've gone mad!" The comment came from the far side of the room. Other voices were raised in agreement.

"Maybe he did go mad from fear of the consequences of that first cutting. And the Silvanii took their revenge."

"We'll all be in for it this time!"

Fabiom leant against the door jamb and took a deep breath. Clearly no one else knew that he had been involved in what had happened within the woods. Had Bathis told his brother, the authorities would surely have come for him already.

He had the chance to walk away from Shakenyew.

Chapter Six

THE MOMENT TAXIANA'S tree fell, Lesandor knew. And even though he had given his word to go home, he would have turned back then had Ralfus not been there to prevent him – which he did resolutely, eventually knocking him senseless with the handle of his belt knife.

Lesandor came to in the early hours of the morning. His head throbbed and his stomach churned. He retched but there was nothing left to bring up – he had a vague recollection of vomiting … shouting … trying to wrestle Ralfus, who was all muscle and sinew and seemingly made of stone.

Meanwhile, Ralfus watched him, pouring water into a leather beaker and putting it on a tree stump then stepping out of Lesandor's reach again. He might have been the stronger of the two, but he had had enough damage inflicted on him the previous night to make him wary of a repeat performance.

In furious silence, Lesandor gulped down the water, threw the cup on the ground and, with Ralfus following, set off towards home. By midday, his anger had given way to confusion; by the time they reached Deepvale, four days later, the only thing he felt was lost.

Casandrina welcomed him with tears of relief, and he wept in her embrace.

They awaited Fabiom's return and he did not come, neither was there any word from the authorities in Shakenyew or Fairwater. Days passed. In the hold-house there was much talk about the consequences of Fabiom's action. Lesandor paid it all little heed. Even if they lost the holding, he hardly cared. He had no desire to have that sort of authority. In truth, he had no desire – at all. He considered his father, awaiting trial somewhere, and found himself glad; until the pictures in his mind twisted and altered and instead of Fabiom he saw himself in Townmaster Florim's office. 'You shall never go home ... you shall never see the woods of Deepvale again ... the Silvanii will dance only in your dreams ... you will forget her face.' No, he was not glad.

Lesandor spoke of returning to Shakenyew, though he was bound by his word to Fabiom that he would stay away.

"No. You must stay here," Casandrina told him, in a tone that would brook no arguments.

The subject came up again and again, whenever the household gathererd.

"I could go," Aelinn suggested, one afternoon when Tarison was at the hold-house. "I could find out where Lord Fabiom is and send you word. I have imposed on your hospitality long enough. It is time I returned to Shakenyew."

"Not yet," Casandrina replied. "Stay with us a while longer, Aelinn. You have been a great help to us." She glanced meaningfully at Lesandor.

"Yes. I.... Thank you. I appreciate all you have done." He took a deep breath. "And not just in looking after Jarin." It was the truth, though he could not help but think he would have felt more whole had he never met Aelinn, but instead committed the triple murder Taxiana required of him.

Casandrina sighed.

"Then let me go, my lady," Calbrin offered.

"He has moved on. Where would you look?" Casandrina argued, loath to lose their house-steward.

"Someone has to go," Tarison said. "I cannot. I need to be here, should things get – difficult." Distractedly, he rubbed at the twisted gold and silver holder's ring that Fabiom had left in his care. "I'm far too old for this," he muttered.

Finally Casandrina agreed that Ralfus should go back, and Philon decided to go with him. They promised to be discreet. Seric, meanwhile, set out to return to Fairwater, promising to send word if he heard anything in the capital, in little doubt that he would.

Deepvale resumed its wait.

Shimmering in the afternoon sun, the river Fairwater and its city, both silver bright. Only over Fabiom did the clouds hang heavy. It seemed apposite that Ravik was in the courtrooms, not at the palace, a fact Fabiom discovered when he went to the Hall of the Assembly to surrender his badges of office, and himself, to the court officers there.

The clerk recognised him, told him that Ravik was attending a hearing that was due to break soon, assuming as he did that Fabiom had come to see the prince. Fabiom nodded, thanked the man and said that he would wait, unsure whether this way would be harder or easier, almost beyond caring.

"The historian Jerynn was right, *Silvanan blood* he called it. Poetry is all very well but tears that are spilled can be dried. Blood is another matter." Fabiom toyed with the amber paperweight on Ravik's desk then replaced it carefully, holding out his hands palms upwards as he turned to face the prince. "And my hands are dripping with it. It will not wash away."

The look on Ravik's face brought home to him what he had done, in a way that neither his troubled sleep nor burning shoulder had managed to do. Fabiom looked away. He could not bear to see such censure on the face of someone he cared for so deeply, and wished fervently that he had gone to the court officers as he had planned, even stayed in Shakenyew. Anything but this.

"Fabiom – why?"

"For Lesandor. She would have destroyed him. Yet that is no excuse. I realise that." He looked up then, though not at Ravik, fixing his gaze on a wall hanging: the tapestry of dancing woodmaids.

"Casandrina –" Ravik began.

"She...." Fabiom shook his head and started again. "I was going to say she doesn't know. But of course she does. Lesandor is home by now and he must have felt.... He would have told her. Anyway, she will have guessed, even if he has said nothing."

Ravik moved towards him and laid his hand on Fabiom's right shoulder, causing Fabiom to wince in discomfort and then to turn his head to look at the prince in surprise. The appalled look that had cut him so deeply had gone.

"Are you telling me that Casandrina is well?"

Despite everything, Fabiom had to smile, understanding Ravik's confusion. "I could never harm her. You must know that," he whispered. "Still, I've done something I would not have thought myself capable of." He told the story in full then, leaving nothing out and making no excuses.

"It was as horribly simple as that," he finished, picking up the paperweight again. "They said the amber seemed like gore dripping from his hands, though it was solid by then. They were right, that's what it was. So Bathis paid the price for what he did. Now I must do the same."

Ravik ignored his last comment and asked instead why he had not gone home. Fabiom just shook his head.

"The legal implications – extreme though they are – seemed preferable to you than the personal ones, perhaps?" Ravik suggested.

Fabiom closed his eyes. "Before I left home, I told Seric there was nothing and no one that could keep me from Casandrina – and yet, here I am."

"So the first thing you are to do is go home," the prince told him. "Come back when you have sorted things in Deepvale with your family. Let the matter go no further meanwhile. Likewise, I will say nothing to anyone here."

Fabiom looked down and sighed. "I have never thought of myself as coward, my lord, but I cannot do that. I cannot face them, any of them."

"Lesandor's life was in the balance," Ravik reminded him.

"That does not mean he will ever understand, ever come to terms with it, or with me. She was his wife."

Yet it was not Lesandor he was really thinking of at that moment, it was Elzandria. A voice in his head told him that he would never see his daughter again; that he had lost her forever. As for Casandrina – for the first time since he had met her he was trying not to think of her at all.

"More than that, I cannot bear to know what Casandrina thinks. If she has turned against me, better by far that I should have died alongside Bathis in the yew woods."

"I lost a son myself, Fabiom, and Raidan's death still cuts me like a knife. As for what it has done to his mother.... Had I been able to save him, do you think there is anything I would not have been prepared to do? How, then, can I blame you for what you have done? How can Casandrina?"

Ravik went to the window, looked out at the courtyard where other members of the Assembly were strolling together, many deep in debate over the matters that had come before them that morning. He smiled grimly. If only they knew what was being discussed in this room.

"There has not been a case like this in my lifetime, nor can I recall having read or heard of one similar. If you insist on publicly declaring yourself guilty, the consequences will be far-reaching. My inclination is to say that, for the time being, as no holding is seeking payment of penalty, or is threatening Deepvale, the matter should rest here. After all, there is little chance you will do the like again."

"Would you say likewise if the holder of Shakenyew came to you and confessed he had committed such an act in Deepvale?" Fabiom demanded.

Ravik merely raised his brows in a quizzical frown.

"What I have done needs meet its just reward, my lord."

"I may not have a choice, but, until my hand is forced, you are a free man. I cannot, and will not, be the keeper of your conscience, Fabiom. Neither am I going to punish you just because you want to be punished," Ravik returned mildly.

Fabiom clenched and unclenched his fists but said nothing.

"Very well," Ravik conceded, thinking to snap Fabiom out of his black mood. "I need someone to go to Gerik, to check on our interests there and to liaise with Robstrom's government. You can volunteer if you will, and give us both time to think this through properly, else you can return to Deepvale and I will send another in your stead."

Not for one moment did he expect Fabiom to accept the commission.

Part
V

Chapter One

PRINCE RAVIK STARED out from a high balcony and saw the plains of Gerik rather than the wooded hills of Fairwater.

"I shouldn't have let him go."

"Lord Fabiom, Uncle?" Tegun asked, though he hardly needed to. Ravik had been fretting since Fabiom had set sail the previous day, bound for Westmouth.

"Fabiom, yes." Ravik turned and looked at his great-nephew for a long moment. The boy was unaware of his scrutiny, head bent over a complicated music manuscript from the palace library.

"I have to go to Deepvale. I shall be leaving in three days and I'd like you to accompany me, Tegun. Will you come? I know you were planning to go home."

Tegun looked up in surprise. "Why, yes, sir. If you wish it."

"I do," Ravik replied absently, turning again to look at the view, missing Tegun's grimace of dismay as he did so.

From the balcony, Ravik observed his third son approaching the main entrance.

"Good. Pharrell's here. Excuse me, Tegun. No – you carry on," he added, as Tegun made as if to put away the music sheets. "Pharrell will visit with his mother first, then I shall speak with him in my office, not here."

"Will you go alone?" Pharrell asked, some time later, when his father informed him of his plans to go to Deepvale. "I could come with you...."

Ravik looked with affection at his son, the first member of the ruling house in almost a hundred years to have won a Silvanan bride, and the only person with whom he had shared the burden of Fabiom's confession. He recalled how Pharrell had been only thirteen when Casandrina had predicted his success, whilst warning that his two older brothers should not make the attempt: "Romarus is too proud, and Laurens too introspective. But Pharrell would find favour in the wildwood." She had said the same about Raidan. Ravik shook his head and dragged his thoughts back to the present.

"I should enjoy your company, and value your counsel. But no. I need you here."

Pharrell helped himself to a date, stuffed with soft cheese. "To do what?"

"Your oldest brother is beginning to flex his muscles. He enjoys it too much when I am away from the capital."

"So, you will take *Romarus*?"

"No! In the name of all that's sacred, Pharrell! Do you think what happened in Shakenyew is something your brother needs to know? I need you to stay here to keep an eye on him, as well as to look after your mother, and, most importantly, to be my ears. Should anything even be whispered about Shakenyew, I want to know." Seeing the dates disappearing, Ravik took one. "As for your question, I shall not be going alone, I have decided to take your cousin, Tegun."

Pharrell shook his head. "Letting Tegun know about Lesandor's marriage, about Fabiom's *solution*, would be as dangerous as telling Romarus, surely? If he lets word slip to Aunt Jaymna...."

"I agree. My sister would use this information against Deepvale with great delight."

"So – why risk it?"

"By nature, Tegun is a gentle soul; besides which, he has suffered enough to empathise with others' distress. Lesandor must be hurt, vulnerable. Two damaged young men – I'm hoping that getting them together now will avert any antagonism that might otherwise arise later."

Pharrell pondered his father's words. "You think Tegun might grow to resent Lesandor, or his heirs, or whoever holds Southernport."

"If it's not sorted now, yes, I do." Ravik sighed. "Sadly, Tegun's condition continues to deteriorate. He is in more pain than he was a month ago. I am told it can only get worse. With his physical difficulties, and his diminished status, his marriage prospects are reduced, perhaps non-existent. All in all, his future is nowhere near as bright as it was. I hate to say this but, if Tegun becomes embittered –"

"Romarus will make use of any antagonism."

Ravik – himself the youngest of four, who never understood how his sisters' minds worked – pondered whether being the middle child afforded a certain degree of insight. For certain Pharrell understood all his brothers in ways none of them understood each other. He nodded. "Should it suit him, yes. I am certain he will undo bonds I have forged, in order to forge his own. That's fair enough, but I can see him doing more: destroying what I have built, bringing down those I have raised up. Simply on principle, Romarus will not court Deepvale's holder. So, I would diffuse tensions between Tegun and Lesandor now, remove one weapon from Romarus's hands. Besides which, if I can ease some of Tegun's burden, I will be well-pleased."

"And the fact that he is about to celebrate his coming to manhood, and Aunt Jaymna will be intending to mark the occasion in her grandest style is coincidental?"

Ravik laughed. "Of course."

Tegun had intended to celebrate his seventeenth birth anniversary and his coming to manhood with his immediate family, as was customary. Instead, with just eleven days to go, he found himself going off across the country.

Being away from Southernport he did not mind too much. His own family could be somewhat overwhelming when they all gathered together, especially when his grandmother was present. She would be furious at his absence from home on his birth anniversary and that, he suspected, was the reason he would not be there. The family had been bickering for years, and somehow he always seemed to be involved, even though few of the rows had anything to do with him. For that reason he was almost glad not to be going home.

But to Deepvale.

They set off, four days later, under clear skies. Tegun played his pipes and kept the company in good cheer. Ravik was not fooled. The sweet piping disguised both the boy's anxiety about his first trip to Deepvale and his intense physical discomfort. Ravik wished he could have spared him the second, knew he could not spare him the first.

They had barely reached the borders of Fairwater and Alderbridge when the clouds, which had been amassing steadily since the previous afternoon, darkened the sky and the air was charged with lightning. Heavy, driving rain soaked everyone and everything. Tegun put away his pipes and hunched miserably in the donkey cart, his legs swathed in leather covers that weighed heavy but at least kept him halfway dry. By the time they stopped at the hold-house in Alderbridge, he could hardly walk.

The rain continued throughout the night, easing off at dawn just long enough to lull them into believing the day was suitable for travel. They were too far from the hold-house to turn back when the skies opened once more and so they went on, across the Deepvale border, and sheltered in the hostelry in Watersmeet. Eventually the downpour eased to a sullen drizzle and they completed their journey.

❦

Over Lesandor's head, the seasons met, intertwined in the artist's depiction of ash trees, all gloriously alive on the nursery ceiling. Even the branches of the winter tree were potent with fat buds, waiting for spring. In front of him, the little bed was empty, as it had been for two days. Aelinn had taken her own child and Jarin, and was staying with Kita and Nissus for a while. Lesandor missed them all.

"We have company, and Casandrina is in the woods." Nek'h touched his arm and was gone before he had time to question her.

His mind still in the nursery, Lesandor made his way to the heart room and there stopped dead, swallowing hard, barely able to meet Ravik's eyes.

"Lesandor." Ravik's voice was kind, as was the hand he placed on Lesandor's shoulder. "This is not an easy time for you, and I have no wish to make it any harder. Yet you have a right to know the facts. Your father has gone to Gerik."

"Did you banish him?"

"I did not. I am not going to condemn one of my closest friends – one of my most competent holders, and a man who has done more to protect the wildwood and the Silvanii than any I know of – if I have any say in the matter, any choice. Though I have to tell you, Lesandor, I do not yet know what choice, what freedom I do have; the law is the law."

Before he could say more, Casandrina came in, shaking the rain from her hair.

"My lady." Ravik took her hands in his, appalled at her dull gaze, the sorrow on her face. "Fabiom came to me. He told me everything."

"I have always been pleased to see you, to welcome you to my home, Prince Ravik. Dare I be pleased to do so now?"

"He has gone to Gerik," Lesandor repeated, his voice hollow.

"It was his choice," Ravik added hurriedly.

Casandrina sighed, like the autumn wind through the branches of a long dead tree. "I cannot go to him there, yet I must see him, speak with him. Does he really believe he cannot come back to us?"

"I think he does," Ravik said. "And he is hurt. He denied it and would see no physician, yet it was obvious enough from the way he favoured his right arm that he has sustained some injury."

Lesandor's jaw tightened and his chin lifted. "My lord, may I go to Gerik?"

"No!" Casandrina said, before the prince could reply. "You are not yet over the trauma of either your time with Taxiana or her death. I have no intention of letting you leave here for quite some while." She turned to the prince, some glimmer of fire back in her gaze. "They are too alike! Quick to act, slow to think."

At her words, Lesandor managed a wan smile and Ravik chuckled.

"I will go myself," Ravik offered. "I will take whatever message you will give me. If he knows everyone here wants him home, that should persuade him."

"Yes," Casandrina replied at once.

Lesandor nodded, not quite trusting himself to speak.

"Elzandria too?" Ravik asked. "Fabiom was concerned that, regardless of what anyone else felt, she would be unable to comprehend his motives."

"Yes, Elzandria too," Casandrina agreed. "Fabiom is wrong. She does understand. Ask her what message she would send, Lesandor."

Lesandor started. "I...."

"You have seen little of your sister since you came home. She misses Fabiom and she misses your company, too. Your father does at least have some excuse – he is not here."

He was afraid to go into the woods. How could he say that to his mother? How could he admit it to himself?

"Very well. I shall go and see her at once."

Outside, the rain slanted down. To Lesandor's relief, Casandrina shook her head.

"Unless Prince Ravik is in a great hurry to leave us, I would advise you to wait until the weather improves. The evening should see a clear sky."

"I am never in a hurry to leave Deepvale, though on this occasion I must not tarry overlong. I agree with your mother, Lesandor. Having travelled in this for much of the last two days, I would not recommend going any farther than necessary, except between downpours."

"Did you come alone, my lord?" Lesandor asked, realising he had seen no sign of any of Ravik's company and glad of a chance to change the subject.

"No, not alone. I had no wish to impose upon you at this time. Those who travelled with me are in the hostelry in the market place, where they will be well catered for. There is only one I would ask you to extend your hospitality to – my great-nephew, Tegun."

"He will be welcome, of course," Casandrina said.

Calbrin was already out, buying provisions, so Casandrina dispatched a nephew of his to go to the hostelry and escort Tegun up to the house.

"While you're in the town, Anuld, try to find your uncle. Tell him we have visitors. He may want to buy extra provisions," Lesandor suggested automatically, knowing such things would never occur to his mother.

The boy was happy enough to go out in the rain and set off straight away.

"Darseus obviously had him at some chore he would rather avoid," Lesandor said. "I hope the rain lets up soon, I shall be glad to see Tegun again."

Ravik hoped the feeling would be mutual.

"That's why I brought him. He was in Fairwater, visiting a specialist physician. I thought a trip to Deepvale might do him more good still. There'll be trouble over it. He was expected home right about now."

Tegun was pleased when Anuld arrived at the hostelry and informed him he was invited to the hold-house. He was less pleased when the boy mentioned Lesandor was at home. The last Tegun had heard, Lesandor was in Windwood, helping the young holder there. That would have suited him better, for though he had nothing against Deepvale's heir personally, indeed, remembered him fondly from Gerik, he was uncomfortably aware that Lesandor's children were due to inherit what he had long been promised.

"How did you get here?" Tegun asked Anuld, wondering if he could bring himself to climb back into another donkey cart after the last two days.

"I walked. His Highness said you came by cart. Shall we take one of yours back up to the house?"

Tegun considered the options.

"No, show me the way and I'll walk. You can go on ahead, I'd rather go on my own, and take my time."

"If you're sure." Anuld hesitated, uncertain whether pointing a royal visitor in the right direction was the same as escorting him back to the house. "I've got to find my uncle anyway, so I suppose it'll be all right, if you're really sure you want to walk."

Tegun smiled bitterly. "I'm certain."

He set out with his head down and a fold of his cloak up as a hood. After he had been walking for a while, the rain eased and the wind changed direction so that it was no longer blowing directly into his face. Tegun looked up and, with a sinking heart, thought he had taken the wrong road. In front of him was nothing but trees. He had reached the woodland edge. Wondering where he had gone wrong, he started to turn and saw that the road divided a short way ahead, the left fork running alongside the wood and through the valley, and the right fork leading up a steep hill, near the top of which he could make out the terra cotta roof of what must be the hold-house.

Wearily, Tegun began the ascent as the rain started to fall heavily again. As he made as much haste as he was able – wishing he had brought two sticks to aid him, not just the one – it occurred to him how unseemly it would be to rush in, little better to arrive soaking wet, to drip all over the place. Thinking that, he decided to take shelter with the gate keeper and tidy up before he presented himself at the house proper.

There was no keeper's lodge, not even a proper courtyard in front of the single-storey house, only a glass room full of rare plants. Tegun paused with his hand against the door, uncertain, eventually deciding to walk around the portico and see if he could find anyone there to show him in. He had taken only two steps when he was surprised by a greeting from behind. Turning, he saw the conservatory door had been opened by a young girl who neither looked like a servant nor a lady of the house. Tegun was disconcerted to find himself socially unsure and he stammered a greeting, of which Lan'h only understood that he had come from Fairwater. She invited him in.

Having stopped, Tegun was not sure he could make himself start moving again. Through the inner door of the conservatory he could make out the heart room. It was not far. Determination had got him from the market to the hold-house. He was not about to give in now.

To his dismay, Lan'h took his arm. A moment passed before Tegun discovered he was neither offended nor embarrassed. She smiled at him, her eyes laughing at his confusion and he smiled back as he realised she was acting purely from kindness, not pity.

"Thank you," he murmured when he found himself before the basin in the heart room. He leant against the marble for a moment before rinsing his hands, hoping that wherever he had to go next would be very close.

"Tegun?"

Tegun turned and saw Lesandor, looking as haggard as when they parted company in Southernport after their disastrous trip to Gerik. Memories stirred: Lesandor telling him that he had done well, holding his hand against the pain as his wounds were dressed, supporting his stretcher as he was moved from one ship to the other.

"Lesandor. It's good to see you." He was glad he could say so and mean it.

"It's good to see you too. Though I would hardly have recognised you. Welcome to Deepvale." Lesandor frowned then. "You look weary."

"My own fault," Tegun muttered, feeling foolish. "I was so stiff after the donkey cart and the rain that I decided to walk from the market. I should know better."

Lesandor helped him into the day room and Lan'h went to fetch hot wine.

"Is it true you have a hot bathing pool?" Tegun inquired, realising there was nothing he would enjoy more than to soak in very deep, very warm water.

"We have. That is a good idea. And we have exceptionally kindly woodmaids, so afterwards you can enjoy the best massage in all Morene."

Lesandor led Tegun through to the pool and, after a relaxing soak and an invigorating massage from Lan'h, Tegun discovered he had left half of his pack behind at the market hostelry. Lesandor found him some fresh clothes of his own to wear.

Calbrin, who had only just returned from the town with Anuld, offered to go and recover the young man's possessions.

"I thought he was the house-steward," Tegun said, bemused.

Lesandor nodded. "Poor Calbrin has to fill many roles. He is well used to it. If we asked anyone else to run such an errand, who knows where they would go, or what they would bring back."

Zin'h, who had arrived with hot wine and light food, strove to look offended, failed, and left the room, giggling.

"Did Prince Ravik bring you here to see Nissus?" Lesandor asked, helping himself to an apricot.

"Nissus? No, I don't know that name." Tegun pulled a small chunk off the loaf of bread and cut a piece of soft ewes' cheese. "I don't really know, but I think he brought me to see you. I was expected back in Southernport a couple of days ago. My uncle dragged me here instead." He looked Lesandor directly in the eye and said, "Princess Jaymna is my grandmother, as I think you know. As Larse is her only son and had already inherited his late father's estates in Riverplain, Grandmother named me as her heir. The Holding of Southernport was to pass to me. I suspect Uncle Ravik wanted to be certain that any, er – problems – were resolved now, so that there would be none in the future."

Lesandor chewed his lip for a moment then answered carefully, "I am sorry, I had no idea. And now, to be honest, I am not quite sure what to say."

"What is there to say?" Tegun asked with a shrug. "You father a second child and the holdership of Southernport passes to that child. If not, then it will go to Jarin's second heir in years to come. It has nothing to do with me any more."

That night, Lesandor lay awake, staring at the stars through the open shutters of his bedroom. Tegun wanted a title and a holding, had assumed all his life he would see that hope realised. A tear slid down Lesandor's cheek and his stomach ached with the knotted emotions he could not unravel. Tegun was angry. So was he. He wondered which of them was the bigger fool.

Unlike Lesandor, Tegun fell asleep immediately, exhausted. The weight of falling beams, pinning his body to the ground, crushing his legs, woke him; the dull leaden ache that told him he had pushed himself too far.

"No," he mumbled, shoving sweat-dampened covers away. "Won't give in." He forced himself to stand, to take one step, then another, ignoring the pain, trying to ignore the fact that everything was harder than it had been this time last year. Through the window he could see nothing but darkness. All he was certain of was that midnight had passed and morning was still a long way off.

Breakfast the next morning was a quiet affair. Other than Casandrina commenting on the fact that neither Lesandor nor Tegun looked as if they had enjoyed a good night's sleep, little else was said, everyone immersed in their own thoughts.

Immediately after he had eaten the small amount he could stomach, Lesandor rose from his place.

"I have to go to visit my sister. Will you all excuse me? Unless," he hesitated, glancing at Tegun's legs. "You are welcome to come with me, Tegun."

Both Lesandor and Tegun noticed Ravik's smile of relief, and pretended not to.

"I'd love to. If you're not in a great hurry. I can't move fast."

"No. There is no hurry."

As they left the room, Lesandor returned Tegun's grin, though a little self-consciously. "I'm pleased to know you can walk at all."

"No one expected me to. Determination is a great medicine. I'd lost so much; I wasn't about to lose that as well."

Something in his tone warned Lesandor it would be unwise to pursue the matter.

"Come on then. Bring your pipes if you like. You can play for her. She enjoys music."

With his pipes tucked into his belt and a stout stick in his hand, Tegun followed Lesandor through the shadowy paths of the wildwood, negotiating his way carefully over streams and under hanging boughs, until they arrived at a grove where two ash trees grew, and where moss and ivy wreathed the already decaying trunk of another, not many years fallen.

"Here we are," Lesandor murmured. "Elzandria, it's me."

Tegun hung back, letting Lesandor go on alone between the trees to place green garlands on low branches of both ash trees and then sit, waiting, with his back against the larger of the standing trees. His mother's, Tegun guessed.

Beauty and calm. Tegun drank in the loveliness of the place and wished at the same time that he had not come. He was intruding, not on the grove, which was welcoming, but on Lesandor's emotions.

Lesandor, as if aware, glanced over at Tegun, his eyes filled with sadness.

"I should not have imagined she would be pleased to see me."

"I've a good sense of direction. I'll go back. You should speak with her alone. Maybe she'll come if I'm not here," Tegun offered.

"No," Lesandor said quickly. "Stay, Tegun, please. Play some music if you will."

With a shrug of compliance, Tegun took his pipes from his belt and eased himself down to sit at the edge of the grove. Choosing a tune was not hard, for the wildwood was filled with its own music. He had only to listen and pick up the melody, joining in with the birds or the breezes. Engrossed as he was, he did not see Lesandor's head rise or the smile that came to his face as Elzandria entered the grove.

"You have brought me a fine gift today, Lesandor. Is he by way of making amends for neglecting me?"

"Yes," Lesandor told his sister with a wry grin. "Maybe he is."

"Then I must forgive you, I suppose. Why do you stay away from me? This is a place of healing. This is where you should be."

"I know that!" He closed his eyes, wanting to weep, refusing to let go of the hurt.

"And you do not want to be healed."

She understood him far too well.

"I do," he protested. "At least, I thought I did. No, you are right. When Father comes home, then, then...."

"Then?"

"I do not know."

"You want to hold on to all your hurt until he comes back, so that you can confront him with it, perhaps?"

"No." He considered that for a long moment. "That is not it, honestly. When he comes home we can put it behind us, that is all. While he is away, I cannot forget. He is gone because of what happened, so it is still happening."

"I do not believe that." She slipped behind her tree, emerged on the far side of the grove, danced lightly back across the open space. *"I like his music. What is his name?"*

"Tegun. I told you about him before. He was hurt in Gerik, in the fire that killed Raidan."

"Ah yes, Tegun. I think you brought him so you would not have to traverse the wildwood alone. You are turning your back on your life, Lesandor. You are hurting yourself. I do not like to see you do that. You know you are safe here."

"Safe, yes." Was it enough, to be safe? Surely he had a right to want something more.

"Open your heart, Lesandor. Let everything good touch you again."

"Being angry, being hurt, that is all I have, all I understand, Elzandria."

The words amazed him, as if they had been spoken by someone else, someone he did not know. Filled with chagrin, he looked up at his sister. She was smiling.

"Now you know that, you can move on. Let yourself understand something else." She brushed his hair with a kiss he could barely feel, making him smile too. *"I am glad you came."*

"Under duress," he admitted. "Now I am glad." He picked a few blades of grass and shredded them thinly. "Prince Ravik is going to find Father. He wants to know if he can bring a message from each of us. Something that will persuade Father that we want him to come home."

"And is that what we want?"

"Elzandria!" Lesandor half rose. She shook her head, smiling still.

"Oh, you misunderstand me; I want him to come back. My message for Prince Ravik to carry is simple: what Father did does not appal me. Leaving you there, at her mercy, that I could not have so easily forgiven."

Lesandor closed his eyes. "Yes," he whispered. "I will tell Ravik." He took a deep breath. "My own message should be a message of gratitude. I do not know if I can go that far yet. But I do want him home."

Elzandria swept away from her brother, towards the edge of the grove where Tegun still played his pipes, lost in his own world. As she neared him, Tegun knew, without a doubt, there was a Silvana present. She moved close to him, an experience he found somewhat disturbing, yet he sensed she meant him no harm.

"Elzandria, this is Tegun, Prince Ravik's great-nephew, and my friend," Lesandor said, as he joined them. "Tegun, Elzandria is very taken by your playing. To be honest, I think she is more pleased you came than that I did."

Tegun could not have sworn he heard the Silvana laugh, but he could not have sworn otherwise, either. He looked up and grinned – foolishly, he imagined.

"I am glad," he murmured. "It is an honour."

"We should get back, I suppose. No, Elzandria, you cannot keep him! Come, Tegun, before she decides to mesmerise you and keep you here to play for her constantly."

Tegun laughed as he got to his feet, declining Lesandor's proffered hand. Being mesmerised by a Silvana and doing nothing for the rest of his life save play his pipes deep in the wildwood seemed like the best option he had been presented with for quite some time. He was almost sorry Lesandor was jesting.

Lesandor was pleased to be able to tell his mother that he had gone to see Elzandria, and pleased also with the message she had entrusted to him.

"Have you sent word to Aelinn to come home, Lesandor, before Prince Ravik leaves?" Casandrina inquired.

"No. Do you think I should?" He considered for a moment. "I suppose it would be a good idea, after what she did for me."

"Is that all?"

"Why else?" Lesandor asked, mystified.

"I am going to ask her to stay with us, if you have no objections and she has no other plans. She has already proved a great help to me, caring for Jarin, also to Calbrin – with regards to the house."

"I do not object. Far from it," Lesandor agreed. "Though Prince Ravik will be quite jealous if we have a little girl to indulge."

"When you met Aelinn and Lyrra in Shakenyew, was it purely by chance?" Casandrina asked.

"I walked into them. I was not looking where I was going. Why? Did I not tell you that?"

"I thought you knew them."

"No. What Aelinn did for me, she did for a total stranger."

"She has a kind heart," Casandrina agreed. "And she would understand your hurt. Maybe that is why she did what she did."

Up until that moment she had assumed he knew who Aelinn was, who Lyrra was. Now she saw it was not so. Lesandor had never been good at dissembling.

The peace he had encountered in the ash grove stayed with Tegun throughout the day. He took it with him to his bed, lying awake for a while, basking in the memory until sleep drifted over him, warm and comfortable.

The comfort did not last long; pain woke him as it did every night, sooner or later. The absolute blackness outside his window told him that tonight it was sooner. He had hardly slept at all. Quietly he rose from his bed and dressed, pushing down the anger and frustration that had become so much a part of his nights that he barely noticed anymore. The house was silent. Faint nightlights, burning in alcoves, illuminated his way to the kitchen and to the door that would let him into the garden.

Undeterred by the darkness, Tegun made his way across the stone bridge that spanned the River Swan, taking the path Lesandor had taken yesterday, following an unerring sense of direction until he arrived at the ash grove.

"I hope you don't mind my coming here like this, Elzandria," he whispered, placing a feathery sprig of sweet-scented tamarisk at the base of her tree. With some difficulty he lowered himself to the ground, beside his gift, resting his back against the trunk.

He closed his eyes. "Everything has gone wrong, I don't know what to do. My legs are getting worse. It's harder and harder for me to walk. In a few years I'll be completely crippled and then what? Without Southernport, I'll have nothing. I'm sorry. I didn't really come here to wallow in self-pity. This is a very special place, and it's so peaceful. That's why I came back."

A song drifted around him, stilling his fears, filling his soul with peace. Music he would never forget drove back the darkness and filled the night; music so quiet that every tiny stirring in the wildwood could still be heard.

"I think I might sleep now," Tegun murmured around a yawn. And he did.

As music had lulled him to sleep, so music awoke him – the dawn chorus of woodland birds greeting the new morning and celebrating the bright, warming sun after days of rain.

Tegun stirred and groaned as his neck protested at his attempts to move his head. Gradually he managed to coax his body to respond as he wanted and got to his feet, leaning heavily on Elzandria's tree. Sleeping out in a damp wood, leaning at an awkward angle against a tree trunk, was not what his physician would have prescribed. Tegun felt better than he had in months.

No one saw him return to the house. He let himself in, washed and changed, and was on his way to the day room when he became aware of a number of voices he did not recognise. Through the columns of the courtyard portico, he saw Lesandor talking with a man and two women.

"Ah, Tegun. There you are." Casandrina smiled a gentle welcome. "We were becoming concerned about you." Her eyes held a glimmer of amusement and he guessed she knew where he had spent the night. "We have friends come to visit. And family returned."

A dark-haired toddler tugged at her gown, gazing up at her with large grey eyes.

"Want lift," he told her.

"This is Jarin, my grandson," she told Tegun, picking up the little boy, as he demanded.

Jarin planted a damp kiss on her cheek.

Tegun smiled at the child, and at the notion of Casandrina being a grandmother.

There were children everywhere. The oldest of them, a pretty girl, whom Tegun guessed to be about ten years old, was doing her best to keep the smaller ones under some sort of control.

"And that is Keran," Casandrina informed him, disentangling her hair from Jarin's fists. "Her mother, Kita, is Fabiom's cousin, and Nissus, her father, is a renowned physician and herbalist. They are in the courtyard with Lesandor at present. Maybe it was presumptuous of me, I asked Nissus to pay us a visit, that you might benefit from his wisdom, should you wish."

"No," Tegun murmured, surprised. "I mean, it was not presumptuous. It was very kind. Thank you."

"You are welcome," Casandrina inclined her head.

"Does he always bring his entire family with him?" Tegun wondered, amused by the antics of two young boys who were quite obviously twins.

"Not always," Casandrina admitted. "We have a house-guest whose daughter has had little opportunity to play with other children, and as Lesandor has not been in the best frame of mind to fulfil the role of father to Jarin, I sent them all off to stay with Kita and Nissus for a few days. So today they are returning the visit, and Jarin has come home."

"Down now," Jarin said. Happily he trotted off to play with his cousins.

"The daughter of your house-guest. That would be the little red-haired girl?" Tegun guessed. "She looks familiar somehow."

Ravik came in, raising his brows at the scene that greeted him. Keran lifted her little sister off a settle so that the prince could be seated if he wished, managing, somehow, to bob a neat curtsy at the same time.

From the courtyard, Lesandor noticed Ravik's arrival, and brought the others indoors. When Nissus and Kita had greeted the prince, Lesandor introduced Aelinn, unaware that his mother was watching the exchange with interest.

"Your father told me of this young woman," Ravik acknowledged, taking Aelinn's hand and raising her from her curtsy. "You are to be commended indeed, Aelinn. It is an arduous enough journey from Shakenyew to Deepvale, without a difficult message to deliver and a young child to worry about."

Aelinn blushed at Ravik's praise, her colour deepening as Lesandor agreed.

"Without her, I do not know what would have become of me, my lord," he told Ravik, and then smiled at Aelinn. "I shall be ever in your debt, Aelinn. And I am glad you stayed. I was afraid you would have left, that I would not have seen you to thank you properly."

"I need no thanks," she murmured. "I was glad to help. None of us can manage alone."

At that moment, Lan'h came in to inform them that breakfast was ready. With the woodmaid's help, Kita shepherded the children through to the dining room, though they needed little encouragement. The adults followed in their wake.

After they had eaten, Tegun went off with Nissus to sit in the garden and talk in private, the twins coerced Lesandor into helping them set up archery targets, and the two toddlers fell asleep. Lyrra, unimpressed by the visitor's rank, and quite cured of her shyness, brought her drawing slate to Ravik and asked him to help her draw a rabbit. He lifted the child onto his knee and together they drew rabbits and birds and squirrels while Casandrina looked on, a secret smile in her eyes.

"Will you seek your husband's family, Aelinn?" Casandrina inquired, draping a light blanket over Jarin while Aelinn did the same for little Mysha.

Aelinn shook her head. "I have no notion as to who they are, or where they are from. He promised to take me to his home when he came back from service. When he came back...." She smiled wistfully. "No, I have no one who will take us in, except perhaps my cousin in Shakenyew, though I have never even met her. Our blood ties are rather distant, I can expect little from her, except perhaps a roof and some food in return for my services. I can dress hair, bake, mend clothes; maybe that will be sufficient."

"There is no question of that, unless it is what you desire," Casandrina told her. "There is a home for you here and you are welcome to stay. What you did for us is beyond value. It was just that I wondered if perhaps you had other plans, and if you had I would have asked you to wait at least until Fabiom returned."

Aelinn laughed sadly. "I have had no plan, other than keeping my daughter safe and warm and fed, for the past three years and more. There is nothing I would like better than to stay here, Casandrina, though I must do something towards our keep. Not only that," she went on before the Silvana could reply, "there is something that you must know, and if you change your mind about us staying I will understand. It was my grandmother who instigated the sale of sericulture secrets to agents in Varlass. That is how we lost everything, including any respect in Morene." She glanced nervously towards Ravik, but the prince was engrossed with her daughter and was taking no notice. "We were banished. I should not be in Morene. But there were family issues. My mother brought me back and left me here when I was but ten years, so where else can I go?" She took a deep breath. "I suspect that is why he never came back to me. The taint must have been too much. I was foolish to believe I could have a normal life, a normal family, after what we did."

Casandrina reached out to Aelinn and touched her hand.

"That was your grandmother, Aelinn, not you." She smiled. "Once, I would not have been able to say that. I have learnt a lot since I have been with Fabiom. Now I understand how things have a habit of turning themselves around. Good from bad, joy from sorrow."

"What do you mean?"

"Had your grandmother not done what she did, this land and Varlass would not have needed to rebuild their relationships. That being the case, Prince Ravik, who is even now teaching your daughter how to draw hedgehogs, might never have met the Varlassian princess, Maedrim, and their children would not have been born. I think that is something neither Ravik nor Maedrim would wish. Neither would we. Their youngest son was Lesandor's dearest friend."

"Was?"

"He died, several seasons before Lesandor went to Shakenyew."

Aelinn sighed. "That's sad. He must have been very young."

Nissus had brought with him a poultice of fresh whitewort roots mixed with the boiled roots of madder and alkanet, blood-red and pungent, which he applied to Tegun's legs.

"This, used regularly, should stop any further deterioration, and hopefully engender an improvement. I'll leave you enough for the next few days and then I'll make up a fresh batch. Meanwhile, I'm also going to consult my father. He has dealt with injuries such as yours before and I think he might have some ideas. Much as I'd like to be able to say that I know as much as he does about all things medicinal, I can't pretend to equal his expertise. Still, I'm working on it!"

The poultice was warm and sent a tingling yet almost comfortable sensation through Tegun's limbs.

"Not to get worse. That in itself will be a great blessing."

Nissus sat back on the bench, gazing up at the sky, scowling.

"I'm just sorry you didn't come sooner. There was no need for this to have happened. Once the initial damage had been tended, your condition should have been maintained, even if it could not have been improved."

311

"Regrets are a waste of time," Tegun told him. He flexed his bandaged knees and chuckled. "Though, to be honest, hardly a day goes by when I wish something or other had or had not happened. It's strange, coming to Deepvale was something I definitely did not want to do, and yet is something I'm never likely to regret. Leaving, now that might be another matter."

"Leaving?" Nissus broke off his contemplation of the clouds and turned his full attention to his patient. "Can't you stay?"

"I suppose so," Tegun said, uncertain.

"Good. You can come to us if you need to. Though we've a houseful of children. Arrange it with his Highness, or I'll tell him, if you'd prefer. You can't leave now."

Nissus was so insistent that Tegun went inside at once to speak with his uncle.

"I didn't know you were so good at drawing rabbits, Uncle."

"Neither did I! Lyrra's been teaching me, haven't you, sweetheart?"

Lyrra laughed as she climbed down from his lap to show her mother her latest drawing.

"I still think she looks familiar," Tegun mused, before telling Ravik what Nissus had said, and that the physician wanted him to remain in Deepvale for treatment.

"He can help you? Stupid! I should have brought you here years ago. Or better still, sent for Nissus to tend you in Southernport as soon as you came back from Gerik. Though I was hardly thinking straight then. Of course you must stay. And don't worry about your grandmother – I'll be going to Southernport to see Jaymna directly from here – I'll tell her myself." Ravik's grim smile suggested that doing so would give him a certain amount of pleasure.

Tegun had no objections, just so long as he did not have to explain his prolonged absence to his grandmother himself.

That evening, Tegun returned to the ash grove where, in between playing his music, he told Elzandria all about Nissus's treatment, how he would be staying in Deepvale and that he was going to meet Nalio the very next morning.

Eventually, guessing the hour to be around midnight, he went back to the hold-house. He slept the remainder of the night, reluctantly waking and rising at Nek'h's dawn summons to see his great-uncle off.

The western sky was still dark as Ravik made ready to leave, taking the messages entrusted to him for Fabiom. The prince bade a fond farewell to Tegun, wishing him well with his treatment, before taking his leave of Casandrina and, finally, of Lesandor.

"Well, Lesandor, what do I tell your father? He will need word from you if he is to be persuaded."

Lesandor checked the harness straps of the prince's donkey cart.

"There is no singing in the yew woods, neither birds nor woodmaids. There are no flowers. Did you know that, my lord? Tell Father I've found the songs and the flowers again. Tell him I'm glad about that."

It was not quite what he wanted to say but it was as near as he could manage.

Chapter Two

TWO DAYS AFTER Ravik's departure, Lesandor brought his son to visit Elzandria in the ash grove.

They made their way through the familiar paths accompanied by the song of an unseen nightingale and Jarin said, "Pretty bird."

Lesandor agreed, remembering the day before his return to Fairwater to complete his service when Mysha had surprised him by suggesting they should take a walk in the woods. A nightingale had been singing and she had asked him what it was, then she told him her news: midwinter would see them parents, adding that she knew the wildwood was the only place to tell him. That was the day he first thought their marriage might work after all, the day he vowed to himself to do his best to ensure that it would. Tears stung his eyes until Jarin tugged at his hand, pulling him back from the edge of the chasm of self-pity he was risking.

"Sweet!" the little boy said, pointing to the strings of creamy-pink flowers entwined about the brambles.

"Honeysuckle," Lesandor told him, plucking a flower and handing it to him. "Are you going to eat them all or shall we pick some for Elzandria?"

Jarin discarded the well-chewed flower. "Pick some for El," he decided generously.

Taking three strands of the flowering creeper, they went on to the grove.

Casandrina was there already, watching Elzandria wander back and forth in the space between their two trees.

"They have seen how contented I am in my marriage, Elzandria.

More than one with seniority over you might well be tempted to leave the woods for a span," Lesandor heard his mother reason.

"What is it? What's wrong?" he asked.

Jarin gave one of his honeysuckle sprigs to Casandrina and laid the other two in front of Elzandria's tree.

"Nothing is wrong. Quite the opposite," Elzandria said, sounding rather petulant. She bent and kissed the top of Jarin's head, making him giggle.

"Were you aware that Tegun is only four days away from his seventeenth birth anniversary?" Casandrina asked her son.

"No, I was not. What of it?" He stared at his sister, realising the answer to his question even as he asked it. "You want him for your husband."

"I do. And I want you to tell him he must come to the Dancing Glade on his birth eve. Tell him, Lesandor."

Lesandor glanced at his mother.

"Are you determined, Elzandria?" Casandrina inquired.

"Yes, I am."

"Very well. He shall be told that you want him. That and no more," Casandrina agreed. "Whether he comes or not will be up to him," she added, as Elzandria began to protest.

"Why should he not come?" Elzandria asked lightly.

"Why indeed?" Lesandor agreed.

"At least Tegun is not known. There is no reason why any other should want him particularly, though he is a lovely young man." Casandrina conceded. "But, Elzandria, if you love anyone in Deepvale besides Tegun, you will back down immediately should you be challenged."

"Will she be in danger?" Lesandor asked.

"Yes, she will."

"Some," Elzandria told him. *"But you are not to worry."*

"I thought it was only the men who came to the woods seeking a bride who put themselves at risk." He looked at his mother askance. "Were *you* in danger when Father came?"

She rubbed her arm absently where two faint scars still showed. "Little enough. He had formed an attachment to my tree, as Tegun must be encouraged to do with Elzandria's if he accepts her offer. And I had seniority few others could match. My tree is as old as any now standing

315

in the woods. Furthermore, Narilina's father was Lord Laurrus, the first holder of Deepvale. At least your sister does share that same breeding, which should place her at an advantage."

"So she will be safe?"

"I cannot promise you that, Lesandor. I wish I could. However, as she is determined, there is nothing I can do." She smiled then. "And, should you succeed, Elzandria, it would be the best that could happen to Tegun. If they have any compassion, the other Silvanii will let you have your way."

The wind stirred the leaves, carrying her words into other parts of the wildwood.

"I do not understand," Lesandor muttered, somewhat ungraciously.

"Why I did not allow my own son to do what I am almost encouraging Prince Ravik's great-nephew to do?"

At that Elzandria laughed again and Lesandor scowled.

"You have read *Tales of a Woodsman*, have you not?" Casandrina said.

"You know I have – several times."

"He was loved too well. Understand that, Lesandor, *too well*."

"I know. Two Silvanii died, wanting him too much."

"They destroyed each other because of what he was."

"He was a woodsman."

"He was Silvana-born."

Lesandor let out his breath slowly and then drew it in again in a horrified gasp, remembering the devastated yew tree, the moans of the dying Silvana. At last understanding what he had heard during the night he had gone to the yew woods; what Taxiana had done. He opened his mouth to tell them but he could not bring himself to say her name there in the safe places of his childhood where she did not belong. Another time he would tell his mother, away from the woods.

They ambled back towards the house together, Lesandor using the time trying to persuade Casandrina that she should be the one to pass on Elzandria's message to Tegun.

Ignoring his pleas, she mimicked the calls of woodland birds for Jarin's amusement and they answered her. Each time she would have stopped, Jarin cajoled her into repeating the performance with cries of, "Again!"

"If *he* asked you, I think you would do it," Lesandor muttered, making her laugh.

"I would not. However, if you asked me to call a nuthatch for you, I would do so gladly," she replied.

Linking his arm through hers, Lesandor effected a rapid trilling in perfect imitation of a nuthatch. An answering trill sounded from the oak tree beside them.

"That, I can do myself, thank you."

"Just as you can speak with Tegun without any assistance from me."

Years ago he had learnt that arguing with her was a waste of time.

"Oh, very well, I shall do it."

"Yes," Casandrina agreed mildly, as if the matter had never been in dispute.

They had just set foot on the stone bridge when they saw Nek'h and Lyrra, across the river, following a string of baby hedgehogs and their mother.

"Hedgies!" Jarin cried joyously, letting go of his father's hand and trotting over the bridge. He tripped, picked himself up without a murmur, and scampered even faster to catch up.

"He is so like you," Casandrina observed.

"I would say I was a little more co-ordinated," Lesandor replied, as his son stumbled again.

Nek'h took one of Jarin's hands and Lyrra the other, and all three trailed after the hedgehog family.

"At least we will be giving Tegun something, not taking it away. He was bitterly disappointed about Southernport," Lesandor reflected, thinking of the task ahead of him.

"Then perhaps you should also tell him that no child of your line is going to inherit that holding."

"Tell him? No, not until I find Cuivah. What if her child did not survive? As soon as Father returns I must resume my search. Taxiana said –" He swallowed hard. "She said that if Cuivah had wanted to be found I would have succeeded already. I believed it at the time. Now, I am not sure."

"Yes, you are sure. In your heart you know full well that you must find her." Smiling, she paused to watch the river and echo the song of the water with her voice, a teasing sound, so that he glanced at her curiously, more so when she laughed and asked, "Have you spoken of this to Aelinn? She has family in Shakenyew. Maybe she could help."

"No." He sighed. "One thing at a time. First, Tegun. What is amusing you so?"

"You are, dear one. Come now, there is a task awaiting you."

Following a trail of wafting aromatic smells and giggling, they left the children engrossed with the hedgehogs under Nek'h's watchful gaze and entered the house through the kitchen, where Aelinn was busy teaching some of the other woodmaids how to prepare a new dish.

"Good, you're back," Aelinn greeted them. "I hope you're hungry; this will be ready soon."

"What is it?" Lesandor asked curiously, lifting the lid from a large earthenware pot. "It certainly smells good."

"Sorrel and watercress soup," Zin'h told him, replacing the lid. "And we're making sweet morel fritters too."

Aelinn began warming some honey for the fritters.

"Nalio is still here. He's staying to eat with us. I wonder where Tegun is."

"Lesandor was just about to see if Tegun was in his room. You can tell him to join us for something to eat, Lesandor," Casandrina suggested.

At least doing it straight away would minimise the ordeal, Lesandor decided, making his way to the sleeping quarters, where he found Tegun applying some of the unguent Nissus had made up for him.

"I suppose it is rather soon to tell if that's any good," Lesandor commented.

"Oh, I don't know." Tegun glanced up at him with a lop-sided grin. "It seems to ease the pain caused by the exercises Nalio devised for me."

Without waiting for an invitation, Lesandor sat down, waiting until the younger man looked up again, questioningly.

Lesandor wet his lips and looked away, staring out of the window at the woods in the distance.

"You have been spending quite a lot of time in the ash grove," he said at last.

"Yes. I – Shouldn't I have gone there? It's so peaceful and my head is so full of conflict. I'm sorry, I meant no harm."

Lesandor laughed shortly. "On the contrary, you are very welcome. Elzandria enjoys your company." He made himself look at Tegun then, even managed to smile. "So much so that she would like to enjoy it on a more permanent basis."

Tegun said nothing, the bewilderment in his eyes confirming he had no idea what Lesandor meant.

"Only three days to your birth eve, Tegun. If you like, I will show you the way to the Dancing Glade."

"Dancing Glade! No! Lesandor, look at me – I'm a cripple. I could never presume to do such a thing."

"You would not be presuming. You have been invited. Rarely does a man get such an invitation. I do not know how you would go about turning it down. Of course that is up to you. Maybe there is someone waiting for you in Southernport."

The incredulous smile that had lit Tegun's face faded.

"No, there's no one waiting for me. My condition is not over-appealing to the women of my grandmother's house or to her friends' daughters and granddaughters; certainly not to those I have so far encountered anyway. Maybe had I a title to offer them – but who wants to be wanted only for something like that?"

The pain behind those words drove all self-pity and resentment from Lesandor's mind. "You can forget about them, and Southernport," he said emphatically. "Tegun, listen to me, Elzandria wants you. She is prepared to risk herself that she might claim you. Will you not go to her?"

"Yes, of course I'll go, if that's what she really wants. What risk? What do you mean?"

Tegun seemed so confused that Lesandor actually laughed.

"She is very young, obviously. And it is not usual for a Silvana to seek a husband so soon. I blame your piping, she is quite smitten. Any other Silvana who decides she wants you is bound to be senior to Elzandria. The only way she can be certain of success, and safe, is by you displaying a definite attachment to her and to her tree beforehand. And there is little time. Tegun, I wish you success, and I want Elzandria to be happy, but if anything should happen to her – I could not bear that."

Tegun rose to his feet, went to Lesandor and embraced him awkwardly.

"Nor could I," he agreed, his voice so quiet that Lesandor barely heard him. He released Lesandor and smiled. "Thank you," he said.

Lesandor was not quite sure what it was that Tegun was thanking him for in particular. Not that it mattered.

"Mother will talk to the other Silvanii, she has promised to. Hopefully she can persuade them to let Elzandria have her way. More immediately, there's food ready, if you are hungry. I gather Nalio is still here. Is he not yet finished with you for today?"

Tegun grinned wryly. "Apparently not. He said something about some new exercises he wants to show me later. It's strange, when my great-uncle brought me, he can't have known what good would come of this trip."

"He might not. But perhaps Princess Maedrim did. Your great-aunt is gifted with star-sight, after all."

"Whatever the reason, I'm glad of it. It's funny how things work out." Tegun laughed an easy laugh that reminded Lesandor of Raidan.

Though the meal was delicious, Lesandor was distracted. Having allowed himself to notice that Tegun was in one small way like Raidan, he now had to admit that there were other similarities between the two. Although they did not look much alike, Raidan having favoured his mother far more than his father, Tegun shared many traits with his late cousin. More than anything, his innate kindness and his sense of humour reopened wounds Lesandor had thought healed.

That night Lesandor dreamt again of the bakery engulfed in flames, struggling against hands that held him back, only to wake and discover it was his mother who held him, not strangers in a Gerish street. He thought that if Tegun stayed, he must go away himself – that he could bear no more grief – until he realised that, for the first time, his grief was for those he had lost before Taxiana.

"I think I will be all right now," he whispered to Casandrina after a long while. She did not reply, instead she sang him back to a more peaceful sleep and sat with him for the remainder of the night.

In the morning he awoke feeling tired yet more relaxed than he could recall. On an impulse he put Sirsha's grey and gold stone back on its bronze chain and wore it again as he had been wont, beneath his clothing, close to his heart.

And as he went along to the nursery to see Jarin, he found himself hoping Elzandria would succeed in her plan. That in itself was in no way certain.

Casandrina's woodmaids intended to do all they could to assist Elzandria. As soon as he was free, they called Tegun into the wildwood. He needed little prompting, for the days he had spent in Deepvale had reawakened his childhood fascination with the wild places of Morene, something he had put aside when his grandmother had taken him into her house and begun to groom him as her heir. That was redundant now, as Southernport was no longer hers to pass on to him or anyone else.

As he followed the singing woodmaids along the bank of a stream and around the open space of a flowery glade, Tegun realised he did not much care who inherited the responsibility for Southernport. The air was fragrant and clear and he found himself singing along with the woodmaids, filled with a pure joy.

He brought Elzandria a garland of rock roses and a new tune that he had composed the previous night, when he had made use of sleepless hours caused not by any bodily discomfort but by his mind's tumult at Lesandor's revelations. Tired as he was, Elzandria had little difficulty in lulling him to a gentle sleep. He dreamt of rainbows.

Evening was drawing in by the time Tegun left the woods. Even from the bridge he could see the windows of the house, golden with the welcoming glow of lighted candles. Aelinn had supper waiting for him and she ate with him, having just settled the children in their cots.

"Lesandor told me about Elzandria. I'm so happy for you, Tegun, though it's scary too."

Tegun helped himself from the dish before him.

"I'm scared for her. Maybe I should refuse. If anything happened to her, how could I live with that?"

"And how could Lesandor?" Aelinn added quietly. "But surely Casandrina would not allow you to go on if there was any real danger.

How can you refuse? And if you did, could you live with that either?"

"No, I don't think I could. When I first met Nissus I told him regrets were pointless. Yet to forgo Elzandria's love, that would be something I would surely regret until my dying day."

While Tegun and Aelinn ate supper, Lesandor told his mother about his first night in the yew woods, the sounds he took to be a rising storm, the torn tree, the amber dripping like blood from its wounded boughs, how the Silvana had gone long before he had thought she would. Casandrina listened and encouraged him to talk, even when he would have stopped. Evening darkened into night, the rest of the household retired to their rooms, and she made him tell her everything about his time with Taxiana. As dawn touched the eastern sky his story ended, then she held him and sang to him as she had done when he was a child, so that he might put it behind him and he let her love and her music heal him and make him whole again.

Over the next couple of days, time hung heavy for Lesandor, waiting for Fabiom to come home, waiting for Tegun's birth anniversary to be certain Elzandria was safe. And, even though Darseus found him as much work as he wanted around the farm and in the mill, still he found it hard to settle to any task. Finally Aelinn suggested he make himself a new bow, having watched him fretting in the mill all morning.

"Zin'h has been teaching me how to reel silk," she told him, showing him her morning's efforts. "I'll make you a bowstring, if you make the bow. Get Tegun to help you. He needs something else to occupy him as well. He's getting a little jittery." She turned back to her pile of cocoons.

"Why not," he agreed, then sighed. "I should tell him about the events in Shakenyew, too."

"Not your father's part in it, surely?" she replied, startled.

"No, not that," Lesandor agreed.

Out in the garden, where Lesandor had invited him, Tegun listened, appalled, to Lesandor's – somewhat abridged – tale.

"When Uncle Ravik spoke of your wife's death, I assumed he was

322

referring to Jarin's mother. I had no idea...." He shook his head. "I can't imagine – I don't want to imagine."

"No. I don't want you to, not with Elzandria waiting for you."

"And your father killed her?"

"I did not say so," Lesandor said, caution etching his voice.

"No. But I am assuming that's what happened. What else could he do? How else could she be dead?"

"If it was known...."

"My great-uncle knows, doesn't he? That's what all the whispering has been about. Not just here," he explained, when Lesandor looked surprised, "at the palace. He had several meetings with my cousin Pharrell and his wife. Since he married his Silvana, Pharrell is rarely at the palace, but he and Luthrina were frequent visitors in the days before we left to come here."

Lesandor was not surprised to hear that. He picked up a length of elm. "No one else outside the family knows, save Aelinn."

"Thank you for confiding in me. I will not speak of it; you have my word."

Lesandor relaxed. "And you can accept what he did? Not hold it against him?"

"I didn't really have a father, to speak of. The idea of one who would risk everything for his child is very appealing," Tegun said, looking curiously at the timber Lesandor held. "Are we making something?"

Tegun was more than willing to help make a bow, though he had no experience and warned he might be more of a hindrance than a help. Lesandor was not put off. Indeed, teaching Tegun the basic skills of bowyery was the best way he could think of to fill some spare time. In the end they made two bows, supposedly one for each of them, except Lesandor made his based on the measurements of an old one of Fabiom's and only realised it when he drew the finished bow and found it marginally taller than he favoured. In his heart he knew it was no accident. Tegun's words had moved him; he wanted to have a gift for his father's return.

When they were nearly done, Aelinn asked him to show her how to wax the lengths of silk cord and then, as she had promised, she made strings and spares for both bows.

Apart from making bows with Lesandor, and doing his exercises, Tegun spent most of his time in the ash grove, where he played sweet music on his pipes. Elzandria listened and sang to his playing, so softly that he was unaware he heard anything at all, save the breeze singing in the leafy branches.

At dusk on his birth eve, fasted and bathed, Tegun presented himself in the Dancing Glade. He heard singing, and knew Elzandria's voice, though he had no idea how. When she suddenly faltered and fell silent, he thought he must surely die from the loss. A number of voices spoke softly and another was raised in song but it could not touch him. Soon that, too, ceased.

"It seems you must have your way. Or else he must perish."

"No harm must come to him. I asked him to come here. He has formed an attachment to my tree. I claim him by that right, and the right of my breeding."

"We know you asked him, Elzandria, and we know your breeding. Yet you must not presume we will all accept your claim, for all the esteem we once held Lord Fabiom in. After all, he did murder a Silvana."

"Gracillia — enough! For Lesandor you would have done no less, even among your own here. Let her have her way."

Early birdsong woke Tegun the next morning and he found himself back in the ash grove, stiff from sleeping on the rough ground, damp with morning dew and amazed at his good fortune.

Six days and five more nights passed. Garlands of flowers and dreams of sweet music made up Tegun's world.

Lesandor went to stay with Kita and Nissus for the duration. He was unconcerned for Tegun now that his birth eve had passed without mishap. He knew his sister's mind, knew she loved the young man already and that he was quite safe.

Being safe was not something Tegun was aware of. Alive, yes. Invigorated and incredibly lucky, definitely. He knew she would be beautiful; he was not prepared for the effect she would have on him.

Everything about her filled his senses to overflowing so that he felt himself unable to move or breathe or think, as if he were drowning in ecstasy.

Days slipped by, overwhelming euphoria gave way to a more manageable joy. Tegun thought himself the happiest man alive. He also felt fitter and healthier than since he sustained his injuries. The severe exercises from Nalio, together with Nissus's poultices, had started a healing process he had long since lost hope of. They had no delusions. He would never be sound. Far too much damage had been done by the fire even if he had received better treatment immediately, yet Elzandria aimed to see even greater improvements.

"With luck your father will be home soon," Tegun murmured as Elzandria massaged his legs with a mixture of Nissus's prescribed herbs, conifer resin, and oil from the seeds of her tree. "I trust he will approve of your rather rash decision."

"Will he be moved by our pleas?" she wondered. "Casandrina wants to go to him, I know that. Yet she cannot do so. Not that she would choose to leave Lesandor at this time." Her hands stilled. "She cannot go. But I could. We could. Will you bring me to, where is it?"

"Southernport," Tegun told her, rolling onto his side and sitting up. "Elzandria, it's a very long way."

"Will you bring me?" she repeated, her beautiful face intense.

Though the wildwood called them and they would have lingered, they set off that very afternoon, accompanied by three of Elzandria's woodmaids.

By unspoken agreement they stayed within the shelter of the trees for as long as possible. Finally there were no more trees. Open fields lay before them, bathed in sunshine.

"Tegun, I do not know if I can do this." Elzandria glanced back into the woods.

"Sit here awhile," he suggested, leading her towards an ash tree there at the very edge of the woods. "We can go back. It's so soon. You have to get used to everything. This journey is too much and too far."

She sat with her back pressed tight against the tree. "And yet I cannot bear to think of him afraid to come home."

325

He sat down beside her and stroked her hair. "I met your father once, did I tell you?"

"No," she whispered. "Tell me now."

"You know he went to Gerik to find Lesandor? It was after the fire. I was in a terrible state. I don't remember much, except that he was very kind to me. All that had happened there and still he sat with me during the voyage and talked to me. I'll not forget his kindness."

Elzandria kissed his cheek, then stood and held out her hand.

"Then can we be less kind to him?"

"I didn't mean to push you," he said, alarmed.

"I want to do this," she assured him.

After a long moment's hesitation, he nodded. Hand in hand they walked out of the shadows.

They borrowed a donkey cart in Watersmeet, found a thick copse in which to spend the night and called on the Holder of Alderbridge the following morning. Three days later they arrived in Southernport to discover they had succeeded in getting there before Fabiom.

Tegun arranged accommodation for them in a small private apartment near the harbour, dreading the possibility of a long delay; Elzandria needed to be at home, close to her tree, even though she was loath to admit it. Tegun kept telling himself that Fabiom had to get there soon.

Princess Jayma had moved into a small house in the grounds of the hold-house when the holdership of Southernport had been stripped from her. Tegun might not have called on his grandmother, had he not been spotted by several people who recognised him. As it was, he was certain word of his arrival was likely to arrive at her house long before he did. Delaying was not the best option. Having made the decision to visit her, the next was whether he dared take Elzandria with him.

In the end, he was forced to compromise. He could not bring himself to leave his wife behind, even though he had awoken twice in the night with the clear understanding that the two women should not meet – under any circumstances.

"I shall be happy in the garden," Elzandria assured him.

"Indeed. You can see for yourself what your mother wrought there."

She laughed, and the spark she had lost, as they travelled further and further from Deepvale, momentarily returned. "You do know what your grandmother tried to do to my father?"

"I – er – heard rumours. But I can put the pieces together, thank you –"

She laughed again and linked her arm through his. "Trying to steal a Silvana's husband is a very bad idea. I would not tolerate it, either."

"I am glad to hear it. Ah, here we are. I do not know how long I shall be. I will try not to tarry." They had arrived at the gate of the walled garden. She hesitated.

"Master Tegun," the gateman greeted him with no hint of surprise, though he looked at Elzandria with some amazement. "Your grandmother...." He lost track of his thoughts and stared open-mouthed.

"Perhaps I shall wait outside," Elzandria decided, smiling at the man, which did nothing to help his composure. She glanced back at the road behind them, winding through neglected stands of almond trees. "I should prefer to be among trees, I think."

Tegun kissed her, reluctant to leave.

"Go!" she told him. "I shall be here."

Even as the bemused gateman unlatched the gate to let him back out, a scant half-hour later, Elzandria flung herself into his arms with a sob of relief.

"I was lost!" she admitted. "I couldn't find you, and my tree seems so far away."

He held her until the tension began to leave her, then reluctantly, he extricated himself from her embrace. "I'm sorry, I shouldn't have left you."

Arm in arm they began to retrace their steps. Below them, the water of the inlet shimmered in the sun, small boats dotted the surface but there were no larger vessels anywhere to be seen.

With no need to hurry, they made their way into the shade of the nut trees and sat down. Branches hung low around them, weighed down by fuzzy green fruit. Fallen almonds from years gone by littered the ground. Something seemed different about the orchards, though Tegun could not figure out what. It occurred to him that everything looked more wholesome with Elzandria beside him.

A melody drifted into his consciousness, whether from Elzandria's lips or from the air around them he could not say. He closed his eyes and leant back against a trunk. "Aren't you going to ask me why I was gone such a short time?"

"Were you? It did not seem so short to me."

He snorted in amusement. "Grandmother was very pleased to see me – until she learned I had not come home to stay. Nevertheless, she had her servants bring me a collection of lavish gifts for my coming to manhood – until she learned I did not intend to lodge with her while I was in Southernport. She sent the gifts away before I could even see what they were, told me I could have them when I returned, and ordered food brought. When I told her I was married she laughed. When she realised I was serious, given my age, of course she figured out I was married to a Silvana – she stopped laughing and ordered the food taken away. I might not have told her where I was living, but she asked. When she learnt that my wife was from Deepvale, she told me to leave." He sighed mournfully. "The food looked delicious, too."

Elzandria kissed his cheek and reached up to pick an almond from the branch above.

Grimacing, Tegun shook his head as she cracked the nut nestled within the dry, green flesh.

"Eat it," she urged.

Looking at her askance, he took the nut and bit into it. The sweet, flavoursome taste was the last thing he had expected: as a child he had vied with the other youngsters of the hold-house to see who could finish even one of the rancid nuts.

"Did you do this?"

Now that he looked more closely, he could see that the orchards looked – softer. It was the only word that made sense: the colours were less bright, the edges less sharp.

"I did. I recalled Lesandor asking once if there was anything that could be done to restore the gardens and orchards. Of course, from Deepvale, there was nothing Casandrina *could* do." Elzandria touched Tegun's hand. "You do not mind that I did this for my brother, do you?"

He gathered her into his arms.

"My beautiful wife, do you think I regret losing Southernport? Lesandor's heirs are welcome to all I have or might have had here. Everything I aspire to is already mine. There is no other desire in my heart."

He glanced about. They were completely hidden from sight, with no chance of being disturbed – it would be some time before anyone else discovered that the fruit was sweet, and ripe for plucking.

Chapter Three

THE AXE SWUNG, biting deep into the living wood. Amber and sap ran like blood. Fabiom listened to the mournful groan of the tree's falling, the tearing crash of its coming to rest, the absolute silence that followed. The silence was the worst, that and the emptiness, the gaping hole in the woods where the great tree had stood. Silver-brown bark ringing the muted gold heartwood of a waist-high stump, all that remained. No, no, the colours were wrong – bright gold and black. Black! Wishing did not make it so, neither did it turn the soft green leaves and winged seedpods into stiff needles and blood-red berries. The wind howled, calling his name as a dying breath.

"Casandrina!" His silent scream woke him from the nightmare turmoil; sweat beaded his brow, fear pumped his heart. "Casi, I'm sorry." But the night paid his whispered words no heed.

He lay absolutely still, letting the night cool him and the darkness erase the pictures, waiting for the new day and wondering what it might bring. Wondering too, why being in Stonehaven should cause him more distress than being in Westmouth, whether it was the distance from Morene and his family or simply that he had more time to dwell on his own misery. In Westmouth there had been too much work to do, much of it tedious, all of it necessary. Not that he had been there very long. Just seven days after he had taken up his post, word arrived from Robstrom requesting a meeting in Stonehaven.

The night held no answers to his questions, nor did sleep come again, so he went over all he had heard about Robstrom from Lesandor, and from Masgor and Ravik also, and tried to imagine why the prince might want to see him.

Morning dawned at last. As Fabiom rolled out of his bed he automatically glanced down at his right shoulder. The wound was not healing, if anything it was getting worse. It occurred to him that if Gerik's waters were indeed tainted by the death curse of dying Silvanii, then cleansing a Silvana-inflicted wound with that water might not be the wisest thing he could do.

As he dressed, using his right arm with difficulty, he considered seeking out a physician in the town, though he doubted if any local physician would have access to many good herbs in this desolate country. Still, it was something to do between now and midday when he had an appointment with Robstrom in the very place where Lesandor had been incarcerated.

They met in the Townmaster's offices and Robstrom immediately dismissed his attendants. Fabiom had learnt to disregard the wood veneer with which such places were habitually decorated but he was surprised to see the incipient Ruling Prince of Gerik had a simple ash bow with him, leant up against the side of his desk.

"One of my most precious possessions." Robstrom nodded towards the bow, seeing Fabiom looking at it. "A gift from your son. One of many, though the others cannot be seen." He touched his head and his heart. "A most remarkable young man. I trust he is well."

"He is…." Fabiom frowned, lost for words. He focussed his gaze on the familiar grain of Robstrom's bow. "No, your Highness, I doubt he is well at all."

Fabiom had not intended telling this stranger what had happened yet he found himself doing so, and Robstrom understood more than Fabiom might have expected.

"You must not lose him, Fabiom. I lost my daughter, my only child. There is nothing in this world that can make up for that. Sirsha was as precious to me as life. I know what I'm talking about."

They spoke about Lesandor then, and Fabiom learnt more about his son's journey through Gerik: how Robstrom had found him washed up on the river bank and how they had travelled together, with Lesandor telling stories that had reshaped Robstrom's perception of Morene.

"I would see Gerik once again like Morene: green and wholesome. No, I would see Gerik reforested. Is that too fanciful, Fabiom?"

"It is a beautiful notion, my lord. Is that why you asked to see me?"

"It is. I would enlist your help. But you already carry heavy burdens —"

Ignoring Robstrom's last comment, Fabiom heard himself promise to do whatever he could.

After the meeting, Fabiom went for a walk, trying to imagine the barren land transformed by tall trees. He stopped after a short while and sat on a mossy bank to catch his breath, wondering what was wrong with him, that he should tire so quickly, and putting it down to Gerik itself – which brought him back to his original thoughts of Prince Robstrom's dream of reforestation. It would be more than a matter of simply bringing in seedlings and planting them; that had been tried many times. Indeed, there was no certainty it could be done at all, if the poison ran too deep. The Silvanii of Morene would have to be involved for the plan to have any chance of success, yet that in itself was unprecedented, Silvanii rarely took notice of what was happening beyond their own environs, let alone in a neighbouring land. Still, Gerik was different. They all knew about Gerik.

As he resumed his walk, he recalled Casandrina's dismay when she learnt he was going there that first time, thirty-five years ago. The deeds done in Gerik in past generations had touched all Silvanii for all time. They did not easily forget the destruction of their own.

Unaware, Fabiom had stopped walking. His nails cut into the palms of his hands and all his muscles were taut, so that his injured shoulder throbbed and burned and the pain brought him back to awareness. Taking a deep breath – which left him coughing – he turned back towards the town and made himself think instead of all Robstrom had told him of Lesandor so that, when he arrived back at his accommodation, he felt closer to his son than he had for many days.

The hostelry in Stonehaven, where Fabiom had taken a room, was an improvement on the accommodation he had endured on his first visit to Gerik – as a young officer in Prince Ravik's service. However the company was nowhere near as convivial; the surly keeper who handed him the folded letter on the fifth morning of his sojourn ignored his polite salutations, as he did every morning, and only curiosity prevented the man's customary hurried departure. One glance from Fabiom sent him away nevertheless. Ravik's dispatch claimed it was urgent Fabiom return to Westmouth immediately but gave no details. Fabiom ignored the food set out before him and toyed with the letter. So soon.

Before he left the dining room he informed the innkeep he would be departing that afternoon, then he made his way to the Townmaster's office to take his leave of Robstrom.

"I made you a promise I may not be able to keep," Fabiom admitted. "Ravik has recalled me. I can only think that the Holder of Shakenyew has contacted him and I am to be made to account for my actions. That is only right, but it may make it hard, if not impossible, for me to do anything personally towards the realisation of your plans. And under the circumstances I cannot tell you to turn to Lesandor. I will speak on the matter to Prince Ravik, of course. If I cannot do anything, I'm sure he'll find someone else to aid you."

"I can ask no more," Robstrom agreed. "I wish you well, Fabiom. I only hope we will meet again in Deepvale."

"If I still hold Deepvale when you visit Morene, you will be more than welcome in my house, Prince Robstrom."

If. It was not a thought he cared to dwell on.

Fabiom was not surprised to find another message awaiting him in Westmouth, ordering his immediate return to Morene. Having no choice, he complied. The captain of the *Galingale* told him that Prince Ravik had waited for him in Westmouth for four days before he had returned to Morene, sending the ship back immediately upon his disembarkation. As he endured a choppy crossing over the strait, Fabiom puzzled over why Ravik had come to Gerik himself. If the prince doubted his edict would be obeyed he could simply have sent a magistrate and some soldiers to make certain.

There would be no soldiers, no magistrate; Fabiom realised that, long before they reached Southernport. Ravik respected him too much to have him arrested in public. The prince would trust him to go to Fairwater and surrender himself – which did not explain why Ravik had come to

Westmouth, unless it was to offer his support. Fabiom was glad Ravik had not been able to wait. If he was going to do this at all, he had to do it alone, for he had to shut his mind to the very real possibility that he would never go back to Deepvale and would never see Casandrina again. He could not bear to contemplate how much unhappiness he had caused her already, how much was still to come or what would happen to her if he did not return. All he could do was go to Fairwater, as he was ordered, and get through each day as it came.

With all his emotions locked away, he collected his little baggage and disembarked when the ship docked at Southernport. He was the only man who did not notice Elzandria waiting on the quayside.

"Father!" she cried, as he walked past her, unseeing.

Turning, he stared at her in disbelief.

"Oh, Father. I have worried so."

He could not mistake her relief, yet still he hung back. She went to him and he held her, wondering at her being there, substantial, afraid she was there to condemn him.

It was nearly twenty-two years since the day she emerged from her tree – the day Lesandor was born – tangible, as all Silvanii were on the day of their emerging. He had held her that day, kissed her, heard her sing her song of blessing to her infant brother. That had been in a different lifetime, when everything was perfect. Yet here she was, flesh and blood, clothed in green and gold silk, as beautiful as her mother.

"Elzandria – I don't understand. What are you doing here? How did you get here?"

"You were lost, so I came to find you. And now I have, and we can go home." She tossed errant strands of silver-brown hair over her shoulder, and the scent of ash flowers, fresh and wild, emanated from her.

"Elzandria." In wonder he stroked her cheek, smoothed her hair, then his hands fell to his sides. "I did a – a terrible thing," he admitted, stumbling over the words.

"No," she said. "You saved your son. To abandon him, that would have been a terrible thing. I am not sure I could have forgiven you for that."

"Even so –"

"Come home, please," she begged. "Lesandor is…. He is worried about you. He wanted to come to you, even in Gerik. Look at me, I have a husband now. Your house and your holding are waiting for you; your family and friends. Come back to us, Father, please."

"I am supposed to go to Fairwater, Ravik has sent for me. Elzandria, what I did, there must be a penalty. I cannot come home."

"You can. Prince Ravik came to Deepvale. He has done everything to help us, to help you. Father" – she touched his face, her smile turning to a look of dismay as her hand slipped from his cheek to his wounded shoulder – "you have more than paid the penalty already. You should not have to suffer so. Prince Ravik seeks no retribution. He is concerned only for you, as I am."

"And your mother?"

Elzandria stepped away from him and stared into his eyes. His own daughter she might be but still he flinched from her gaze.

"I have only been married to Tegun this short while, yet if I thought he doubted me I would be offended beyond words. You and Casandrina have been together so much longer, and you question her feelings for you?"

"No!" he protested. "It's just – have I not forfeited all rights to those feelings?"

"You have not," Elzandria told him.

He smiled, allowing himself to enjoy the relief her loving presence afforded. And sensing that, she laughed, so that heads turned, eyes stared.

"Tell me about your husband. I presume he is here with you. Tegun, you say? Am I to meet this most fortunate young man?"

She linked her arm through his. "He is waiting for us. You know him already. And I believe you were once acquainted with his grandmother."

Tegun's first words to him settled any remaining doubts Fabiom harboured about going home.

"Thank all that is good!" the young man exclaimed, seizing Fabiom's arm. "My lord, you are surely weary after your journey but we must set out for Deepvale immediately."

"You worry too much, Tegun," Elzandria chided, but Fabiom looked at his daughter closely then, and knew her husband was right.

"Casandrina found this distance hard to bear, and she had been used to the world beyond the woods five years before she came all this way. I am ready to travel, Tegun; and you are right, we should go at once."

❦

Aelinn arranged some fresh flowers in the largest guest suite. According to Lesandor, Tegun and Elzandria should have come to the house before now; he had returned from his cousin Kita's home a few days since, expecting his sister and her new husband to be there already.

"Mother says they have not been in the ash grove for some time," Lesandor said, as he handed her some twigs of red willow and a small bunch of silvery-pink peonies.

Aelinn took the flowers and smiled her thanks. "You are not worried about them, are you?"

"Not really." He sighed. "It is stupid, but I just want them here so that I can get used to – to Tegun having what I always wanted. I need to know I *can* get used to it."

"No." She touched his hand. "That's not stupid. But you like Tegun, don't you? And it's obvious you adore Elzandria. You will get used to them being here and being married."

"Will I?" he wondered, absently stripping leaves from some of the remaining peonies.

"Yes, you will," she told him emphatically, rescuing the near-leafless flowers. "You are too kind to resent other people's happiness."

Late that afternoon, two of Elzandria's woodmaids came to the house to announce that Fabiom was on his way home. On hearing the news, Casandrina's woodmaids busied themselves with the task of bedecking the house with flowers, and with branches of their own varieties of trees, to greet his return. Aelinn took charge of the rest of the preparations. It had not taken her long to realise how, other than Calbrin, few of the household were very concerned with any sort of organisation. She was pleased there were things she could do to help, for it gave her a reason to accept Casandrina's invitation to stay. Despite the Silvana's assurances, she knew she would have to justify her continuing presence

336

once Fabiom came home and Lesandor recovered fully. All she had done was carry one message. That hardly obligated them to give her a home for life.

The pair of swans searched for food among the reeds just beyond the river bridge, close enough to each other that their wings brushed from time to time.

"They stay together for life, mourn the death of a mate. Am I to be less loyal?"

"And they will risk their lives for their young," Casandrina answered her son, who glanced back at her and smiled wryly.

"I know."

They had spoken frequently and at length since his return from Shakenyew, and Casandrina was confident she knew Lesandor's true feelings, less confident that he did.

"Will you not go and meet your father? It would mean much to him, to me also."

The swans drifted upstream, side by side.

"He would never forgive anyone who so much as threatened you, let alone...." He could not bring himself to finish the sentence.

Casandrina did not disagree.

Lesandor sighed. "Yes, I will go."

"And when you come home we shall celebrate."

Celebrations were a long way from Fabiom's mind as he made his way home. Despite Elzandria's presence, her reassurances and her songs, he had little hope that Lesandor would feel anything but antipathy towards him, regardless of the awfulness of his marriage. He could not imagine how Lesandor felt about Taxiana. It was pointless trying to draw a comparison between his own relationship with Casandrina and his son's relationship with the yew Silvana, yet he could not pretend his feelings for Casandrina were based solely on her merits. He had been besotted from the moment he laid eyes on her, so many years ago.

"Lord Fabiom, we are arrived." Tegun's voice brought him back to the present, to the fact that they had reached Alderbridge and that evening was drawing in.

They were expected at Alderbridge's hold-house, for Tegun had arranged it on their way to Southernport. Fabiom, cold – despite the warm weather – breathless, and in constant pain from his shoulder, was more than ready for a rest, relieved too that he did not have to see Lesandor just yet, for until they met he could go on believing everything would be well between them. Not that he could put off the meeting for much longer. The morrow would see them in Deepvale.

Lesandor knew the Holder of Alderbridge, knew he would be welcome in his house, but he had no desire to meet his father in someone else's home, so he travelled no farther than the border of the two holdings and waited there. It was nearing midday when he heard the sound of a woodmaid's laughter and then his sister's voice affirming the joy of being so close to home again. For a brief moment he considered hiding somewhere, even behind the boulder which marked the boundary between the holdings. With a strangled gasp he quashed all such thoughts and took just one step, to the side of the boulder, to rest briefly against the solid stone.

When they saw him standing there beside the road, Tegun drew the donkey cart to a halt, leaving Fabiom to go on alone and on foot into his holding and to be reunited with Lesandor.

Lesandor would not speak at first, and Fabiom could not bring himself to say he was sorry, for he was not, though he ached for the grief he knew he had caused his son.

Lesandor studied the ground for a while and finally said, more to the earth than to his father, "I was so angry, so appalled. I felt betrayed and betrayer both, as if I should have guessed your intent yet did nothing to prevent you. Then I realised you had given me back myself. That I could feel such anger meant I was alive again, and the anger went away." He looked up, met Fabiom's eyes. "I pray that if Jarin ever has such need of me, I will be as able and willing to help him as you were to help me."

Chapter Four

CASANDRINA GREETED FABIOM wordlessly, holding him in a brief embrace. Over his shoulder a look passed between her and Elzandria. It was a look that sent shivers deep into Lesandor's core.

"Everyone is weary; celebrations can wait until tomorrow," Casandrina suggested, releasing Fabiom, "and you must all be hungry." She moved away from him to draw Aelinn aside; Fabiom looked after her sadly.

Shortly afterwards, Aelinn left the house, her face pale and drawn. Lesandor would have gone after her but Lan'h stayed him, sending him to the nursery where, she claimed, Jarin was fretting at his absence.

Tegun joined him in the nursery moments later. He too looked strained, though in his case it was the rigours of the journey that were taking their toll.

"Something's amiss," Tegun muttered.

Lesandor glanced up from his position on the floor, where he was wrestling with his son. Though he laughed with the game, his eyes were serious as they met Tegun's. "Whatever it is, Elzandria knows. Has she said nothing to you?"

"Nothing." Tegun tousled Jarin's hair. "I thought it was the distance from her tree that was distressing her. Yet now we're back she seems little better."

"And where did Aelinn go?" Lesandor scooped Jarin off the floor, into his arms. "Let's go get some answers. And – welcome home!"

They did not have to go far. Alone in the courtyard, Lyrra was playing with a spinning top. Lesandor nodded to Tegun.

"Where is your mother, Lyrra?" Lesandor asked, squatting down beside her, balancing Jarin on his knee.

"Mama's gone to get Nalio," Lyrra told him. "I heard Lan'h say so. Make it spin faster, Lesandor."

Lesandor set Jarin down on the ground and, kneeling, whipped the top into a frenzied spin, eliciting gales of laughter from both children. He glanced up at Tegun. "Maybe Elzandria is concerned about you. That was some journey you undertook."

Tegun looked doubtful.

"Now you, Tegun!" Lyrra insisted, holding out the whip handle.

After his own successful spin, Tegun helped Jarin have a go. The top wobbled in all directions, Jarin clapped his hands.

"Your turn," Lyrra chortled.

Lesandor looked up. His father had come over and was watching with an indulgent smile.

"Not now, sweet. I wouldn't be very good at it," Fabiom apologised. "I'll just watch."

Frowning, Lesandor rose to his feet. "Prince Ravik said you were injured and I noticed you were favouring your right arm. Are you hurt? Is that why Aelinn has gone for Nalio?"

"Has she? Well it's not on my account, though I will need to pay him a visit. I let a graze become infected, I think. Certainly, whipping tops are beyond my capabilities at present."

"And drawing a bow, I presume. I made you a new one," Lesandor added, without waiting for confirmation.

"Did you? Thank you. I'll look forward to trying it out. I won't pretend I'm not surprised; I wouldn't have imagined you making gifts for me."

"I was somewhat surprised as well," Lesandor admitted. He looked over at Tegun, still playing with the children. "And surprised how happy I am that he and Elzandria are here, together."

Fabiom sat down on one of the stone benches.

"I hadn't thought of that." Then he chuckled. "Our household seems to have grown considerably. Your mother wants Aelinn and Lyrra to stay, which is good; isn't it?" He glanced down at his hands, clasped together on his knees. "She's said little else to me of any substance. And I don't

340

know what to say to her. Forty years. There has to be something I can say."

"But, Father, I do not think she is angry with you – about anything. She has been longing for you to come back, and so concerned."

Fabiom shook his head and did not reply.

"If you really cannot talk to her, why not go for a walk in the woods together. Words might come easier there, to both of you."

"I could ask her, I suppose," Fabiom agreed, not entirely convinced.

Fabiom had to look for Casandrina, finding her eventually in the rooms she had prepared for Elzandria and Tegun. She smiled when she saw him; a smile so distant it almost made him change his mind about following Lesandor's suggestion.

"They will want their own house," she murmured, strewing rose petals about the floor.

"Yes," he agreed. Then, sensing an opportunity, asked, "Where, do you think? There are a few sites that might be suitable. We could go and see where might be the best to offer them; maybe go to the woods as well. I'd like to walk with you there. I need to. Casandrina?"

Her fingers tightened around the few remaining petals she held, releasing a warm perfume into the room, and her voice was as clenched as her hand as she refused him.

"Later, perhaps. At present there is too much I need to do. You should rest for a while." The crushed petals fell to the floor. He could not hide his dismay and, relenting, she touched his lips with damask-scented fingertips. "I will come to you soon."

Alone in their bed chamber, he waited, his heart aching. He was exhausted yet there was no way he could sleep and each passing moment seemed like an eternity. It was quite some time before she came, and when she did she was not alone.

"Nalio is come. I have asked him to see you."

Nalio placed his apothecary's bag on the foot of the bed. "They've been telling tales on you. I understand you have a shoulder in need of tending." He grasped Fabiom's arm. "It's good to have you home."

"I would have come to see you tomorrow," Fabiom replied, returning the greeting gesture, relief in his voice as well as surprise at Nalio being summoned when he had said nothing to anyone about his injury. At Nalio's indication, he unfastened the shoulder of his tunic and undid the makeshift dressing he had applied, missing the brief horror that darkened his friend's eyes, seeing only the easy, practised smile of the physician when he looked up.

"That looks nasty. And it's not new. You haven't had it seen to, have you?"

"I saw a physician in Gerik. He dressed it."

Nalio grunted noncommittally as he measured out a dose of some pungent liquid. "Let's start with this potion. Swallow it all and lie down." He stood back and waited, his smile fading even as Fabiom's eyes grew heavy. When they closed, he rubbed his face and groaned. "This should have been tended at once. Even then...."

Casandrina moved closer to the bed and stroked her husband's brow. He did not stir.

"Oh, I am aware of that fact, Nalio. And now the poison has spread far. I can feel it if I so much as touch him. Yet we have to try. I feared he was lost to us before, but he has come home. We cannot lose him now."

"Nothing in my training or experience... This is beyond my abilities!"

"As it is beyond mine," she admitted. "Yet, perhaps it is not beyond you and me together."

Nalio probed Fabiom's damaged shoulder and grimaced. "What can I do?"

"Treat it as you would any deep wound in need of cleansing. I may be able to counteract the poison with sap and bark from my own tree."

"Sap? Bark? You mean to damage your tree?"

"I mean to help you save his life."

Cutting deep, Nalio removed the necrotic flesh around the five livid track marks that scarred Fabiom's shoulder, releasing a thin stream of malodorous pus as he did so, then he flushed the wound with vinegar and packed it with freshly picked yarrow, which Kir'h brought at his request.

Meanwhile Casandrina spoke urgently with her other woodmaids, sending Nek'h to find wild honey and Zin'h to look for willow and comfrey, before slipping out of the house, unseen. Carrying a woven satchel containing a small flask, she hurried across the garden and the bridge, into the wildwood and on to her grove.

Cream and pink honeysuckle blossom, star-bright anemones, and periwinkles as blue as Fabiom's eyes adorned the ash grove. The wildwood thrummed with vitality in its summer glory – there had to be healing for her beloved husband here. Casandrina placed her hands against the etched bark of her tree, its grooves and fissures as familiar as the lines on her palms. High above, a multitude of seeds encased in their delicate pods were ripening to gold, bright against the great tree's soft green canopy. Though she had no real concept of numbers, she was aware of every single seed, every leaf.

She began to sing. A shiver ran through her body as a corresponding tremor shook the tree. Winged seedpods spiralled towards the ground all around her. They were not ripe enough to fall naturally and the sensation was disconcerting, uncomfortable. She quickly gathered the fallen pods and filled her satchel. Closing her eyes, she felt again the dread she had experienced when she had held Fabiom on his return. For his sake, she would do anything. So thinking, and still singing, she rose to her feet, caught hold of a small branch growing out of the main trunk, and twisted it off. Her voice faltered. For a moment her sight darkened and she could not think, until, with tremulous fingers, she unstoppered the clay flask and held the lip to the oozing tear in the trunk. Blood seeped between the fingers of her other hand, pressed against her side.

Zin'h was the first of her woodmaids to arrive, with Lan'h close behind. "Why are you here? I set you tasks –" Casandrina scolded.

"We have completed them." Zin'h took the flask from her mistress as Lan'h reached for a freshly spun spider web to dress Casandrina's side.

On the trunk, the sap began to solidify to a thin amber scar. Zin'h stoppered the flask and went to place it in the satchel, but Casandrina stayed her.

"I must carry that. Help me home as quickly as possible. This cannot harden or it will be useless. With my voice I can keep it fluent for a short while." She took a shuddering breath and began to sing again.

Zin'h carried the satchel, as she and Lan'h supported Casandrina back to the hold-house.

Nalio was laying loose bandages on Fabiom's shoulder and arm when they returned.

"That's all I can do for now," he said, straightening up and stretching taut muscles. "My lady, you are so pale! Sit down."

With the woodmaids' assistance, she sat on the bed by Fabiom's head. Then, without a word, the woodmaids began pounding the ash seeds into a paste.

Nalio lifted the bandage he had just applied, and carefully removed the yarrow. He glanced at Casandrina. She nodded and he tipped the flask. Thicker than honey, the sap was the colour of sunlight. As the final drop slipped from the flask onto the open wound, Casandrina dipped her finger into the vessel to get the sticky remnant, which she touched to Fabiom's tongue.

The woodmaids, confident Casandrina was resting, went to look after Jarin, and help prepare food. The day crept by. Nalio repacked Fabiom's wound, this time with the ash seed paste and honey.

"It is helping, but it is not enough." Sitting beside her husband, Casandrina rested her hand on his chest. Still his heartbeat was too fast, his breathing too slow.

"If we could get him to ingest some, that might help," Nalio mused.

"You mean, we need more sap?"

"My lady, I'm so sorry. I didn't mean to say that aloud."

"We *will* save him, Nalio. We must." She pulled herself to her feet. "Ah!" She reached out to steady herself against the wall, but her hand caught only air and she stumbled.

"Another tree –" he insisted, reaching for her.

"No. Mine is more potent. But, I cannot do this alone, not again."

He helped her sit back down. "My lady, you cannot be suggesting...."

She looked up at him, a small smile on her lips, pain in her eyes. "He has always trusted you, utterly and without reservation. You must do this for him." When he did not reply, she sighed. "Would you have me ask Lesandor?"

"No. He.... No!" He tried, and failed, to suppress a shudder. "Very well. I shall go. Tell me what to do, and call for Elzandria, let her look after you. Would one of your woodmaids come with me, show me the way? Or would they not be able to let me damage your tree, even at your behest?"

She shook her head. "I dare not tell Elzandria, for she would surely want to help her father in the same way, and she needs to care for Tegun, and Lesandor. We cannot both be weakened. Besides which, I must come with you – to keep the sap from solidifying and turning to amber."

With some care, she got to her feet. "See, that is better. I was unprepared last time."

At the grove, Casandrina sat on the ruin of her mother's tree, contemplating the damaged area of the tall ash before her. "You can see where I have broken a small branch. There is another, right beside it. You must break it or cut it off in such a way as to pull a strip of bark with it. We will bring the bark, as well as the sap. You must not hesitate once you begin. For your sake, and mine."

"Now we're here, I do not know that I can do this." Nalio looked at her imploringly. "From earliest memory, the sanctity of your trees is drummed into us children of Morene."

She smiled, acknowledging that fact. "And yet, Fabiom managed to fell a full-grown Silvanan tree."

Nalio closed his eyes. "Yes. I know – for a loved one, anything is possible."

"Indeed, it is." She rummaged in the satchel, removed the flask and a shapeless, cloth-wrapped lump. "I brought some beeswax."

"Beeswax?"

Dividing the mass into two, she offered him the pieces. "For you, to stop your ears."

"If I hurt you, then I do not need to be spared knowing it," he insisted, with a shake of his head.

She smiled. "To stop the sap hardening I must sing to my tree. It is not a song you should hear."

There were small branches growing from the limbs of the tree, some low enough to be easily broken. Casandrina had chosen to take one from the tree's trunk instead, so that the corresponding wound on her torso would be easier to hide. It had seemed sensible when she had made the decision, but she had not allowed for how much more it would hurt. In her life she had known little physical pain. Apart from her altercation with Gracillia, which had resulted in two scars on her upper arm, and her recent furious uprooting of the yew tree in the garden, which had left her hands raw and aching, she had not had enough experience to judge where would be the least debilitating place to be injured. Even Lesandor's birth had been merely tiring and uncomfortable. This was different. But now that she had damaged her tree she could not bring herself to mutilate another part. She would continue what she had begun.

Taking a last moment to draw strength from Narilina's memory, Casandrina rose to her feet and made her way to her own tree. She leant against the trunk, pressing her face against the bark, trying to concentrate on the sensation against her cheek, and the need to keep the sap from hardening through the power of her voice.

"Do it now," she whispered.

She began to sing, tuning in to the fluidity of the tree's sap as it flowed through the outmost layers of the trunk, her song becoming a gasp of anguish as the branch was twisted and then cut, the gasp turning into a drawn-out groan as a hand-measure of bark was ripped away.

As before, the deed was barely done when two of the woodmaids arrived. Wordlessly, Lan'h brought clean gossamer to dress Casandrina's reopened and enlarged wound. Kir'h glared at Nalio as if he was to blame, so that he busied himself with stoppering the sap-filled flask and carefully wrapping the piece of sundered bark until the woodmaid's attention turned to the damaged tree, which she tended much as Lan'h tended Casandrina.

Chapter Five

ONLY A FEW slivers of early-morning sunlight eased through the shutters into Fabiom's room but they were too bright, hurting his eyes. He turned his head away, towards the shadows, and gasped as the movement drove knives of pain through his shoulder. Taking quick, shallow breaths and trying to lie as still as he possibly could, he realised that his shoulder felt only marginally worse than his head.

"How do you feel?" Nalio's voice seemed to come from somewhere very far away.

"I hurt all over, and I feel nauseous," Fabiom groaned. "What did you do to me?" Talking was painful too, for his throat and mouth were dust dry.

"I'm sorry," Nalio said. "I wanted to knock you out quickly and be certain you stayed that way for a while. Mandrake and henbane. Not too pleasant, eh?"

Fabiom risked opening his eyes and, after a while, Nalio's face settled down to its familiar shape.

"I don't want you to move for a couple of days," Nalio told him unnecessarily. "Your shoulder was seriously infected, as you must have realised. I had to open the wound to clean it, and may have to again." He held a cup of ash-leaf-infused water to his patient's lips and Fabiom managed to drink a little.

"It's true then, Gerik is poisonous." Fabiom risked a deeper breath, grimaced then relaxed. "I promised Prince Robstrom I would aid him in his plans if I could. Maybe they're too ambitious. Maybe nothing could grow there."

"Hush," Nalio admonished. "I've no idea what you are talking about, but now is not the time. Tell me about it later."

Fabiom yawned. "Later," he agreed, and slipped back into an uneasy sleep.

Evening light begloomed the bed chamber before he stirred again, waking to see Casandrina standing beside the bed, gazing down at him. Unable to read her expression, he closed his eyes; fearful that she had not forgiven him. Her lips brushed his eyelids, reassuring, tender, and she sang him back to sleep. When he next awoke it was morning once more.

Under Nalio and Casandrina's ministrations, Fabiom's shoulder and arm began to heal, though slowly. Casandrina's tension had vanished and she was beside him constantly, so that he was happy to do nothing other than bask in her loving solicitude and in the joy of being home.

On the second day, more awake and aware, he saw he was not alone in being injured. Casandrina had a wound on her side, a full hand's span wide, that she had been trying to keep from his notice.

"You're hurt! What happened?" he demanded, fear in his voice. "Did someone come from Shakenyew? Casi – I'm sorry! I meant to keep you from danger; you know that's why I went alone."

She silenced him with a lingering kiss. "No one came; no one did this to me. A small branch was torn from my tree, and some bark, that is all."

He touched the wound. "It looks new –"

"Shush," she warned. "You are to relax, not fret. You really do not want any more of Nalio's sleeping draught, do you?"

That was enough of a threat to make him drop the subject. She snuggled up close to him on the bed and laughed at his expression.

"Shall I tell you about Tegun and Elzandria instead?" she suggested.

"Please do," he said compliantly. "Talk to me about anything – just stay with me."

Even had she not stayed with him, he would not have been short of visitors. Masgor sat and talked with him, wanting to know all about his meeting with Robstrom and the current situation in Gerik; Yan, who had been sent back to Deepvale by Prince Ravik to await Fabiom's return, visited, as did the rest of his family; and, daily, Nalio called in to check up on him. After three days he was allowed to leave his bed, on strict instructions that he did nothing strenuous.

Lounging beside the bathing pool alongside Casandrina, watching Lesandor and Aelinn attempt to teach Jarin to swim, and Lyrra – who already swam like a little porpoise and needed no help from anyone – was sedentary enough to comply with Nalio's strictures and was more entertaining than lying in bed.

After a while, Lesandor lifted Jarin out and handed him to Casandrina who wrapped the child in a cosy towel while Lesandor dried himself off in a cursory manner.

"I'll be glad when I'm allowed in the pool again," Fabiom sighed. "Nalio is being very authoritarian about this."

Lesandor threw his wet towel aside and regarded his father uncertainly for a moment.

"Was it Taxiana? Did she do that?" He looked away. "I tried not to believe it, but I think I knew, the day you came home – when Nalio was summoned with such alacrity."

Fabiom nodded, and rubbed his shoulder absently, trying to choose the right words, but Lesandor was already saying, "You were fortunate then. She told me once she could kill a man that way; that she was as poisonous as her tree. Perhaps she was lying."

"She was not lying," Casandrina replied.

Both her husband and son looked at her in horror.

"You came home just in time," she told Fabiom gently. "The scars will stay but the poison is gone." She looked away briefly. "I feared you had come too late."

Fabiom shivered but he had no wish to dwell on that revelation. He reached across and took her hand, holding it firmly in his.

"Those scars are not all I brought back from Shakenyew," he said, deciding to take the opportunity to talk about what else occurred in that holding while Lesandor seemed reasonably at ease with the subject. He kissed Casandrina's hand then rose, still somewhat unsteady, from his couch.

"Where are you going?" she asked, concerned.

"I need to fetch something."

"I can go, what do you need?" Lesandor objected. "Nalio said...."

Fabiom glared at his son. He left the room, returning only moments later with a small silk pouch, which he handed to Lesandor. He did not tell them he had sent Nek'h to fetch the pouch from the bedchamber for him.

"I discovered this in the marketplace, as I was leaving Shakenyew, on my way to Fairwater. It cost me considerably more to buy it the second time than it had done initially. But then *I* did not have to pay for the amber that first time."

Once again, he reached across to his wife, this time to trace the barely visible scars on her arm.

Lesandor studied the silver clasp carefully, turning it over twice, then he closed his eyes and groaned. "She *was* there! That is why I went to Shakenyew in the first place, but I could not find her. Why would she have sold it? Did she think Raidan had abandoned her?" He handed it back to Fabiom. "That is not the clasp I was wearing. I still have that one; I brought it home with me."

"Who was there? Who were you looking for?" Fabiom asked, confused.

"Father, you made me promise to stay away from Shakenyew, and I am bound for half a year after losing that wager. Release me, please. I must go back. I made a vow I have not yet kept and it is long overdue."

"A vow? To whom?" Fabiom asked suspiciously.

"To Prince Raidan," Casandrina answered for Lesandor. There was a sparkle in her eyes that made both her husband and son look at her curiously. "Tell me, Lesandor, are you really determined to find her now? To do anything, go anywhere?"

"I am," Lesandor replied. "I have let myself be distracted too often and for too long already."

"One of you, please tell me of what and whom we are speaking," Fabiom insisted.

Casandrina leant against his side, turned her head and kissed him but did not answer. Instead she said to Lesandor, "I advised you a while since to ask Aelinn for her assistance. You should do so now. She is becoming somewhat anxious about her position here and might be glad of something to distract her. This clasp and your quest would, I think, distract her considerably."

After much cajoling, Aelinn persuaded Lyrra out of the pool then stepped out herself. Lesandor handed her a warm towel to wrap Lyrra in.

"I have a delicate matter I need to discuss with you," he told her, then turned to Fabiom. "I can tell you both at the same time, and I would be glad of any help you can suggest." He laid more towels on a couch for Aelinn and Lyrra.

"Of course I'll help, if I can," Aelinn said, uncertainly.

"Prince Ravik has a daughter-by-marriage and, I believe, a grandchild – both of whom he is unaware of. I have been trying to find them, unsuccessfully as you can deduce. The only firm lead I had suggested they had gone to Shakenyew, a year ago or maybe more."

Fabiom said nothing, only shaking his head in mute amazement.

Aelinn began brushing her daughter's hair. "I had only just arrived in Shakenyew when I met you, and, besides my cousin, I knew no one there," she told Lesandor. "But surely such a family would be known to the lord holder." Her hands stilled. "Do you want me to go back? My cousin's husband has connections in the holder's house. He might be able to help you."

"We could go together," Lesandor suggested, glancing at his father for permission.

"Yes," Fabiom said distractedly, trying to take in Lesandor's words. "So the cloak clasp I bought was hers, is that what you're saying? Yet he must have given it to her, so why would she part with it?"

"Maybe it was stolen from her," Lesandor guessed, and the implications of that thought filled him with dread.

"Fabiom, show Aelinn the clasp. It may be she recognises it," Casandrina suggested.

"It is most unlikely...." Aelinn began, then her words turned into a gasp as she caught sight of the amber and silver clasp in Fabiom's hand.

"What is it, Mama?" Lyrra asked, then she too saw the clasp. "Your brooch," she said, in delight.

"Yours?" Lesandor's voice was incredulous. Yet, as he tore his eyes away from Aelinn to stare at Lyrra he wondered how he had not realised it before. Petite, red-haired and with more than a sprinkling of freckles across her small, tip-tilted nose, the child was the image of Princess Maedrim, and of Raidan. One look at his mother confirmed his suspicions – and told him she had known all along.

"I had to sell it. I felt terrible. He said it was not his, that he was looking after it for a friend, but I had no money left and nothing else of value. I could not have made the journey here otherwise," Aelinn explained, then looked askance at Lesandor. "What's the matter? What's wrong?"

"He told me your name was Cuivah."

Cuivah was a family name, borne by the eldest daughter for the past eight generations, a name which linked Aelinn to the shame her grandparents had brought on them all. Raidan alone had known her thus. When he did not come back from Gerik, and she found herself alone and with a new baby, she had reverted to the name she had adopted since the family's illegal return to Morene.

"No wonder I could not find you," Lesandor sighed.

"No, but I found you." And she wept, then laughed, for all she had lost and gained.

Chapter Six

LESANDOR WENT TO Valehead that very afternoon, to tell Yan their quest had resolved itself successfully, sharing their secret with Tarison and Marid at the same time.

Now that Fabiom was home and recovering, Yan was preparing to return to the capital to take up the position of tutor to Ravik's eldest grandson, six-year-old Davin. Tarison's suggested that Aelinn and Lyrra should travel with him when he returned to the city in two days' time, and that Lesandor should go with them to break the news to Prince Ravik in person.

When Lesandor returned home the following morning, he found Aelinn less than enthusiastic about the proposal.

"No, no. I cannot!" she protested. "We were exiled forever. I will be in the most terrible trouble if it is ever discovered I came back. And Lyrra – what of her? She could be taken from me."

"Aelinn, Ravik is not that kind of man. Trust me." Lesandor took her hand. "He is kind and just and generous – indeed very much like his youngest son."

She scowled at him. "That's not fair! And even if you are right, it's too soon. I am not yet used to the things you've told me." Her eyes were wide and imploring. "If you must tell him now, will you not go alone?"

"It is not as if you have never met him," Lesandor reminded her. "Remember how well he and Lyrra got on? How could he be anything but delighted to be told she is his granddaughter?" He echoed his Great-Aunt Marid's words to him the previous day, when he had expressed his own doubts and fears.

Aelinn hugged her arms around herself and did not reply.

"All right," Lesandor said gently. "How about this: we all go to Fairwater. You and Lyrra go with Yan to his apartment while I see Prince Ravik. If he is in any way hostile to the notion, I will not mention that you are in the city. If he can accept it immediately, then you and Lyrra can come to the palace."

"Yes, I suppose so." She tried to smile, failed and gave up. "Excuse me, Lesandor, I think I will walk in the garden. I need to be alone."

"Before you go –" Lesandor paused as she turned back to face him. "I think we should let Tegun know; he was close to Raidan, and took his death hard. I wouldn't want him to learn of this by chance."

"Yes, of course. But please, will you tell him?" She touched his hand and did manage a brief smile before leaving.

The early summer garden was a wondrous tonic, alive as it was with sweet scents and vibrant colours that filled the senses and left little room for anything else. Aelinn picked a basketful of arum lilies and carried them to the portico, where Casandrina was watching over the two children. In the distance they could hear the muted twang of bow-strings and the soft thud of arrows, interspersed with talk and some laughter, as Lesandor informed his brother-by-marriage of Raidan's newly discovered family, in between instructing him in the finer points of archery.

"Our young men seem happy," Casandrina observed, referring to the sounds of gaiety emanating from the yard.

"The children too," Aelinn agreed. Lyrra and Jarin were close by on the lawn, playing with a half-grown orphaned fox cub, which Casandrina had found and fostered; giggling with pleasure each time the little animal pounced on the piece of knotted rope they wriggled in front of it.

"Something is troubling you," Casandrina guessed. "Will you not tell me?"

"I don't want to go to Fairwater," Aelinn answered quietly. "I'm afraid to meet the prince and the rest of Raidan's family. I'm afraid they'll despise me, and almost equally afraid they'll welcome me – and want to keep Lyrra close by, for Raidan's sake. What shall I do, Casandrina?"

"What do you want to do? In your heart."

"Stay here," Aelinn admitted. "I know that's not possible now. It's just that, after everything that has happened, I would really like to stay in one place, with people I know. And Lyrra is so happy. Before we came here I'd feared for our future. Even when I went to my cousin in Shakenyew I had few expectations. We did not know each other. She owed me nothing. Her life had turned out well, mine less so. I do not know if she would have done anything for me. As it was, I never found out. I never even saw her." She smiled, remembering.

"For which I am ever grateful," Casandrina assured her. "Lesandor's letter was of no use. We had no idea where he was. He said only that he had married again. Had it not been in his own hand, we would not have known it was from him. We knew something was amiss but there was no help in that. You and Lyrra were the ones who found him."

They travelled slowly, talking about Raidan, mostly, and Aelinn's life over the past four years, enjoying the leisurely pace they allowed themselves. They made their way to the city by donkey cart, their vehicle pulled – to Lyrra's delight – by the little white donkey which had once been Mysha's.

"He left me money, enough for half a year, he said. But I had never been used to such wealth and hardly needed a quarter of it, which was as well. When I had no choice but to accept that he was not coming back, we lived more frugally still and so I had enough for three years. A distant cousin of mine had married a minor official from the holding of Shakenyew, part of the lord holder's household. I wrote to her. She replied saying I might go there, and that's where I was bound when I met you," Aelinn told her travelling companions.

"But were you not supposed to go much sooner? I only went to Shakenyew because I believed you were there already, yet I arrived several months before you did," Lesandor said.

Aelinn shook her head. "Going to Shakenyew was a last resort. I put it off more than once, until I had run out of options." With a smile, she added, "It's very strange to think that somebody was tracking me across Morene. And for so long. Many people would have given up."

"How could I? I promised him I would find you, somehow. Though I did not expect it to be in my own home."

"Promised him?"

"He carved your name – Cuivah – in the wood beneath the ship's bunk he slept on. I found it on the way home, your name carved by his hand. It was as if he was there, and I made an oath to him and to you and your child." He let out a deep sigh. "I was very nearly forsworn. Any longer with Taxiana and I would not have cared what I had promised, or to whom." He glanced at her teasingly. "I may have been able to outshoot your husband but I would have to concede that he had far more talent than I when it came to choosing a wife."

The setting sun silvered the white stones of Fairwater, and the waters of the estuary were mirror-clear, reflecting trees and boats, buildings and lights, in perfect detail. For Lyrra's benefit they had to lead the donkey close to the edge so they could see her reflection in the water.

"Look at Whisper upside up!" Lyrra chortled, and passers-by smiled, amused at the child's delight.

"Whisper will have to go to the stables, upside down or not," Yan told her. "I live on the second floor of a building in the middle of the city, and we'd never get her up the stairs."

Lyrra giggled even more, turning in a circle then stopping to gaze at the palace, high on the hill. "Look up there. Look, Mama. It's so pretty. I want to see inside."

Lesandor grinned and raised his brows; Aelinn pretended to ignore him.

Leaving the water behind, they followed Yan through the dusky streets, first to the stables and then to his apartment, settling themselves while Yan's manservant, surprised at their arrival, made hasty preparations for supper.

When it came, Aelinn had little appetite.

"I'm sorry," she told Yan. "I can't eat. Now that we're here.... Well, I just wish it was over with. Maybe I should come with you tomorrow," she said to Lesandor. "I don't think I could bear to stay here, wondering what's going on."

"Decide tomorrow," he suggested. "Look at Lyrra. She does not care, so why should you?"

Lyrra was sound asleep on a couch, her thumb in her mouth. Aelinn regarded her daughter enviously.

After a night of little sleep, Aelinn took one look at herself in her travelling mirror and decided she would let Lesandor go up to the palace alone.

"Probably the wisest decision," Yan concurred. "Prince Ravik might appreciate a little time to get used to the idea, even if he is pleased at the news – as we all hope he will be."

Lesandor had no real opinion at that moment for he was almost as nervous as Aelinn about facing the prince. Quashing his anxiety, he went as early as was seemly, arriving at the palace to be met with a surprise himself: Robstrom was there, come to Morene to look further into the possibility that Gerik could be reforested. They met in a cool marble corridor, both of them startled and then delighted.

"You look better than I might have expected," Robstrom said as he grasped Lesandor's arm. "I was sending a messenger to your father's house this very morning, to ask if it was a convenient time to take both you and him up on your invitation to visit Deepvale."

"I am glad you can come, my lord." Lesandor bit his lip, stopping himself from voicing the thought he had nearly spoken aloud.

Robstrom said it for him: "I am just sorry my beloved Sirsha cannot."

Before either could say more, Ravik's voice brought Lesandor's mind firmly back to his immediate concerns. "Lesandor! This is a surprise. You have not come to accompany Prince Robstrom to Deepvale, for you could not have known he was arrived. So what brings you to Fairwater?"

Lesandor glanced at Robstrom.

"You go ahead. I'm just exploring," Robstrom told him. "Your prince and I have already talked – a lot!"

"I do not want to intrude," Lesandor told Ravik, despite Robstrom's assurances.

"You're not intruding, Lesandor. I'm pleased to see you. I would have come to Deepvale soon enough – I received Tegun's letter...." He shook his head in amazement. "There's nothing amiss, is there?"

"No, my lord, all is well with us. Father sends his greetings, as does Tegun, of course. I have come to you on another's behalf and regarding the holdership of Southernport. I would speak with you in private, if I might."

Ravik nodded and indicated a door to the left. "What about Southernport, Lesandor? I thought the matter was settled." He closed the door behind them.

"You did say that it was to be held on Raidan's behalf?" Lesandor confirmed. "That Princess Jaymna forfeited the holding because of her part in the events that led to –"

"His death. Yes," Ravik agreed.

Lesandor drew a deep breath. "Then there is one with a far greater claim than any child of mine. My lord, the little girl you met in Deepvale, Lyrra, she is Raidan's daughter. He and her mother met in Rushford before he left for Gerik."

"Lesandor –" Ravik sat down, one hand covering his mouth. "I don't ... Aelinn and Raidan ... yet you said nothing when I came to your father's house."

"I could not tell you then, my lord, because I did not know. And she had no idea either. Raidan did not tell her who he was. He was planning to bring her home on his return. I have to tell you this," Lesandor hurried on, fearing to stop in case his resolve crumbled, "I have known all along that he had a wife, who was with child when he left. It has always been my intention to find them. I knew it would not be easy, I had so little to go on. I had no idea how hard it would actually be. Aelinn is not even her name; not the name of the woman I was searching for. And then my own life took such unforeseen turns."

"What is it you're not telling me, Lesandor?" Ravik asked. "And why did Raidan keep such a secret from us? Why did you?"

At that, Lesandor did hesitate. He squared his shoulders. "Her given name is Cuivah. She is granddaughter to...."

"Cuivah? That is her actual name? Then I can guess who she is granddaughter to. It is a name gifted to few infant girls in the past thirty years. I thought I recognised the family likeness, yet I did not recognise her name. Not surprisingly as it is false."

"I owe her my life," Lesandor said.

The prince looked at him for a long moment. "And Raidan loved her?"

"Yes, my lord. Very much."

"And I have a granddaughter, to whom you are content to relinquish any claim on Southernport."

"Yes, my lord," Lesandor repeated quietly.

Ravik sighed heavily, through gritted teeth. "I have sealed their fate with my own hand: any member of that family who steps foot on Morenian soil shall forfeit their life. Can I ignore my own ruling because it suits my heart to do so?"

Though the words were not directed at him, Lesandor answered. "You did no less for my father. We both know what *he* did, what the penalty should have been –"

Ravik snapped out of his reverie. "Have you not forgiven him?"

Lesandor looked away. "Sometimes I wake at night – those nights I sleep at all – and I … I hate him. It passes in a heartbeat. And fully awake, I feel quite the opposite. Nevertheless, I bolt my door when I retire – in case I sleepwalk – in case I *do* something I would bitterly regret. However, what I feel changes nothing: there is a written and sealed penalty for" – he frowned, swallowed – "for deliberately felling a Silvana tree. Yet that penalty was waived. I am glad, beyond words, you found a way to spare him, my lord. How could I live with myself if a mistake I made cost him – of all people – his life? But now, can you not make the same allowance for your own granddaughter – and her mother? *They* have done nothing wrong, save be born to the wrong bloodline."

With a wry smile, Ravik leant back in his seat. "You are your father's son, Lesandor. You will make a fine diplomat one day." He looked at the young man appraisingly. "I suspect they are not too far away, am I correct?"

"Indeed, my lord. I brought them with me, in the hope that you would receive them."

"You had better send for the two ladies, and introduce us properly." Ravik's smile broadened. "And while we await their arrival, tell me the whole tale, in detail, so that I may break this wonderful news to my wife." He closed his eyes briefly. "This could be the very thing which might help her."

Lesandor rested his right hand over his heart, in a gesture of shared hope.

As Robstrom was desirous to visit Deepvale almost immediately, Lesandor had to leave Aelinn sooner than he would have wished, yet she seemed content enough, if still a little bewildered, when he went to say farewell.

"I was nervous enough about meeting your mother, given my family history. Prince Robstrom has my sympathy," she told him. "You will come back soon, won't you, Lesandor? Just in case...."

"When Robstrom returns I shall travel with him and then I shall see you, but there is nothing to worry about. No two people could be more welcome anywhere than you and Lyrra are here," he assured her.

And as Lyrra waved him off that afternoon, sitting up on the shoulders of Prince Dilon, her youngest uncle, Lesandor knew he had done the right thing.

Chapter Seven

"THIS IS MY home. You are very welcome."

Robstrom followed Lesandor into the heart room, rinsing his hands in imitation of his young host.

"I like this ritual," he reflected, handing his towel to Calbrin with a slight nod of thanks. "It makes for a sense of belonging. Such a feeling would not go amiss in Gerik, I think."

Lesandor handed his own towel over. "Calbrin, would you tell my parents we have a guest."

It took a moment for his words to register with the house-steward, for Robstrom's reference to Gerik had caught Calbrin's attention.

"I'm sorry," Calbrin murmured after a slight hesitation. "They're not here, Master Lesandor. They're both at the silk mill, there was a problem with the dyes."

Robstrom looked distinctly relieved.

"No matter," Lesandor decided. "You'd as soon rest and refresh yourself anyway, I would imagine," he suggested to Robstrom, who he knew had serious qualms about meeting Casandrina. "Is, er, Tegun about, or Elzandria?" he asked Calbrin, deciding this was not the time to reveal that there was a second Silvana living in the hold-house.

"They are at the site your father has granted them to build their new home."

From the sounds in the house, or more precisely, lack of sounds, Lesandor deduced that all the woodmaids were with either his mother or his sister.

"Is *anyone* here?"

"There is one person."

Trying not to smile too broadly, Lesandor introduced the Ruling Prince of Gerik to Masgor and then left the two of them alone while he and Calbrin made arrangements for Robstrom's stay.

Eventually, tired out, Masgor's head began to nod and Robstrom left him, closing the door to the day room very quietly.

"Such an astute and learned man. It's a pity he's not younger or I'd ask him to come back to Gerik. He's sleeping now."

"He does that a lot these days. Calbrin has a light meal for us and then I thought we might go for a walk."

"A walk?"

Robstrom looked out of the window at the woods beyond the garden.

"Before I left Gerik, I tried to imagine what they would be like. Nothing prepares you. If you've never seen one tree there is no way to imagine what a forest will look like. I won't lie to you, Lesandor, the prospect of walking where the Silvanii dwell fills me with dread. Even on the way here, travelling along roads lined on both sides by trees was daunting."

"You do want to go, though?"

Robstrom laughed. "Oh yes. Anyway, I can hardly come to Morene and not set foot upon a woodland path; neither can I claim to dream of Gerik reforested if I have not the nerve to stand surrounded by trees here. That doesn't mean I will find it easy."

Lesandor grinned. "I think there is someone who might be able to help you."

Robstrom regarded him suspiciously. "And who might that be?"

"My son, Jarin. He is two years old. See the wildwood through the eyes of a small child and you will see it is a place of wonder and beauty."

Jarin already knew the names of many of the trees and birds and happily told Robstrom what everything was, even when he was not quite sure himself.

"Berry!" the little boy said, pointing out the white flowers and the fat red fruits of wild strawberries growing on a bank.

"Strawberries," Lesandor told him. "You want some, Jarin? Robstrom?"

Robstrom had never tasted strawberries and he sampled the sweet fruit tentatively before pronouncing it delicious and then eagerly joining in the hunt for more.

After the strawberries, they walked for a while in companionable silence until Robstrom stopped and slowly turned full circle.

"There's nothing else, is there? It's as if the rest of the world doesn't exist any more and this is all there is." He reached a tentative hand out to touch the stem of a hazel. "How do you know which ones are Silvanan?"

"You don't, necessarily. If you are familiar with the Silvanii you can tell; I can tell."

"This tree?" Robstrom looked up at the branches of the hazel, all full of unripened nuts.

"No. Hazels are the abode of woodmaids and there is no Silvanan tree hereabout, so no woodmaids' trees either. Come on this way, I shall show you one."

"I'd rather not, if you don't mind. This evening I'll meet your mother. Maybe tomorrow I'll ask you to bring me here again. I think I'd be happiest doing it in that order. It must be hard for you to understand, Lesandor."

"Believe me, you have come farther than many even in Morene would dare go. We will go back now. My parents may be home by the time we get there, if not I shall ask someone to find them."

Fabiom came back from the silk mill, alone, and was surprised to find Masgor sound asleep in the day room, even more surprised when the old tutor woke and told him that he had enjoyed a long conversation with Robstrom.

"He's gone off for a walk with Lesandor. Did you say you were going to get me a drink of wine?"

"Lesandor's in Fairwater and you know Nissus said you weren't to drink wine. I'll get you some morat, it's gentler on your stomach."

"Lesandor's home. He came back with Prince Robstrom. I thought I was the one who was becoming hard of hearing."

Fabiom grinned and went to the cellar to find a new flask of morat. As he came back through the heart room, the conservatory door opened and Lesandor and Robstrom came in.

"Prince Robstrom! Masgor said...." Fabiom shook his head slowly. "To be honest, I thought he had imagined you'd come. Though he'd never forgive me for saying so."

Robstrom grasped Fabiom's arm. "It's good to see you again, and to see that everything is resolved. As for Masgor, I won't tell him you questioned his soundness of mind," Robstrom promised. "He's a very old man, even so I didn't get the impression there was anything wrong with his reason."

"Oh, there's not," Fabiom agreed, leading the way through to the courtyard. "It's just that meeting you has been his wish, ever since Lesandor came home from Gerik. And it was a wish he did not expect to see fulfilled."

"Then I'm glad to have been able to meet him, especially as my own wishes are being granted. Now only one thing remains."

"The hardest thing of all," Fabiom warned. "I'll send a message to my wife. She'll join us shortly."

All Robstrom's nervousness at the prospect of meeting a Silvana vanished as he took Casandrina's hand in his. Instead, he was overwhelmed by grief and shame that his people had been responsible for the murder of so many of her kind. There was no censure in her eyes, only welcome and maybe a little amusement as she invited him to resume his seat.

"You have persuasive voices speaking on your behalf, Prince Robstrom. Fabiom has told me of your desire to see Gerik reforested, and Lesandor speaks very well of you. I know what you did for my son; for that reason, if for no other, I would try to help you. Yet you must understand, my support is of little more value than that of anyone else. There is nothing I, or any Silvana, can do to make trees grow in Gerik. They will not thrive in that land until some of the damage has been undone, and that may take many seasons. Yet there are smaller plants that might grow, with the proper care, plants that would draw the poisons away and others that could mend and strengthen the soil and purify the water," Casandrina mused.

"I have learnt to be patient, my lady. A lifetime of waiting has taught me that virtue. To see one new flower bloom in Gerish soil I would account a triumph, and an augury of hope for the future. I may never see a tree grow there, but if I can believe that my ... that future generations might walk in a Gerish wood I will be content."

"Flowers, I think I can promise you," Casandrina said gently.

Over the next few days, Casandrina and Elzandria gathered seeds and cuttings from the woods, while Nissus and Kita brought samples from their garden and hothouse. Meanwhile, Robstrom let Lesandor lead him further and further into the woods, to visit Silvanan groves and even a Dancing Glade.

It was there, upon the grass of that sacred space, that Casandrina vouchsafed the hope that some Silvanii might, in fact, be waiting, dormant in Gerik's soil. Elzandria was beside her and all around them – imperceptible to Robstrom – others were gathered to see the man who would atone for the murder of their Gerish sisters.

Robstrom was fascinated. "Dormant? How so?"

"Seeds," Lesandor speculated, looking at his mother for confirmation. At her smile he added, "I have wondered about it, but it seemed too fanciful to even mention."

"No, not entirely fanciful," Casandrina told him. "At least, we hope not. If a tree was dying at the exact time the Silvanii were destroyed – and there were many trees, so it is likely that one, at least, existed in that state – the Silvana of that tree would have left it and be waiting to regenerate within one of her tree's seeds. But the soil was cursed, the land doomed, the seed would not germinate and yet, that seed might have survived, and its Silvana with it." She shook her head. "We do not know how long she could wait, and so many seasons have passed. But it is our hope, and has been all this while."

"How would she know it was safe for her to grow?" Robstrom asked, the childlike eagerness in his voice prompting a susurration of pleasure from the gathered Silvanii.

Casandrina shook her head. "That is difficult to answer. If there are others, should one grow the roots of her tree would begin to cleanse the surrounding land, which would inspire her sisters to awaken. But, as for the first, all we can hope is that some of the healing plants we shall give you will send the same message."

Fifteen days later, when Robstrom returned to Gerik, Nissus went with him, with herbs and flowers they might sow to begin the healing of the land. As Morene's foremost herbalist he was going to select a suitable area for cultivation and oversee the initial tending of the young plants.

Since he had promised Aelinn he would return, Lesandor accompanied Robstrom and Nissus as far as Fairwater.

In the fountain square they were met, by chance, by Prince Dilon, who sent word immediately to his father that they had arrived, before dragging Lesandor off to spend time with Pharrell and Luthrina. The couple had been visiting that day and were anxious to know about Robstrom's visit to Deepvale. The four ate together and talked for some time before Lesandor was summoned.

Ravik was alone when Lesandor was shown in to his private room. The Prince was as pleased to see Lesandor as his two youngest sons had been. Having questioned his visitor about his health, and about Robstrom's visit, and having been reassured regarding both Fabiom's and Tegun's wellbeing, Ravik informed Lesandor that he would visit Deepvale immediately after Festival, and bring Aelinn and Lyrra with him.

"Were it not for you, we would never have known them – they are as much your family as ours. You have given us a great gift." He shook his head. "Furthermore – not only have I gained a beautiful granddaughter but my dear wife is restored to me; my sons have their mother again." He allowed himself a contented sigh. "Speaking of Maedrim, she will be glad to greet you. And upset if she learns you are here without attending her –"

Up on the palace roof, surrounded by pots of vines and flowering shrubs, Aelinn and Maedrim were sitting side by side, heads almost touching. On a small loom, the princess had set out warp threads in russet and chestnut, interspersed with cream. Maedrim guided Aelinn's hand as the younger woman worked an amber-shaded weft thread in and out, in an intricate pattern.

"Lesandor!" Maedrim looked up and smiled. She looked radiant.

Lesandor blinked and cleared his throat. "I am glad to see you, my lady."

"And I, you." She rose to embrace him and kiss his cheek. "Do you know, Aelinn's grandmother taught me to weave? How strange that life has come full-circle in this way," she whispered.

Aelinn had glanced up briefly, but her concentration was on her work.

"Leave that, dear one," Maedrim suggested. "We can continue later. Go fetch your daughter; she has been asking when she will see this young man again."

Maedrim linked her arm through Lesandor's as she led him to a cushioned bench. "Tell me about your parents. How are they? I must visit them soon, it has been far too long."

Lesandor's reunion with Lyrra was ecstatic, as the little girl threw herself into his arms where she chattered non-stop about all the wonderful things she had done and how her grandparents and uncles spoilt her. "But I miss you lots," she said, snuggling in to him.

Lyrra was thrilled with all she had seen and done and all she had been given in Fairwater, though none of the presents she had received compared with Whisper, the white donkey, which Lesandor presented to her on the day he left.

"Look, Mama!" Lyrra called. "I'm riding!"

Prince Dilon had seated her up on the donkey's back and was leading the animal around the garden.

"You're a very lucky girl," Aelinn told her. "Be careful now."

"I will," Lyrra promised, holding on tightly.

In Lesandor's mind, Dilon – walking beside the gleeful child – was replaced by Raidan; he could almost feel his friend's pride and delight in his beautiful family. On an impulse he unfastened his bronze chain and offered Aelinn the grey and gold stone that had been in turn Sirsha's, Raidan's and his own.

"You deserve something special, too," he told her. "This was once your husband's."

A tear slipped down her cheek as she bent her head so that he might fasten the chain around her neck.

Chapter Eight

MIST, LIKE A silver-grey shroud, covered the garden; shimmering cobwebs draped each shrub; red and gold painted the trees. Festival was over, the harvest was plentiful, and Deepvale's hold-house was looking forward to a visit from Prince Ravik, who was bringing Aelinn and Lyrra to visit and would arrive in a few days. Given the riches of field, vineyard and orchard the harvest had bequeathed, they lacked only one thing.

"Do you want to come hunting?" Lesandor asked his father.

Darseus, Calbrin and a half-dozen others were armed with bows and knives and ready to set out.

Fabiom hesitated. "No, you go on, I've things that need doing here. And your great-uncle is due some time today. I should be here when he arrives."

Lesandor nodded, disappointed yet unsurprised.

When they had gone, Fabiom went out into the garden. He was not expecting Tarison for some hours. With him he had the most flexible bow he possessed, and a quiver full of arrows. He aimed, shot, aimed, shot. Seventeen arrows. Only four hit the target and none of those anywhere near the centre.

He shook his head as he collected the arrows he could find. Three were missing somewhere in the shrubbery.

"You always were a serious hazard to the flowers in this garden."

"Mother! I didn't see you. How long have you been here?"

"Long enough. You paid a high price for his freedom, didn't you?"

Fabiom grimaced and flexed his shoulder. "I've shot enough arrows on mark to satisfy anyone. If that's all I've lost then I count myself blessed."

"So why are you here, trying to hit that target?"

He laughed shortly. "I didn't say I was happy about it. I do not like the idea of no longer being able to train bowmen for Ravik, nor of having to rely on others, even Lesandor, to provide meat for my household. I shall have to learn to live with it though."

"Perhaps. Perhaps not. Let us sit, Fabiom – not in the shade."

"Is Tarison not with you? Ah, no – he has business at the port, hasn't he?"

They made their way to a garden bench made from the yew tree Fabiom had felled the day Lesandor was born. The irony was not lost on either of them.

"What are you suggesting?" he asked, spreading his cloak for her to sit on.

"I recall when you were eight, nine at most, your father tried to teach you how to shoot with reversed hands. He said it was a good skill to master, and you did."

Fabiom frowned and then smiled. "I remember. I stopped doing it after a while, but I did practice for a month or so. Fancy you recalling that. It was nearly fifty years ago!"

Vida sighed and pulled her shawl about her shoulders, though the day was hot. "Sadly, these days I find it easy to conjure memories from long ago, not so easy to remember yesterday."

"But good memories?"

"Oh yes." She smiled. "I made my peace with your father some time since. Which is just as well as I feel it won't be long before we're together again."

She smiled again as Fabiom shook his head.

"Oh, don't worry," she assured him. "I'm not being morbid. Maybe I just miss him more these days. I've less to do to keep busy, more time to think. Too much time."

He took her hands. Her fingers were stiffened now, making it hard for her to spin or weave the way she used to, and he knew her eyesight was not as good, either, so that she could only read in good light, and even then, only for a short while. "It's a good thing you have a great-grandson and great-nieces and nephews to entertain, and to entertain you."

"It is indeed. Now, enough of me. Go and try. You know what your

370

father would say. He'd not want to see you wallowing in self-pity."

"I'm doing no such thing!"

"Oh? So why did you let them go off on a hunt without you? Don't tell me you're too proud to risk being bettered in the chase by your own son."

"My son has long been able to match me in the field. He has his mother's instincts and ability to be silent in the wild. And I have taught him well in the more human aspects of archery."

"But you could still outshoot him at a fixed target – for which we are all grateful."

"I had the skill when it mattered," Fabiom agreed quietly. "It is of no import now."

She slapped his arm, none too gently. "For goodness sake! Don't be so melodramatic. Use your left hand to draw!"

"Yes, Mother."

It was not easy. Yet, as he practiced, the memory came back to him – the time she had referred to – when Tawr had endeavoured to teach him to shoot with reverse hands.

By the time he went back into the house he was exhausted and his shoulder throbbed, as much with the unusual exertion of bracing the bow instead of drawing the string.

Casandrina chided him as she rubbed a liniment, made from the seeds of her tree, into his aching muscles.

"Your mother is here, as is Marid," she told him, planting a tender kiss on his shoulder.

"Yes, I have seen Mother already; I should greet Marid. I believe they left Tarison at the quay, to finalise details of the last three-hundred barrels of wine bound for Fairwater. Had I remembered earlier, I would have gone down to meet him." He sighed contentedly and leant back against her. "You are good to me."

Tarison arrived in the late-afternoon, at the same time as Lesandor returned from his hunting foray.

"Uncle!" Lesandor greeted his great-uncle with a warm embrace. "See, Father, you could have come out with us, after all. And Grandmother!

Who else is here? It is a good thing our hunt was successful."

"Your father will hunt with you next time. Won't you, Fabiom?" Vida said, before kissing her grandson fondly. "You make certain he does," she instructed, close enough to Lesandor's ear so only he could hear. "So, dear one, what did you bring us for supper?"

"Pigeon and rabbit for tonight," Lesandor replied. "And we brought down a boar – but that is for another day; Darseus is dealing with the carcass. There is extra pigeon, too, Princess Maedrim's favourite."

"I can hardly believe she is travelling. That little girl of Raidan's has been such a blessing," observed Marid, who had come out of the house to greet Lesandor.

The next morning, having little choice, Fabiom accompanied Lesandor and Calbrin on the hunt. On the way to their destination he sighted a fallow buck. He let it go without drawing. Over the years he had brought down more animals that he could count, but only when he was certain of a clean kill. The others had not seen the buck and they moved on, across the meadow and through a narrow strip of trees to the river. It had been Fabiom's suggestion that they should go line shooting, for it was less effort for him to shoot downwards. Four fat salmon proved his idea sound. His son and his house-steward were so impressed with his newly-honed ability to shoot with opposite hands that they determined to learn the skill themselves, an effort that ended in much joking and several lost arrows.

Lesandor's mood became more serious as they made their way back to the hold-house. Half-way there, he asked Calbrin to take the catch home so that he might speak with his father. In unspoken accord, he and Fabiom changed direction and soon were in the cool shade of the wildwood.

"The badgers are back," Lesandor commented.

"In the copse? Yes, I know. There are brambles there; they seem to like the berries. But you didn't send Calbrin away to talk about badgers."

Lesandor chuckled. "No. I –" He bent and picked up a handful of acorns, letting them fall through his fingers. "I wanted to talk to you about Aelinn. About me. About marriage."

"You are not seriously thinking…"

"No! On the contrary. That is what I need to speak with you about. I might be imagining things, but Princess Maedrim said something, nothing specific, but she hinted at a connection, something I presume she had seen in the stars. She seemed amused, pleased. Father – I do not want to be coerced into another marriage and I am not ready. To be honest, at this point, I cannot imagine I ever will be again."

"Don't say that." Fabiom put his hand on his son's shoulder. "You are twenty-two years old. I had not imagined you being married once, let alone married and widowed twice by this point, not since you were unable to present yourself in these woods."

Both looked at the trees surrounding them.

Fabiom shook his head. "Perhaps five years from now, I would have looked to arrange a marriage for you. After all, it is wise for the firstborn son of a high house to wed and get himself an heir sooner rather than later, especially for a man with no siblings. But you *have* an heir: you have a fine, strong son. You have no need to marry at all, until it is what your heart desires. Certainly, I have no intention of pushing you to do so, for Deepvale has no need of it – your sister's presence means that even when I'm gone, should you have no wife, the holding would have a formidable Lady. Furthermore, with Lyrra discovered, even Ravik's commission to you to sire a holder for Southernport no longer holds sway. Having said that, I sincerely hope you will find someone – or allow us to find someone for you – when you are ready."

"Thank you. But that does not help if our ruling prince decides I should wed his widowed daughter-by-marriage. Would you deny him?"

"Why should he do such a thing? He cannot imagine you are over what happened in Shakenyew. And why would he want to part with Lyrra? Unless you think he would separate mother and child, and I cannot imagine that." Fabiom frowned. "What, exactly, did Maedrim say?"

Lesandor shook his head. "Something about time passing, and families being united, and trees. And that it involved Aelinn. But it was as much the way she looked at me as what she said."

As it happened, nothing was said that related to future plans for either

Aelinn or Lesandor, and the visit was delightful. Jarin was overjoyed to have both Lyrra and her mother back, as were the woodmaids.

After supper on the second day, finally able to take some time alone, Ravik told Fabiom that he had found an ancient precedent for sparing Fabiom from any consequences for his actions in Shakenyew.

"It was way back in Lincius's day – a Silvana lured many men to the wildwood and to their deaths. There are few details, not surprisingly, except that her tree was felled and those responsible absolved from all blame." He raised a glass of Deepvale's finest wine in a gesture of salutation. "Should I ever be required to defend my decision, it is good to have history on my side. But, as far as I am concerned, it is finished."

Wordlessly, Fabiom lifted his own glass in reply.

Ravik swirled the dark wine in the glass, clearly preoccupied.

"But...." Fabiom prompted, his voice wary.

With a chuckle, Ravik glanced up at him. "Curiosity. Perhaps I shouldn't ask."

It was so unlike the prince to be hesitant that Fabiom's own interest was piqued, though he would truly have liked the subject closed for all time.

"Ask. I owe you everything, the least I can do is answer your question."

"They had not been together long."

"Half a year," Fabiom agreed.

"Perhaps there was not yet a sapling to be seen, a result of their union?"

Fabiom hesitated. "There was."

Ravik raised his brows.

"I spotted it as soon as we arrived in the grove, and made certain it didn't get trampled or crushed. It is safe." He refilled their glasses. "In twenty years from now, Lesandor will have a daughter – a yew Silvana. He has not mentioned it, but I do not know if that is because the thought has not occurred to him, or if he dare not ask me what befell her tree."

"Perhaps it is best he remains unaware," Ravik mused. "No good could come of that relationship."

❦

Prince Ravik was not the only person who needed little reason to visit Deepvale's hold-house. They came and went, relatives, friends and acquaintances, calling socially or on matters of business or state. Cavan was just another visitor. He arrived near autumn's end. An acquaintance of Lesandor's, he said, and of his friends in Windwood. He was made welcome.

Lesandor was in the municipal centre with Fabiom and Tegun, so the woodmaids brought the old man food and drink in the day room, and made him comfortable. Some time later, Fabiom returned alone, the younger men having stayed in town. He greeted Cavan warmly.

"Lord Fabiom, I have heard much about you – I had hoped to meet you. I brought a gift," Cavan told his host. "Some wine. I have settled down of late. Maybe you have heard Lesandor mention my name, my wanderings?"

"No," Fabiom admitted. "I think not. Then I was away for some time. He may well have spoken of you to the others. Thank you for the gift."

"Yes, I made it myself. Need to keep busy, you see. Less time to think and brood if you're busy."

Fabiom agreed that it was true. He had found the same himself.

"Shall we wait for Lesandor, or open it now?" he asked, watching amused as Cavan caressed the flask lovingly. The old man had not seemed overly pleased with the wine he had been offered from their own vineyard.

"Let us have some now. There's plenty to go around later. I'm not so fond of grapes. That's not grape wine you see. Try it. I think you will like it."

"Your health!" Fabiom said, as he took a mouthful.

Cavan nodded and drank deeply himself.

Fabiom frowned. "An unusual taste, not unpleasant." He took another draught.

Cavan drained his cup. "With the compliments of the inhabitants of Shakenyew," he whispered.

Casandrina was in the garden when Fabiom fell. She ran into the house, falling to her knees as she reached his side.

Curled around his pain he did not register her presence until she wrapped her arms about him.

"Casandrina!"

"I am here, beloved, I am here."

He clung to her before a spasm of pain made him struggle onto his side, away from her. As it subsided, she gently turned him onto his back and cradled his head on her lap.

"I killed her, Casi. A Silvana –"

"Hush, my love. You did what you had to do."

"Did I? I didn't know what else to do." He arched his back against another wave of pain.

"You did what I would have done."

"That's different."

"No! How is it different? You and I, we are one. You made a poem for me. Do you remember? When you went to Gerik, that first time and we were apart. You came home and told it to me:

I dreamt – again – that you were in my arms,
Our bodies, breath and heartbeats
in perfection merged.
That where you ended, and I began –
I had no sense, no notion –"

He tried to laugh, coughing blood instead. Tenderly, she wiped his mouth.

"But now I've got to leave you, Casi. I'm sorry. I'm so sorry."

"Sssh. You have nothing to be sorry for. My love, my sweet love. You will wait for me. This season too shall pass. We will be together again."

His eyes held hers. "Yes." He reached up to her face, though his hands shook. "I am enthralled, and ever will be, un –, u –"

"No! No, Fabiom."

"Un – til –" He struggled for air.

"Until my dying breath," she whispered.

"Yes." His eyes closed.

"No, Fabiom, not yet. Please, my love, stay, stay with me."

His fingers clenched around hers. A terrible spasm passed though his body and his eyes opened wide, searching desperately for her face.

The light faded from Fabiom's eyes. With great care, Casandrina closed them – bending to place a final kiss on each lid.

Tears fell onto his face, as if he wept. Yet he would never weep again. His features were relaxed now. Peaceful.

Heedless of those gathering about them, Casandrina stroked Fabiom's hair, the voices meaningless. Her whole attention was on what remained of the man she loved. Every posture, every expression that had ever crossed his face was etched in her mind, nothing was lost. Every moment they had shared, she could recall with total clarity and yet, despite that, letting him go was so hard. But he was not there anymore. That kind, loving heart no longer beat; that sweet breath no longer filled his chest. His voice was silenced, except in her mind.

As she sat there, caressing his brow, pain – like she had never known – coursed through her, so that she cried out before she could stop herself. "It hurts!" She was vaguely aware of Elzandria and she bit back the next cry. Her daughter could not know how much it hurt to be unmade again. Narilina had known. Casandrina half wondered and half understood why Narilina had not warned her. Though, in a way, she had: *"So, when the time comes, you will have no regrets."*

Through the terrible pain, she focussed on the beloved face of her husband. No, she had no regrets.

Chapter Nine

WREATHED IN DARK foliage and bitter herbs, the holding mourned. On the streets, Deepvale's people spoke in hushed whispers, while on the trees and vines, the remnant of the harvest remained ungathered.

Bound in sheets of wine-red silk, with wild thyme, lemon balm and other fragrant herbs, Fabiom's body was brought to the grove and laid beneath Casandrina's tree. Casandrina had gone. Her song of mourning would linger in the grove for all time but never again would she walk substantial in the world of men.

Lesandor stared at the wrapped body of his father, unseeing.

"Why Cavan?" Tegun asked, his voice still hollow with shock.

Lesandor shook his head. He had no answer. He knew that the old man had never come to terms with the loss of his own Silvanan wife, never forgiven those who cut her tree, yet had he really set himself in judgment over others? Sworn revenge on any who committed such an act? Nothing he had ever said to Lesandor suggested such a thing.

Already they had buried Cavan's body in a deep gully in one of the most far removed parts of Deepvale; Tegun had taken care of that.

Rain fell, dripping off the leaves of the trees. Lesandor shivered and Elzandria took him by the arm, led him away from the ash grove and back to the house.

"Lord Lesandor." Calbrin bobbed his head apologetically as Lesandor started.

'Lord Lesandor'. So he must assume his father's title: Lord Holder of Deepvale. He would rather have waited.

"Yes, Calbrin."

The house-steward had in his hand a ring of gold and silver twisted together and set with chalcedony. The ring of the Holder of Deepvale. Lesandor stared at it for a long moment before he took it and placed it on the first finger of his left hand.

"Thank you." He closed his hand over the ring and tried to draw strength from it. There was much to do and it was all his responsibility now, whether he wanted it or not. At least he was not alone.

Fabiom's death had upset Masgor so badly that he had taken to his bed. Lesandor feared the shock would be too much for the old tutor. He sent for Nalio, though the holding's senior physician had been such a close friend of Fabiom's that he, too, was in shock. Nalio spent some time talking with Masgor and left some gentle sleeping draughts for him, suggesting to Lesandor that he should not be left unattended for too long.

Kita had come to the house with Nalio and, on hearing his suggestion, arranged to leave her children with her mother while she stayed to take care of Masgor, and help in any other way she could. Lesandor suspected she was also staying, on her father-by-marriage's instructions, to keep watch over him. He could not object.

Over the days that followed, couriers from other holdings arrived bearing condolences; friends, from all over Morene, came to offer comfort. Yan travelled from Fairwater with the Princes Dilon and Pharrell, and Luthrina, Pharrell's beech Silvana wife. They arrived in time for the final day of mourning – the day of the funeral pyre.

That evening, flames illuminated the overcast sky in a mockery of sunset. The fire died down as night descended, until, in the faint, pre-dawn light, they took Fabiom's ashes and scattered them beneath Casandrina's tree.

Afterwards, Pharrell took Lesandor aside. "Father says you are to attend him as soon as you feel able, but you are not to rush. And Mother wanted me to tell you –" the prince paused, considering his words. "I think you are aware that, due largely to Lyrra's presence, my mother has begun to engage once more with the world?"

Lesandor nodded. "Yes, and I am glad of it."

"Indeed. It is a great blessing." Pharrell gazed upwards to where a single morning star glimmered through a rent in the clouds. "You might also know that since Raidan's death she has not looked to the heavens?"

"I was not aware of that. In fact, I thought she did little else."

Pharrell shook his head. "For certain she locked herself away in the star-tower my father built for her. But no – she abandoned her gift. Now, however, she has taken to showing the constellations to Lyrra. Of course, she cannot do that without seeing – whatever it is star-seers see. She asked me to tell you that she saw hope, for you and your endeavours. And joy." Pharrell shrugged. "She would not elucidate. Yet perhaps there is some comfort in that?"

"There is," Lesandor confirmed. "Father –" He frowned and drew a steadying breath. "Father often told how she comforted him when he feared he had lost my mother, all those years ago. How her star-sight gave him courage and determination when he was so afraid. Thank her, when you return home – from both of us."

The house was filled to overflowing, yet still more visitors arrived.

Trisran and Dulcissa had set out from Windwood as soon as word came to Dulcissa, whispered, across the land, through the tracts of wildwood. Petron travelled with them and the three arrived together. Lesandor would have been surprised, had he really noticed; Petron and Trisran might both be friends of his but they had hardly become friends to each other, and for Dulcissa to travel so far – he had not realised she held him in such regard. He was glad she and Trisran had come, for they, more than anyone, knew Cavan. Perhaps they could help answer some of his questions.

Dulcissa held him like a child. "I am so sorry, I did not know. Maybe I should have sensed something was terribly wrong with him. We put it down to all those years of loneliness. Foolish! Foolish!"

They were in the courtyard at the centre of the hold-house and all their friends gathered around to listen, half afraid.

Elzandria moved closer to her brother. She took his hand whilst saying, "Speak, Dulcissa, please."

They were not alike, ash and elm, yet there was something they shared that marked them apart from such as Taxiana. Lesandor wondered how he had been so stupid as to go to the yew woods. Why had he listened to Cavan? Indeed, why had Cavan given him such advice?

"His own wife was from the yew woods," Dulcissa said, answering his unspoken question. "We did not know. He never said."

"How is it you know this now?" Kita wondered.

Unexpectedly Dulcissa looked to Petron, who answered, "Not long ago I met a man travelling through Windwood who had lost his Silvanan wife when her tree had been destroyed by an earthslide, during the great floods the year Prince Ravik's father, Darseus, acceded to his title. He came to the hold-house and when I heard his story I sent him to the silk mills to meet Trisran."

At that, Trisran took up the tale. "When he came, I showed him around and then invited him home. Naturally he recognised Dulcissa as Silvanan and stayed and talked with us. He's still in Windwood, helping at the mill. He's of an age with Cavan, more or less, and like him he has carried his great sorrow for most of his life, yet we saw at once that he was not as Cavan, for he had known such happiness that the memory of it sustained him. He shared that with us."

"And we guessed the truth about Cavan," Dulcissa concluded. "Things he said, things he left unsaid, all made sense in the light of that."

It began to rain and they went indoors.

As Calbrin poured out more wine and Elzandria's woodmaids brought in small morsels of food for the guests, Kita sat down on the arm of Lesandor's couch and put her arms around him. "Cavan must have gone to Shakenyew to find you, Lesandor, and discovered what had transpired there. The yew Silvanii must have sent him here, just as Taxiana tried to make you exact revenge on her behalf on those who cut the other tree in the yew woods."

"Unlike you, Cavan had no misgivings," Tegun said.

Trisran nodded. "Their poison had been at work in him for more than fifty years."

381

Lesandor shuddered at the thought. He had felt the absence of all that was good after only a few days. Fifty years, it was a long time, as Cavan himself had once pointed out.

"They are evil, and they are death. Always," Elzandria said, echoing Casandrina.

"And is it over now?" Petron asked. "Or will they still be out for revenge?" He glanced at Lesandor anxiously.

Dulcissa shook her head. "I think it is over."

"Yes," Lesandor murmured. He managed a wan smile. "At least Father had the best of lives, if not the best death."

Elzandria smiled at that. "Better by far for him to end his life here at home among those he loved than dying on the barren plains of Gerik, as Casandrina always feared he would." She touched Lesandor's face. "Now it is your turn to have a good life. That is all they ever wanted for you."

And Lesandor knew it was true, knew he owed them that much, that he should at least make a great effort. His mother had not deserted him. She was close by and would be forever; her tree would outlive him by many years. His sister was with him, as was his son. The future looked bright enough; bright as the sunlight that poured through the rain clouds, edging them with silver, bright as the autumn leaves that bejewelled the wildwood, bright as the Silvanii, bright as hope.

About the Author

Belinda Mellor currently lives near the beach in Tahunanui, at the Top of the South Island of New Zealand. After a decade of milking goats and collecting eggs on a lifestyle block, she now runs a motel with her husband, Peter, to whom this book is dedicated.

At the age of five Belinda won a school award for 'free expression' and has not stopped writing since. She was an inaugural winner of an Ian St James literary award for her fantasy story *Bronwen's Dowry* (published with the eleven other finalists in the Collins anthology *At the Stroke of Twelve*). Since then she has been awarded a literary bursary and an award for a character-driven story, had numerous non-fiction and occasional fiction pieces published in magazines and local newspapers and a play for children performed by a theatre-in-education company. *Bronwen's Dowry* has been more recently republished in another prize anthology: *All These Shiny Worlds* and she has several other short stories in the 2022 New Zealand and Australian authors anthology: *Down Under Fantasy Realms* (which includes two short stories from the same world as The Greening).

A background in Theology and Applied Spirituality, a lifetime interest in myths, legends, folklore and fairytales, and a passion for wild places and the environment all inform her writing.

Find out more at belindamellor.com

Acknowledgments

As this second book was once very much part of Book 1, all the 'thank yous' that applied to that apply equally to this part.

Once again, my brilliant editors, Teresa Bassett and Chrissie Ward. Thank you so much.

For this part, I have to give special thanks to my beautiful daughter, Iona, to whom *The Turning* is dedicated. Just as Fabiom and Casandrina were journeying through the uncharted waters of parenthood, I was learning alongside them. It has been interesting to watch my real child and my fictional child grow up side by side.

To my beloved husband, Peter, thank you for supporting my writing dream and never suggesting I should get a 'real job', nor complained about the housekeeping (or lack of).

I also have to say a huge thank you to readers of *The Greening* for all the encouragement and kind reviews. Knowing that people are eager to read on makes the dark days of final edits a lot easier.

Also, and once again, thanks to Holly Dunn of Holly Dunn Design for another lovely cover and gorgeous chapter headings.

Finally, CP Books, who are always great to work with. Suzanne, as artistic as always – and patient! And Dave – always supportive. Thank you both, and the rest of the team, too.

THE
SILVANA
CHRONICLES

BELINDAMELLOR.COM

www.ingramcontent.com/pod-product-compliance
Lightning Source LLC
Chambersburg PA
CBHW012358130726
47904CB00020B/2567